PENGUIN
RITES OF P.

Sanjoy Hazarika was born in Shillong, then capital of the undivided state of Assam, in 1954. He studied at Shillong, London and Cambridge, Massachusetts, at Harvard University, and was a correspondent for the *New York Times* out of South Asia between 1981–1996. Formerly a member of the first National Security Advisory Board, he is now part of the National Commission to Review the Working of the Constitution. He has also set up a Centre for North East Studies and Policy Research. A Senior Fellow at the Centre for Policy Research in New Delhi, Sanjoy Hazarika is a columnist for several newspapers. He also makes documentaries, especially on the North East, and is completing a film on the Brahmaputra. Sanjoy Hazarika divides his time between the North East and New Delhi where he lives with his wife and daughter.

RITES OF PASSAGE

Border Crossings, Imagined Homelands, India's East and Bangladesh

Sanjoy Hazarika

PENGUIN BOOKS

PENGUIN BOOKS
Published by the Penguin Group
Penguin Books India Pvt. Ltd, 11 Community Centre, Panchsheel Park, New Delhi 110 017, India
Penguin Group (USA) Inc., 375 Hudson Street, New York, New York 10014, USA
Penguin Group (Canada), 90 Eglinton Avenue East, Suite 700, Toronto, Ontario, M4P 2Y3, Canada (a division of Pearson Penguin Canada Inc.)
Penguin Books Ltd, 80 Strand, London WC2R 0RL, England
Penguin Ireland, 25 St Stephen's Green, Dublin 2, Ireland (a division of Penguin Books Ltd)
Penguin Group (Australia), 250 Camberwell Road, Camberwell, Victoria 3124, Australia (a division of Pearson Australia Group Pty Ltd)
Penguin Group (NZ), 67 Apollo Drive, Rosedale, North Shore 0632, New Zealand (a division of Pearson New Zealand Ltd)
Penguin Group (South Africa) (Pty) Ltd, 24 Sturdee Avenue, Rosebank, Johannesburg 2196, South Africa

Penguin Books Ltd, Registered Offices: 80 Strand, London WC2R 0RL, England

First published by Penguin Books India 2000

Copyright © Sanjoy Hazarika 2000

This book was written under the auspices of the Centre for Policy Research, New Delhi

All rights reserved

10 9 8 7 6 5 4

Typeset in Sabon by Mantra Virtual Services, New Delhi
Printed at Deunique Printers, New Delhi

This book is sold subject to the condition that it shall not, by way of trade or otherwise, be lent, resold, hired out, or otherwise circulated without the publisher's prior written consent in any form of binding or cover other than that in which it is published and without a similar condition including this condition being imposed on the subsequent purchaser and without limiting the rights under copyright reserved above, no part of this publication may be reproduced, stored in or introduced into a retrieval system, or transmitted in any form or by any means (electronic, mechanical, photocopying, recording or otherwise), without the prior written permission of both the copyright owner and the above-mentioned publisher of this book.

For Myron Weiner, friend, scholar, social historian,
well-wisher of India and its North East

Contents

Foreword   ix
Acknowledgements   xii

Chapter One
Introduction   1

Chapter Two
Mahesh: Encounters of the First Kind   9

Chapter Three
Crossing Thresholds: Land and People   16

Chapter Four
The Roads to Nellie   25

Chapter Five
'Where Are the Bodies?'   49

Chapter Six
The Roads Away from Nellie   54

Chapter Seven
A Place Called Home   75

Chapter Eight
An Inner World: Chars, Islanders and Diwanis   100

Chapter Nine
Where is Suleman?   122

Chapter Ten
Memory is a Fickle Companion   137

Chapter Eleven
Kurigram and Keramat   151

Chapter Twelve
The Story of Keramat Bhai   179

Chapter Thirteen
Bangladesh: Standing Room Only   204

Chapter Fourteen
Seeking Partnership, Renouncing Confrontation   239

Appendices   269
Bibliography   334
Index   341

Foreword

Over the past years, Sanjoy Hazarika, a former reporter for the *New York Times* and currently a Senior Fellow at the Centre for Policy Research, has been engaged in a study on an extremely relevant issue in eastern India which has defied a solution. The question of migration has spread much bitterness and tension in the North East of India, not to speak of violence, and troubled relations between India and Bangladesh. But many of the substantial issues have been lost in rhetoric and political posturing.

Bangladesh's official position is that there are no illegal migrants and that India is deliberately pushing out its principal religious minority. India says that Bangladeshis are pouring into its territory. What is the truth? Why do people move? What are their stories, beyond the debris of statistics and sharp rhetoric which obfuscate the real issues?

The phenomenon of illegal migration is not limited to the geographical area of South Asia, or even Asia taken as a whole. It is an international problem that has led to conflicts in different parts of the world and an exacerbation of social, economic and environmental pressures. The Centre for Policy Research has long taken an interest in issues of population and population movements and this book is part of a larger concern in CPR about peace, development and security in the South Asian region.

The reasons behind migration, where people move from and where they are headed, the lack of a comprehensive strategy to tackle the economic and social roots of these difficulties, the use of religious radicals for purposes of ideology and destabilization, and the personal stories of tragedy, despair and hope—these combine to make an extremely readable book, written in a non-academic style that will make it appeal to a wider audience.

Rites of Passage's passionate style and rich narrative prose plus rigorous research, are typical of Mr Hazarika's despatches as an international reporter for the *New York Times* out of South Asia, and his earlier acclaimed books, *Strangers of the Mist: Tales of War and Peace from India's North East*; and *Bhopal: The Lessons of a Tragedy.*

The voices of the unheard in the entire debate on migration are heard through this book. These are what should help determine policy on a subject as difficult as the movement of people.

Migration has resonance for the subcontinent. It raises extremely touchy emotional issues, for India and Pakistan were born in the bloodshed of Partition, and Bangladesh had a similar, bloody birth.

In parts of India, especially its North East, migration is not just an emotive question but one that is seen as related to the very survival of communities. The Assam students' movement of the 1970s and 1980s, and other agitations elsewhere have forced even national political parties to take the issue on board. This is an important part of democratic change and debate, to bring greater understanding on a sensitive issue. Unfortunately, much of the discussion has become bogged down in rhetoric. This is where Mr Hazarika's work comes as a breath of fresh air in policy advocacy.

There are numerous innovative ideas in *Rites of Passage*. Not only do they shed light on macro issues which need discussion, but they point to the direction of strategies at the ground level which can transform extremely complex problems, in a very difficult area, into opportunities.

Mr Hazarika is acknowledged as a specialist in issues relating to the North East and its neighbourhood. Through other initiatives, he also seeks to promote dialogue and understanding in civil society in that region.

The CPR is glad to have given him a base for this study. We wish to acknowledge the role of the Population Foundation for India as well as HIVOS, the Humanist Institute for Cooperation with Developing Countries, of the Netherlands, both of which funded the research.

Dr V.A. Pai Panandiker
President
Centre for Policy Research
New Delhi
21 November 2000

Acknowledgements

Without question, the first line of credit must go to Dr V.A. Pai Panandiker, President of the Centre for Policy Research (CPR), who backed this idea from the very beginning and placed the superb facilities at CPR at my disposal. Dr Pai, who has been supportive in other areas of common concern—the North East and Indian policy-making—has built up a unique institution at CPR with a good team. CPR has been a kind host to me, and my office, with greenery bursting through the windows, has been both base and sanctuary.

The Population Foundation of India (PFI) deserves many thanks for its financial support which helped fund part of the project. I am especially grateful to Dr Bharat Ram, Dr K. Srinivasan, Executive Director of the PFI, and Dr R. Natarajan, former deputy director and leading demographer. All of them must have despaired at my work ever seeing the light of day.

HIVOS, the Dutch NGO, with its South Asia base in Bangalore, provided the other funding for the study. Ben Witjes, whose initial interest led to HIVOS extending this support, was extremely helpful and so was Ms Susan Mathews.

Without this support provided by all three groups, *Rites of Passage* could not have been completed.

The responsibility for the delay in putting this book together is entirely mine. Filming of the documentary on Brahmaputra river in India, Tibet and Bangladesh, membership of the first National Security Advisory Board and frequent travel in India and abroad ate into both time and energy.

My family, Minal and Meghna, gave immense support and showed abounding generosity; a writer under stress, or at any time, is more than a handful.

Anindita Dasgupta of Guwahati, between a full-time job teaching history at Cotton College, Guwahati, and finishing her Ph.D., showed initiative, courage, patience and persistence in conducting extensive fieldwork, interviews and documentation in Assam and Meghalaya under difficult conditions. I still have a lot of material which I hope to publish gradually—but all of which couldn't be put in here. Although we may not agree on some issues, I think we respect each other's perspectives.

In Bangladesh: Anwar-ul Raquib of Dhaka University made several trips to Kurigram and other research sites, collected data and helped with my travel. His associate, Firdouz, was a cheerful companion in the last field trip. I wish them well in their plans for the future, in management and in government respectively.

Others in Bangladesh who were supportive and kind: my dear friends and frequent hosts, Shaheen and Mahfuz Anam and their daughter, Priti, who so willingly parted with her room in their old home in Dhanmondi, particularly on one occasion when the Ambala Inn cancelled my booking and I found myself without a place to stay! There were many wonderful meals and conversations.

Others I wish to thank include former Foreign Secretary, Farooq Sobhan, and Rehman Sobhan, Executive Director of the Centre for Policy Dialogue; Imtiaz Ahmed, C.R. Abrar and Ameena Mohsin of Dhaka University for their openness and frankness; Dr Iftekar Ahmed (Ifty), formerly of the Regional Centre for Strategic Studies in Colombo, the Bangladesh Institute for Development Studies for their library facilities and discussions with faculty members Debopriya Bhatta-charyya and Dr Sharifa Begum; the Bangladesh Institute for International Strategic Studies, especially Dr Abdur Rob Khan.

Thanks are also in order to Shyamal Roy and others in Terres des Hommes in Kurigram and the staff at the Rongpur Rural Development Society, and particularly Keramat Bhai and his friends in Chilmari and around, whose stories are the core of this book.

In India:

In Assam: Sunil Baruah of the State Census Department; Chief Minister Prafulla Mahanta; police officers in Guwahati, Dhubri and elsewhere; former Deputy Commissioner of Dhubri, L.M. Singhvi ; Dilip Chakravarty; members of the Asom Sahitya Sabha and the Bar Association, Dhubri; Jahnu Barua, film-maker; Gautam Bora, film director and cinematographer; Dilip Chandan, editor, the *Asom Bani*; former Home Commissioner Tapan Lal Baruah; Justice S. N. Bhargava of the IMDT; Prof Monirul Hussain of Guwahati University; Dhiren Bezbaruah, editor, the *Sentinel*, Opu Dutta-Chowdhury of Bellevue Hotel, Guwahati, and his incredibly helpful staff; Manoj and Vineeta Jalan in

Dibrugarh whose hospitality and support appear unending.

In Meghalaya: Niketu Iralu, my mother Maya Hazarika, my brother Suzoy and Sandi S. Syiem

In Calcutta: Ranabir Samaddar and Paula Banerjee, Subir Bhowmick and Prof Barun De; the family of Shri Mahadeo Jalan for their generous hospitality

In New Delhi: My cousin Sumita for getting hold of Supreme Court documents and decisions; Dr M.R. Vijayunni, then Registrar-General of India, and the staff of the Census Commission; Jaswant Singh, External Affairs Minister (EAM) and friend of the North East; R.S. Jassal, spokesman of the Ministry of External Affairs; Lalit Mansingh, Foreign Secretary; Salman Haidar, former Foreign Secretary; Arun Kumar, Joint Secretary, Ministry of External Affairs (Policy Planning); S. Deb-Mukherjee, former High Commissioner to Bangladesh; Ranjit Rae, former Director in the EAM's office; Raghuvendra Singh, former Personal Secretary to the EAM; Chaman Lal, Special Rapporteur in the National Human Rights Commission; K.P.S. Gill, and G.K. Pillai, Joint Secretary, Ministry of Home Affairs, who was a source of information. It was a pleasure to discuss issues related to the North East with him. He made time even during the most demanding of schedules.

At CPR: Prof B.G. Verghese, K.C. Sivaramakrishnan, former Urban Development Secretary, Rajmohan Gandhi, Ved Marwah, recently appointed Govenor of Manipur, and Gen V. K. Nayar.

Kamaljit Kumar and the CPR library staff who were always helpful.

Mr P. Dhokrekar, Chief of Adminstrative Services, and his accounts team, P.K. Rao, P. Khanna and M.C.

Bhatt helped me keep track of the health of my project's finances.

Among others, Kamini Mahadevan, my editor at Penguin Books India, who prodded, pushed, cajoled and made key suggestions.

Preeti Gill, for reading the initial drafts, and urging me to discipline my writing hours.

In Switzerland:

Rajiv Kapur of UNHCR and his wife Smriti for their help and hospitality in Geneva, and the solitude of their farm house in Delhi, and Mohan Ram's quiet efficiency which helped fine-tune a chapter and other work.

In Britain:

Belinda Wright, Barbara Harrell-Bond, David Turpin of Oxford University's Refugee Studies Programme; also Dr Amrita Dhillon and Dr Fabian Essler.

In the United States:

Dr Amartya Sen, then of Harvard University, and Dr Sharon Stanton Russell of MIT and her many colleagues and assistants in Cambridge, Massachussetts; Prof Ashutosh Varshney and Vibha Pingle, and also Michael Teitelbaum of the Sloan Foundation.

But above all, my thoughts go to the one person to whom I owe this interest and involvement in issues of migration, displacement and refugees, and the deeper underlying questions: the late Myron Weiner. This book is dedicated to his memory.

Myron was without doubt one of the extraordinarily gifted persons I have had the privilege of knowing. His interest in the world and especially the subcontinent and our little North Eastern corner was deep and abiding. I had the privilege of sharing a platform in December 1993 at MIT with Myron in the chair and Prof Amartya Sen as one of the speakers. I was also the second listed speaker on Ayodhya: India, a year later. I suppose I was asked to speak since I had reported on the situation for the *New York Times* after the destruction of the mosque at Ayodhya.

Representing the BJP was a Dr Mody from New York. Myron steered that discussion through a potential minefield with skill and sensitivity, silencing an angry scholar who interrupted Dr Mody, and ensuring that everyone got a decent hearing. Of course, we can all guess what the sentiment of the house was!

His intellectual brilliance apart, Myron was an extremely warm and caring man who wrote with dedication every summer at his Vermont home; he loved the winter skiing at Vermont and spent time with his family. He had the instincts of a first-rate investigative journalist and field researcher: he could 'smell' a situation that was blessed with many opportunities and complications and swiftly see ways to move forward.

We miss him and his energy, curiosity and honesty which touched all those who had the privilege of knowing him.

Sanjoy Hazarika
New Delhi
14 November 2000

Credits

1. Map of Assam and North East courtesy Survey of India

2. Map of Bangladesh Administrative Units courtesy Bangladesh Bureau of Statistics, Dhaka

CHAPTER ONE

Introduction

For more than three years, I have been working on issues relating to the demographic and cultural crisis arising out of the migration of people from Bangladesh into Assam. Constituting a wedge of fertile land in India's North East which is watered by the Brahmaputra, Assam is hemmed in by Bangladesh, Bhutan, Tibet/China, and other Indian states of the region.

This project and other associated ones have taken me several times to Bangladesh and various parts of Assam as well as elsewhere in the North East. And as my knowledge of the area and its issues has grown, so has despair at the realization of how much more needs to be done, urgently, desperately, beginning with making available better information about the area. Home to nearly 150 million people, set amid the stunning landscapes of fertile valleys, here we find back-breaking poverty and a rich cauldron of ferocious and ancient ethnic divisions and feuds. Yet, for the rest of the world, this geographical and cultural entity may as well not exist, so little is the interest in or knowledge about it. And this indifference is well known among the local people. It is a wound that festers and worsens with every passing day. After more than fifty years of independence in India, people in its North East now realize how marginalized they have become in relation to the policy-making apparatus in New Delhi and their own ruling elites at home, and how great remains the ignorance of officials and politicians who govern them, despite all attempts to educate them. The mindsets in Delhi and Dispur remain largely unchanged.

My present concerns also flow out of interactions with villagers, scholars, professionals, politicians and bureaucrats during the course of my research, as well as with non-governmental groups and the media. Though a detailed study of relevant documents, and other theoretical literature on the subject has been done, my approach is not purely academic—anyway I am not particularly qualified to pursue such an enquiry. Our knowledge of the depth of the problems discussed here and their interconnectivity with other concerns is limited; they need to be understood through a multidisciplinary approach. The mere collection of data or compilation of interviews is inadequate for this task. Alejandro Portes writes: 'Data, whether quantitative or qualitative, may accumulate endlessly without producing any significant conceptual breakthrough. Indeed, much of what we do as part of our everyday work is simply to produce information on one aspect or another of social reality within the intellectual frameworks already in place, without altering them to any significant extent. Ideas, especially those of a broader reach, are few and far between and certainly do not emerge out of masses of data.'[1]

---

1 'Immigration Theory for a New Century', in *Immigrant Adaptation and Native-born Responses in the Making of Americans*, (eds.) Josh DeWind, Charles Hirschman, Philip Kasinitz, *International Migration Review*, Vol. 31, Winter 1997

If the problems are multidimensional, so also must be the search for answers. A purely humanist or purely scientific and theoretical approach will not do.

I stumbled along in this search, looking for a concept that would encapsulate my longing for a multi-dimensional set of answers. Late one night, I looked at a review of the brilliant work of that great scientist and philosopher Edmund O. Wilson in a special number of *World Watch*. And I knew that I had found what I wanted.

A professor at Harvard and a devout Baptist as well as a dedicated biologist, Wilson talks about the unity of knowledge, or consilience (a concept that was given this name by the scientist William Whewell as far back as 1840), which is essential in the logical study of any complex issue in today's world. He urges us to span disciplines, and jump across the boundaries of fact and theory.

It is an exhilarating thought—that the 'experts' do not have the answers. That it is only through the weaving together of many strands by different disciplines of work, study and thought, that we will be able to break away from the deadening influence of fragmented knowledge. Wisdom is never piecemeal—it is complete, and rounded.

According to Wilson, it is that leap across the frontiers that will enable us to address long-term problems by following the path of interconnectivity, not of separate sciences and disciplines. Thus, for example, we have to look at land degradation and crop loss in the context of the fragility of our ecosystems, the instability of political groupings, the gross over-exploitation of water resources, the need to educate all levels of society on these questions, and the need to integrate this knowledge into information systems.

These are seemingly disconnected strands. But they appear disconnected since we have made them so. Problems will remain intractable so long as we divide them into comfortable and neat compartments and rationalize ways of tackling them. Take, for example, migration.

It is the outcome of a series of factors which, as in the case of Bangladesh, a focus of this book, appear to be disconnected. Some of these factors are slow to develop, like land degradation; others are dynamic and immediately visible, such as devastating floods. The reasons for migration thus range from population density, land pressures and land-carrying capacity, erosion of river banks, to even a drop in fish catch and the pull of those who have gone before. There are religious anxieties among smaller groups. These are multidimensional issues.

People may also move because they are attracted by the prospects of 'a better life', not necessarily because they believe they will actually have one. They know that while life may be 'better', it may not be easier, at least as far as social interaction with the host community is concerned. The latter may be hostile, at least for an initial period. For example, locating Bangladeshi migrants in Assam was not an easy task. Few would acknowledge that they had come from across the border because of fear of harassment by the local police and anti-immigrant activists.

This book is an effort to place the Bangladeshi migrations into India, especially into Assam, in a perspective that seeks to reflect a multidisciplinary, multidimensional approach. The book has been organized into fourteen chapters. In the first six, we look at the problem of thresholds—of what comprises 'carrying capacity' in nations: the thresholds of population, land and water as well as food and energy. The pressures that make people move, the places where they go to and how they are received there, are examined. We look at the scale, scope and concepts of migration, differentiate between refugee flows and migratory movements, and then view the disasters that overtake societies when these basic problems are ignored or not understood adequately. Chapters seven to thirteen analyse the dynamics, and tragedies of the Bangladesh–Assam/North East situation. Built on extensive fieldwork and conversations in Bangladesh and Assam, they tell the stories of both those who move and others who stay behind. The last chapter addresses policy alternatives, questions of nationality and citizenship from the perspective of the people as well as that of government. It looks at what, in my view, can and must be done—now and in the near future.

The telling of this story has been shaped both by my personal experiences and views, as well as by the facts of the situation. I have deliberately avoided placing large chunks of statistics in the body of the book. Readers will find extensive statistical material in the appendices and in footnotes.

As with my other books, I have chosen to follow the narrative style of writing here, one with which I am comfortable. There may be obvious drawbacks with such a style but I risk taking this approach because I want the book to engage people and provoke them, not to languish in some distant library. I want it to force a debate, to shake up governmental and societal approaches to the issue of migration. Perhaps that is being too ambitious—but innovative thinking must shape the agenda of our governments, whether it is the result of inputs by people outside the 'system' or those who are in it.

We need to think with our heads. For too long we have thought with our hearts.

This approach becomes even more important when we look at the literature of migration. This can be broadly organized into two segments: one, academic writing, focusing on theory and using case studies as opportunities to establish a particular legal, philosophical or political point; two, documents from international conferences, seminars and 'projects'. In much of this literature, the people who move, who are at the heart of this phenomenon, are mere footnotes, if even that. They are statistics not stories as they should be: voices of people resonating across time and distance, telling us of their tales, forcing us to listen and heed. They do not form the core upon which a 'project' rests but only 'materials' to forge a case and develop an idea.

Rites of Passage is an effort to give migration a human face, merging narratives and analysis. It is based on my own background as a reporter for the *New York Times* and other publications, my travels, especially over the past eighteen years, and the research material I developed and gathered from Assam, Bangladesh and other parts of the world. I have been engaged in this process of dialogue and policy development through my columns and lectures, seminars and workshops over the past several years, as well as through my work with the National Security Advisory Board, the newly-formed Centre for North East Studies and Policy Research and the National Commission for the Review of the Working of the Constitution. In the present work I have sought to stitch together this body of work, built up over the years.

People are on the move and their movement tells the story of a changing world.[2]

For migration, forced and unforced, is our history. The latter encompasses those who move, voluntarily, across state borders in search of livelihoods and cultural compacts. The former are those who have been pushed out by governments or political and social groups hostile to their very existence. They leave because they fear for their lives.

Bangladesh is an extraordinary example of a nation that has seen both trends. The best known was the 1970-71 outflow of more than nine million refugees who fled a brutal Pakistani crackdown on pro-liberation East Pakistan in 1970-71 before Indian army troops and Bangla guerrillas brought freedom to that land. But preceding and consequent to that tragic chapter in the life of the subcontinent, the movement of people for economic and environmental reasons was (and continues to be) a factor in the Brahmaputra, and Barak valleys, in tiny Tripura, not to speak of West Bengal and even across India. Visibly reshaping and transforming the demographic, ethnic, linguistic and religious profile of large parts of the population in these areas, it stirred a potent brew of hatred, suspicion and fear.

The social, demographic and political tensions spawned by this problem are too deep to gloss over or to seek quick-fix solutions like 'throwing' foreigners out. Some extreme, parochial groups take refuge in the Italian political philosopher Niccolò de Bernado Machiavelli, without knowing that it is him that they quote. Many ideologues of the extreme right-wing who accuse Bangladesh of trying to swamp the North East and take it

---

2   *State of the World*, World Watch Institute, 1995, p 132

over demographically, and thence politically (not to speak of economically), indirectly quote Machiavelli when they raise these fears. The Italian had declared in the sixteenth century that 'sending immigrants is the most effective way to colonize countries because it is less offensive than to send military expeditions and much less expensive.' It is doubtful if there is an active 'conspiracy' to Bangladeshize Assam and the North East, as some would have us believe. There are different reasons why people are moving and triggering the fears, hopes and concerns that they do. The fundamentalist surge in the lower districts of Assam is one of the factors for worry, but not the only one.

We need to look at the issues dispassionately and find out what solutions will work. Can anything be resolved given the complexities of the issues? During the course of our fieldwork, my researchers and I met extremely pragmatic people on either side of the border. They knew what they wanted, how it could be achieved, but they had little hope that political leaders could do it. They saw the benefits of local choice, local decisions being translated into national and regional realities. Their views as much as, if not more than, those of scholars, social theorists, politicians and officials must direct policy-formation.

Rites of Passage seeks to record and affirm their voices, besides my thoughts, and to span boundaries in a leap across disciplines, and a vision born of history.

CHAPTER TWO

Mahesh: Encounters of the First Kind

T he first 'migrant' I met was Mahesh, our bandy-legged cook who was fond of going '*O mai go!*' whenever he wanted to emphasize a point. Stretched a bit, it could sound like 'O, my God.' But translated from Bengali into English, this means 'Oh, my mother!'

Mahesh Chandra Das was born in Sylhet, a Muslim-majority area of the then East Pakistan that was dominated by Bengali speakers. This chunk of territory had, even before Partition, voted to be part of the separate Muslim-majority provinces, instead of staying with Assam. To this day, there are Sylhetis who like to talk about their close connections with Assam and especially with the former capital of Shillong, where many went to school—even after Partition.

Nostalgia is a hopelessly all-encompassing vice; and it is hopeless, because it constructs a world that is never a 'now' but one that 'was' or 'could have been'.

Mahesh had moved to Shillong, the capital of Assam province to find work. He ended up as a cook at the Reid Chest Hospital, the main tuberculosis treatment centre of the North East. My father was the superintendent or chief administrator at the time. But how Mahesh got in is a story I don't know.

Mahesh is central to this book not because he has a great story, but because he doesn't. He was illiterate, yet, could sign his name with a flourish. Many of the people who move from nation to nation, village to city, often illegally and silently, are simple folk with simple tales, often faceless and voiceless. Often, they do not even exist as statistics because they are not enumerated. Until perhaps much later. By then they have developed a fiction of their lives: one identity in this land, another in the nation of their birth and growth. You won't know who they are until you engage them in a conversation and that too after winning their confidence, a process that could take weeks, if not months. Because they're always afraid that the *sarkar* would be watching their every step, waiting to harass, extort, pressure and oust them through its many agencies. Or worse, the sarkar would turn its back on harassment, extortion, pressure and ousters by local thugs and dalals.

Which of the two is preferable? Which is worse?

Mahesh was a Bengali-speaking Hindu, which did not really matter to us. Growing up and studying in an Irish missionary (Roman Catholic to boot) school, with a classful of other boys from all communities, labels of caste, religion and language did not really matter. I think I learned more about secularism just by being at St Edmunds' all my school life than by reading about it, or later, through observing majoritarian or minority chauvinists at work in India and abroad.

Mahesh was a great cook; everyone used to rave about his *ilish* (hilsa) curry. I preferred his chicken and mutton, not being much of a fish-eater those days. It's only now that I realize how much I missed.

If there was one thing I found obnoxious about Mahesh, it was the horrible-smelling *biris* which he smoked. He had this rather unsettling habit of sucking in the smoke with a long hissing sound. His cheeks would cave in, his lips would disappear and he would, ostensibly, savour the moment. Then, at the right time, with a sibilant hiss, the smoke would flow out of his nostrils and mouth. Life would be normal again, except that his lips remained stained from the last *paan*.

In summers, Mahesh would wear a loose *kameez* (shirt) and a dhoti. In winters, to this he would add a sweater and a woollen scarf or a woollen *galabandh* to keep out the fierce hill chill of Shillong, which sat snugly among pine trees, rolling hills and swift streams at nearly 5,000 feet above sea level. Frost would form on winter nights, the taps would freeze and the coldest place would be bed—at least for those freezing first few moments when you jumped in, before your body heat, the thick razai and the hot water bottle at your feet restored some sense of normalcy.

Mahesh had a wife and several children. And every year, he would disappear for a couple of weeks—he was going home, he would say. My parents, of course, knew where 'home' was. But it was not until I was about twelve or thirteen that I understood.

I forget whether it was my father or mother who mentioned to me that he went to East Pakistan. 'This is wonderful,' I thought. It was the very stuff of adventure—our bandy-legged cook, slipping across treacherous terrain, deep into enemy territory, meeting secretly with relatives and then slipping back. Better still, what if he were a spy out on a special mission. One had read about such innocuous or ordinary-looking people being recruited as secret agents in World War II comics. For an imaginative mind, the possibilities were endless.

Mahesh went up a few notches in my esteem, despite his biris.

So when he came back, I asked him about the trip.

'I went to Sylhet,' he said. 'Yes, but how did you go?' I asked. I recall that he misunderstood the question. 'I have many relatives there still.' I repeated the question. The answer was short and bland: 'I went to the border and paid ten rupees to the Pakistani police and then walked across.' He then caught a bus and went to Sylhet, which is about 100 kilometres from Shillong. On the way back, he would invest another ten rupees in the Indian police officer on duty (few people even today make the fine distinction between a policeman on duty or a border security guard but they do differentiate between a policeman and an army soldier) and slip across. No papers, no hassles. A nice balance it seemed: pay the Pakistani on the way out and the Indian on the way in. Keep parity.

In similar fashion, Mahesh added, his numerous relatives would come to savour the fresh air of a hill station at Shillong (this was the nearest hill station for East Pakistan and remains so for its successor state, Bangladesh). Everyone eventually got what they wanted—the policeman got his money and the relatives their trip to India without going through the bureaucratic labyrinth of first seeking passports, then visas and then dealing with the travel sharks and touts. It seemed, to my young mind, a very easy and sensible thing to do.

But, I asked, suppose he didn't want to pay the twenty

rupees to the policemen. Couldn't he just sneak across? He said he could, but, if he was caught, not only would he be soundly thrashed, he would have to part with much more money. So he preferred to play safe.

So much for wild ideas about Sylheti cooks from Shillong functioning as undercover agents. But later that year, my elder brother, Suzoy, and I travelled with our parents to Dawki on the India–East Pakistan border, about 200 kilometres south of Shillong, a five-hour run by car then. There are several things that I remember about the trip, including that the border point was a bamboo pole, one end fixed to a pillar and the other tied to a rope. This was the actual 'gate'.

The Assamese policeman (he could have been a customs officer, at that age I could not tell) told us quite cheerfully how they had come under fire the other day. 'We were dodging the bullets,' he said, playing to our wonderment. 'And then, *saala, aami enekuake guli marilu je ekebare teulookor ghar-sor sob uri gol.*' (in simple terms, 'We just blew them away.')

'Damn good. Taught those bloody Pakistanis a lesson,' I thought, caught up in my schoolboyish excitement, looking across at the Pakistani side.

Many years later, Dawki is a major trading point between India and Bangladesh. Through it flows an unending stream of trucks carrying coal to India's neighbour. Other goods which move include areca nut and betel leaf, fish, meat, consumer goods and cattle (especially during Ramzan in Bangladesh. Otherwise, from where would they get their meat?). Skinny-looking creatures, these cattle, plod along on the Guwahati–Shillong highway.

I've often wondered where they come from. Probably

from different parts of Assam and Meghalaya. But also from as far as the Punjab, I've been told. Though this can't be confirmed, I can well believe it. There are many 'cow corridors' through which these animals are pushed into Bangladesh. And indeed, the biggest illegal export from India to that country is cattle—nearly two million of them every year, specifically for meat. We don't slaughter cattle in most parts of India (on religious grounds, ostensibly) but that doesn't prevent us from marketing these beasts there. It makes for an interesting marriage between religion and commerce.

There was little meat on the cattle when we first saw them decades back; there's little meat on them now. But smugglers and buyers aren't too fussy about looks. At feasting time, what matters is whether meat is available, to feed relatives and friends.

So, what has changed? The cattle still trundle on. Dawki is still an entry and exit point. People still sneak in and out of India and Bangladesh. But what has dramatically and irrevocably changed in the past decades has been the seamlessness, the speed and the scale of this movement and the devastating way it has made international borders so vulnerable. I've lost track of Mahesh so I don't know if he goes to Sylhet any longer or even where he is.

These days, there are tens of thousands of people like him who move in steady file, visible only when they emerge in statistics in the villages of Assam, the North East and other parts of India, marching in unison to the beat of an unseen but loud drummer. That drummer is poverty; the land they flee is Bangladesh—but it could be anywhere in the world. Their numbers are surging and growing, frightening 'local' people into fearing for their future and their identity. It is a relentless march and as it moves across the subcontinent, it reflects a phenomenon as old as time and visible across the planet: migration, unstoppable.

Understandable and unstoppable.

The march is made more complicated, and is difficult to tackle because now the walkers have among them Ring Wraiths, as in J.F. Tolkien's magnificent fable, *The Lord of the Rings*—the shadowy dealers of death: in weapons, explosives and drugs. Some dance to the tune of a different piper in a different land, not Bangladesh. And there are stirrings of anger, of violent claims, of demands for religious and ethnic supremacy and fundamentalism.

The seamlessness of the movement, added to these spasms, give it a critical, even dangerous, edge especially as they take place in an area already troubled by insurgencies. A fundamentalist Islamic front in the soft underbelly of eastern India, where governance is poor and infrastructure close to collapse, has the potential of causing havoc. Where will it head? Who will direct it? Can its formation be curbed, if not stopped? Are there opportunities for change, for social mobilization, for hope?

We must face these issues head-on if we are not to despair.

CHAPTER THREE

Crossing Thresholds: Land and People

I f life is about stretching our limits, then the world is about crossing thresholds and knowing when we have done so. The tragedy is that we are waking up to the dangers facing our world far too late. We are realizing how one crisis after another has overtaken us, only after we have been enveloped by it. Thresholds give us a benchmark for knowing what those danger levels are, and where they have already been passed. They can be gauged from the signals we get from a polluted river where marine life has simply ceased to exist, killed by chemicals and waste poured into it day after day; or a drop in land fertility as a result of the overuse of chemical fertilizers and pesticides; or unending traffic snarls in towns and cities because of the lack of foresight to know that broader roads would be needed to support a galloping vehicular population.

It has been a few decades since the spread of environment consciousness began. Yet, it is not as if human beings have been destructive of nature since the very beginning of their existence or unaware of the need to conserve. There are enough examples going back to the river valley civilizations of China, India and Europe as well as even the hunter-gatherers of ancient times, environmentally-friendly communities that existed even then.

More than a century ago, the scientist and philosopher Baron Alexander von Humboldt developed the belief—which was further expounded upon by his follower Charles Darwin—that interdependence was the key to the world's existence and the health of its many species.[1] Humboldt talked of a 'chain of connection' holding life on earth together and that, within the chaos of the world, there was also harmony, what has been called as 'unity in the vast diversity of physical phenomena.'

The environmental buzz of this century started with the UN Conference on the Environment at Stockholm in 1972, and the brilliant and powerful testimony of Rachel Carson in her *Silent Spring*, against the long-term impact of pesticides in the life chain. Perhaps, no other book has influenced the world's perception of and policies toward environmental issues as Carson's has.

These were followed by the development of Greenpeace and other environmental activist groups in the First World and then in the Third, the influence of think-tanks such as the World Watch Institute in Washington and a series of toughly-negotiated international treaties on climate change, protecting the ozone layer, the resources of the sea and bio-diversity.

Over these years, we have been witness to the development of a new language where phrases such as 'sustainable development', 'eco-friendly regimes', 'eco-friendly industry,' 'eco-efficiency,' 'carrying capacity' and 'social thresholds' have become both commonplace and

---

1   The references here to Humboldt's work are taken from Aaron Sach's essay, 'Humboldt's Legacy and the Restoration of Science' , *World Watch*, March/April 1992

meaningful.

These words or group of words carry greater weight than they have ever done before, especially within governments and, generally, in civil society. The signals have gone out far and wide and they are beginning to be reflected in actual policies. But, still, too many people are unaware of the vastness of the task ahead, and the interconnections to every sphere of life; this makes the business of tackling these tasks all the more challenging and critical.

Without restrictions on a population's use or access to natural resources, the very existence of the latter can be imperilled. In many cases, overuse has meant that a resource cannot be replenished. This has happened with natural soil fertility in many places and selected fish species, to take two examples.

At the start of the twentieth century, 1.6 billion people inhabited the earth. In October 1999, the world witnessed the birth of its six billionth child, wrapped in swaddling clothes, in Serbia. The United Nations Secretary General, Kofi Annan, flew specially halfway across the world to welcome the new arrival, to the popping of flashlights, questions flung by the world's media at him and the rolling of television cameras. The child slept on, safe in the arms of his smiling, young mother, oblivious to the enormous publicity.

In the past fifty years, human population has soared by more than 3.4 billion, putting enormous pressure on the earth's basic resources: air, water, energy, and land. Environmental, economic, social and political problems have shown a commensurate, dramatic surge, whether in terms of crime or conflicts, food shortages or rising aspirations, leading to political instability.

The critical element is the demographic trigger, when populations sweep past the ability of land, river and air to sustain them. When that trigger is pressed hard, it forces social groups and individuals to move for the sake of survival, at gunpoint as it were, to other areas. Indeed, as Myron Weiner has remarked, migration is the story of our world. People move internally, within nations. People move externally, to other countries, even to poor and underdeveloped lands, which hold out some promise of a living. This puts pressure on the host communities, more so if they are already poor, fearing marginalization by the new, hardworking and mobile settlers. Often, this in turn, leads to a backlash against the immigrant.

Bangladesh represents a classic example of this demographic tragedy. But it is the bloody harvest that has followed since the late 1970s in the remote north-eastern state of Assam, which neighbours that country, that is of special significance. The violence has grown out of an inability by the state and communities to understand or even to begin plumbing the depths of the sheer reactive rage that is spawned by these pressures.

That the demands made by an increasingly aggressive human population have begun to outstrip the capacity of the earth to sustain them is becoming more and more starkly visible. There are social conflicts such as fishing clashes between Canada and Spain over turbot near Canada's eastern coast or between Asian nations such as Indonesia and the Philippines in the Celebes. Water shortages have led to riots in Delhi, as people revolted, suffering in the furnace-like heat of the summers; underground water levels are dropping swiftly in the major bread and grain baskets of the world—the Great Plains of the Midwest in the United States; the 'Green

Revolution' states of Punjab and Haryana in India: farmers are overpumping these reserves.

In the hill regions of North India, women walk longer and longer distances every year to fetch firewood for cooking their meals—the forests are in retreat. The demands of lumber, energy and paper are spreading quickly, forcing the decline of the forests in South America, in Africa, and in Asia and consequently, of the wildlife and ecosystems that have sustained them and us for centuries.

Environmental degradation and population pressures are but two of the major reasons which fuel poverty around us. We have the capacity to feed ourselves. In 2000, for example, India had a glut of foodgrains in its reserves. But as rats and poor storage nibbled away at this cornucopia, there was another question: why was the food rotting in godowns when it should be reaching the poor through fair-price shops? The problem lies not in our numbers or other cited factors: the real crisis lies in a poor distribution mechanism, official lethargy and what farmers see as a lack of adequate support prices.

Disparaties within nations are also reflected starkly among nations as the gap between the rich and poor grow. Thus, the world economy is today seventeen times the size of what it was a century ago. Nations are industrializing faster than ever before. Billions live healthier lives and life expectancy in most countries has doubled in this period, thanks to a combination of better diets, health care and incomes. Yet, more than 800 million people go hungry every day, are malnourished and underweight, and over a billion—or one-sixth of the earth's population—do not have access to safe drinking water.

The gap between rich and poor nations remains

greater than ever, and more iniquitous. As a result, the ratio between incomes in the richest one-fifth of countries has widened from 30 to 1 in 1960 to 61 to 1 in 1991, 'creating tensions between those on the upper rungs of the global economic ladder and those stuck on the bottom steps,' says the World Watch Institute.[2]

Our vulnerability and dependence on natural resources is even more obvious when nations, and powerful interest groups within nations, confront each other over, for instance, the distribution of river waters. In many cases, the rights of riparian, upstream states compete with those of riparian, downstream ones. Water is not just a critical input to sustain agriculture and feed populations. It has the force to be a powerful political issue, especially when communities and nations feel deprived of what is perceived as their 'just' rights, of water needed for irrigation, fishing and energy requirements. One of the best examples of this in recent years has been the political struggle between India and Bangladesh over sharing the waters of the Ganges river.

The dispute here was between a water-controlling country, India, and a weaker, lower riparian, Bangladesh. The Ganges emerges from a Himalayan glacier at Gaumukh in northern India and flows through the heavily populated states of Uttar Pradesh, Bihar and West Bengal before moving into Bangladesh. It later joins the Brahmaputra to form the vast Padma. Through its course in India, the Ganges is tapped by millions of farmers and tens of thousands of villages and towns for a variety of purposes, including irrigation, bathing, and household as well as industrial use. In the process, it has become one of the filthiest and most bio-degraded rivers in the world,

---

2   *State of the World*, World Watch Institute, 1999

receiving the untreated garbage, industrial and agricultural effluents, as well as human and animal waste (including human corpses and animal carcasses) before flowing into Bangladesh. The water is a health hazard in places, leading to fish kills, where tens of thousands of fish are poisoned by its pollution. In other places, the world's holiest river harms the skin, causing ailments to villagers, for example, in Uttar Pradesh.[3]

In the 1970s, India completed the Farakka Barrage which diverted water from the Ganges to Calcutta, to help flush the silt from its port. This reduced the flow to Bangladesh, which anyway was the last in the line to receive the water. An argument can be made that Calcutta anyway did not need this water because it was a dying port, incapable of taking in deep draught vessels. This in turn forced the large ships to follow the cumbersome procedures of transferring their cargos out at sea to smaller boats for carrying into the city. Calcutta's silting has not eased and the condition of the port has not improved over the past twenty-five years.

Indeed, as B.G. Verghese, a specialist on water resources, has said, Calcutta should have been maintained as a river port, as in the British days and pre-colonial times. Indian planners should have set in place a network of other ports in the hinterland of Bengal, Bihar and broadened this to include Bangladesh. Such a strategy would have enabled Calcutta to play a bigger economic role. Instead, it drained water from the Ganges and still failed to redevelop as a great port.

'Calcutta has had its day,' says Verghese, referring to the future of the port.[4]

---

3   Interview with author, Kanpur, 1995
4   B.G. Verghese, *Waters of Hope*, Oxford & IBH, 1990

In Bangladesh, more than 30 million people depend on the waters of the Ganges for their livelihood and sustenance. The water at this low flow time is especially needed for irrigation.

Bangladesh's dependence on river waters is reflected in its ballads and culture as well as the intensive manner in which its people use the rivers as regular highways for transport, commerce and in their daily lives. Indeed, more than three-fourths of the country's entire land area falls within the flood plain of the Ganga-Brahmaputra-Barak rivers which ultimately fall into the Bay of Bengal. According to B.G. Verghese no other country anywhere 'faces a flood problem of the nature and magnitude that Bangladesh does.'

The Ganges water negotiations have been among the most protracted and difficult endured by the two countries in the last quarter of the twentieth century. Of course, the discussions began before the creation of Bangladesh in 1971.

An initial short-term agreement took place in 1977, defining the lean seasons when water supply was critical to Bangladesh and specifying the amount that was to be guaranteed under this accord. By the mid-1980s, both goodwill and political resolve had evaporated on either side and the agreement collapsed.

Emotions ran high in Bangladesh. Desultory discussions continued, stalled, governments came and fell in both countries, angry words were exchanged. In 1988, Bangladesh was devastated by the worst floods of the century; the same surge of the Brahmaputra river had overwhelmed Assam earlier.

Nothing came of the negotiations until 1996 when Prime Ministers H.D. Deve Gowda and Sheikh Hasina

Wajed of Bangladesh signed an agreement on water sharing, after months of tough negotiations between river experts from either side.

Men like Verghese and others played a significant but background role in the shaping of the accord, which involved figures such as External Affairs Minister (and later Prime Minister) Inder Kumar Gujral when they were out of government, in an informal process of dialogue consultations and joint research that has come to be known as Track II. These informal talks discussed the water-sharing problem in an open manner, had the tacit backing of either government and drew specialists, scholars and policy-makers from both sides.

This is one aspect of the Bangladesh-India relationship that has been resolved bilaterally and the agreement appears to be working. But there is another area that has remained impossible to untangle, one that involves both countries, as well as communities within the North East.

The problem of illegal migration from Bangladesh into India, and especially into its North East, brings together all the skeins of the problems that have been outlined earlier, to produce one gigantic brew of bitterness and conflict that is constantly churning and erupting and shows little or no sign of abatement. What makes any solution of it difficult is the fact that two neighbouring nation are involved, both poor—one more so than the other—with the outflow from Bangladesh being basically a strategy for survival. Matters are not helped by the scant global or even regional interest in helping India and Bangladesh do the simple things which could ease this crisis and improve conditions. The most brutal illustration of this confrontation was seen in 1983, on the rice-fields outside the little roadside town of Nellie in Assam.

CHAPTER FOUR

The Roads to Nellie

In February 1983, the Government of India and the Election Commission—at that time nothing but a compliant lapdog of the government—undertook the organization of elections to Assam's 126 state legislature seats and fourteen seats to the Lok Sabha. The decision to hold the elections flew in the face of logic and showed crass insensitivity to local concerns and rising emotions.

Assam was a tinder-keg of hatreds and suspicions, of animosity and confrontation. For just under four years, a group of young men from the All Assam Students Union (AASU) had seized the political initiative and captured the imagination of people in the Brahmaputra Valley by picking on a theme that was to spark both fear and anger. AASU said that the original people of Assam were being marginalized by a relentless flow of illegal migrants from Bangladesh, patronized by political parties, especially the Congress Party. The immigrants, they said, were largely Muslim and their presence in Assam threatened to overwhelm the local ethnic groupings and to take political, economic and social power out of the hands of the Assamese. Citing highly inflated figures, AASU triggered spasms of protests that wrecked the local economy and virtually brought the government in the state to a halt. The Assamese, it said, were already a minority in their own land and the state would soon be consumed by Bangladesh. There were not less than four million Bangladeshis in Assam and demands were made for the deportation of those who had come to India after 1951. This demand was scaled down to post-1961 and finally to post–1971, when Bangladesh was created.

The students and their political advisors declared that Bangladesh was renewing the unfinished agenda of Partition—when Pakistan's founder Mohammed Ali Jinnah saw Assam snatched away from under his nose by a determined effort from Assam Congressmen led by Premier Gopinath Bardoloi, who was strongly supported by Mahatma Gandhi.[1]

Bardoloi was Assam's hero of the hour, the man who saved the province from going to Pakistan and becoming absorbed in East Pakistan under the Grouping system devised by the Cabinet Mission of 1946. Under this scheme, Assam, which was largely Hindu, would have been clubbed with the Muslim-majority, but larger Bengal state. They would then have drawn up the constitutions of their respective areas—but it does not need much to understand that Bengal would had decided the fate of Assam. This was rejected by Bardoloi, with the support of Mahatma Gandhi, and over the objections of Jawaharlal Nehru and Sardar Vallabhbhai Patel, who were extremely irked as what they regarded as Assam stalling the independence process.

Assamese nationalism, or what Sanjib Baruah

---

1   Sanjoy Hazarika, *Strangers of the Mist*, Viking/Penguin, 1994; also see the private papers of Sir Mohammad Saadulla and of Gopinath Bardoloi, Nehru Memorial Museum and Library, New Delhi

describes as subnationalism[2], has always ranged itself against the outsider, be it from Bengal or Rajasthan or other parts of India. The Assamese perception and concern over the illegal migrant, or any migrant and settler, has been articulated as early as the 1930s by politicians and writers. An influential thinker and organizer in the pre- and post-independence movement was Ambikagiri Raychaudhuri, a revolutionary poet, a radical and member of the Congress Party. Raychaudhuri proclaimed the need for Assamese to 'ensure full control . . . over Assam's land and natural resources, agriculture, commerce and industry, trade, employment, language and literature, culture and ethos.'

That long list hardly leaves out any subject of regional discourse!

Gynanath Borah wrote in a collection of essays in 1935 that the different provinces of India needed to recognize their own unique qualities. Borah strongly questioned the wisdom of trying to unite different literatures, languages and communities under the banner of 'one language, one literature and one nation.'[3] He believed that India would flourish as a federation of entities, each enriching the nation with its own special virtues and gifts.

Thus, the Assamese construct of the historical threat from the perceived outsider/foreigner is not a new one. The concept of the *bidekhi* too is different to that of mainland India where many communities have accepted 'outsiders' and settlers as part of their own land. In Assam, anyone who is not an Assamese speaker or one who does

---

2   Sanjib Baruah, *India Against Itself: Assam and the Politics of Nationality*, University of Pennsylvania Press, 1999
3   Baruah, S. ibid.

not speak any of the original aboriginal languages, whether Bodo and its numerous dialects, or Ahom, Tiwa, Rabha and Mishing to name a few, is viewed as an outsider, no matter how long he has lived in the region.

Religion is a factor although the Assamese-speaking Muslims (who are converts going back only a few centuries) or Assamese-speaking Sikhs are largely exempt from this rule. Thus, Bengali-speaking Muslims, both by language and religion, are prime suspects as these factors are common to the majority of the population of Bangladesh. In addition, the Bengalis have long been resented by various linguistic and ethnic groups in the Brahmaputra Valley as a group which allied with British colonizers to undercut Assamese interests. It is part of public memory that Bengali officers helped to inflict Bengali as the official language on the province briefly before American Baptist missionaries, with the publication of the first Assamese language magazine, *Orunodoi* (meaning Sunrise), persuaded the British that Assamese was a separate language which should be used for official purposes in the province of its birth.

Nationality is not viewed as a gift bestowed by the Indian Constitution but one that owes more to customs stemming from a group's view of history, however small or narrow that vision may be. Such a historical approach is also determined by oral traditions of the community, passed down several generations.

All these came into play during the anti-immigrant movement in Assam of the 1980s. The agitators took the line that Bangladeshi Muslims were pouring across porous borders and the Government of India was disinterested in the issue.

1980s and Agitation

The Government of Assam, then run by a portly Socialist named Golap Borbora, appeared unable to shake itself out of a daze. The students called the shots and negotiated directly with the prime minister.

Ah o ah
Ulai ah
Khed oh khed
Bidekhik khed

(Come, come
Come out of your homes
Chase, chase
Chase the foreigner away)

This pithy slogan became the rallying point of every meeting, the call to arms of every procession and protest, during daytime or with *mashaals* or torches at night; of pickets and sitdown demonstrations outside oil refineries and government offices. Schools and colleges closed for weeks at a time: the students were all out at pickets and protests, ignoring their studies, a decision that many of them later rued.

The atmosphere was electric, crackling with excitement and the romance of passion, of conviction. The student leaders appeared to be setting the agenda and forcing the government to yield, time and again. Curfews were declared and defied, forcing administrators to withdraw their orders.

Assam lurched from round to round of confrontation but Prime Minister Indira Gandhi refused to budge. Talk in practical terms, she told the agitators in several rounds of talks in New Delhi and Assam. Agree to 1971 as the 'cut off year', she said, the year of the Bangladesh war when Indian troops, aided by Bengali liberation fighters known as the Mukti Bahini, crushed Pakistani troops, forcing their ignominious defeat within a few weeks of the outbreak of war.

The reason for selecting 1971 was clear: it marked the creation of a new nation. Those who came from the new entity, Bangladesh, were not entitled to settle in India without valid papers, she argued. Detection of the immigrants could begin right away with intensive revisions of electoral rolls and census data; deportation could then follow.

The students were also adamant, although they had eased their demands. First of all, they had sought the deportation of all 'illegal immigrants' from Assam after 1951. Then they scaled this down to those who came after 1961. The Government of India had problems with this as well—among the nearly one million people who came between 1961 and 1971, illegally, of course, not less than 920,000 were Bengali Hindus who had fled the pogroms of the late 1960s in East Pakistan.

As the talks faltered and finally failed, Mrs Gandhi decided to try and break the movement by political force and put the students through a crucible—she would ask the people to give a mandate on their demands and her responses. Voting was ordered for the Assembly as well as for the eight out of fourteen seats to Parliament which had not been filled since 1980 (there were boycotts organized by the students that year which blocked voting in these constituencies although in six others, the voting came through). The 1980 general election returned Indira

Gandhi to power after a three-year period in opposition. Leading the Congress Party's charge in Assam was Hiteswar Saikia, a stocky politician with the guile of a fox and the organizing skills of an army general.

Assam: a Profile

It is important at this point to survey the condition of Assam. A land of 82,000 square kilometres, watered by the vast Brahmaputra river, prone to severe floods, it is inhabited by a medley of communities professing a range of faiths: Hindus, Muslim, Christian and Sikh. Its nearly 25 million people are bunched together in the narrow Brahmaputra Valley, barely 90 to 100 kilometres wide at its broadest.

The land is bountiful, bearing fruits and crops of different varieties—oranges and grapefruits, bananas and mangoes, rice and mustard, tea and coconut, areca nut and betel leaf. During the summer rains, the place is washed clean and covered by a rich, deep green carpet which, from the air, appears to be an incredible patchwork of geometrical patterns. In the winters, the farms are, for the most part, quiet and fallow. The fields are almost barren; dust lies where rice stalks flourished in the monsoon rains, when women with saris and skirts wrapped around their legs walked with military precision through knee-deep water and slush, holding porous, delicate-looking but strong cane baskets. These baskets are fish traps but they would not look out of place as an exotic artifact in the drawing room of a wealthy family in Delhi, Bombay or Calcutta. Mud-spattered and deeply tanned from the sun and humidity, these women wear *japis* or cane hats on their heads and cane trays on their backs during the thunderous monsoons for protection from the heavy rain.

These are vignettes of gentleness and social peace among communities used to a slower pace of life, whose worlds are gentler and kinder than ours. Such postcard-like lives conjure up visions of South-East Asia and one would not be far wrong in linking the two. For India's North East is where South and South-East Asia meet and merge to form new identities, rooted in either tradition and possessing a uniqueness of their own.

But with astonishing abruptness and brutality the calm of these societies is being torn apart.

Much of this has to do with the location of the region, geographically so distant from Delhi, and the terrain which makes it difficult to establish connections. Placed between what is now Bangladesh, Tibet, Myanmar (the former Burma) and Bhutan and with a thin land corridor linking it with the rest of India—the Chicken's Neck near Siliguri in West Bengal and the Assam border—the North East today comprises of seven states, each vigorously different from the other. Assam and Meghalaya, Arunachal Pradesh and Nagaland, Manipur and Mizoram and finally, Tripura. The hill states surround Assam, abutting on the other nations of South and South-East Asia. Ninety-eight per cent of the borders of the North East touch these nations. Only two per cent is connected to India, pointing to the North East's tenuous geographical and political connectivity to the Indian mainland. Through this narrow land corridor run the only road and rail connections as well as the oil and gas pipelines connecting India to its North East. This lack of connectivity and isolation has bred extreme inequity and promoted the growth of enclave industries which are dependent on the rich natural resources of the area—tea, oil and gas as well as timber. The beneficiaries of this lopsided development have been large companies owned by a handful of individuals, especially in the tea and timber sectors, with their main offices located outside the region.

Tea has had by far the greatest social and economic impact, employing nearly 600,000 workers in Assam alone and supporting another 3.4 lakh dependents. A major exchange earner for India (in 1999, the figures were twenty billion rupees or about 500 million dollars), tea is cultivated on a major portion of the arable land in the narrow Brahmaputra Valley. This reduces the land available for 'ordinary' consumer crops such as rice, other cereals, vegetables and fruits. Dependence on other parts of India for imports of these products has grown and farm technology, especially the use of fertilizers and pesticides as well as of high-yielding varieties of crops, has fallen far behind other states of the 'mainland'.

Oil and gas have been a monopoly of the Government of India for the past decades. Only in the past years has this opened up to private investment. Domestic and foreign interest in this sector has been low because of the violence and confrontations which have erupted since the North East's first face-off with the Indian state led by the Nagas in 1952. Since then, the North East has been a simmering cauldron of ethnic divisions, militancies and insurgencies which have ripped aside the fragile veil of peace.

As Arun Shourie, journalist and a leader of the Bharatiya Janata Party, remarked in a powerful, investigative essay: 'Each community that was a victim in one place was the predator in another.'[4] Shourie was referring to the explosions of slaughter in Assam in 1983 and particularly to the killings of Bengali-speaking Muslims at Nellie, north-east of Guwahati, the main commercial hub of Assam. Yet, his grim words, which conjure up the vision of a nasty, even primitive condition of the human mind and spirit, have an eerie ring of relevance when measured against almost every conflict situation in the North East.

I personally dislike the 'North East' label because this term makes it appear as if it were a homogenous mass while, quite to the contrary, it is a bustling terrain sprouting, proclaiming, underscoring a million heterogenities. Yet, the 'North East' has become common and accepted usage even in the area, among the seven states and the nearly 350 distinct communities, large and small, which inhabit them. Many of these groups appear to have been transplanted from South-East Asia.

Thus, the Khasis of Meghalaya speak a language akin to Mon-Khmer which is still in use in present-day Kampuchea. The Khamtis have travelled from the Myanmar-China border and settled in Arunachal Pradesh's Lohit district in the eighteenth century. The Mizos are kin to the Kuki-Chins of Myanmar and the Lisus have come from as far away as Yunnan Province in South West China where they are a 'large' minority with their own district and vice-governor. In Arunachal Pradesh, they number a few thousand!

There are other groups such as brahmins and the kayasthas or middle castes among the Assamese speakers. The latter are principally writers, chroniclers and keepers

---

4   Arun Shoune, 'Assam elections: come what may,' *India Today*, 12 May 1983

of accounts although they were also called upon to do military duty for king and country in the days of the Ahom Kingdom (1228 to 1826 AD). What is truly amazing about this diversity is that most of the hill communities do not have their own scripts but use the Roman script to communicate. This is a 'legacy of the Christian missionaries of the West (primarily British, American and a handful of Italian Jesuits) who came there in the nineteenth century to preach the gospel and win converts. In the process, they helped push the use of English and that of the Roman script. A significant number of tribes in the North East live in the hills where they have settled over hundreds of years. Their size is especially significant in those states which are ethnically dominated by non-plains communities.

To communicate with each other is a difficult task in the North East. In the Assam valley, while Assamese is the lingua franca, there are substantial pockets of Bengali speakers and smaller linguistic groups. The Bodo community, the largest among the plains tribes of the state, prefer to communicate in Devanagri or Hindi. There are variants, of course: some speak either a broken form of Hindi or a combined version of Assamese and a local language or dialect. This patois is called Nagamese in Nagaland state and Nefamese in Arunachal Pradesh (the earlier name for Arunachal was North East Frontier Agency or NEFA).

All this may sound and seem quaint. Yet, behind this romantic veil of social coexistence is a witches' brew of suspicion and hatred which has destroyed the concord and social compacts which have existed here for generations, where one side adjusted to the concerns of the other.

Primordial Passions

For centuries, the North East has constituted India's frontiers. It has received, welcomed as well as opposed settlers, intruders, conquerors and would-be conquerors. As noted earlier, communities moved from as far as Kampuchea and Burma. The first Muslim presence in Assam was noted in the eleventh century when an Iraqi prince was allowed to set up a shrine near the banks of the Brahmaputra, on a hill near Hajo. That shrine still flourishes at Pua Mecca where the muezzin's call welcomes the rising dawn and where Hindus and Muslims come to worship in an expression of communal solidarity that is rare elsewhere in the world, leave aside either Assam or India.

The Mughals, descendants of Babur and Akbar, tried hard to conquer the region. They failed miserably for the most part although the Mughal general, Mir Jumla, succeeded in the 1660s, in inflicting a decisive defeat on the kingdom of the Ahoms. A community of Thai-Burmese origin, the Ahoms settled in the Brahmaputra Valley in the early part of the thirteenth century. To get to Assam, the Ahoms trekked from the Burma-Thailand border, from the land of the Shans, across the Patkai range that separates Burma from the North East and into the valley of the Brahmaputra. The defeat at the hands of Mir Jumla was avenged after his death—the great general died during the monsoon rains which spread disease and despair among his men. He is buried at Mancachar (in reality, the town is Maniker char or the char of Manik). A char is an island formed by the vast amounts of silt brought down by the Brahmaputra river during the annual floods and which surfaces once the river retreats in winter. Manik, one presumes, would have been a man of substantial means many years ago. What is also interesting to note is that the Brahmaputra must have once flowed by or over this place, but it has now moved about twenty kilometres to the west of Mancachar.

The Ahoms ruled Assam for six centuries, until 1826, when the East India Company responded to an appeal from Purnadhar Singha, the then Ahom monarch. The Burmese had invaded and devastated Assam, and Purnadhar sought British help to drive them out. The British were successful but Purnadhar Singha paid a high price for this alliance—his kingdom. Under the terms of the 1826 Treaty of Yandaboo, Burma dropped all its claims on Assam and the state became a protectorate of the British. It became a formal part of the British Empire in 1842.

As a result of this takeover, the Ahoms lost their lands and influence. Other groups which suffered deprivation or were marginalized included the Motoks and Dimasas, the Bodos and Cacharis. Tiwas and Rabhas, Hajongs and Deoris. These groups, of Tibeto-Burman stock, were located in various parts of the Brahmaputra Valley. Of them, the most significant to our story are the Bodos, Motoks and Tiwas. These were ruled by princely clans or chiefs who were at times assisted by a council of advisers or ministers, known as durbars.

In 1842, following Assam's becoming the latest jewel in the Crown, the British extended their influence to the hills around Assam—the Khasi and Jaintia Hills, to the Naga and Lushai Hills, to the Mishmis, Adis, Noctes and Daflas (now better known as Nishis) and to the Manipur valley and hills. Some of these intrusions and controls were not backed by an extensive administration. The

British preferred to rule through local representatives although they also placed a handful of British officers in district headquarters or at an office in Assam.

The British were among the latest in a succession of waves of immigrants that changed the demographic profile of the North East—these included the Tibeto-Burman groups of Arunachal Pradesh to the Kuki-Chins of Mizoram, Manipur and Nagaland and the Austrics of South-East Asia who travelled to present-day Meghalaya.

As this process was underway, the older communities like the Bodos were pushed to pockets in the hills and the plains. Scholars often raise the question about the identity of the 'original inhabitants' of a place—who they are, where did they come from and when. Such views are important but not really relevant any longer in today's changed political and social environment. They matter in terms of emotional links to the past and in the formation of a political identity. But what truly matters, in addition to historic roots, is the ground reality of who, or which group dominates a region.

Bodos, Motoks and Tiwas

The Bodos are of Tibeto-Burman stock and introduced settled agriculture, the cultivation of rice, the use of domesticated cattle and silk weaving into the Assam valley. They are regarded as among the aboriginal groups of Assam but which are now scattered and settled under different names in various parts of the region.

Thus the Bodos or Boros of western Assam are to be found in the Kokrajhar, Bongaigaon districts and are part of the Bodo-Cachari stock. They have settled in a dispersed manner, along the north bank of the Brahmaputra. They are known as Mechs in Bhutan and in Bangladesh. In the eastern part of the North East, they are the Dimasa-Cacharis of Nagaland and Cachar district, where they have been marginalized by Naga groups and Bengali settlers.

In recent years, the Bodos, who number just over one million and are the dominant plains tribal community in Assam, have come into conflict with the powerful Assamese-speakers of the Brahmaputra Valley who are predominantly Hindu and have held political control of the state since the end of the nineteenth century. Smarting with resentment at what they regard as the Assamese attitude of superiority, the Bodos of western Assam have in the past decades been demanding a separate state which they called Udayachal in the 1970s, and now Bodoland.

Such is the depth of Bodo bitterness against what is perceived as Assamese exploitation and their own underdevelopment, that they rejected the Assamese script as the medium of education and communication and turned instead to Devanagri or the Hindi language. At one time, even the Roman script was considered as a possible lingua franca.

The language issue is still alive among the Bodos. In early 2000, Bodo militant groups demanded the use of English as the language of communication. This has been rejected by the main Bodo literary society, the Bodo Sahitya Sabha, and an influential student group, the All Bodo Students Union. These organizations said that changing the script and language at this time would create confusion in the community and negate the advantages it had gained during the past years.

The rationale behind the demand for English was

fairly obvious: it would have meant the severance of any connection to the Indian heartland.

Since 1993, the Bodo demand for separation from Assam has become extremely strident, assuming a violent character that aims at ousting non-Bodos from an area which militants have claimed as, their traditional homeland. This geographical belt stretches in their lexicon from the Sunkosh river that flows down from Bhutan and joins the Brahmaputra to the once-thriving river port of Sadiya, near Arunachal Pradesh.

Sadiya, of course, no longer exists, having been buried deep in the bosom of the Brahmaputra after the great earthquake of 1950. But rhetoric often buries reason as well. In this region, the Bodos do not add up either to a numerical majority or a community that has the advantage of linguistic and geographical contiguity. They are dispersed for the most part and are small minorities in many areas.

That is why when the Government of India, under the direction of the Minister of State for Home Affairs, Rajesh Pilot, and the Assam government under Hiteswar Saikia agreed to set up an autonomous Bodoland Council, they were asking for trouble. The Bodos kept up a stream of demands to include areas with non-Bodo populations in this territory. The other side was equally adamant in refusing these demands.

Bodos began moving from the Kokrajhar belt to other parts of northern Assam with the support and connivance of local politicians in the 1970s. But this became a significant trend in the 1990s as part of a strategy by the National Democratic Front of Bodoland of Ranjan Daimuri, which wants an independent country, to change the demographic profile of districts like Sonitpur.[5] A substantial part of this movement took place quietly.[6]

When negotiations kept stalling and failing on the inclusion of more areas, Bodo militant groups, led by the Bodoland Security Force (later to become the Bodoland Tiger Force) and the National Democratic Front of Bodoland (NDFB), organized pogroms of communities which had lived in these areas for generations. The major target were Santhals, a group which had been settled there since the latter part of the nineteenth century. At the time, they were transported by the British to work as labourers on tea plantations. Over the years, the Santhals settled on the land in their traditional style—in isolated hamlets practising subsistence agriculture. In fierce attacks on the Santhals in May 1996, the Bodos drove tens of thousands from their homes and forced them to take shelter in refugee camps set up by the state government. The Santhals, no mean fighters themselves, retaliated with their traditional weapons—bows and arrows as well as *daos* (machetes).

Nearly 200,000 persons, non-Bodos for the most part, and Bodos, continue to live in unsanitary conditions, cheek by jowl, with little sustenance but irregular government doles. Some who went back to their homes have become refugees a second time after the Bodos descended on them again and made them leave.

The Bodo example shows how land and language have become important tools in the development of political identity in the North East. There are other examples

---

5 Interview with police official, Tezpur, February 1998. Sonitpur has been long viewed as a bastion of 'Assamese' culture. The great singer Bhupen Hazarika has his roots here.
6 ibid.

which show how this process has been accelerated in other parts.

One is of the Motoks and the other of the Tiwas. In each case, marginalization caused by dispossession of land led to conflicts.

The Motoks are a sub-group of the Bodo family and dominated the region in Upper Assam near the business town of Tinsukia in medieval times. Their capital was Bengmara, the site of Tinsukia town today, and their lands were rich and fertile. After Assam was annexed to the British Empire, many young British entrepreneurs and other from the middle and lower-middle class, in search of quick money, descended on Assam and the Duars in neighbouring Bengal to tap profits from a new industry—tea. The Chinese monopoly of tea was to be undercut if British commercial interests were to survive and do well. And this economic battle was fought in the plains of Assam where vast tracts of land was brought under tea plantations.

British companies and planters took over large parts of land in the Tinsukia-Dibrugarh area. The Motoks who were dispossessed received little or no compensation in return.

More than a century later, the revenge of the Motoks was felt most sharply by the tea planters and companies which continued to sit on these lands and extract large profits from them. In the 1980s, a powerful new political group was rising in Assam, one that demanded independence from India and also which extracted huge amounts of money from the tea industry—refusal to pay could mean kidnapping or even death. Unused to dealing with this new situation, most tea companies took the safe way out and paid up.

It was only later when they analysed the profiles of leaders of this militant organization, the United Liberation Front of Asom (ULFA), that government officials realized that several of ULFA's top men were Motoks. They included Paresh Baruah, the commander-in-chief of the organisation and Anup Chetia, the General Secretary of ULFA. Both were from the same village near Chabua air force station in Dibrugarh and had married sisters. Without articulating a historic fact and perhaps even without realizing it, the Motoks in ULFA were avenging the past.

If the Motoks have one set of grievances, further south, in Nogaon district, Central Assam, another older community, the Tiwas, a sub-group of the Bodo-Cachari race, have been deeply angered by dispossession.

Nogaon is a rice bowl located in the very heartland of Assam. Indeed, it falls almost directly at the centre of the entire North East. Its summers are blisteringly hot but its winters are pleasant. It is watered by a few small rivers, the Kolong being the dominant one.

My brother and I spent our winter vacations from school in Shillong at Nogaon, then known as Nowgong. The latter, I think, has a better ring to it. It used to take nearly five hours in my father's black Ambassador which had succeeded the cute but tiny Morris Austin in Shillong. The Ambassador was replaced by a white Fiat a few years before my father's death.

The journey used to be divided into various stages. The first part would be the segment to Nongpoh, 50 kilometres down from home. We were still in the Khasi hills. Then we would pass Jorabat, which as its name suggests was a *jor* of *baats* or a road junction. One road led to Guwahati, the commercial capital of the region, and then went on to the southern and western parts of Assam and the Khasi and Garo hills. We would travel on the other road, which snaked up a group of low hills before descending to the Brahmaputra valley. And what a landscape!

Kilometre after kilometre of paddy fields, gentle and dry in winter, with cattle ambling over the dry land, turning up puffs of dust as they walked. Jacaranda trees and *seemul* with its red-silk blossoms lined the roadside. Large throngs of goats, being prodded and bullied en route to a market or a slaughterhouse, would slow our progress. A few village pie dogs would run along yapping and barking at the vehicle and their own reflections in the hub-caps.

The edges of the roads abutted in places on shallow ponds and streams, their surface covered with water hyacinth. Once, I remember, we were stopped by the flood waters of the Brahmaputra. The river itself is not less than 50 kilometres west of the road that runs along the plains. But in a petulant, final surge of its high water—it was the fourth wave of floods that year—it breached the highway in many places, forcing travel to a halt as water got into distributor heads and engines. Finally, villagers pushed the cars across—for a price, of course.

Hundreds, were perched on the edge of the road, which happened to be the only high land in the neighbourhood at the time. It was a very long time ago and I do not remember it that well, but for the image of rice heaps placed to dry on bamboo mats by the road, a few inches above the water level, and a handful of weary, old men staring hopelessly at the cars struggling by.

Usually, we would drive into another small hamlet, Jagiroad, by lunch time for a helping of spicy chicken and *parathas* served at a Sikh hotel. Parathas were so novel to us—since Assamese eat rice both at lunch and dinner—that we looked forward with hungry anticipation to the *rotis* and the chicken curry. And then onwards, past the hillsides scarred with dynamite blasts for rock and rubble needed for road construction and other projects, past the hamlet of Nellie and to the warmth and affection of the home of my grandparents. Till much later, I did not even know of Nellie's existence.

As evening fell—shorter days meant that it would become dark by 5 p.m.—the smell of smoke from firewood and from dry cow dung pats would waft past the road. It was a peculiar, rich but tangy smell. As dusk grew close, clouds of this smoke would gently float across the fields. If we reached late—and that happened quite often—fireflies would light up the darkness. There were no streetlights along the highway. That remains unchanged even today—and I see little chance of this changing in the future.

In our childhood ignorance, we knew little of the angers and passions that were to bloody this pleasant land. But on 18 February 1983, all this changed for good.

In the space of six hours, Tiwas allied with other plains tribal groups and a number of Assamese to avenge two perceived wrongs.

The first and immediate provocation appeared to be the reported abduction and rape of four young Tiwa women by Bengali-speaking Muslim immigrants. The second was a longer-held, deep-seated grievance: the gradual, sure march of the *miyahs*, as the settlers from the old Mymensingh district of the former East Pakistan (now Bangladesh) were known, over traditional Tiwa lands. The miyahs worked them, first as sharecroppers and then as tenants before finally acquiring rights, if these could be called that.

Essentially, these rights were illegally sought, bought and acquired. For these were traditional lands governed by British-made laws that banned non-tribals from acquiring in any form or shape, land which belonged to the tribals. Not even a government seal on a piece of official paper could change this status. In the case of Nellie and its surrounding villages, those who sold their lands were the Tiwas. Their bitterness grew as they saw the immigrants nourish the soil and grow more crops, making profits on fields which were, until recently, their own.

All roads led to Nellie as the Tiwas, their resentments growing, sharpened their daos, oiled their muskets and twanged their bows and arrows, preparing for what they regarded as judgement day. Perhaps it would be better described as pay-back day.

So much of life is about revenge, so little is about reconciliation. In these twin streams, the primordial passions of love and lust, anger and grief, play central roles.

As Rajmohan Gandhi says, 'A nation cannot be judged by a city, nor a city by a season, but the wall, the lathi and the knife are not, alas, a figment of the imagination.'[7]

'History will not dissolve resentments and suspicions. Selective history will, in fact, harden them,' Gandhi writes in his celebrated study, *Understanding the Muslim Mind*.[8] Speaking of Hindu-Muslim conflicts, he says further, 'Yet

---

7   Rajmohan Gandhi, *Understanding the Muslim Mind*, Penguin Books, New Delhi, 1987.
8   Ibid.

a frank and non-partisan look at the past can at least tell us of the blocks to Hindu-Muslim partnerships and tell us, too, of what went wrong, and why, in the efforts to remove them. If it informs us of times when the other side, too, was large-hearted, and of other times when our side also was small-minded, that awareness may make us, whoever we are, less prickly. History will then have served the cause of national, and subcontinental, understanding.'[9]

These are noble thoughts, remarks, which make us feel the need to reach out to the other side as well. To try and delve into the minds of people who involve themselves in a frenzy of hurt, anger and bloodshed that may seem inconceivable to others.

Gandhi has dwelt on this in another extraordinary book, *Revenge and Reconciliation*, which captures the pain and tumult of South Asia. Here he bemoans the fact that not enough attention is given 'to the history and continuing culture of settling scores, or to the fact that over time triumphs and defeats ... have led not to stable treaties or settlements but to oaths of revenge and preparations for new rounds of battle.'[10]

This book does not pretend to be a bridge-builder between communities. But it seeks to take an honest look, naturally burdened by the limitations of the writer himself, at what has gone wrong and continues to go wrong in Assam, especially among old and new settlers, in the light of land scarcity and population pressures in neighbouring Bangladesh.

---

9   Ibid.
10 *Revenge and Reconciliation: Understanding South Asian History*, Penguin Books, 1999

We will look at ways at which these can perhaps be addressed and even tackled. This is necessary because the events at Nellie show how terribly things can go wrong when the political, economic and social foundation of a host community comes to breaking point—or is shown to be close to that.

CHAPTER FIVE

'Where Are the Bodies?'

O n 20 February 1983, I travelled with four other journalists to Nellie. We represented different newspapers and news agencies: there was Najmal Hasan of Reuters (later killed in a mine explosion in the Iran-Iraq conflict), Satish Jacob of the British Broadcasting Corporation (BBC), Anand Sahay of the *Times of India* and Sabita Goswami of *Blitz*, the sensationalist weekly from Bombay.

We were a team, covering those bad times together. And the previous night we had gathered around the teleprinter at the Press Trust of India in Guwahati which rapped out the bare facts of a massacre in Nellie, some fifty kilometres from the city. Initial reports spoke of scores dead and many injured. We decided to drive out there first thing in the morning.

The magnitude of the tragedy hit us when we reached the town: hundreds of people had taken refuge in a school; others were outside the building in makeshift tents. The tiny dispensary was overflowing with the injured, most of them suffering from savage cuts inflicted by daos to the head, neck and upper torso. Other clinics had been set up, by the Red Cross, voluntary groups, by the army and paramilitary. Outside, people wept in pain and grief, from the hurt of physical injuries, or mourning the death of a relative or friend. A long queue of patients waited for treatment.

Those few hundred metres on either side of the road were a testament to brutality, hatred and bloodshed.

We drove past a dusty lane toward the dry rice-fields beyond Nellie. A young man came running toward us. When he learned that we were journalists, he began crying. 'Sir, it is very bad, there are hundreds of bodies lying all over the fields,' he said, introducing himself as Motalib Rahman. 'Sir, I will take you there.'

We got off the vehicles and marched in single file behind Motalib, who wore a shirt and a green *lungi*, over the tiny paths by the dry land. We had walked for nearly a kilometre and I had begun to doubt the truthfulness of our guide. Were there any bodies? I snapped with the cynicism of a journalist. 'Yes, sir,' said Motalib, 'just a little further, sir.' A few minutes later, we saw a group of men with spades and shovels, digging a ditch. But it was not a ditch; it also a burial pit for the bodies that had suddenly begun to appear.

These were mostly children, although there were a few adults. Their heads and necks had been slashed and battered. We walked on, suddenly silent and grim. Were there more bodies? I asked Motalib. 'The worst is across the canal, sir,' he said. 'You will not believe it until you see.'

A young woman was sitting under an umbrella near our path, obviously injured in the attack. She asked hoarsely for something. I bent to listen and saw the gashes on her face and neck—one blow had virtually sliced off her left ear and the other had damaged her throat. She spoke again: she was asking for water. I had none.

We walked on and came to the canal. A small dugout took us across. As I clambered up the small bank, my eyes were attacked by perhaps the most hideous scene that I have seen in all my years. An entire family was laid out at the top of the bank: parents and five children, of varying ages—the youngest was no older than an infant. Each one was dead, stabbed, slashed; the tiny one had been beheaded. Its head lay beside the body.

I looked up and saw more bodies. I think that after that, we became numb to feeling—the paddy fields were full of young women, older women, old men, young children who were struck down. In one small patch of land, I counted 200 bodies which lay where they had fallen. Yet, how had the young men survived?

The answer was simple: because they could run faster than the women, the old, the infirm and the children.

A cluster of huts peeped out of a grove of coconut and betel leaf trees. That was Bhagduba Habi.

The survivors talked of how they had been chased from the Nellie side and had crossed the canal, believing that they would be safe in the rice-fields. Then they saw two other column of Tiwa tribespeople coming in from either flank, moving to cut off the last bit of open space in a pincer movement. That was when all hope died. The old, the weak, the women and the very young fell to the rushing mob and its spears, daos, bows and arrows and muskets. The young and fit ran the fastest, fleeing from certain death, and staggered their way to a small Air Force station about five kilometres away. That was how the world came to know of Nellie.

Motalib and others said that they were attacked by strangers as well as by people with whom they had grown up. 'We went to the same school,' Motalib said as he

51

recounted the killings. 'I still don't know how they could have done this.'

After the killings, which had been planned meticulously, most of the Tiwa men fled to the surrounding hills. After some weeks, the tension appeared to have abated; they began returning home stealthily. Scores of Muslim children who had been orphaned were settled in a Save Our Souls (SOS) children's village, some waking to repeated nightmares of horror and death. These began to abate as they grew to adulthood.

Despite extensive police operations, only a handful of the killers were held. A Congress Party leader from Nogaon town spoke to a few of them. 'An evil wind blew, sir, and overwhelmed us,' one of the Tiwas remarked.

Be that as it may, few of the Tiwas were prosecuted for the slaughter. Indira Gandhi, then prime minister, rushed to Nellie in a helicopter from Guwahati. While the other reporters were kept at bay, by some fluke I landed up next to her, asking about the violence and whether the Government of India would take any responsibility for the tragedy. No, she snapped, the students and the agitators were to blame; they had created a climate of violence by spurning talks with the Government.

Mrs Gandhi drove off in a dusty convoy, saw a few burned out hamlets, met no one, kept her counsel and helicoptered back to Guwahati. The police were tense.

Two decades later, the issues raised by the killing fields of Nellie continue to haunt Assam and to a larger extent, the North East and India. The killings—1,753 according to one Muslim social worker of the area—were significant not just because of the scale of the violence but also because it underscored the core fear about land alienation. As noted earlier, the immigrants and every single non-tribal sitting on Tiwa land had no business to be there. Even their presence was not acknowledged under existing law. Yet they were there, in reality, in the fields and the villages. As the dispossession of the Tiwas grew, so did their rage. The boycott of the elections called by the students gave them an opportunity to strike.

Land or *maati* is critical to identity-formation especially among agrarian societies. Take away the land and what happens to the people who once tilled it, who trace their roots there over the centuries? They become dependent on others, mindful of the disregard and silent sneers of others. Their own shortsightedness is reflected every day when they contemplate their former tenants as owners of this ancestral land. The rage becomes deeper, blinding those in its grip to their own follies.

But how much land is needed for identity protection?

CHAPTER SIX

The Roads Away from Nellie

For years, the middle of the road *Asomiya* (and this term, in my view, embraces all the people of the Brahmaputra Valley who profess Hinduism and Islam, both speaking Assamese or a dialect of it) had been fed up of the growing political influence and clout of settlers from outside. The Congress Party, which had a powerful Muslim group, was seen as the villain of the piece—getting migrants from the former East Pakistan (now Bangladesh) to come over in exchange for their votes. In response, the Mymensinghias (people from Mymensingh district) and other immigrants declared Assamese as their mother tongue and were promptly baptized the *natun Asomiya* or new Assamese. This act was resented by the Assamese who saw a Congress conspiracy to reduce the Hindus to a minority in their own land and seize political power from them. The cases of Tripura and Sikkim were cited as a mantra to whip up emotions and passions—the original groups here were marginalized and pushed out of power by aggressive immigrants. In the case of Tripura it was the Bengali Hindus fleeing discrimination and riots in East Pakistan. In Sikkim, the Bhutia-Lepchas, who have ties to Bhutan and Tibet and are predominantly Buddhists, were marginalized by Nepali speakers, who were without exception, Hindus.

'Save Assam to Save India' became a rallying cry of the main body leading the agitation. The latter was also seen as an opportunity to avenge lost honour and power, to settle scores with those who supported the Congress plan of fragmenting the vote in Assam and settling 'outsiders', be they Bangladeshi Muslims or Nepali Hindus. The All Assam Students' Union (AASU), whose most prominent leaders were its president, Prafulla Kumar Mahanta, and the general secretary, Brighu Kumar Phukan, spearheaded the movement. Their demands included revision of the electoral rolls on the basis of the 1951 National Register of Citizens; that Bangladeshis should be struck off these rolls and deported to their country; further, the border with that country should be 'sealed.' How appropriate and relevant were these demands? We shall deal with these problems one after the other, while considering the prelude as well as the aftermath of Nellie.

The core issue raised by the AASU in April 1979 of 'foreigners' swamping Assam and the need for a national response to what it called a national problem remains at the heart of Assam's political agenda even today—and to a lesser degree that of other states in the North East, especially Tripura. It has acceptance among most political parties, even though groups like the Congress tend to shy away from taking an unequivocal stand and instead try to hedge their bets and positions.

While it is important to analyse why this problem arose, or what are its roots, much has already been written about this. A more serious issue is the extent to which the Indian State has failed to respond adequately to such concerns. We need to see how much of these problems are hype, how much is reality.

For decades, charges have flown around that the local Congress Party, especially in the 1960s and 1970s, patronized the influx of Muslims from East Pakistan and later Bangladesh, to retain political power in the Brahmaputra Valley. The strategy was to allow the miyahs or the Muslim Bengali-speakers from Mymensingh, Rongpur and other border districts of East Pakistan-Bangladesh to enter and settle in areas where older settlements of migrants existed. These were to be found in the lower valley segments of Dhubri and Goalpara as well as Kamrup and Darrang, going up through Nogaon (earlier known as Nowgong) and Jorhat, right up to Dibrugarh and Sibsagar. To move in and claim legitimacy was easy—one could always claim that one had moved from another part of the state and cite a fictitious parental address or name of a relative. Who was to check? Who cared, anyway?

But the fact of the matter is that no politician has ever been caught for pushing foreigners into this country. The names of the former President, the late Fakhruddin Ali Ahmed, and of Moinul Huq Chowdhury, a former Cabinet Minister under Prime Minister Indira Gandhi, came up time and again. It should be noted here that Chowdhury had been an extremely active Muslim League youth leader until independence, demanding the creation of Pakistan. He had even wanted Assam to join that ill-fated country. He failed in his efforts and, when the Muslim League shut shop in India, he went over to the Congress where he became an influential leader from the Bengali-dominated district of Cachar, bordering East Pakistan.

But the game of 'settlement for vote' continues to be played. In the 1989 general elections, a Congress leader from Cachar sought re-election as a Member of Parliament from Tripura. He had been a minister in successive Congress party governments: Indira Gandhi's and her son and successor, Rajiv's. Later, he was a part of P.V. Narasimha Rao's council of ministers. The politician's clout came from his family wealth in Assam where they owned large properties, including a cinema hall. He was also known for his tough, abrasive methods. One day, he called a senior official from the Border Security Force (BSF) with a request. The BSF man held the rank of an Inspector General of Police (IGP). At the time, tension was mounting in Tripura and there were public expressions of concern that the vote would be rigged. The police was on alert as political parties traded charges against each other. The IGP listened in stunned silence to an extraordinary demand.

'He [the politician] wanted the BSF to look the other way and allow 50,000 Bangladeshis to come into the constituency, vote and return.'[1] The officer in Tripura checked with his bosses in Delhi. The answer was clear and categorical: under no circumstance were the Bangladeshis to be allowed to enter. The decision was conveyed to the politician who did not appear to be surprised.

In this case, an upright officer stood his ground and won. But there are many cases of such blatant intervention by politicians. Even without their support, there is the law of basic economics—that products which people wish to sell (whether it is a manufactured good, or fish and

---

1 Interview with author, New Delhi, 5 May 2000

vegetables, or their skills, or their labour) will find their own levels.

Bangladeshis walk into Tripura every day to work as rickshaw-pullers or daily laborers; there are petty smugglers and traders too who come and conduct business during the day and go home by nightfall.

A former BSF official recalls cases when he allowed people to come across the border, to watch popular Hindi movies at the local cinema across the border in Tripura because there were no cinema halls in that part of Bangladesh. 'They would come and then melt away into the darkness as they went home. But that cannot be compared with the demand to allow Bangladeshis to vote,' he added. What the politician had wanted to do was clearly illegal. Yet, it was, by no means, regarded as unusual as these kind of 'requests' are made often.

The decision to prevent any influx for the specific purpose of the vote was appropriate, but not the harsh measure that were sought by the militants in Assam. A good example of an alternative was the tough approach taken in Assam nearly three decades earlier by a man who later was to become a legendary, if controversial, Indian Police Service (IPS) officer. His name was Kanwar Pal Singh Gill, better known as K.P.S. Gill.

In the early 1960s, Gill, then a fresh entrant into the IPS, was assigned to Assam as his parent cadre. As anyone at that age, he was young and enthusiastic. There was no Bangladesh at the time but East Pakistan. One of the problems that was affecting even his district of Nowgong (now Nogaon), in the Assam heartland, was the surreptitious entry, and settlement of men and women from the neighbouring country. Public opinion, even at that time, rode high against the illegal immigrants, and the state police worked out an elaborate strategy or tackling them.

First, Gill recalled,[2] the district police officers would go to Muslim village elders ('the older settlers') and explain to them that the new groups could turn against them and harm their interests. So the effort was to develop a process of voluntary disclosures. Police officers would take down the details of those who surrendered. These individuals were herded into the Jubilee Field at Nowgong before they were placed on trains headed to the East Pakistan border. At the time, the Pakistani border guards made no effort to resist this push-back policy. Gill feels that the 'surrender' scheme was 'the best scheme, it actually worked and there were virtually no complaints against the police on grounds of harassment.' Those who filed cases against the police challenging the legality of the decisions lost their appeals, strengthening the validity of the moves. As Nowgong's superintendent of police, he supervised the organization of a system that pushed out more than 100,000 East Pakistanis in two years. Another 100,000 were sent out from other parts of Assam, he adds.

But the border guards did not distribute the returnees to other parts of Pakistan. Instead, they were settled on the India-East Pakistan border. From here, slowly, the East Pakistanis began pushing out the Hindus into Assam, Tripura and West Bengal.

Thus, the wheel of migration turned full circle, adding to the hurt and pain of the story. Economic migrants of one religious group were pushed back from a neighbouring country, resettled in their own, and then they went about forcing another religious community out

---

2   Interview with author, New Delhi, May 2000.

of their own country. In times of migration, there is always one group which is 'more aggrieved' than the next one. It was a point to which Arun Shourie referred in his essay on Nellie and the bloodletting of 1983.

The religious cleansing had the support of the East Pakistani government. This was also evident in the brutal anti-Hindu riots that erupted across that part of Pakistan in 1964, forcing hundreds of thousands of Hindus to flee assault, murder, kidnapping, robbery and rape. These refugees were housed in temporary camps before being allowed to settle permanently in different parts of the North East and West Bengal. There were corresponding anti-Muslim attacks in these areas and in parts of Bihar as well.

The riots in both countries were so serious that the home ministers of Pakistan and India held talks in New Delhi on the issue. Prime Minister Jawaharlal Nehru wanted the Assam Chief Minister, Bimala Prasad Chaliha, to go easy on the deportations and even stop them. Chaliha refused, saying that the problem was so critical that Assam's demography and culture would be permanently changed. The Delhi talks broke down but eventually the violence ebbed and abated.

The 1965 war between India and Pakistan also changed perceptions of the issue. The Pakistanis then adopted a policy of aggressively rejecting everyone the Indians sent across. There were push backs. Concern about the immigrants also diminished. 'It just fell by the wayside because we got involved in tackling law and order situations' with new campaigns by the All Assam Students Union.[3] Chaliha's health was failing and he had enough problems on his hands with a furious revolt by Muslim

3   Ibid.

60

MLAs against another anti-migrant programme.

But Gill says—and this is an extremely controversial position—that the Congress was not involved in settling immigrants. Whenever men like Fakhruddin Ali Ahmed or Moinul Huq Chowdhury received complaints about harassment of Muslims, they would pass them on to the concerned district officers. They did not interfere even once in Gill's district or, to his knowledge, anywhere else. The former police official blames corrupt land revenue officers who would take money from settlers to place them on records and thus give them the sanction for getting on voters lists. That was the equivalent of 'virtual citizenship' without signing any papers for it!

To battle the influx, the state government had armed itself with a special law: Prevention of Infiltration from Pakistan (PIP) Act of 1964. The PIP had been predated by the Immigrants (Expulsion from Assam) Act of 1950 which distinguished between Hindus and Muslims. The latter were illegal aliens, the former were refugees. This was surely a formula that would have gladdened the heart of the Bharatiya Janata Party faithful had they been around at the time! This blatantly discriminatory law was repealed in 1957 although, on the sly, the Government of India passed an administrative order which enable Hindus from East Pakistan who had been resident in India for more than six months to be granted citizenship by a district magistrate.[4] This too was later withdrawn.

The PIP raised a special border police force of 1,914 men under the leadership of a Deputy Inspector General of Police. A total of 159 watch posts (towers) were built and 15 patrol posts. Another six passport checkpoints were

---

4   Sanjib Baruah, *India Against Itself; Assam and the Politics of Nationality*, University of Pennsylvania Press, 1999, p 119

also set up.

The 1965 war between India and Pakistan intervened as the project was coming into place. That conflict led to the raising of another border patrol force, the Border Security Force (BSF), which has since taken responsibility for the monitoring and security of India's frontiers with its neighbours. The Assam Border Police's work was handed over to the new paramilitary organization and the state forces were relocated inside Assam. The mandate was similar yet different: to identify and deport illegal migrants who had escaped the eye of the troops at the border and smuggled themselves into the countryside.

Later, as public interest in the situation diminished and political pressure decreased, they melted away—in the darkness or the shelter of anonymity in the Muslim-dominated riverine areas of Assam, neighbouring East Pakistan.

In 1987, the strength of the Border Police went up with support from the Government of India and the state Government: a total of over 2,000 men and officers were inducted, increasing its numbers to more than 4,000. But the effectiveness of this group as well as the BSF is open to question, as we will see.

It is worth examining here why the high-profile campaign launched by Chaliha, Gill and others collapsed so rapidly. Several reasons have been cited; but the core issue was political.

A furious revolt had erupted inside the Congress Party as a result of the anti-immigrant campaign. At the time, Chaliha was among the most respected political leaders of the country. He had battled hard to prevent the Congress split in 1969 and his integrity and compassion had won him the respect of even the Naga rebels fighting against Assam and India. For a brief time, he was part of the three-man peace mission to Nagaland.

Despite all these things in his favour, Chaliha's political survival depended on a powerful Muslim vote and lobby. He simply could not afford to alienate them. They were outraged by the apparent targeting of Muslims. At a meeting of the Muslim members of the Congress Legislature Party (there were about 20 in the 126-member house and Chaliha had a fragile majority—a few defections and his Government would fall), the rebels made it clear that they were prepared for the collapse of the ministry. Chaliha had to chose between political expediency on one side and the long-term interests of Assam and India.

Within a few months of its issuance, the PIP was put in cold storage. And there it has remained.

In 1979, the issue erupted again after more than a decade of dormancy. Until then, only a few voices spoke against migration and illegal settlement. The political power of the Congress was enough to drown out dissenting voices. But by the late 1970s, a major political change was sweeping India. Assam and other parts of the North East were also touched by this transforming wind.

There was a popular backlash to Mrs Gandhi's dictatorial 1975-77 state of Internal Emergency, when thousands of opponents were detained and a reign of terror unleashed on an entire nation, including forced sterilizations. In this anti-Gandhi wave, the Congress lost power for the first time at the national level and in many states which were regarded as its fiefdoms.

One such state was Assam. This was a time of transition which marked the end of the Congress triumvurate in the state: Chaliha, Fakhruddin Ali Ahmed and Dev Kanta Borooah. The first two had died; the third was fading into political obscurity despite his intellectual brilliance and cultural genius.

Delhi's hold on Assam was lessening—so was Assam's connection to Delhi, through the triumvurate and its allies. In their place came a rag-tag bag of Socialists, former Jana Sanghis, and former Congressmen. But within a year of the Janata Party coming to power in Assam, a group of scrawny students gave notice of a national struggle that was to transform Assam for good.

The All Assam Students Union, the most influential of the student organizations in the state and indeed in the entire North East, launched a movement against 'illegal migrants' in Assam. AASU's declaration of 'Save Assam to Save India' was the decisive blow that changed Assam's social fabric irretrievably. A revision of electoral lists in the Parliamentary constitutency of Mangaldoi turned up more than 60,000 names of people who had no business to be there—who could not prove their Indian identity and had clearly registered recently. Where had they come from? They were, in addition, Bengali-speaking Muslims. The revision of the voters' lists was necessitated by the death of Hiralal Patwari, the Member of Parliament who had won the election to the seat. The process of delineating the 'illegals' from the genuine Indians, smacked of bias against the Bengali-speaking Muslims.

By this time, Assam was in ferment but not in flames. The latter was to follow, as a logical culmination to the mess. Marches, protests, pickets and dharnas were the order of the day. Some events were supported by government officers, who defied official orders and courted arrest, demanding the ouster of the aliens. If it was not xenophobia, then it was patriotism of a very jingoistic quality.

The agitators led by Mahanta and Phukan, with a handful of failed politicians on their side, used innovative Gandhian tactics to paralyse economic and business activities as well as the adminstration. Governments in the state came and went until finally, the Centre imposed direct rule from Delhi and ordered a crackdown against the agitators. Mrs Gandhi's patience was running out.

Until then, the students had garnered national support and media mileage as their pickets outside oil installations and government offices blocked oil from being supplied to other parts of the country and prevented the administration from its normal function. The oil blockade was broken at least once by the use of the Indian Army and widespread arrests followed.

The movement grew around several founding principles. One of these was that the means adopted for the struggle had to be non-violent Gandhian style satyagrahas. Virtually every ethnic group of the state, student associations from other states, government officers, business people, lawyers, journalists, artistes and other creative groups, as well as professionals, joined the protests in those first few years before the momentum slowed as its popularity slipped.

The other goals of the agitation were the three Ds: Detection, Deletion, Deportation. Detection of foreign nationals; their deletion from electoral rolls and finally their deportation. It was so pat, so glib. And impossible to implement as we shall see in the following chapters.

The issue leaped into the headlines of the national

media, putting additional pressure on both the state and Central governments. But there was always a extreme fringe, which did not believe in peaceful protests and used force to secure financial gain for themselves and terrorize the prosperous business community. They later coalesced with the ULFA. Indeed, one of the initial 'actions' of ULFA was the killing of a prominent Marwari businessman in Guwahati. He was killed not because of an ideological bias but because of a dispute about the amount of money demanded from him as a 'contribution.'

However, the basic contention of the students put the Government of India in a bind. The students were not asking for anything that went either against the Constitution or common sense. Indeed, for the first time, the North East had an influential group which wanted a Constitutional settlement of their problem, not one that was outside it, like that demanded by the Nagas, Mizos and Meiteis and later the Assamese too, through ULFA.

The students were raising a very basic question: who had the right to vote in an Indian election? Indians, of course. So why should Bangladeshis, or people from any other nationality, exercise that right? This had long-term implications that Assam found very disturbing—accepting this situation was, in effect, sanctioning 'foreign control' of the politics of the state and other parts of the country.

The Assam movement and its demands thus raised the question of whether the Indian Constitution was an adequate tool to deal with a problem of such far-reaching consequence, having its roots in foreign soil. (This is an issue I propose to tackle in the concluding segment of the book.)

Tired of the inconclusiveness of the political situation,

Indira Gandhi decided to force her way out of the logjam. She called fresh elections to the state legislature along with the elections to the fourteen Lok Sabha seats which had been unfilled since she returned to power in 1980 (at that time, AASU had blocked the elections to eight of fourteen elections in the state and also stalled the census operations: the latter was a foolish decision for it set Assam back by a decade in terms of census data—raw material that could have helped the agitators to better showcase their own issues.

The run-up to the election was ominous. With every passing day, the rhetoric became shriller, the political temperature a little higher. Atal Bihari Vajpayee, then leader of the rump Bharatiya Janata Party (it was barely four years old, having been formed after the three-way split in the Janata Party in 1979), declared that the 'rivers of blood' would flow if the Government went ahead with the election. The BJP had just two seats in Parliament out of a total of 542, including Vajpayee's own. Barring the Congress and the Left group, most other parties decided to fall behind the agitators and boycott the elections. Vajpayee was in Assam to campaign against the vote. His voice and that of many others added to the growing hysteria.

It was at this time too that a distinguished soldier from Rajasthan made his entrance on the political stage: Jaswant Singh of the bushy eyebrows and gravelly, ponderous voice was selected by the BJP to be the observer for the state. It was, as he said many years later, his 'karmabhoomi'.

Many rumours did the rounds. One evening at the Bellevue Hotel, where many of us hacks had camped, a shout went around that a group of miyahs in a boat had landed on the river front and were rushing towards the hotel. Frantic calls were made to the police; a search party went out from the hotel. Of course, there was no one to be found.

In another case, someone's fevered imagination reported that men in black (this was well before the popular film about Extra Terrestials!) were being dropped from helicopters to start riots! And the local media lapped it all up, adding to the general confusion.

Despite the rumours, the Congress Party won the elections handsomely. In some places, no one participated in the polling. In others, voting was about 1 per cent of the total electorate.

Few remember that Hiteswar Saikia, the short, stubby Ahom from Nazira in Upper Assam then became chief minister. What they do remember is the violence and the brutality as the hate and anger of a hundred years poured out of the hearts and minds of communities across the Brahmaputra Valley, from Kamrup to North Lakhimpur, from villages to islands in the river.

However, one area remained peaceful—at the time, it appeared as if the Barak valley was in a time warp. There was hardly a single incident of violence. But then this area had never supported the anti-foreigner movement anyway. The population of the Barak valley was overwhelmingly Bengali-speaking—both Hindu and Muslim. Calls for bandhs in the Brahmaputra Valley rarely found an echo here. They would be ignored while the Bengalis would organize their own anti-Assamese bandhs, decrying the agitators as parochial, narrow-minded and anti-minority. Reflecting on this, Shekhar Gupta, then the resident correspondent of the *Indian Express*, and now its chief editor, said that the story of

Assam is that of two valleys—the Brahmaputra and the Barak.

One of the more significant developments of the twentieth century in Assam was the formation of an Assamese upper class which was politically astute and proud of its linguistic and cultural heritage. The core of this identity is the linguistic tradition of the Assamese and their resentment of the Bengalis. This antipathy stems partly from the manner in which the Bengalis took it upon themselves in the nineteenth century to pass off the local language as but a poor relative of their own. It took the tireless efforts of American Baptist missionaries, led by R.Moffat Mills, to convince the British that Assamese indeed was a sovereign language.

The wound inflicted by this struggle—of having to fight for what was rightfully theirs and sought to be taken away—is still unhealed in the Assamese pysche. This attitude is reflected in open resentment toward Bengali speakers. It is a hostility that knows no bar of religion and is equally critical of those from Bangladesh and West Bengal.

Over the years, the Congress with its activist pro-minority plank was seen as a party which supported the interests of settlers. It was thus labelled pro-'Bangladeshi' by its opponents, especially the agitators. One doubts, however, whether any Congress leader in the state would have the courage to oppose the general consensus that all those who came after the 1971 creation of Bangladesh should be deported. Yet, in its desperation to hold on to its Muslim votes and anticipating that these would be wooed by other parties, including the regional

Asom Gana Parishad and the leftist groups, the Congress has boxed itself into a corner.

It has declared repeatedly that it will not stand by and permit the harassment of Indian minorities (for that read 'Muslims' and sub-divide that word to read: 'Bengali-speaking Muslims') in the name of ousting illegal aliens. This controversy has largely risen as a result of legislation pushed through Parliament in 1983 called the Illegal Migrants Determination by Tribunal Act (IMDT). The Act set up tribunals in each district, which were to be presided over by retired district/additional district judges. Appeals are heard by an Appellant Tribunal of two retired High Court judges. The tribunals were to decide upon complaints about the presence of illegal migrants with the assistance of the local police. They had the power to summon witnesses and pronounce verdicts.

But between 1983 and 2000, the sixteen tribunals in various districts have functioned at far below their capacity. They have located about 10,000 illegals of which a bare 1,400 have been deported.

There have been several hurdles in the implementation of the Act. One clause specified that the complainant should live near the suspect and deposit twenty-five rupees to back up the complaint. This was later reduced to ten rupees. This was an extraordinary clause and stood the concept of laws governing foreigners elsewhere in the world on its head: the complainant and not the person complained against was being put in the dock! The declared objective of the clause was to prevent the filing of frivolous complaints. But it appeared that the Congress Party, whose government had introduced the Act, did not have any intention of implementing it.

As the fears of the agitators grew, minority

groups—and these included both Hindus and Muslims of the Bengali ilk—joined hands and formed a political party, the United Minorities Front under the leadership of a former Congressman, Ghulam Osmani. Osmani was also a prominent lawyer in the Guwahati High Court.

The Congress and UMF were the most prominent opponents of AASU's policies and politics because they felt politically challenged. There were others too who opposed the movement on ideological grounds. These included the leftist parties, the Communist Party of India (Marxist) and the Communist Party of India. Those holding the middle ground like the Janata Party virtually abdicated their role and took shelter behind AASU. The state's political canvas was essentially divided between those for detection and deportation, however far-fetched these may appear now, and those against.

At this point it would be appropriate to consider the context in which these developments were taking place: the changes in the demographic composition of Assam leading up to the 1980s.

A Little Bit of History

Assam was a part of the Bengal Presidency between 1826 and 1873. For another thirty-one years, until 1905, it remained a province without a legislature. The Partition of Bengal by Lord Curzon in that year disrupted the system and Dacca became the capital of East Bengal and Assam. This did not last long and in 1911, the Partition was annulled amid protests from anti-partition groups. Assam reverted to being a chief commissioner's province.

In the following years, Assamese nationalists expressed their concern over the unchecked immigration from East Bengal. The British were prevailed upon to introduce the Line System. Under this system, a line was drawn which segregated those areas where migration was allowed from the rest of the territory. A Colonisation Scheme was set up in 1928 to back up the Line System but the effectiveness of both steps was questionable. In an unpublished paper, Virender Singh Jafa, a former Chief Secretary of Assam, was to say[5] that the 'failure of both measures was evident as the immigrant settlers from East Bengal were in occupation of 37.7 per cent of land by 1936 in Nowgong District alone.' In the space of a decade, the population of settlers from East Bengal rose from 300,000 to half a million or an increase of 200,000 from 1921 to 1931 in Nowgong.

'The immigrant army has almost completed the conquest of Nowgong. The Barpeta sub-division of Kamrup has also fallen to their attack and Darrang is being invaded. Sibsagar has so far escaped completely but a few thousand Mymensinghias in North Lakhimpur are an outpost which may, during the next decades, prove to be vulnerable for major operations.'[6] Those remarks by the Census Commissioner for Assam, C.S. Mullen, along with other pithy statements buttressed local fears about being swept aside by an invading tide.

This passage of Mullen's report is perhaps one of the most celebrated in any study of Assam's demographic crisis. The British official went so far as to say that the 'most important event' in Assam over the past quarter century 'has been the invasion of a vast horde of land hungry Bengali immigrants, mostly Muslims from the

---

5   V.S. Jafa, 'Insurgency and the Problem of the Migration: the North East in a Historical Perspective'. Unpublished paper, 1999.
6   C.S. Mullen, Census of Assam, 1931.

districts of Eastern Bengal and in particular Mymensingh.'
He predicted that this influx would 'alter permanently the
whole future of Assam and to destroy more surely than
did the Burmese invaders . . . the whole structure of
Assamese culture and civilisation.'

Mullen declared that the first Bengalis that
immigrated were officially taken note of in the 1921
census on a few pitiful islands in Goalpara. By 1931, the
official said, more than half a million people had swept
into Assam making the whole thing appear 'like a marvel
of administrative organization on the part of Government
but it is nothing of the kind; the only thing I can compare it
to is the mass movement of a large body of ants... it is sad
but by no means improbable Sibsagar district will be the
only part of Assam in which an Assamese will find himself
at home.'[7]

Fifty years later, these concerns were reflected in
similar language by the student activists of the 1980s,
showing how little has changed in the Assamese psyche.

But how real are these worries?

To assess this, we will need to head back a little in
time, to when a few years after Mullen's dramatic
declaration.

For most of the years between 1937 and 1946,
Mohammad Saadulla of the Muslim League held office as
Assam's Premier. In July 1941, his party announced a
Land Settlement Policy which opened up the region to
immigrants, allowing them to settle on government land
anywhere in Assam and enabling them to seize as much as
thirty bighas of land and more for each homestead. Four
years later, Saadulla was to boast in a letter to Liaquat Ali

7   Ibid.

Khan, then Mohammad Ali Jinnah's chief aide and later Premier of Pakistan, that, 'In the four lower districts of Assam Valley, these Bengali immigrant Muslims have quadrupled the Muslim population during the last 20 years.'

Saadulla claimed that all this was part of the war effort: that as a good and reliable ally of the British, he was doing his best to meet Allied needs for food. But Lord Wavell, the then Viceroy, was not taken in one bit.

Wavell remarked cynically, 'The chief political problem is the desire of the Muslim Ministers to increase this immigration into the uncultivated Government lands under the slogan of "Grow more food."' But what they really wanted was to 'Grow more Muslims.'[8]

In the space of a few years, the profile of the migrant had changed: from sharecroppers eking out a survivalist existence, they had become land owners who had set up their own farms, leading a settled, pastoral existence. By Saadulla's own admission, those four lower districts had seen a massive inflow of Muslims from East Bengal. These were the old undivided districts of Goalpara (which included Dhubri), Kamrup and Nowgong.

This was to be the pattern for future migrations.

---

8   Penderel Moon, ed. *Wavell; The Viceroy's Journal*, London: Oxford University Press, 1978

CHAPTER SEVEN

A Place Called Home

The history of the world is migration. Our forebears have come from elsewhere, settled in the place we know, or knew as home and we have moved to newer homes and homelands, raising families and shaping careers, making choices and developing the societies in which we live and work. At the same time, we maintain connections with those individuals, communities and larger societies to which we are tied by bonds of loyalty, be they ethnic, linguistic, religious or nationality.

The pace of migration has quickened with each passing year, more and more people being drawn to developed countries, as well as to places with better conditions even in underdeveloped lands. The pull of technology, economic growth, global communications as compared to illiteracy, unbridled population growth and falling living standards in the many underdeveloped nations continues to force this inexorable march of the wretched of the earth—though often these communities count among as the most resourceful and dynamic.

Those who live in the 'second half' of our world see the opportunities in any place, near or distant, as providing a breathing space, a chance to live and survive—and who knows, even prosper.

'Recent profound changes in the world political and economic order have generated huge movements of people in almost every region,' says Nicholas Van Hear of the Refugee Studies Programme at Oxford University.[1]

'As migration has proliferated, so too has the diaspora or transnational communities, leading to increasing numbers of people with allegiances straddling their places of origin and their new homelands.'[2]

What Van Hear is saying is that many migrants now have dual loyalties: one to the land of their birth and the other to the land which gives them work and sustains them. Which of these loyalties is the greater?

There are few instances, for example, of Bangladeshi migrants to Assam or New Delhi or Mumbai marrying local Assamese speakers or even Bengali speakers or Hindi or Marathi speakers of the same faith. But the preference is for partners from the same country, same religious and linguistic identity and even from the same neighbourhood. In addition, few 'locals' would want their children to marry immigrants from another country, despite a common religion or language. It is seen as an undignified diminition of one's status.

Refugees as Migrants

At this point we must make a distinction between migrants and refugees. The two are related but they are also very separate, with their own categories and sub-groups. Thus a refugee is, for purposes of argument, also a migrant. But a migrant is not necessarily a refugee.

---

1   Nicholas Van Hear, *New Diasporas: the Mass Exodus Dispersal and Regrouping of Migrant Communities*, London: UCL Press, 1998
2   Ibid.

Definitions have become more complicated with the international acceptance of the term 'environmental refugee' which is different from internally displaced persons. An internally displaced person in India, for example, is one who is forced to move from his home and village to another place within the country because of a development project such as a large dam or the building of an embankment along the river. Or he/she could have been harmed by natural disasters such as floods or earthquakes. Of course, man-made disasters such as unplanned industrialization, the poor location of hazardous industries are other reasons for such displacement.

Extreme care needs to be taken about the how such descriptive terms are used. The Norwegian social scientist, Astri Sukhre, warns against the dangers in using these terms loosely, when she compares the problems of what she describes as Minimalists and Maximalists.[3] Opinion is divided between these two groups of thought. One school, the Minimalists, holds out that it is enonomic growth, especially employment-related motives, which predetermine and dominate the way people move within and outside a country. Environmental factors are but one of a series of factors which force people to move.

On the other hand, the Maximalists take the position that environmental refugees are people who have been uprooted from their homes by a natural calamity such as flooding and drought. Circumstances may well force them to seek shelter in a neighbouring region or a neighbouring country.

3 Astri Sukhre, *Pressure Points: Environmental Degradation, Migration and Conflict*, American Academy of Arts & Science, Toronto University, April 1993.

The most prominent of the Maximalists—and they are better known and perhaps more articulate and media-savvy—is Essam El-Hinnawi, whose work on environmental refugees[4] is very influential. In 1985, in *Environmental Refugees*, his innovative book for the United Nations Development Programme, El-Hinnawi wrote that 'all displaced people can be described as environmental refugees, having been forced to leave their original habitat (or having left voluntarily) to protect themselves from harm and/or to seek a better quality of life.' He further elaborated by specifying three sub-categories:

- Those who temporarily have to leave their traditional habitat due to a natural disaster or similar event
- Those who have been permanently displaced and resettled in a new area and
- Those who migrate on their own.

In my view, El-Hinnawi's proposition blurs the distinction between refugees and migrants to an unacceptable level. This, according to Sukhre, violates 'common sense' and inflates the numbers of those on the move—of either category.

There are generalists among academics and journalists who dramatize the situation by talking in broad, non-specific terms and define environmental refugees as those 'fleeing from environmental decline.' This is a rather imprecise definition for it makes no distinction between people who are displaced internally and those displaced

4   Essam El-Hinnawi, *Environmental Refugees*, United Nations Development Programme, 1985.

internationally. Such sweeping statements create confusion and spread disinformation. New paradigms are developed without adequate discussion, research, preparation or logical consideration of the issues.

The Bracero Programme Versus Guest Workers

Different countries have tried different methods to deal with the problem of migration, ranging from strong-arm methods such as pushing people back and building fences as in India and Bangladesh or United States and Mexico, to the absorptive approach which accepts migrants but expects them to return after they have completed their stay. The latter also includes the United States and its Bracero programme and the Guest Worker programme in Germany. It is interesting that the United States should be prominent in following both approaches. But that is surely to be expected, for it is the biggest recipient of immigrants (legal and illegal) in the world.

The Bracero programme was evolved to regulate the flow of legal and temporary Mexican workers. The south-western states of the United States, having once been under Mexico, are run by conservative establishments which oppose immigration from Mexico. There is concern that the immigrants would bring down the wage rates of labour because they would be prepared to work for less than the average American. Further, there are fears that as this labour is largely Hispanic, the Hispanics would overwhelm the local white, Anglo-Saxon communities.

The Bracero programme was put into place during the Second World War, as a temporary measure to make up for labour shortages in the American war effort. It was continued to overcome worker shortages during the Korean War. The programme was unilaterally terminated by the United States in 1964 after a record five extensions—all under pressure from the American farm lobby which needed cheap Mexican labour.

To soften the blow of abrogating Bracero, the United States helped Mexico set up a Border Industrialisation Programme. The idea was to provide alternative employment to those Mexicans who would be displaced by the closure of Bracero. Factory units to process semi-processed components shipped out by US firms were set up. There were trade preferences for investors and most of these were American. Duty was to be paid only on the foreign value-added.

By 1990,[5] as many as 2,000 factory units were functioning along the US-Mexico border. Border towns which are industrializing, whether they are at Ruili on the Myanmar-South West China border or along the Mexico-US border, function as a magnet, drawing potential workers from the distant countryside. They employed close to half a million workers—but there was a catch here: most of the workers were women. The history of Mexican migration has shown that most migrants were men, especially in the seasonal agricultural worker sector. Thus, argued Sergio Diaz-Briquets,[6] the goal of creating employment for returning migrants or would-be migrants seemed not to have worked. It is believed that large numbers who came to the industrial belt travelled on to

5   Sergio Diaz-Briquets, 'Reltionships Between US Foreign Policies and US Immigration Policies' in *Threatened Peoples, Threatened Borders—World Migration and US Policy*, ed. Michael S. Teitelbaum & Myron Weiner, New York: W.W. Norton
6   Ibid.

the United States.

Guest workers can create a problem for policy-makers back home. There is a growing reluctance worldwide to accept immigrants. The dilemma is posed by the rights and expectations of the host community or the voters where adult franchise is practised and the demands of those who have moved and need sustenance.

'Respect for the human rights of the asylum-seeker might be in conflict with the understandable concern of resident communities to protect finite resources from unrestricted access to those from without,' says the summary of an international seminar on environmental impacts resulting from mass migrations.[7]

Those, who have been environmentally displaced, move because they have no other choice. This has been asserted earlier in this book. Displacements may occur either en masse, following a major disaster such as a cyclone or flood, or in waves and ripples. The latter may be caused by a fall in the availability of common resources and could be triggered by a range of factors including desertification. These causal factors are growing in scale and diversity because of the pressures on our earth. As we have seen population growth is the chief reason. Others include prolonged drought, soil erosion, diminishing water supplies and deforestation, all of which force people to seek livelihoods and homes elsewhere.

Environmental Displacement

Experts have defined five categories of population

7   *Environmentally-Induced Population Displacements and Environmental Impacts Resulting from Mass Migrations*, Symposium Summary, 21-24 April 1996, Chavannes-de-Bogis, Switzerland.

movement caused by environmental factors:[8]

- acute onset movements with the possibility of return. This is one of the most visible forms of flight, caused by natural disasters such as cyclones, earthquakes, floods and volcanic eruptions. Man-made tragedies such as industrial accidents such as the Bhopal gas disaster in India are also behind such temporary displacements.
- acute onset movements, without the possibility of return. This is applicable to groups displaced by nuclear contamination or dumping of other hazardous wastes or destruction by especially severe natural disasters.
- slow onset movements with predicability without possibility of return. In this case, displacement is caused, for example, by dam construction and other large-scale development projects.
- slow onset movements, with the possibility of return. Chronic water shortages, deforestation, agricultural failure and land-related problems such as unclear land tenure and even extensive pollution of resources (land, water and air) are major causes of flight in this category.
- low onset movements, without the possibility of return because of natural conditions in the area of departure. This is a reference to irreversible natural phenomena, such as desertification or rising sea water levels.

This ordering completely leaves out the other major

8   Ibid.

migrant who comes in the shape of a refugee, fleeing not destitution or an environmental crisis but seeking succour from a threat to his life and liberty. A political refugee is not a migrant. The former is regarded as a temporary traveller, while the latter is viewed as a settler and thereby a competitor for space in every form: land, water, services and jobs.

The political refugee has a chance of returning to his homeland after the threat to his personal life or that of his community has abated. This has happened time and again, not just in Rwanda-Burundi, witness to the Hutu-Tutsi civil strife. In 1970-71, nine million refugees fled a Pakistani military massacre of Bengalis in East Pakistan. They returned from India only when their land gained independence as Bangladesh, and the Pakistani killing machine had been crushed by the Indian Army and the insurgent Mukti Bahini.

Among the cases of refugees not returning to their country of origin are the Ugandan Asians who were driven out of Uganda by the dictator Idi Amin; they settled in Britain. Then there are the two million Afghan refugees who continue to live in Pakistan's North West Frontier Province, more than a decade after the exit of the Soviet Army, which intervened in 1979. Bitter ethnic fighting and civil war continues to ravage Afghanistan.

But these refugees are not to be confused with economic and environmental migrants. Across the world, the number of political refugees continues to swell. At last count it was not less than 20 million. But it is still less than the number of environmental refugees. According to one estimate,[9] there are not less than 25 million environmental

---

9   Norman Myers, 'Environmentally-Indued Displacements: The State of the Art.' Paper read at international symposium on environmentally-induced

refugees worldwide, of people forced to move by environmental reasons beyond national boundaries. And not less than 100 million move voluntarily, within nations and outside their borders, by 'virtue of being drawn (not driven) by economic opportunity.'[10] The number of illegal migrants still remain, guesstimates at best. The fact is no one really knows! Alarm sirens are now shrieking across communities and countries as nations seek to put up barriers of fences and laws to stop the desperate and the impoverished from coming in. Fears of a 'swamping' are voiced, especially by the extreme right-wing.

Myron Weiner outlined a set of ideas which sought to end the confusion in the popular perception and among some academics and activists. He tried to separate concepts of refugees and migrants, by classifying two categories of people who moved across international boundaries: Rejected Peoples and Unwanted Migrants.[11]

The Rejected Peoples

The Rejected Peoples were taken to be political refugees. Such groups would comprise, for example, the Tibetans, who have been driven out by the Chinese and leave their country out of fear of persecution and threat to their lives because of political and religious beliefs. A majority of the 120,000 Tibetans who have left Tibet since the 1959 flight of the spiritual leader, the Dalai Lama, live in India. They use a number of travel documents, including those

---

population displacements and environmental impacts resulting from mass migrations. Geneva, April 1996.

10 Ibid.

11 Weiner Myron, 'Rejected Peoples and Unwanted Migrants: The Impact of Migration on the Politics and Security of South Asia,' Paper read at MIT, December 1991.

use a number of travel documents, including those indicating United Nations refugee status and those issued by the country where they have settled. The more affluent and resourceful have settled in developed countries where they have acquired citizenship, making international access so much simpler.

There are other large populations which have fled genocide and threats to life and liberty, the most vivid being the flight of refugees from Afghanistan and from the civil war in Rwanda in Central Africa. In the case of Afghanistan, the direct military intervention of the Soviet Union to overthrow a leftist despot led to the beginning of anarchy and civil war which continues today although the Russians have long since left. In Rwanda, a series of economic factors led to the mass killings. The country's grainland acreage per person shrank to less than 0.03 hectares per person, less than one third that of Bangladesh which is the world's standard bearer for poverty and land scarcity.

This was disastrous for a nation which was entirely rural. The land could not sustain the huge population that it was carrying. From 2.5 million in 1950, Rwanda's population went up to 8.5 million in 1994. Old ethnic hatreds between the Hutus and Tutsis came to the fore. Once ignited, there was no stopping the fire and more than half a million Tutsis were slaughtered.

Here again, as in other cases closer to home, we find that land scarcity was a major factor in ethnic conflict, reaffirming the connection between population pressure and land. The wounds still remain, many of them unhealed; the memories remain, many of them whole; the hatreds remain, many of them unforgiven.

Other such groups in the Rejected People's list include the Muslim Rohingyas of Myanmar, who periodically escape a savage regime at home and settle near Chittagong port and Cox's Bazar in Bangladesh. The first such exodus took place in 1978 when Myanmarese troops attacked Muslim villages and mosques; in 1992, a furious onslaught by Myanmarese troops sent an estimated quarter of a million refugees to Chittagong. Many were housed in camps supported by the United Nations High Commissioner for Refugees (UNHCR). Several international aid groups also operate in these camps including the World Lutheran Organisation and OXFAM, organizing shelter, food programmes and medical assistance.

Despite an on-again, off-again repatriation programme, most of the refugees have returned barring about 20,000 who say they will not go back because they are threatened by an unforgiving military junta. The international agencies as well as Myanmar and Bangladesh are divided on the identity of these groups, their ideologies and the level of their popular representation.

Other groups which would fall in this list are the Sri Lankan Tamils who have fled the civil war in the north of the island to southern India, where they have lived in refugee camps set up by the Government of India in Tamilnadu state. Most of these camps have since closed after the Tamils were repatriated to their homes. But ethnic strife in that region continues to send floods of Tamil refugees and displacees to other parts of Sri Lanka.

Then there are the 'Biharis' of the former East Pakistan who live in squalid slums in the heart of Dhaka, the capital of Bangladesh, and other towns. There are sixteen such camps in the country and one of the best-known is Geneva camp, a fetid, fly-infested place, a place built of cardboard sheets and tarpaulin. Here live an estimated 10,000 people whose leaders once supported the former military regime in Pakistan during the 1970-71 crackdown against Bengali nationalists.

More than half a million were killed and not less than 100,000 women raped or molested in that slaughter. After the liberation of Bangladesh, this group, known as the Biharis because of their origins, were attacked, intimidated and finally herded into places such as Geneva Camp. Negotiations to get Pakistan to accept them have failed time and again; they remain a stateless people, despised in Bangladesh and unrecognized in Pakistan.

But occasionally situations arise which defy compartmentalization. Take the case of the Chakmas of East Pakistan, now Bangladesh. More than 25,000 were displaced in 1964 from their native Chittagong Hill Tracts, a tribal-dominated district, by a dam on the Karnaphuli river. (It is of course a different matter that migration encouraged by the Bangladesh government in the 1970s and 1980s has reduced the indigenous population to a bare majority, while the Muslim Bengali settlers have risen in numbers from a few thousand to half the entire population in the Chittagong Hill Tracts!)

Those displaced were not given compensation and left for India in anger and disgust. Here, a protective central government took them under their wing and settled them in what is now the Changlang district of the state of Arunachal Pradesh, near the border with China. These were internal displaces who became environmental refugees or developmental refugees and finally were accepted by the federal government but not by the local hosts, the Arunachalis, or their state government.

In fact, the Arunachal Pradesh government has been

87

trying to evict this community, which has over the years, swelled to a population of nearly 70,000. The Chakmas in the state are denied basic facilities such as education, healthcare and rations from ration shops, rights accessible by all Indians. They are still not Indians, in the full sense, despite various court rulings in their favour. They lack opportunities and the desire to return to their original land which still exists but under the name and powers of a different nation: Bangladesh.

The Supreme Court has had to intervene repeatedly as has the National Human Rights Commission, a statutory watchdog group on civil liberties without any powers of conviction or punishment, to assert the rights of the Chakmas.

Indeed, the case of the Chakmas was used to demonstrate the innovative power of the Supreme Court as well as the Constitution's ability and the responsibility of the State to protect all people who resided in India and were not just citizens of the country. The Chakma issue reflected the affirmation of equality in the eyes of the low (if not the state!) despite difference of creed, caste, gender and even nationality.[12]

---

12 Article 14: The State shall not deny to any person equality before the laws
or the equal protection of the laws within the territory of India
Article 19: (1) All citizens shall have the right—
to freedom of speech and expression
to assemble peacefully and without arms
to form associations or unions
to move freely throughout the territory of India
to reside and settle in any part of the territory of India
to acquire, hold and dispose of property; and
to practise any profession, or to carry out any occupation, trade or
business.
('There are various other clauses in Article 19 which sanctions powers to
the State to take action as it deems proper to curtail these rights in special
circumstances such as the security of the State, friendly relations with

But the story of the Chakmas does not end here: in 1978, more than 25,000 Chakmas were driven out of the Chittagong Hill Tracts in a military crackdown. They took shelter in the adjoining, underdeveloped Indian state of Tripura. The Chakmas returned only after India exerted pressure on both the leaders of the Chakmas and on Bangladesh. A decade later, not less than 60,000 refugees fled to temporary camps in Tripura after a fresh bout of military pacification. The Bangladeshi excesses, which were not acknowledged by Dhaka until many years later and which were never highlighted by the media until the late 1990s, were especially surprising after Bangladesh's own suffering at the hands of a brutal Pakistani regime in 1970-71, at the time of its birth as a nation.

The Bangladesh military actions in the Chittagong Hill Tracts followed attacks on them by a rebel army called the Shanti Bahini, which was supported and trained by India's external intelligence agency, the Research and Analysis Wing (RAW).

The people who fled the crackdown in 1988 included political activists as well as ordinary villagers—predominantly farmers and their families, labourers and others. They were settled in three camps near the Bangladesh border and supplied rations and some cash by the Indian government. Yet, no external refugee agency was allowed access to these refugees or the camps. Neither Bangladesh not India are signatories to the Convention on the Protection of Refugees, though India has had a long history of treating refugees with tolerance and compassion.

Foreign States, public order . . .') Article 21: No person shall be deprived of his life or personal liberty except according to procedure established by law.

After years of fruitless negotiations, the pace of bilateral discussions, which also involved Chakma exile activists, picked up after the pro-India Awami League government led by Sheikh Hasina Wajed, daughter of the late Sheikh Mujibur Rahman, came to power in 1996. A settlement was thrashed out which gave greater powers over local government and issues affecting the Hill Tracts such as forests and land alienation to the Chakmas. The settlement does not mean that the political problems of the Chakmas are over. New issues and demands have cropped up. But this example is aimed at showing the different stages of migration, and forced migration in a border community. Here, at first, an internal problem forced the environmental outflow and created a problem that remains unresolved in the receiving country. Then, a military drive resulted in the classical refugee syndrome: thousands of frightened civilians crowding camps in an alien land.

Yet, strange though it appears—given the experience of the world—the refugee crisis was actually easier to handle than the problem of migrants or the internally displaced. This latter group shares the fate faced by external displacees, especially since the state government in Arunachal Pradesh fiercely opposes efforts to confer citizenship on them. A domestic political concern, created by an influx from across the border has thus become more intractable in the subcontinental context than a bilateral problem.

The Chakmas are victims twice over: in Bangladesh and in the land they chose over the country of their birth. If their experiences in the Chittagong Hill Tracts and in Arunachal Pradesh were not enough, their compatriots have faced harassment, eviction and discrimination in Mizoram state. The difficulties here have arisen over questions of religion (the Mizos are predominantly Baptists, while the Chakmas are Buddhists), ethnicity, language and demographic change.

Mizoram is a jagged sliver of land which is hemmed in by Assam, Bangladesh, Tripura and Myanmar. Mizo leaders say that the Chakmas are moving illegally into their tiny state (population of about 700,000) from Bangladesh, settling on agricultural land, increasing in numbers and posing a threat to their traditions, lifestyles and political power.

Bhutan too has been a sender of refugees. Here, Nepal has been the receiving country. Those who have been forced to leave Bhutan or who have left on their own, without coercion, are of Nepali-stock. Their forebears from Nepal had settled in Bhutan over the past 50 years, clearing wastelands and malarial-infested forests and swamps in the humid south, bordering India, turning difficulties into opportunities. New migrants kept trickling in until the ruling Drukpa, who are Tibetan in origin and Buddhist by faith, felt alarmed enough to launch a campaign to drive out 'illegals.' In the process, many genuine Bhutanese citizens of Nepali origin were harassed and pushed out of Bhutan.

For nearly a decade, these refugees have lived in UNHCR supervised camps in south-east Nepal, near the town of Jhapa, in neat settlements where there are schools but no work for the able-bodied. Not less than 1,20,000 live in these camps and another 20,000–25,000 have moved to the borders of Assam and West Bengal, where they have settled temporarily.

They continue to wait, hoping for a return to their

homes. But several rounds of discussions between officials from Nepal and Bhutan have failed to move the situation around. They remain in the camps, the question of their nationality as far from resolution as when they first came, nearly a decade back. But the longer they stay in camps, the greater the danger of being infiltrated by radicalism and extremism and of groups taking to arms as an alternative means of struggle.

One of the best known exodus of refugees in recent times took place only a few hundred kilometres from India's borders. More than two million Afghans have streamed out of their war-devastated country since 1979 and taken refuge in Pakistan and Iran. Some have returned to Afghanistan but the majority stay on in sprawling camps near Peshawar, in Pakistan's North West Frontier Province, bordering their homeland, and in camps on the Afghan-Iran border. They live in these settlements, fearful of the fighting that rages on in the country, of the land mines that devastate life and limb, of the lack of a stable government, and are worried about the capacity of the land to bear crops.

These are examples of how social definitions, analysis and academic discourse break down in the face of human prejudices and concerns.

Unwanted Migrants

The other 'category' which Weiner defined as Unwanted Migrants embraces those groups which have crossed international and domestic provincial boundaries in search of economic benefits, or those who have moved as a result of economic and environmental factors. They are unwanted because they have been rejected by the host community. Thus, the Russians who settled in Estonia over many years and, who, after the breakup of the former Soviet Union, became targets of Estonian nationalism, fall in this list.

Hosts don't turn against migrants until they begin feeling politically and socially threatened. Or put more simply, until the settlers begin to assume numbers which make the 'native' community feel that they are being undercut, both culturally and physically.

The Lothsampas of southern Bhutan also fall into this listing: they went as migrants and were thrown out once their usefulness was perceived as over by the ruling Bhutanese elite. Migrants became refugees in another land.

But the most enduring example of Unwanted Migrants are the Bangladeshis of North East India. But even they are 'unwanted' only up to a point, as our travel to Bangladesh in search of these people will show. One needn't go even as far as Bangladesh—a look around eastern India should suffice. Immigrants Bangladeshis form a substantial chunk of the cooks and maids, servants and rickshaw pullers, fishermen and construction labourers there.

It needs to be stressed here that urban economies have greater capacity to accomodate migrants more easily than a sustenance-based land economy. Competition over fixed land resources can explode into violence as we have seen in Assam, or it can lead to a longer and more arduous trek for migrants, as I personally discovered in 1988, in the Punjab.

On the Move

In May of that year, I, and a number of fellow journalists from the international and national media, found ourselves reporting on the siege of Sikh militants holed up in the *Golden Temple at Amritsar. In dispatches filed for the *New York Times*, I likened the Temple to the Vatican for the Sikhs.

This was sacred land for them.

On a blistering summer day, the imposing, glittering domes of the Temple were silent and deserted. The sprawling complex, comprising of a sacred artificial lake, the Akal Takht, the spiritual seat of the faith, the clock tower and the offices, dormitories and the langar or dining area for the pilgrims was being cleaned up. The militants holed up inside had surrendered to security forces led by K.P.S. Gill, Punjab's imposing Director-General of Police, who began his career in the plains of Assam, driving out migrants as we have seen in an earlier chapter.

Nearly ten days of fighting between the militants on one side and Indian army troops and Gill's forces on the other had ended. The songs of the *ragi* or religious singer rang out in the morning, bouncing off the walls of the empty sanctuary for the first time in several days. The place had been ceremonially washed and cleansed of dirt and death during the night by local Sikhs.

I walked up the broken steps of the Guru Ram Dass Serai, which as its name suggests is a hostel for travellers and pilgrims named after the fourth Sikh Guru. At the first level was a battered room, strewn with rubble and glass fragments, its windows blasted to pieces. It had been a place where some of the militants had been based before they were driven out by fierce fire from the security troops. A few spent cartridges were lying around.

As I bent to pick one up, a small dark booklet lying nearby caught my eye.

I picked up the booklet; it turned out to be a passport. A Bangladeshi passport; or, rather, the jacket of one. The passport owner's identity was missing, all those pages which sketch a person's life in bare outline—date and place of birth, identifying marks ('if any' as such documents invariably say), father's name, home address—had been ripped out and thrown away. I looked elsewhere in the room, without luck, for the missing pages.

An examination of the jacket turned up other basic and important information. It turned out that the passport had been issued in the Bangladeshi town of Comilla, about 1,300 kilometres south-east of Amritsar. In fact, Comilla borders on Agartala, the capital of the distant state of Tripura in the Indian North East.

The passport had been issued on 24 March 1988, barely six weeks before the operation at the Golden Temple. Even at that time, the Punjab was a transit point for Bangladeshis in search of work and seeking a future in Pakistan. Some were keen to travel on through Pakistan, especially via the port city of Karachi, to the Middle East where they could secure their dreams and perhaps even become rich. That was the ultimate goal of their desperate rush to leave behind the impoverishment of their homeland.

I do not know what happened to the passport holder. Perhaps he reached Pakistan or whatever destination he was seeking. Perhaps he died while crossing over. Perhaps he died in an exchange of fire in the Golden Temple itself.

There were occasional media reports at the time of

Bangladeshis being shot while trying to cross the international border between India and Pakistan along the Punjab. Later, during a visit to Rajasthan in 1992, security officials spoke to me about scores of Bangladeshis dying in the Barmer and Jodhpur/Jaisalmer sectors every year as they sought to enter Pakistan. In the space of four years, the area of transit had changed from Punjab to the deserts of Rajasthan.

The modus operandi was simple. And those who drew them to the border were ruthless. Bangladeshi labourers wanting to go out to Pakistan and the Middle East were contacted by travel touts in Dhaka and other large cities who demanded part of the payment in advance. The figures cited to me at the time were between 15,000 rupees and 25,000 rupees per person. Through a network of agents in Bangladesh and India, the men, often with their families, would be transported to near the border.

'The last agent would take them to the desert, away from the nearest Border Security Force post and then point westwards and say, "Pakistan is just there",' an intelligence official said.[13]

'Over there' invariably meant getting lost in the sand dunes, with no identifiable landmarks or guides. Scores, some say hundreds, have perished in this manner under a merciless sun and a hostile environment. At times, entire groups of men, women and children (in one case over forty bodies were found) have died of dehydration, sunstroke and starvation.

Far from their lush-green land, watered by fifty-two rivers and innumerable streams, washed and flooded by monsoon rains, home to rich traditions of music, song and

---

13   Interview with author, Jodhpur, December 1993

dance, their bodies collapsed and dried up in an alien environment, under a pitiless sun.

In some cases, they were shot by guards from either side—suspected of being Pakistanis or Indians. The Indians say that there have been incidents where Pakistani Rangers have captured groups, shot or imprisoned the men, raped the women and then thrown them back into the desert to die. Of course, stories about the same treatment being meted out on this side also do the rounds.

Tremendous desperation in addition to an equal determination is what drives a person to go to such lengths to leave his own country, breaking the bonds of familiarity, family and social comfort, and to put himself and his close relatives at such terrible risk. It is a sign of the power of passage, of the allure of a better life, of the destitution that people flee.

There are an estimated one million Bangladeshis in the city of Karachi alone, according to Pakistani scholars and journalists. They comprise the city's labour, including construction workers and menials such as cleaners and domestic help.

'The aim is to go to the Middle East but they are rarely able to go beyond Karachi because once they settle down, they find it difficult to move again,' said the intelligence official in India.[14]

The long-term aim is El Dorado: the Arab Middle East, as well as Iran and Iraq, the Mecca to all prospective migrants from South Asia, where the seductive lure of dirhams and comparatively well-paid, if menial, jobs beckons.[15] A passage to the Middle East means several things: status at home, a steady income and, for the

14   Ibid.
15   Ibid.

unmarried, an upswing in the marriage market. But in many cases, the hopefuls end up not in El Dorado but as helpless prey of touts, mercenaries and border guards—as in the brothels of South Asia.

Mixed Migration

The importance of handling these economically-driven outflows, in addition to the refugees and displaced people that move across the world, was highlighted by Sadako Ogata, the then United Nations High Commissioner for Refugees, when she travelled to India in May 2000. Calling for a separation of migrants and refugees, she defined the category of economic migrants as the 'third dimension' of the problem of displacement.

'Poverty, under development and unemployment are also contributing to population movements in search of economic opportunities. Population flows are therefore increasingly becoming mixed in nature. Some are migrating for economic reasons; others are fleeing from conflict and persecution. Managing mixed migrations poses serious challenges, if the rights of asylum seekers and refuges are to be safeguarded,' Ms Ogata declared to an attentive audience in Delhi.[16]

Ms Ogata, one of the world's best known advocates of refugee rehabilitation during her tenure as UNHCR chief, recognized a crucial issue in her visit to India that many other refugee rights' specialists had forgotten. That in some nations, such as India, migrants are more significant as a political and economic issue than refugees.

This was a message that went home to her hosts for it

16   On the Humanitarian Frontlines. Sadako Ogato lecture at Vigyan Bhavan, New Delhi, 5 May, 2000

was a theme close to the heart of the Bharatiya Janata Party government in Delhi.

She spoke of the increased mobility among communities internationally as they struck out for better lifestyles. 'Increased mobility and the disparity in resources also mean that population movements will be, more and more, a mix of refugees and economic migrants. We shall encounter with increasing frequency the case of a person fleeing his or her own country for a variety of motives: fear, danger, persecution, certainly; but also, equally compelling, the legitimate urge to seek a better life.'

The urge to seek a better life is indeed legitimate. The problem arises when the means to fulfil that aim are illegitimate.

CHAPTER EIGHT

An Inner World: Chars, Islanders and Diwanis

The Circuit House at Dhubri commands a splendid view of the majestic Brahmaputra as it begins the last of its great bends southwards, plunging like a giant arrow into the heart of the flatlands of Bangladesh. Just outside the main gate to the Circuit House, at the bottom of a gentle slope, is the office of the District Superintendent of Police (SP). After a brief conversation with the then SP, a burly and helpful Ahom officer, Anindita Dasgupta, my researcher for Assam, and I were ushered to the records room. We were permitted to take down notes from any documents, but not to take away any material from there. It was windy and warm, I remember, and Anindita, who is smart as well as pretty, got straight down to the task of noting the number of foreigners held under the Foreigners Act, the number of illegal intrusions over the years, the changing routes for the influx, and some case histories.

We ignored the curious stares of the policemen, the whispered comments of officers wondering what two 'civilians', especially a young woman, was doing in their office. Over the next days and months, Anindita painstakingly noted down material from dusty offices in

Dhubri and other parts of the state, as well as neighbouring Meghalaya, culled out important information, and interviewed villagers, policemen, bureaucrats and politicians, professionals—lawyers and journalists as well as NGO groups.

Our fieldwork took us to different parts of Assam, from Guwahati to Nogaon, to Dhubri and villages on the Indo-Bangladesh border, and Meghalaya.

Dhubri is near Bangladesh; Guwahati is about 400 kilometres north-east of it and Nogaon is another 120 kilometres further away, about three to four hours drive on a pleasant and surprisingly smooth road from Guwahati.

Dhubri is a small, sleepy, dirty town of tiny lanes and bylanes which was built on the banks of the Brahmaputra and then moved inland. The commercial hub of the region is Guwahati, a busy, bustling, overcrowded, noisy city, flooded with rickshaws, autorickshaws, people, cars and fume-belching buses and trucks. It is a city of temples, the most famous being the Kamakhya which is especially sacred because an unmentionable part of Padmini, Siva's consort, fell there when Krishna was busy cutting her body into little pieces. This extreme act, according to legend, was forced by Padmini's death and the acts of her grieving *swami* who carried her across the world, dancing the *tandava* and destroying it without realizing what he was doing.

Nogaon is a sleepy town in Central Assam where nothing seemingly happens—but even in this laidback place, where summer's blistering heat and dripping humidity scorch the plains, the ULFA has had a major presence. It is also a district that attracted large numbers of immigrants, right from the years preceding independence.

These places were not huge distances apart but the roads connecting them were bone-rattling, car-shuddering, and pot-holed, looking as if they had been blasted by an evil apparition, seeking to torment travellers. The biggest culprits in damaging those roads (including the notional national highways and state highways) were the overloaded, lumbering trucks and buses, most of which seemed to be in the same stage of acute disrepair as the roads. It need hardly be added here that the construction quality of the roads was so poor that the first strong burst of monsoon rains was often enough to devastate them. A common enough sight was that of trucks with broken axles or trucks lying on their sides, their goods scattered on the road and the wet grass alongside it, with weary drivers and mechanics waiting for help and marking time. In many cases, the drivers would be Sikhs who had been plying these roads for years, if not decades. But the landscape would always be stunning—acres and acres of lush green countryside with overcast skies and the hint of rain.

Fieldwork

The documentation of this study has not been easy. In the course of collation of material, one travelled—with researchers or without them (and at times, as in the case of Assam, the researcher travelled without me!)—to sites selected for the fieldwork. Fieldwork in any area of the world is not easy, especially in those where poverty and conflict are frequent visitors, if not permanent settlers. Time and again, we were struck by the openness shown by people who we had never met but who agreed to talk with us on the basis of local contacts whom they respected. At one research site in Assam, on the southern bank of the Brahmaputra, Anindita located a former student of her, making for a natural entrée into the village. Others spoke because of a genuine interest in our work, and also because they felt the need to share their views on issues where they were being defined as the victims or as the protagonists, without them having a say in the matter. Their voices had never been heard or reflected in the discourse of politics, policy-making, and in the extensive writing by scholars or the media. Their vision of these concerns was strengthened by their own experiences. These views may have been subjective but, undeniably, they had a ring of truth and honesty about them, rarely heard in such discourse. It is this element of opinions and experiences from the ground level that have helped to shape our approach.

The massive bureaucracy whether on the Indian side of the border or the Bangladeshi was visible throughout our work. People whom we called upon were questioned by the police about the reason for our visits. They spoke up for me and my work. Many elements in the bureaucracy, in uniform or out of it, were helpful with contacts, information and opinions.

The places selected for research were chosen so that they were both close to the border but not too far away as well.

To pilot one's way through this maze, gathering vast amounts of material, took the best part of three years: there were interviews to be conducted, documentation to be collated, discussions to be held before one could begin to feel a sense of satisfaction. Our resources were limited, forcing us to focus on specific areas in the border areas, both in India and Bangladesh. There was another reason for picking these hot spots: a smaller area meant better accessibility to research sites. In addition, we reasoned that those interviewed would drop their initial suspicions after repeated visits.

Indeed, visitors to most parts of rural India travel with a natural companion, suspicion. Suspicion of outsiders is a quality that we would do well to respect—how is a villager to check our credentials? He has only our word for it, or our display of an identity card (which may make no sense to him). The pleasant young man who is asking careless questions could well be a plainclothes police officer out to extract information. Consequently, the villager could be in deep trouble, not just with the police (for what reason he knows not and is too scared to ask), but even with his neighbours and fellow villagers. Why have all this *jhan jhat*, goes the reasoning. Better just to smile and avoid direct answers.

This is especially true of areas such as Assam and the North East whch are constantly on the boil.

The complexity of the fieldwork and the difficulties of data-collection were driven home at our first meeting over breakfast with Nurul Islam, the then Congress MP from Dhubri. Islam was a tall man, a chain-smoker whose ponderous gait disguised a sharp political mind.

'You want to know about foreigners in Dhubri?' he asked, rather brusquely. I explained to him the project and its nuances, the need for data and fieldwork here and elsewhere, the importance of looking at the whole picture. 'There are no foreigners here, all this is propaganda, innocent people get victimized, poor people suffer,' he snapped at us.

It was not an auspicious beginning; I think Anindita started to wonder if our journey would end before it had really begun. I persisted, talking about the history of the region, the demographic changes, the need to replace emotionalism with logic and facts. His bushy eyebrows picked up at that.

'I'm getting a boat to travel across my constituency tomorrow, would you like to come?' he asked. I responded positively although I was not too happy about travelling with a Congress MP and his aide, the Congress MLA from South Salmara, Wazed Ali Choudhury. But here was a chance to talk to people on the chars, the islands and the banks of the river and its many channels.

It was a hot sticky day in June. The engine of the boat, a capacious motor launch lent to Islam by the Deputy Commissioner, the top civil authority in the district, coughed into life and shuddered away from the ghat to the main current of the Brahmaputra. The early morning weather was fine but by 10 a.m. it was cruelly hot and humid. We stopped at numerous hamlets and islands, the MP chatted to his constituents; we talked to settlers, trying to win their confidence.

The vessel eased its way into estuaries and smaller, quieter channels as it docked at the chars. Huts appeared amid clumps of coconut and banana trees; in some places there were groves of tall bamboos. The *khas bon* or stalks of high grass, crowned by their unique puffs of powdery fluff, grow well here during the winters; their stems are used for thatching roofs and walls. There were rice-fields and the yellow mustard flowers bending in the wind. Once away from the boat, a person could be forgiven for believing that one was living on the mainland.

I was told how to make out the difference between an old char and a newly emerged island. The old one would have jack fruit and mango trees; the new char would have only grass or shrubs and some banana trees, showing the evolution of plant species as lands became more enduring and were settled.

The channels would narrow, became shallower and then broader and deeper as they spread their network across the lands of the river. To get off, we would step on to a wooden plank connecting the boat to the nearest bank and then leap across the last few feet separating the land from the vessel.

Collecting data in any part of the world is a tough job. On the Indian subcontinent, it is even tougher. No sooner than one takes out a notebook and pen, that people who have been conversing fluently till then suddenly develop a peculiar paralysis of the mouth. It's a metamorphosis that many journalists are especially familiar with—a surprised expression on the face, followed by one of acute suspicion; a frown replaces the smile and a glazed look suffuses the face, rendering the subject virtually deaf and dumb.

But we had to make contact and the presence of the legislators actually did help—they were able to banter with their supporters and the islanders, telling them that we were out here to search for the elusive foreigners from Bangladesh. There was good-natured surprise and remarks that such things did not take place. We got the distinct feeling that people were telling us that we were wasting our time and energy.

The answers were predictable: one old man said that he had been born here and his parents had come from the former East Bengal in the 1920s. He gave his age as seventy. All of them claimed to have been born and brought up on these islands. They spoke confidently in the presence of their political leaders, knowing that they were safe.

But on an earlier morning, I, Anindita, and Dilip Chakravarty, a senior journalist from Dhubri, made our way by car and then on a shaky dugout to the home of Noor Mohammad, the headman of Barholla village. We found a different story here.

Mohammad was seventy-five. Bare-chested, lungi-clad and with a frown on his face, he talked about the 5,000 people under his care. 'At independence, there were more than 1,000 houses, now there are just 347; so many people have left because of the floods,' he said. But even Mohammad made a distinction between locals and outsiders. While most Muslims were local, there were some who were Bhatia or *bideshis* (foreigners).

He was firm on one point—the local government, whether at the district level or at Assam's capital, Dispur, had done nothing for them. There was no electricity, no paved roads or piped water.

The char-people were tough and articulate. We were struck by another fact—most of the population appeared to be either quite young children (below sixteen) or above thirty-five and forty years of age. One generation— that between these groups—appeared to be missing. We were told that many people had gone to Dhubri, Guwahati and other parts of the North East to ply cycle-rickshaws or work as labourers on construction sites. At one village, on the trip with Nurul Islam, we sat by the side of a village road and chatted with the islanders. It was dusk and the mosquitos were attacking us in swarms, obviously delighted at having some new, fresh victims. Where were the young men, I asked.

Some had gone to Delhi to work on big projects, we were told.

Were they local boys or from elsewhere?

The answer did not say much. 'They are from here, people keep coming and going.'

By this time, the MP and his followers had returned from their trip, standing precariously on a dugout as it wended its way across a small pond inside the island. Islam was doing the 'right thing' by his people: he had opened a playground at a school. Both projects were financed under funds provided by the Government of India for each Member of Parliament. They were given one crore rupees or ten million rupees each to finance development projects of their choice in their constituency. The money was routed through the district administration and Islam had spent a few lakhs on building schools and playgrounds. These were important, for even if the latter were covered by water during the five months of floods, the buildings at least doubled as refugee quarters during this period.

Everywhere, the story was the same.

If there was poverty on the mainland, the impoverishment in the chars was many times worse. There were no roads, only mud paths; there were no colleges, only a handful of schools; there was no electricity, it was too expensive to build transmission towers that would carry power lines across this huge waterway. The technology didn't exist, we were told.

We stopped at a Congress supporter's home for lunch. The women were taken inside and we were served rice with an excellent chicken curry, a dal and a dry vegetable. Earlier, we sat and talked in the courtyard with the householder, a man with large properties and farms. I used my notebook to fan the still, warm, moist air. Nurul Islam and the MLA had villagers fanning them with bamboo and cane fans. They were being treated like visiting potentates—and why not? They controlled substantial funds which could be distributed among key supporters in their constituencies.

A young, bearded, college teacher was among those waiting for us. He wore a white shirt and dark trousers and a small white skull cap. He had travelled by cycle from another village about five kilometres away. Part of the journey was covered on a dugout or *nouka*, steered by wiry boatmen heaving on oars and sticking as close to the banks as possible. The cycle was loaded on to the boat. The rest of the yatra was completed on the cycle. A sudden surge of water or a storm could easily destroy these flimsy boats and their passengers.

'You do not understand how bad conditions are in the chars,' he remarked. 'There are no doctors for miles, no decent colleges or proper schools, no jobs beyond what the land and the river give; no officer deigns to visit us. There are no veterinary doctors for the livestock.' And it is the chars which feed the towns in southern Assam.

This is obvious to anyone who visits the small ghat at Dhubri early in the morning. By the time it is bright daylight—on a summer day, it is light as early as 4 a.m.—scores of country boats, most of them powered by diesel engines, others driven by sturdy oarsmen, are chugging into the river port, disgorging people and goods. Those disembarking include daily labourers as also people in search of jobs and government favours. Some have come in response to a summons, others to work at shops and businesses.

The boats chug into the tiny harbour with goats and

milk, chickens and fruit, fresh vegetables and fish—even grass for cattle and other livestock in Dhubri town! The chars are also the greatest producers of labour: most of the construction workers in Guwahati claim they are from 'Dhubri', according to one survey, a whopping forty per cent of all rickshaw pullers in Guwahati are from 'Dhubri.' But is it the real Dhubri or the imagined one, that which stretches across political boundaries into a neighbouring country?

'Dhubri' has become a major exporter of human resources and unskilled workers to homes and businesses across the state. Women and young girls work as maids in middle class and affluent Assamese households in the towns of the Brahmaputra valley, saying that they are natives of Dhubri. Few believe their stories and they are described to friends and relatives as 'Bangladeshis.' But they stay on because their employers are not interested in sending them away; it would mean a drop in a comfortable standard of living.

The situation of dependency on imported labour is such that in Dhubri, come late evening and if one were visiting a friend or relative, one could get stuck without any transport to get back. Most of the rickshaw-pullers return to their homes on the islands by the evening boat.

In return what do the chars get? Very little. Even with regard to veterinary services, the areas which feed the towns of Lower Assam receive virtually nothing either in the form of visits by government vets or medicines or even information about better breeding and feeding. Thus, people move out in search of better opportunities and their place is taken by new dwellers, from other chars and, not unlikely, from Bangladesh. We shall examine this phenomenon in the next chapters.

It struck me forcefully here, more then than at any other point in my travels, that just as Assam protests against its alleged neglect by the Central Government, the people of the chars have the right to make a more vigorous plea of being discriminated against by Assam's rulers at the capital, Dispur. Despite physical proximity (about 400 kilometres) the mental and spiritual distance between Dhubri and Dispur is many times greater than that between Dispur and New Delhi.

In broad-brush terms, three worlds have emerged in Assam: one is of Dispur, another is that of the districts and a third of the chars which few people have even seen at first hand, barring those who have to live and work there. These are watery lands which are easy to settle upon and easy to leave. Documentation here is either old or non-existent.

South of Dhubri, the inhabitants are virtually completely Muslim. In one particular char, we were told that one Hindu family lived amidst about 500 Muslim families. Yet, one did not hear of any trouble directed against this tiny Hindu population!

Transport is by dugout and small boats, used also for fishing. Large families survive on little bits of land and the bounty of the waters. Both are gifts of the Brahmaputra whose silt nourishes the chars and gives the farmers a bounty of rich soil for cultivation every year. Yet, the river also creates havoc and devastates lives and property.

The neglect of the chars is spawning much trouble for Assam and the North East. This is seen in what the college teacher said on that muggy afternoon in 1997, a view backed by Islam. 'This is not just a feeling of frustration but of alienation and alienation is a dangerous trend.'

'Look around you, where is the infrastructure, there is

not even proper drinking water and we have not less than 500,000 homeless during the floods every year in my constituency alone,' he declared, tapping his cigarette case on his office table for emphasis.

The Muslims, Islam said, would back the demand for a separate state by a group calling itself the Kamatapuris, comprising basically of the Koch-Rajbonshi community, one of the martial races of the plains of Assam with a demographic imprint also in West Bengal and Bangladesh. There now is even a Kamatapur Liberation Organisation that has the tacit support of the char dwellers and other Muslim communities in the border areas and the unequivocal backing of ULFA.

The Assamese ruling elite at Dispur has woken up to the trouble that the underdeveloped chars are spawning and spreading but it is already late. In these lands and sand bars that separate the waters as the Brahmaputra widens and steadies from its Himalayan rush, the presence of the river and its overpowering influence is elemental. 'We live and die by the river,' said one char dweller.

This was evident from the notes of our fellow traveller, Wazed Ali Chowdhury, the MLA. His constituency, South Salmara, has one remarkable achievement. For decades, it has maintained its population and the number of voters at a consistent level. It has not seen the sudden demographic surges or drops visible in other parts of Assam. The river is taking huge bites out of South Salmara, remorselessly eroding its banks and washing land downstream. My brother, who is a doctor at Tura, Meghalaya, and a keen cricketer, recalled playing at the local cricket field one season, by the Brahmaputra. The next year, he said, 'Arre! the field was gone, just like that, swallowed up by the river.'

What is also striking about South Salmara is that only thirty-six per cent of the population has landed property in their own names; the others are labourers. Ninety-five per cent of the population of 1,65,000 is Muslim. Literacy is low and outbreaks of water-borne diseases like dysentery and malaria are common.

People don't stay long at South Salmara: if they can, they like to get out and move to other parts of Assam, especially the neighbouring areas. This is not surprising—out of 201 villages, 135 are severely eroded. In one case in Dhubri, where the river showed its lack of respect for authority by swamping a police station. 'There lies the old thana, in the middle of the Brahmaputra,' said one police officer, pointing in the general direction of where the building rests under water today. The land disappears under the flood waters and reappears as chars, but rarely in its original position. This sets off disputes over custody rights, claims and counter-claims.

The Diwanis of the Chars

The local government is rarely bothered about such disputes; its presence there is minimal and the chars, a world unto themselves, are governed instead by a network of powerful zemindars called Diwanis. The latter are a combination of local power brokers, landlords and businessmen; each has his private army, men armed with lathis and traditional weapons such as daos and spears. They are often connected to political parties.

These gangs are called *lathials* and it is their job to seize fresh land deposited during or after the flood surges. Indeed, these terms have a cross-border resonance. There are lathials in Bangladesh too, a nation where land is infinitely more precious than in Assam, and who perform the same tasks as their counterparts in India.

The Diwanis are not elected to their jobs; far from it, they are hereditary barons, backed by muscle power. Occasionally, they are challenged by new pretenders, leading to open conflicts on the soft soil of the chars. These events are barely reported even in the local media. For most of us, this is an uncertain, dark world about which we know little; we are content with that lack of knowledge.

The Diwani has extensive, informal powers. He receives a multitude of complaints. Should a person come before him seeking the eviction of people who have settled on his land, the Diwani can force their evacuation, for a consideration, of course. This is payable in cash or in kind—a part of the harvest from this very land.

During her travels, Anindita ran into another Nurul Islam, this man being the Assistant Settlement Officer for the char of South Salmara. Islam's job is to settle claims arising out of flood destruction and displacement (hence the title). One of his toughest jobs is presented by the appearance of new land after the retreat of the floods in the winter season. The lathials appear to enforce the orders, not of the government, but of the Diwani and whoever he chooses to support as owner of these fresh islands and sandbanks.

'Sometimes, might is right,' said Islam. Everyone claims to be the owner of the land and some establish possession by sowing dal or gram on it. 'In some cases, the government settles matters, especially if it is *patta* land. In others, the Diwani does.'

In the old days, when erosion was not such a major problem and Assam was one large political unit, South

Salmara was the constituency of one of the state's most influential leaders, Sir Mohammed Saadulla of the Muslim League. Saadulla held office as Premier of Assam in British India. His political battles with Gopinath Bardoloi of the Congress party in the 1940s is the stuff of legend.

Today, it is a place that most people wish to leave. Its influence has vanished and its very survival is at stake with the rushing waters of the Brahmaputra gouging out great chunks of land every year. But if the locals do leave, then who takes their place? Would it be far-fetched to assume that there is an inflow from Bangladesh, barely twenty kilometres from South Salmara's southernmost tip? I don't think so, even though Chowdhury disagrees vehemently.

To the Chars—from Bangladesh?

Those who live on the chars do so under extremely trying physical and psychological conditions. Why would people migrate to such places? Only because they have no choice in the matter. To those leaving Bangladesh, it is a habitat with which they are familiar, even the struggle accompanying it is not alien: an unending jousting with the forces of the rivers. But here, at least there is land to settle upon and build a future. Without land, no community, village or nation can endure, or sustain their histories.

In Bangladesh, the man:land ratio is officially over 750 per square kilometre. In Assam it is 265. The latter figure is somewhat misleading for it does not indicate that the Assam valley is bisected by the Brahmaputra river which takes up not less than 15–20 kilometres of the valley at any given point; cultivation on its sandbanks is difficult and there are the hills not far from the river where high yields are not possible. The cultivable area is shrinking in a region where the maximum width of the valley is rarely much beyond 80–100 kilometres.

But what motivates the seekers of passage and settlement to uproot themselves and their kin from a known identity to an unknown one, where they would be at the mercy of their hosts and neighbours? This is still a question in the minds of many. Why would people come and settle in such difficult conditions on the chars even if they eventually were to move inland?

We get some answers to this in chapter ten, the story of Keramat Bhai. Yet, it is worth reflecting here that those who come are driven not just by absolute destitution and deprivation but also by determination to succeed and get out of the swamp of poverty. As far back as 1991, a wizened old patriarch called Mugha ul-Khand talked to me at the village of Modhupur, about 150 kilometres north of the Bangladeshi capital of Dhaka, about the crisis that is pushing people across the border.[1]

'Every year our land holding is shrinking, our families are growing. My father had twenty-four bighas of land. (one bigha equals about 0.35 acres or 0.15 hectares). Now my four sons have two bighas each. What can you grow on two bighas?' One son had already sold part of his land, and each of the sons had several children.

Mugha ul-Khand declared that his people were prepared to go anywhere 'to Assam, if necessary, if we can get land and live with dignity. But will the Assamese have us? There are man-made frontiers and prejudices.'[2]

1   Interview with author, February 1991
2   Ibid.

Here was a man, then aged not less than eighty, who declared that his family would be prepared to move away from Modhupur to an unfamiliar land. The rumours of anger against settlers in Assam had reached even this placid village. But that did not seem to affect their thinking—they were still prepared to consider the possibility, that if the worst happened and their land holdings became unsustainable, they would migrate to a foreign country and face a hostile atmosphere. The old man said that none in his family had gone to Assam.

These days there are well-organized gangs who organize travel and settlement to India for a fee. This illegal system of organized movement has been around since the beginning of the influx into Assam, at the start of the last century. These days, it is much more profitable and better tuned.

People do not go merely from Bangladesh to the North East. But for a premium, they can find themselves in cities such as New Delhi and Jaipur. Of course, getting to Calcutta is easy pickings.

In June 2000, the Delhi police unleashed a drive to oust illegal settlers from Bangladesh. Their goal was to identify these groups and push them out, placing them on trains to send them back to their homeland. This was not the first such effort as we have seen from K.P.S. Gill's campaign in Assam in 1964. A campaign against Bangladeshis was launched in 1996 in New Delhi when about 200 terrorized 'Bangladeshis' were herded into a train and sent toward Bangladesh. The were pushed across the border, in the face of protests by Dhaka. To add to their humiliation, a number of men were forcibly tonsured by the Border Security Force before being sent away. The Marxist government in West Bengal was appalled and public opinion in India reacted sharply to the images of the tonsuring and the forced repatriation.

In 1998, the West Bengal government refused to allow a train of 'Bangladeshis' detected by the right-wing Shiv Sena-BJP government in the western state of Maharashtra, to pass through its territory. It said that the move violated human rights and that the men, women and children who were being chased out were Bengali-speaking Indian Muslims, not Bangladeshis. They claimed the group was being targetted by the right wing in Bombay because of their religious affiliation. Human rights groups protested, the media wrote in anger and the effort fizzled out.

But a few months later, in January 1999, Chief Minister Jyoti Basu of West Bengal decried the influx into his state to visiting Bangladesh Prime Minister Sheikh Hasina Wajed.[3] Basu said that his government had pushed back 20,000 infiltrators in the past few years. This is, to me, a pitifully small estimate of the real problem as his own government had already told the Supreme Court in Delhi that not less than 1.2 million Bangladeshis who had visited the state on valid visas between 1972 and 1996 had 'vanished' from records. In other words, they had merged with the larger Bengali-speaking population of the state.

The Chief Minister added, 'I know that . . . Bangladeshis enter the border districts of Malda and Murshidabad every day to earn wages and go back. They come here due to economic reasons, so we do not generally object.'[4]

In the June 2000 exercise, Delhi police targetted

3   The *Telegraph*, Calcutta, 29 January 1999
4   Ibid.

Bangladeshis on the western side of the Jamuna, where resettlement colonies have sprung up since the 1970s. There was a significant difference: the state government in power was that of the Congress, a party which had cried itself hoarse about the anti-minority beliefs of the BJP.

This time, however, the target population hit back and a riot erupted. A police jeep was burned and an enraged mob surrounded the local thana and was preparing to set the place ablaze when reinforcements arrived and scattered the rioters. At least one person was killed and several injured in police firing.

Those who were mute and submissive until a few years ago are now sufficiently well-organized and in large enough numbers to fight an attempt by the State to dispossess them. This is a significant step forward in the radicalization and empowerment of such groups in India, and it sets an extremely troubling precedent—foreign nationals, who have settled in a region with the connivance of local authorities and political parties, are now prepared to engage in conflicts with law enforcement authorities because they feel that their 'rights' are threatened.

Although the Supreme Court has ruled that the right to life and liberty are indivisible, regardless of nationality, creed and caste, this does not confer upon any individual or group, especially one whose nationality is doubtful, the right to attack a law enforcement agency. Such an attitude undermines the basis on which governance rests and cannot be tolerated by any government of any political hue. If not tackled firmly, such events could trigger similar confrontations with these communities in other parts of the country.

Neither 'secular' or 'non-secular' parties can claim

they did not know about the influx. The fact is they did nothing to prevent it from happening because they had a vested interest in settling these people—the votes of the migrants.

What is also important about this incident is that many of those arrested later said that they had paid substantial amounts to *dalals* to get to where they were. So, these people were not only protecting their livelihood but also their investments.

At the end of our boat journey together in Dhubri, Nurul Islam sat at on a chair on the deck, visibly tired, his white hair ruffled by the wind. We were gliding through darkness, heading to the town and Islam was chain-smoking. He was weary but happy from the tour, although it was not a journey which he did neither very often or liked doing.

'So, have you seen many foreigners?' he asked with a chuckle. 'No,' I replied. I would reserve judgement because none of those we had met would proclaim anything but their Indian-ness. I added the conditions were appalling and needed to be tackled by the government in Dispur. Without development, the chars would become breeding grounds of instability, radicalism and violence. Once that had begun, where would it end?

He nodded.

'So many rivers go into Bangladesh, it is not practical to restrict people or goods. Everything is going on but innocent people are being harassed. There is seasonal migration; if you have thirty per cent landlessness here you have sixty per cent landlessness there. They come round the year and the local people react favourably to them,' he said.

120

Before we pulled into the tiny harbour, he leaned forward to emphasize a point: 'The Kamatapur Liberation Organisation—we will be in the background, we will give support but will not lead, let the tribals do it.'

A couple of years later, Islam was dead but the idea he spoke of is becoming a reality.

The Kamatapur Liberation Organisation, comprising of the Koch-Rajbonshi community as well as Bodos, Bengali Muslims and some Assamese Hindus, has become active on the Indo-Bangladesh border especially in Dhubri district. This group has connections with the National Democratic Front of Bodoland as well as the ULFA. It is believed to have strong links with Pakistan's Inter-service Intelligence (ISI). The Koch-Rajbonshi community as well as the Bodos (known as Mechs in Bangladesh) and the Muslims, are to be found in Bangladesh as well as Assam and West Bengal. Ethnicity spans national and international boundaries with ease. This latest group finds shelter and succour in the homes of brethren on either side of the border and is steadily emerging as a distinct threat to the soft underbelly of Assam and the North East: the riverine regions as well as the Chicken's Neck and its bordering areas.

The nether world of the chars and of the Diwanis has opened up to radicalism, to a network of fundamentalism and anti-India hate campaigns, which have access to arms and easy connections to sanctuaries across a porous international border. A new 'front' has emerged to plague governance and peace in the North East and its ethnic and religious composition makes it that much more difficult to comprehend and address.

CHAPTER NINE

Where is Suleman?

There is a story about a man called Suleman which is often told by an intelligence officer from the Border Security Force (BSF). 'Suleman was from Bangladesh; he managed to infiltrate and even migrate to Guwahati.' For twelve years he lived there before he was detected. The BSF officer claimed that Suleman even befriended an Indian Army officer and passed on classified army information to Bangladesh. Suleman was then arrested along with an accomplice, a Hindu from Dhubri. They were tortured and 'confessions' extracted; Suleman was imprisoned for three months and then pushed into Bangladesh.

Three months seems to be a rather light sentence for alleged espionage, so one tends to question the whole story. But, interestingly, some months after Suleman's departure to his homeland, the same BSF officer was hailed at the border by a Bangladeshi. It turned out to be the same Suleman. Only this time, he declared, 'I have become a fisherman.'

How easy is it to cross the border? Mahesh talks about this in his story in chapter two. But I, too, have experienced what it is to walk across.

In 1984, I was on an assignment for the *New York Times*. I came down from Tura, capital of the Garo Hills district, to a small border post called Dalu, manned by the BSF. The Indian flag fluttered in the morning breeze as the young post commander ordered for sweet tea and biscuits at the small brick and cement building. His surname was Yadav. A few metres away, a band of various ranks from the Bangladesh Rifles (BDR), the counterpart of the BSF, stood and watched. The Bangladesh flag flew proudly above their building.

In the aftermath of the Assam agitation, the students and other leaders had demanded the 'sealing' of the Indo-Bangladesh border with a fence and a road alongside, to patrol and keep a lookout for Bangladeshis trying to sneak in. We were assured by Yadav and others that the border was, indeed, closely monitored and was difficult to cross.

After tea, we decided to go for a little drive along the border. Out of sight of the BSF, especially its watch tower (there was supposed to be one at a distance of every kilometre), we stopped our sturdy Ambassador at a turning in the dirt road. There was no sign of people; the sound of birds and crickets filled the air. A few hundred feet across the bushes were the paddy fields of Mymensingh district in Bangladesh.

We walked those several hundred feet, looking backwards from time to time to check if the BSF or the BDR were coming after us. It was a lazy late morning and the cows on the fields looked at us with scant interest. What did it matter to them if we were Indian or Bangladeshi? Do cows have a nationality?

But cows and cattle have an interesting history in the

history of the two countries, dating back to the days of East Pakistan. Cattle rustling by Bangladeshi gangs was a common enough event, especially on this sector of the border. Indeed, many years later I learned that the biggest single export by India (in the informal, read, illegal, sector of bilateral trade) was that of over 1,700,000 cattle to Bangladesh every year!

At Dalu, we had been warned about the sudden appearance of thugs and thieves by the BSF, and had shrugged off their offer of assistance (in the form of an armed guard). But our driver had been worried by the advice.

He called out to us several times from the apparent safety of the car, asking us to return. When his hailing had no effect on the intrepid band of explorers (comprising of my brother, a Garo friend of his and me), he resorted to a more direct method of persuasion.

He sent his deputy, a scrawny Bengali boy of about eighteen who doubled as car cleaner, with the following message: if we did not get back in the next fifteen minutes, he was going to leave and return to Tura. With an ultimatum like that, we were in no position to argue. When we turned on him in the car and shouted at him for getting us back, he only raised his hands in embarrassment and helplessness and said: 'But, *saar*, if the car was attacked, then I would have to pay for the damage from my own pocket. Why take a chance, saar.' Our telling him repeatedly that we would cover the costs in the event of any mishap had no effect.

We returned to Tura.

Of course, since that time, we are told that border patrolling has improved: that some fencing has come up and that there are segments of tar-topped roads along these lines of human division. It would be another thirteen years before I returned here, to another part of the border, both from the Indian and the Bangladeshi sides.

In 1998, Anindita Dasgupta managed to put together a micro-level map of one little bit of the border between the two countries. A quick look helps even a casual observer understand how easy it is to cross parts of this border: the river and its many channels are the key. There is another major factor—human greed, of those in uniform and out of it, that helps sustain the profitable business of people smuggling.

How on earth can anyone control the stealthy movement of people over nine channels of the main river? There are rivers which are slashed by the boundary markers of either country. So are the chars. What is there to prevent people walking from one part of the char to the other and thus crossing into another country? There are no barbed wire fences here, no rolls of concertina wire, the BSF patrol boats are few and far between. Anyone who thinks that patrol boats can keep a watch on these many streams, which wend in and out among the many islands, is badly mistaken.

The story of movement in these areas is that of literally hopping from one char to another, from one channel to another, until you hit the main channel, or a large enough char near an old settlement and then, through existing contacts, to move in here before travelling to a further point.

In the patch of the river border shown on this map, there are not less than sixteen islands of differing sizes. In addition, there are ten chars and islands through which the international boundary runs. This is an administrative and policing nightmare. Just how is this policing to be done? Even if there are a few dozen kilometres to be covered, even if the Government of India posts 100 men to every kilometre, how are they to patrol? How are they to live on their boats, day in and day out, every day of the blistering summer, the cold winter and cope with the explosive power of the flooded river and the monsoon rains?

Many, on the small BSF river force already do that—but to what avail? The BSF Bay Wing, as it is called, has twenty-three speed boats and forty engine-fitted boats. The latter are basically country boats and much slower and less manoeverable than the former. These boats are responsible for patrolling the border areas as well as further inland.

Another factor that border officials must wrestle with is, literally, the shifting sands of the river. This poses an impossible task for cartographers and for the police. Where is the line to be drawn? What happens if India or Bangladesh 'seize' or sit upon a new bit of land that has been washed down by the Brahmaputra and has suddenly been spat out by the current in mid-stream?

A heavy downpour can cause the resetting of the border: a land mass which defined one part of the border may disappear if the river shifts course. The border could advance or be set back (depending on how you look at it) several hundred metres, causing enormous problems for border staff and the char dwellers.

The latter are pragmatic, tough and resourceful people anyway. But of which country are they nationals, especially if the border shifts from time to time for reasons beyond their control? Those who call themselves Indians

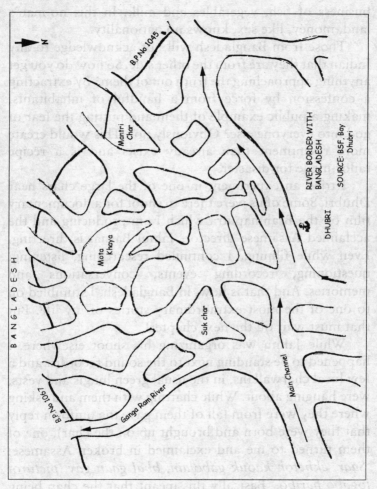

Courtesy: Anindita Dasgupta

move to India. Indeed, most of them do just that. They use the Bangladeshi taka and the Indian rupee to conduct their business of fish, vegetables and milk. In this no-man's land, money, like sex, knows no nationality.

Those from Bangladesh will not acknowledge to any Indian that they are from the other side. So how do you get anything approaching the truth out of them? By extracting a confession by force from a handful of inhabitants, making a public example of them and putting the fear of god into everyone else? Obviously not. This would create more resentment than already exists and is a recipe tailor-made for disaster.

I tried an experiment in one of the large chars near Dhubri. Some of us were there to shoot for a documentary film on the Brahmaputra which I am producing and the acclaimed Assamese director, Jahnu Barua, is directing. Even while filming, I continued researching, listening, questioning, recording events, conversations and memories. And that is how, in Bangladesh, I stumbled on to one of the most extraordinary stories of my life. But that must wait till the next chapter!

While Jahnu was organizing his shoot elsewhere, I happened to be standing next to the sound recordist and a few local charwallahs, in the usual green lungis and vests, were hanging about. While chatting with them and asking where they were from (all of them gave the uniform reply that they were born and brought up on the char), one of them turned to me and exclaimed in broken Assamese: '*Saar, ekhetok kaouk gabolain, bhal gaan gay, picturot logabo paribo.*' Basically this meant that the chap being presented to me was a good singer and we might find his *sur* useful for the film.

I asked him to sing and got Sanjoy Chatterjee, our

sound recordist, to record him on his large tape recorder: the song was in Bangla, the Bhatia dialect, but as I listened I was astonished. The man said he was a rickshaw-puller in Guwahati and had taken a few days break to return home. He filled his lungs and sang a strong yet melodious song in the Bhatiali style. This style is far more prevalent in the northern districts of Bangladesh, especially Rongpur and Kurigram, than anywhere else though there are echoes of it in the Dhubri region.

The young man sang beautifully about the travails of people living on the banks of the Dharla river which flows through Kurigram, a few kilometres distance, and which is just across the border in Bangladesh.

So, when I asked him why he sang about the Dharla river in Bangladesh, he smiled in embarrassment and quickly left the place. The others stood by and sniggered but would not say anything, either for the record, or off it.

There is another incident, this one of April 1998. About twenty-eight kilometres west of Assam's principal city of Guwahati is a famous religious site known as Hajo. This place is special to Hindus, and Buddhists and the Muslims. A short distance from the small town is the Islamic shrine of Pua Mecca, where a wandering Iraqi prince had brought the word of the Prophet Mohammed to the region in the eleventh century. For centuries, Hajo has been an excellent example of the traditional tolerance that has been a characteristic of society in Assam. On a hill, rising above the plains and paddy fields below and flanked by the Brahmaputra and sundry streams on three sides, it represents the first foothold of Islam in the North East. These days, you can watch aircraft take off and land at Borjhar airport, a few kilometres to the east across the river. It is a splendid setting, especially at dawn and at dusk.

On that muggy April afternoon, I had gone with a television unit to Pua Mecca to get some shots of the river, to show its calming and civilizing influence. We were talking with the maulvi, or head cleric of the masjid. He was an elderly Assamese Muslim, and a middle-aged man, thin and gruff-voiced, in a lungi and t-shirt was keeping him company. The man spoke a horribly convoluted Assamese, mixed with many Bengali words and phrases. Without realizing it, he let out the truth: 'In our *desh*, Bangladesh, we have high respect for people like the maulvi saheb, we respected educated people.'

Then, becoming conscious that he had committed a horrible mistake, he laughed aloud, muttered something about respecting one's elders. When I asked him when he had come to Hajo, he shuffled his feet and mumbled about having been here for a few days and that he would soon be moving on. Shaken by the turn of the conversation, he slipped away. I wish I had grabbed him by his shirt or at least reported his presence to the police in Hajo. One can find many excuses for not doing what one should have done—in this case, the fact we needed to return to Guwahati at the end of a long and tiring day's shoot.

These vignettes hold up a higher, greater truth. They inform us of the scale of the human flood entering Assam and its neighbourhood.

Now back again to the char dwellers near Dhubri and those who keep losing land to the river, who are constantly see-sawing between two nations in their own inner world. Who or what are they? How many of them are there? Can their conditions be improved? Are they Indians or Bangladeshis?

If there is any place on earth where there are environmental refugees, then surely they are to be found here—in the children of the chars.

We shall show, in the next chapters, that Bangladeshis do come, in large numbers to India. Some of them stay and settle. Others use it as a transit, en route to Pakistan or to the Middle East and South-East Asia. There are also those who work as seasonal labourers and return home having made some profit.

The Puzzle of Identification

But once you catch a 'Bangladeshi,' how do you establish his or her identity?

This is one the toughest hurdles that laws, the courts, the police system and diplomats have not been able to overcome in decades. Trying to locate or ferret out even the facts can be an extremely tedious and frustrating business. One of the places where information about the complaints against foreign nationals and material about cases against them can be found is at the courts of the Illegal Migrants Determination by Tribunal (IMDT).

Anindita Dasgupta, all of five feet tall and sporting a neat bob cut, marched into the Registrar's office in Guwahati, and later, in other courts elsewhere in Assam, to demand information. She met a portly, cheerful man at Guwahati who happily admitted that their records were 'very badly maintained. That is how we function.'

The job of these courts is to identity and order the deportation (through the local police) of those so identified and confirmed as Bangladeshis. So when Anindita charged about in righteous indignation, seeking some very elementary facts such as the records of the IMDT, she found that even these were not available. 'The lower tribunals,' she found out, 'do not prepare monthly or even yearly reports for the apex court, which is the Appellate Court at Guwahati.' The lower courts do not even maintain figures of those acquitted or sentenced.

The IMDT was passed hastily in 1983 by the Lok Sabha as part of the Congress party's bid to undermine the student movement in Assam. One of the main promotors of the legislation was Prime Minister Indira Gandhi, who supported it under the guise of protecting minority rights (read here Muslim rights, whether immigrant or 'local'). Its very creation was an act of blatant discrimination: the act applies only to Assam and to no other part of the country. Should this be taken to mean that the government of the day believed that there were no illegal foreigners in other parts of the North East, not to speak of the rest of India? An instrument of discrimination, the IMDT needs to be removed without delay or compunction. A law that promotes discriminatory treatment is no law at all.

The IMDT has numerous clauses but the critical one is Clause 3 (1) C which states that the person who can be proceeded against as a foreigner is one who has entered India after 25 March 1971, and has done so without proper official documents.

Let's walk through how the IMDT functions. Basically, there are eleven steps. The first action against a 'Bangladeshi' can be initiated after the police receives a written complaint, either from a government officer or a private citizen, questioning the nationality of a resident of the region. The inquiry begins under the supervision of a sub-inspector of police. This stage involves the filling of two forms, namely Form 1 and Form 2 that involve a deposit of ten rupees by the complainant who must live within the precincts of the local police station. The initial testimony of the accused as well as that of witnesses is recored here.

Next, the investigation report is submitted to a Select Committee comprising of the Superintendent of Police (SP) and the Sub-Divisional Officer (SDO). The latter is usually a young person fresh out of university, fired with enthusiasm in his first, or at least, new posting, and not yet overcome by corruption and insensitivity.

The SP then sends the Select Committee's report to the Government, having discussed the issue with the SDO. The state government then orders the Lower Tribunal (the IMDT court at the district level) to begin proceedings. Only then is the case registered, notices issued to the accused to respond to the charges and a date fixed for hearings. Case hearings take place and eventually there is a judgement. If there is an appeal against the ruling, the petitioner will go to the Appellate Court at Guwahati, which functioned for many years under a former High Court judge from Rajasthan, Justice S.N. Bhargava.

This entire process can take several years and one must emphasize here that the structure of the IMDT makes the involvement of the local police, already overburdened with law and order problems of the day, including armed insurrection and communal strife, mandatory. How can an overloaded and understaffed police force do justice to either? Without fail, the IMDT cases get postponed because the investigating officer has little time to follow up and conduct the necessary interviews. He is too busy dealing with day-to-day emergencies.

The problem gets even more complex when documents are used to buttress a claim by the accused. Under the discovery proceedings that are mandatory under the Indian Evidence Act, every document provided by one party can be examined and verified by experts from the other side. Delays, already endemic in the Indian judicial system, become even more protracted and pronounced.

But this is not the end of the IMDT procedure. There's more in store for those brave enough to fight it out to the bitter end:

Once the Appellate Court has completed its hearing and passed judgement, the accused may go and appeal to the High Court of the state under Article 226 of the Constitution. And finally, the Court may, in its wisdom, send it all back to the Appellate Court for a revised opinion.

The procedure could last years, if not decades.

What are the other laws under which a foreigner, Bangladeshi or otherwise, can be detected?

The main legislation used to locate and evict foreign nationals living in India without formal permission or those who have overstayed their official welcome is the Foreigners Act of 1946. The crucial section of the Foreigners Act is Clause 3, which grants sole authority to the police to detect and deport foreigners.

This clause attracts much criticism for the seeming unlimited powers that it bestows on the police; there are complaints that these powers are abused. There are clauses in the IMDT and the Foreigners Act which overlap. But there is one crucial difference: under the Foreigners Act, the accused is presumed guilty until proven otherwise. This is an internationally established practice—the 'foreigner' must prove that he or she is a national of the country entered or in which he or she is residing. Under the IMDT, the burden, of proof is on the accuser. This is the exact opposite of what is acceptable internationally, the opposite of good law. For reasons not very difficult to fathom, the Congress party firmly supports this flawed concept.

The going is tough too for foreigners' tribunals. A study of the records between 1983 and 1997 showed that only 15,921 out of 46,882 cases against alleged foreigners in Dhubri were found to have merit by the Superintendent of Police. Of these, by the time the cases came to trial, 7,940 had died; another 2,838 had 'shifted' their homes and not less than 5,143 were declared 'untraced'. The last category defies reason: it means that these individuals were never located. Either they had never existed or they just vanished, moving on to other places as in the second category where the pressure was less.

Only 2,314 cases went before the foreigners' tribunal; of these, 2,260 were completed and only 908 were declared as foreigners. Those who were not found to be foreigners were far more in number: 2,233.

As far as the IMDT is concerned, the Congress and other parties are opposed to its possible abrogation, saying that this will harm the interests of minority groups. They have failed to understand the basic point. It should not matter whether the IMDT is repealed or not. Because of its inability to enforce either a substantial number of convictions or deportations, the IMDT is as good as dead!

At times, the functioning of the system borders on the farcical. In one case, the police went searching for a suspected foreigner to serve a notice on him. Having failed to locate him, the exasperated police party finally stuck the notice on a tree and told the court that the summons had been served.[1]

In the first four months of 1997, for example, a total of just four cases were initiated under the IMDT at Dhubri. All of these were launched in April; not even one case was filed in between January and March that year. There are more ways of getting rid of the unwanted foreigner. To this day, there exists an archaic system called the Quit India notices, a procedure put in place by the British, as the term suggests. These are issued by local police to suspected foreigners after the IMDT courts have deemed them to be so.

The number of such notices issued in Assam between 1990 and 1993 were 637. Of these, 407 were actually served. Notices could not be served on 112 as the foreigner had either shifted elsewhere or was 'untraced'.

The Quit India notice is issued on a piece of paper by the local Superintendent of Police. It informs the person to whom it is addressed—a foreign national—that his or her presence is illegal and he/she must leave the country through the nearest available exit point as soon as possible. These orders can be challenged in court, as can all orders of government, ensuring further delays in the deportation process.

Quit Notices, court orders, whatever—once in place, people stay or move on.

---

1   Interview with Justice S.N. Bhargava, Chairman of the IMDT Appellate Court and Chairman of the Assam State Human Rights Commission.

CHAPTER TEN

Memory is a Fickle Companion

Sushil Das of Satrasal village, from where the Indo-Bangladesh border is within touching distance, is a Koch-Rajbonshi, a descendant of the proud, martial race which ruled over southern and western Assam, extending its influence over parts of today's Bangladesh and West Bengal. In a conversation, he spoke of how 'hundreds of refugees' had crossed over during the 1971 Indian war with Pakistan. That exodus followed the crackdown on the Awami League of Sheikh Mujibur Rahman and mass massacres by the West Pakistani army in its Eastern province.

The refugees at Satrasal, 400 kilometres south-west of Guwahati, were initially housed at the local high school. But as the numbers swelled, epidemics of dysentery and diarrohea broke out and the Bangladeshis were transported to the town of Gossaigaon, north of Satrasal and now located in Kokrajhar district. 'Where they all went after that, we do not know,' said Das.

Das' home town of Satrasal is still identified in revenue records and election lists by another title: Ram Rai Kuti. This should really have been Ram Rair Kutir, or the home of Ram Rai, a relative of the great Vaishnavite saint and reformer of the sixteenth century, Sri Sankaradeva.

The sleepy settlement of small lanes and houses with tin roofs and mud-plastered walls is dominated by a sixteenth century *satra*, a monastery where celibate monks still live, set up during Sankaradeva's time and where his sister is said to have married the great Koch general Silarai. The wood panels, recently restored, show flashes of eroticism, desire and torture, elements which seem out of place at a major religious centre. But then, so are the temples of Khajuraho where sexual love is celebrated in diverse forms and positions.

A short walk from the satra, along a small unpaved, dirt road, which is hemmed in by homes and fields, is the Indo-Bangladesh boundary. Actually, one passes the fenced border before reaching Satrasal. The fence appears on one side of the road and then on the other, as the border changes direction. There are not many problems in driving along the narrow road that runs parallel to the barbed wire fence, not less than 10 feet high with rolls of concertina wire before it. There are several gates which allow Indian farmers and their livestock access to farmlands on the border. No construction is allowed for a distance of 200 metres from the actual border.

These gates control the approach to the frontier and are manned by guards from the BSF. To get through them, a villager must produce either identification or give details about himself and his residence to one of the guards, who writes it all down on a lined register book. The worker is then issued a cardboard token, which he or she must carry until the gates close for the night.

As I watched, a few boys flying kites wandered over to the Bangladesh side and then returned, intent on their sport. Some goats also trotted around. Were it not for the guards with automatic weapons and the barbed wire fences, the scene would have been quite pastoral.

Before the fence went up, says a resident of the satra, 'Bangladeshis were entering Satrasal all the time.' The man, Subhash Chandra Sarkar, a portly 43-year-old, said that in earlier days Bangladeshis would migrate to Delhi through Assam, return home after some years, marry there and again return to Delhi.

The conversations with Sarkar and with his fellow villagers recorded below were conducted in Assamese.

'These days, they don't return to Bangladesh to seek brides. There are enough Bangladeshi young women in Delhi and other parts of the country from whom they can choose!'

What is interesting about the movement of Bangladeshis into Assam, to Delhi and elsewhere is that it is predominantly male. The women who come work as maids or household helps, whether it is in Guwahati or in NOIDA, the New Okhla Industrial Development Area, on the northern edge of New Delhi. The men are invariably employed in unskilled areas as rickshaw-pullers, or petty traders (selling fish or the exquisite *jhamdhani* and *tangail* sarees of their country), or labourers. They come in, said Sarkar and others, under false names and make their way along established routes in Assam, Tripura, Meghalaya and West Bengal.

Mahesh's story tells us that.

Many do not stay in places such as Satrasal, which is dominated by Assamese speakers and the Koch Rajbonshi community. Except in the *diaras*, the chars, an immigrant Muslim would stick out like a sore thumb. Through a network of dalals (middlemen) and contacts, people travel on night buses and specially chartered vehicles from towns like Dhubri to Guwahati.

A police officer at Dhubri, who had handled infiltration over the years, including at Cachar District which also borders Bangladesh, described how they had once stopped a bus en route to Guwahati from Cachar. The bus had its windows closed tight, the curtains were pulled across dark-tinted glasses. It was a hot day, making the closed windows even more intriguing. When the police opened the door, they found not less than forty Bangladeshis, sweltering in the oven-like heat and cowering in fright.

They were immediately arrested and sent back to Cachar's border with Bangladesh.

'I don't know if they were pushed back, that wasn't my job, we apprehended them and sent them on their way—but I won't be surprised if they managed to get back or were not sent out of India at all,' he remarked.

Keshab Pradhani, a priest at the local satra, remarked that there were very few Bangladeshis in the neighbourhood since they would draw attention. 'We look completely different to each other,' said Pradhani, who is a Koch, or one of the aboriginal, Mongolian communities of the Brahmaputra Valley. The Kochs ruled western Assam for many years and were especially prominent in the fifteenth and sixteenth centuries.

But Pradhani was not untouched by the immigration agitation. 'We have read in the newspapers about this but have not seen such people with our own eyes,' he remarked.

Pradhani's scepticism is rare among Assamese-speakers. It is healthy for, too often, one meets with academics and journalists, officials and politicians in the country, especially in the North East, who are absolutely convinced that every Bengali-speaking Muslim is an illegal migrant who has come over into the area in the past decade or so. Such an attitude borders on xenophobia and scepticism is necessary if we are to look at such emotive issues with rationality and common sense.

One has to stand above the melee, as it were, to get the big picture and then walk into the pandemonium, to understand the ground situation better.

We have, in earlier chapters, looked at the broader picture. What are the voices in the melee?

Village Voices

On a warm afternoon at Satrasal, Upendra Nath Sen, a member of the Bharatiya Janata Party held forth to a small audience of family members and two researchers. He was joined by a nephew, Dipak Sen, an activist of the All Assam Students' Union.

Sen Senior was talking about border crossing routes and zeroed in on Jhaukutty on the West Bengal side as a corridor. Five rivers, including the Sunkosh, the Kaaljani and Tursha, divide the flat plains, making travel extremely strenuous and long. Sen said that instead of crossing all the streams, Bangladeshis would go through Jhaukutty, Satrasal and Agomoni from the Kurigram side of their border.

And then, he went on, they would get into buses and spread out across Assam. Very pat, very organized. But not a shred of evidence to support it.

We went to another side of the hurly-burly. Listen to Bablu Roy, a Koch-Rajbongshi, who, at thirty-one, was preparing for his law exams. 'Guwahati is the main attraction for daily wages and jobs. If you ask them where they are from, they will tell you that they are from

Agomoni. If you press further, they will say they are from Satrasal in Agomoni block. This is because while passing through, they get to know a bit about the place and the people here. Sometimes, they can even tell you the names of people living in Satrasal. That is why most of them say they are from this area and people think that a lot of immigration is taking place via Satrasal.'

Roy sounded a bit more convincing then Sen Senior. He seemed to know what he was talking about. And he was certain that much of the movement took place on the other side of the river, from Mancachar. Those who migrate to Mancachar, Roy said, did not move out of the area because the population there was homogenous. 'It is constituted mostly of erstwhile migrants from East Bengal which is not the case in Satrasal-Agomoni area. In Mancachar it is near impossible to tell an illegal immigrant from an earlier migrant . . . there they all look alike, speak the same language, wear the same clothes. But in Satrasal-Agomoni, you will find Bengalis, Assamese, both Hindus and Muslims, Koch-Rajbongshis . . . It is not possible to hide here.'

The people of Satrasal had, wonder of wonders, actually caught one live Bangladeshi in 1986 (there is no record of anyone else being intercepted and caught, which makes one wonder about the super-efficiency of our smartly-attired BSF. 'He had entered through Jhaukutty and moved to Guwahati, there he pulled rickshaws for some time; he even had a rickshaw license issued to him by the municipal authorities in Guwahati. We handed him over to the local police.'

That was the end of Roy's story about the lonely Bangladeshi rickshaw-puller from Guwahati.

On to Ronendra Chandra Das, a gram sevak or

village-level, local government worker in Agonomi since 1980. 'There was some immigration into our area before 1973-74 but not any longer. Some people still enter through West Bengal and spread out over Assam, even to the chars. Do you know that Bangladeshis come to Mancachar for their weekly shopping? They use the river channels to enter India. In Bengal, the restrictions are not as strict. Truckloads of illegal goods are moving out daily from Dinhata, Sahebgunj in Cooch Behar. What are the police or the BSF doing about that? They get their share from the traders and the illegal immigrants.' And the latter enter 'through the Muslim villages.'

Again the voice of wisdom speaks of information from a distant land, a faraway district but with much vehemence. The reason for this clarity is simple: Das and Roy have travelled to these areas and seen the situation for themselves.

Walk a little further to the Muslim mohalla in Satrasal and five Abduls, one Fatema, one Moslema and a Khalilur gathered around our little party. One of the Abduls, Abdul Barek Ansari, called himself a Diwani—one of those men with power over life and death, over land and landlessness in the chars. This very man, Ansari traced his ancestry to Dinajpur in West Bengal and claimed to be a direct descendant of the man who built the first mosque in Satrasal. On top of that he said he was a member of the Asom Gana Parishad, which has on its agenda the detection and deportation of Bangladeshis from the state, although it has done little for this cause.

'Initially, everybody said that the border fencing would have evil repercussions on the Muslims of this area. Now we feel that we have only benefited. If such immigration had continued, it would have spoilt our relations with the Hindus.'

The next Abdul piped up, this time a Jalil and a forty-five-year-old school teacher. And he was the most vehement of the lot: 'Only fools can believe that the border fencing can check illegal immigration. They were fools to put these up. The fencing can, at best, stop our cattle and goats from crossing over, not people. If people can cross the seven seas, what is a little wire fencing to them?'

His mind strayed to family planning, which he furiously opposed saying that this was all the will of the 'Uparwalla'.

'People say there are too many people in Bangladesh, there is no family planning there. But this is the rule of the 'Uparwalla'. It is a sin to stop this. If there are too many people there, it is not surprising that they will have to go somewhere else. People will leave that place for here, anywhere else. What is there to be so upset about?'

Jalil had put his finger on what scholars have sought to prove with statistics and embellish with analysis and 'considered' views: that Bangladesh just has too many people for the land that they inhabit.

There were others to be met. Romen Das's home is next to the fence in Satrasal. A former policeman who was awarded the President's Medal for Bravery in 1978 (he single handedly captured a gang of dacoits), he was in an expansive mood and talked with the team as two other Das's , Bharat and Sushil, both aged about forty, joined the conversation about migration.

Bharat: Illegal immigration is taking place along South Salmara, Kedar, Binnachoorra, Jhaukutty, Balabhoot even at the present. Also smuggling. These areas are predominantly inhabited by Muslims. We, the Assamese people, are a timid lot and do not go for smuggling and all that. Only Muslims are involved in all this. The immigrants cross the borders and then move towards Delhi almost immediately. Those are big cities, they can hide there and there are more jobs. Since we have objected against illegal immigration, they do not like to come here anymore.

Romen: This is how it happens. First one person comes. He stays here for six months and then returns. Again he comes back with his wife. Next he brings his brother. Slowly they encourage their kith and kin to come. But they go to Guwahati, Dibrugarh and so on.

Bharat: No, they do towards Delhi; they do not stay in Assam nowadays.

Romen: Yes, a large number do go to Delhi but many stay back in Assam, too. But not a single person stays back in Satrasal. There are no jobs to be had, no chars.

Bharat: They enter mainly through the river border. There is no barbed wire fencing along the river border. The BSF has links with the dalals who organize largescale border crossings. The BSF even takes a share of the money.

Romen (who has since retired from service in 1989): I have worked at the border for thirteen years and I know about the dalals. There are dalals on both sides of the border. They escort the immigrant up to the bus stand at Agomoni. There is a man in Jhaukutty, about my age, lives near the Border Observation Post. Right next to his house lives a dalal who owns a small rice mill. He charges 100 rupees per head for border crossings. He also smuggles goods across the border and is hand-in-glove with the Bangladeshis.

Sushil: You go and tell him that you have no passport

but you want to visit relatives on that side. Will you please help me? That is all. He will agree. This is his business. You have to give him only 100 rupees. He will take you across the border.

Bharat: The people of Guwahati have to share the blame. The immigrants go there, work there and get licenses from the municipal office there. Who gives them the license? It is our own Assamese people who do so. We are a greedy people. We sell ourselves cheap. If six Bangladeshis are caught today by the police and you offer the police 50,000 rupees to let them go, do you think they will refuse the offer? Never! I have seen many Bangladeshis in Guwahati. We used to know them. They used to come here and drink tea, eat food in our area before the AASU movement. Now they are in Guwahati, pulling rickshaws.

Romen: The BSF should appoint local boys who know the ways of the illegal immigrants. More and more of our boys must enter the BSF.

Some fifty kilometres across the river lies Kalapani, amid the flat countryside that rolls eastward from the banks of the Brahmaputra. Its very name says a lot. Black Water. The phrase conjures up a place of punishment, of exile such as the Andamans was to Indian freedom fighters during the independence movement.

During the monsoon, much of the village is flooded, with only a few pukka houses, built on slightly higher ground, escaping the wrath of the river. There is one pot-holed road that leads to Kalapani; the hills have been stripped of trees and there are settlements of both tribals and non-tribals, especially Bengali-speaking Muslims, inside areas where forests once were. All this is of course illegal. But no group, least of all the forest department seems either perturbed or prepared to take action to protect its own legacy, its own rights.

In this backwater, there has been an extraordinary development.

The population of Kalapani has increased 300 per cent in the past decade. This must be among the highest growth rates registered anywhere in India. As we have noted elsewhere, Assam's population growth is about the national average although there are substantial variations for Hindus and Muslims. Thus the Muslim population in the state grew by 77 per cent between 1971 and 1991, an average of 38.5 per cent for each of those decades. The Hindu rate of growth was considerably lower, about 68 per cent or 34 per cent per decade.

Kalapani is dominated by Muslims. Where have the new numbers come from?

One local leader says the increase was caused by the devastation wrought by the Brahmaputra in South Salmara. 'Everyone says they're from South Salmara, that they have lost homes and property there and have come here to earn a livelihood. Who's to check?' he asked.

Clearly, very few do. Even local officials, while acknowledging the growth in the population pattern say that there is little that can be done to verify the extent of the problem. Old records are unavailable, especially land records of places that have been eroded and submerged.

Chandan Bhowmick, the former president of the Samabhay Samiti, said that the data has been damaged by the floods. 'Here and there, you will find bits and pieces.' Bhowmick said he was unsure of the reasons behind the stunning population growth. 'Maybe some foreigners have come, some might be from nearby villages, chars, some as a result of natural growth.'

The Kalapani figures make interesting reading: on 30 June 1991, the population was listed at 643, including 278 Hindus and 365 Muslims. In 1999 it read 500 Hindus and 1,000 Muslims for a grand total of 1,500. That represents a nearly three-fold growth for the Muslims and less than half for the Hindus. Saadullabari rose from 1,730 Muslims (there are no Hindus there) to 3,551 in the same period or just over double.

Kalapani falls in the arc of greater traditional illegal migration, on the southern bank of the Brahmaputra. Even the then Deputy Commissioner of Dhubri, L.C. Singhi, a large, cheerful man, declared in 1998 that while immigration was still taking place, it was more through the Mancachar corridor, below the Meghalaya hills, near where Kalapani is located. Dhubri, he said, was not an area of settlement because local people were against outsiders coming in and edging them out of the holdings and few privileges which they enjoy.

The extensive devastation caused by the river was forcing people to move away from their homes. 'Where will all these people go? Where is the land to be shared with Bangladeshis? The entire labour force of Assam is supplied by Dhubri; there is not enough land for them here, how will they accommodate new settlers?'

In Kalapani, one man declared himself to Anindita as a 'leader-type *manuh*' (person in Assamese) and in addition declined to give his name. He spoke about how the new immigrants were Muslim. 'They have local supporters who give them shelter.'

'The old settlers have land of their own, the new ones do not have . . . they are daily wage labourers, mostly,' according to this leader-type.

Abu Hossein Bepari, a landowner on a char, spoke of how he once owned 150 bighas of land. Today, much of this family property is under water. Three sons work in other parts of the state; two were in Guwahati and the third was at Sibsagar,

Recruiting agents come to chars such as his own, known as Bandihana Char (pronounced *sor* by those living there) to take young men to towns in Assam for work in unskilled professions. They pull rickshaws, drive auto-rickshaws and work at construction sites. Not less than 500 young men from this char leave for the cities every year.

But then, a question arises here.

How does the population of young men replenish itself so quickly, every year? The char has a population of not more than of a few thousand. People may come from other chars, where they are forced to leave by the flood and high water. But not in such numbers. Additional numbers would come from across the border, notwithstanding many protestations, because they too face similar conditions of displacement and penury. Without this factor, an outflow of young men at the rate that Bepari spoke of is impossible.

And what is more, Bepari, who was seventy years old, white bearded, spry and bare-chested acknowledged that 'most' people on his char were facing IMDT cases. Many residents of the chars are suspects in the eyes of law enforcement authorities of harbouring Bangladeshis. Bepari said he had two wives and thirteen children—six sons and seven daughters.

The failure of the law of the land to protect citizens and prosecute the illegals rings out clear and loud. This was most evident when Anindita visited an IMDT court hearing in Guwahati. The name of the accused was the same, Shanti Debnath in the case under hearing. But the sexes changed in the course of filling the forms for the case. In one, Shanti was thirty-two years old and a woman. In the other, 'she' became a forty-year-old man.

The charge of illegality could not be upheld in this case because one prosecution witness declared his suspicion was based upon the fact that Shanti spoke 'colloquial Bengali.'

Which court would accept such evidence? The case was dismissed.

It is for lack of preparation, lack of interest and lack of proper investigation that many cases under the IMDT have failed. Procedures are not followed and government lawyers seem totally disinterested in the proceedings.

The IMDT is as good as dead. All it needs is a decent burial.

CHAPTER ELEVEN

Kurigram and Keramat

W e had risen early that morning, about 4 a.m., at Kurigram, the capital of the district of the same name in northern Bangladesh. It was October 1997.

There were about a dozen of us, mostly from Assam and other parts of India, to film in Bangladesh for a documentary film that Jahnu Barua, the film director, and I were making on the Brahmaputra river. We had completed filming in Assam and Arunachal Pradesh. Our arrival in Bangladesh had been preceded by some of the most exasperating red-tape that I have experienced in many years of dealing with governments, especially bureaucrats. The discussions with the Bangladeshis went on for several months over the script, the itinerary and locations for filming. In fact, at one point, I was quite convinced that the permissions would not be forthcoming.

These finally came through, thanks to support from people within the system like the dapper and astute diplomat, Farooq Sobhan, then his country's Foreign Secretary, and figures like Mahfuz Anam, the amiable and erudite editor of the *Daily Star*. Mahfuz is a popular, influential man who had been a debating star in Dhaka University before the West Pakistani military crackdown in 1970, in which hundreds of thousands of men, women and children were butchered. He also was a Mukti Bahini or a guerilla fighter during the war of Liberation, as were other men and women who have since become academics, senior government officials and political leaders in Bangladesh. His network was formidable, indeed.

We had driven to Kurigram, a small town tucked away by the Dharla and Dhudhkumar (also known as the Teesta in India) rivers, after an exhausting week on the river and the Bay of Bengal, on a small vessel. After returning to Dhaka, we travelled all day to get to Kurigram, a sleepy, uneventful, very warm and dusty place. We were to reach there by late afternoon, and decided to take a brief detour to Chilmari, a river port that was once a major trading centre. At one time Chilmari had welcomed British steamers and deep draft vessels bearing silk and jute as well as tea and foodgrains to its shores. Now the river's constant buffeting and resulting erosion had reduced the port to a short stretch of sand where small fishing boats plied.

Chilmari was a place I had visited two times earlier for my field research for the migration project and I thought it would also be a good site also to film.

After looking around the area briefly, Jahnu, cinematographer Sudheer Palsane (him of the thin frame, untrimmed beard and studious, lost look) and I decided that we would return very early next day to capture the awakening of this river village.

As producer of the film, it was my special responsibility to ensure that crew members were awake on time, that tea was served, packed lunches ready and vehicles primed to roll out from the guest house where we were located. This meant that I had to get up at 3:30 a.m., to ensure that everything was in order. The lot of a small filmmaker is a thankless one; with a very tight budget, we had to complete a number of shooting schedules in North-East India and Bangladesh, and finally cross the Himalayas into Tibet during our quest for the Brahmaputra. Every moment counted and it cost cash. A delay of an hour or two meant cost escalation down the line.

Of course, everyone had to be fed (and fed on time—there are specified times for breakfast, lunch and dinner breaks, according to trade union regulations in the film industry—otherwise the unions could give producers a tough time later); they needed decent accomodation and were not to work beyond a certain number of hours per day. The Brahmaputra unit was a remarkable one—it maintained the rules as much as possible. But when necessary, the unit members took physical risks, endured long hours, worked tremendously hard, and made quick decisions on their own at difficult times.

The making of the film and our accompanying travels are separate stories, with different characters, for another telling.

That morning in October, 1997, we got out of bed before dawn and staggered into the 22-seater Toyota Coaster which took us to the last point before Chilmari Ghat. It was still dark, with the gloaming of early morning barely able to penetrate the thick fog. We walked down the embankment and started putting up the cameras; the sound recordist got busy capturing the morning sounds: water drops falling off the side of a boat, plip! plop! Fishermen yawned as they stretched and stepped down from the boats to wash, hawk and spit; small waves lapping against the shore and the boats; the cries of river birds, and the chugging of the first motors as their owners set out to fish, with music issuing from radios on board and on shore.

Jahnu and Sudheer decided that the spot chosen for the first shots weren't right. So the camera was shifted again. The boats stood in silent silhouette against the mist. The light of dawn was warming the mist and the water, the land and people. Slowly, both boat people and land settlers came out as part of their daily ritual and then stopped to watch our small group of characters with numerous cameras, tripods, instructions and dialects.

I was standing not far from the camera when a deep male voice rasped in my ear, 'Sir, you should go about 100 yards further away, from there you will get a perfect shot.'

Of course, the voice did not speak in English. That is a literal translation of what it said. Nor did it speak in Bangla or Bengali, the national language of Bangladesh and West Bengal. It spoke in Assamese, the language of the Brahmaputra Valley, my language.

I jumped in surprise and saw a dark, lean man in a blue and green checked lungi and a long shirt. He was standing by Joseph, the tough, all-seasons and all-purpose man from Assam with a gigantic appetite for rice and an equally prodigious capacity for hard work and physical labour. It was Joseph's first visit outside the country and he was enjoying every moment of it. However, he thought and said so, in his characteristically simple way, that there were too many Bangladeshis in Bangladesh, that the place was too crowded and abysmally poor. 'We do not have this kind of poverty in Assam, such wretchedness, such misery,' he would exclaim as we passed a village market or a town, where the principal food on sale appeared to be mounds of ripe, golden-yellow jack fruit with its loamy, rich smell and taste.

'*Oho*, Joseph, since when have you become such an expert on camera angles and that too in a place we hardly know?' I snapped at him in mild irritation. The reason for this was that the voice had interrupted a pretty shot of the silhouetted boats with some ducks waddling in front of them. I later did get the photo, without the ducks—they didn't wait for me to recover from my surprise at the next part of the conversation.

The dark, wizened man smiled, revealing teeth stained by decades of chewing paan. 'I was talking, sir, not him, I'm from here, sir.' The sir was pronounced *saar*.

By this time, I was quite stunned. 'But you speak Assamese, good Assamese, how do you speak it so well, you are from here, aren't you?'

'Ah, saar, I am from here but I've lived for thirty-five years in Assam, I know it well and I learned Assamese quickly.'

The name?

'Keramat, Keramat Bhai.'

I was filled with a strange exultation. It was only well after the conversation was over that morning with Keramat and three others (who had visited or lived in Assam for a number of years), that I recognized the feeling that was building up. It was of elation, of unbridled triumph. Triumph against the politicians and bureaucrats, the academics and pseudo-intellectuals in India and Bangladesh who tried either to prove or disprove the border crossings between these countries, based on statistics, or polemics, or propoganda, or theory especially, the shallow ideology of the left.

Here I was, a non-graduate, dabbling in things like demography and international relations, not to speak of international journalism, untrained in the social sciences and the decent skills of social analysis. This was both an advantage and a disadvantage. Such skills are necessary. But they can be learned, even informally. But, more important, I felt, was the fact that I was coming to the field with an uncluttered mind, ready for fresh thought and initiatives, unmindful of set and pet theories and bombast. I carried no ideological baggage or prejudice.

To my untutored mind, that single, simple incident proved beyond any doubt that Bangladeshis came to Assam; they worked, lived, voted, ate and fished there. 'It's all come together for me in this little village by the Brahmaputra,' I noted in my daily journal that evening.

Since 1996, I had spent months with Jahnu and others working on the film, travelling along the river, scouring the world for research material on the Brahmaputra, including maps and historic details, networking through the Internet, writing a script, interviewing hundreds of writers and scholars, scientists and engineers, economists, bureaucrats and politicians, and businessmen. In the process of this yatra, I had been to Tibet, with a tiny unit, filming at altitudes of above 16,000 feet and hardly ever lower than 13,000 feet, following the course of the river as it sped towards India; then in Arunachal Pradesh and Assam and finally in Bangladesh, voyaging across the waters to Bhola and Hatia Islands in the Bay of Bengal.

At the same time, I was working on my study of migration. I had always felt that the two projects were interlinked. But I had not expected it to be defined so clearly and in this fashion.

Here, in a flash, the river had rewarded my interest and friendship with an incredible gift. It shared its knowledge of the reality of migration, a problem that has plagued and continues to plague our region. I had not sought this gift but it turned up anyway in the person of Keramat Bhai.

Some may respond to this perception as an example of my own credulity and non-logical approach to matters. But this is part of my larger philosophy—that if you work for your beliefs, you will be rewarded in ways that are totally unexpected and which may ultimately benefit and enrich what you are then working on.

As a journalist with almost thirty years of experience, I also have realized that the best stories are those exclusives which land in your lap without having to work too hard for them—and that too because the other person (or persons) giving the information is prepared to share it at that specific time. Not earlier, perhaps not later. Well, later, the story would be all over the place anyway so it no longer would be unique. This has happened to me in Sri Lanka and Afghanistan, with the riots in Bombay and the Babri Masjid tragedy at Ayodhya, the revolution in Nepal, the insurgencies of Punjab and Jammu and Kashmir, as well as the Bhopal gas disaster.

But, especially, in the North East, time and again, people have appeared out of the blue or situations have developed where a number of things have meshed at a particular time, telling a particular story. I remember sitting outside the office of the chief minister in Tripura in the late 1980s and virtually dozing off as I waited interminably. There was no light, the soft drink I ordered was warm and it was extremely hot and humid. It was all very, very tiring. A police officer took the chair opposite me and sensing that I was a journalist asked if I had come to scout for stories. We introduced ourselves to each other. I thought to myself, what the heck? Let me tell him that I'm looking for the Government of India's connection to the Chakma insurgency in Bangladesh. He smiled and in the next quarter hour gave me details, locations and names. But he was not to be quoted. This was off the record—any publication of sources would get him into trouble. We understood each other well. He was then summoned to the chief minister's office and then left soon after with a cheerful goodbye. I never met him again.

But I had my exclusive for the *New York Times*. So, when the chief minister blandly denied the whole thing, I could afford to smile. The accuracy of the officer's assertions and briefing was borne out by a visit to one of the sites he had named, and interviews with underground leaders.

The event at Chilmari Ghat was similar yet different. I became personally involved, even though to a limited degree in this 'story.' In the other situations, I was an excited but uninvolved reporter doing his job, exposing the government, or revealing various aspects of life which were not known to the public in India and abroad—whether it was the secret police-organized killer gangs in Punjab, or the Indian army running riot in the Tamil areas of Sri Lanka, or the secret negotiations for an out-of-court settlement of the Bhopal gas disaster.

With my own visits, as well as those of researchers, over the next years to Keramat Bhai village near Chilmari Ghat, his story acquired a life of its own as it shaped the writing of this book as well as my own understanding of an irreversible flow, of an immutable situation.

First of all, the location.

The difficulties of a place like Chilmari emerge from a

map that is over two centuries old. A look at maps over the centuries, including those with satellite imagery details, show a conflict that is as old as the land itself. The conflict is between familiar foes—land and water. In this case, the flatlands of what is now Chilmari and Kurigram and their veteran opponent and destroyer, the Brahmaputra and its tributaries.

This problem is graphically brought out in a report commissioned by Bangladesh's Ministry of Local Government, Rural Development and Cooperatives called 'Change in Chilmari.'[1] It was edited by a tall American with a lazy drawl, Bruce Currey, of the Technical Asssistance Team. Like most major projects in Bangladesh, this was funded by three international donors—the Danish aid agency, DANIDA, the Norwegian agency, NORAD, and the Swiss with their SIDA, or Swiss International Development Assistance.

A map by a British cartographer named Renner showed in 1765 that Chilmari was on the western bank of the river. The Brahmaputra appears to flow close to the Garo Hills, near present-day Meghalaya of North East India. And Chilmari was in truth a place where 'seals' (chil) were stamped (mari) on the cargo of ships.

What makes this etymology interesting is that on the Indian side, about fifty kilometres north of Chilmari, just before the river crosses the unseen frontier into Bangladesh, there is a little cluster of huts known as Chapamara or 'The place where seals are stamped.' The Indian tricolour flutters above the huts where men from the Border Security Force live and work.

---

1   Change in Chilmari, Intensive Rural Works Programme- Bangladesh, Ministry of Local Government, Rural Development and Cooperatives, ed. Bruce Currey, October 1985

A second map of Chilmari in 1856-57, more than ninety years later, shows chars or islands that have grown as a result of upstream silt deposited in this slower, meandering phase of the river. The chars are shown as covered with grass jungle. Elsewhere the area is seen to be heavily settled. The numerous village roads built at this time and the number of villages, as many as 128, testify to the development of the area.[2] New words were to be found on the map: *haat* (market) and *golahor* (warehouse). Currey says that these are 'all probably relics of the indigo crop and industry which the British introduced to the area in the form of a plantation economy for the East India Company.'

The problem of erosion was noted even in those times. Thus, a man named Glazier wrote in 1873 that at Chilmari, the police station 'has been twice removed further inland within the past five years.' One wonders how many more times it must have been uprooted by the Brahmaputra's marauding waters.

Fifty years later, the settlement by Bengalis on the fertile char areas was evident. There was an extensive network of ponds, providing evidence of the high ground water levels. Jute was an important crop by the early part of the twentieth century. The ponds were used as part of a processing chain for jute, as heaps of stalks were tossed on the water to 'rot' before they were transported to mills for manufacture into rope, twine, sacking and other material.

The fourth map in Currey's list was completed in 1933 and shows a new development: the pressure of the police. There were uprisings in the area and across north Bengal of the peasants who demanded a one-third share of all

---

2   Currey, p 3

crops to be given out to the labourers. The Government reacted the only way it knew to a political and economic demand: brute force. Little seems to have changed in the subcontinent over the decades! From a *thana*, Chilmari has graduated to the level of a police station.

As a result of constant river erosion, the amount of stable land available for agriculture steadily shrunk in the districts to the north and west, but it grew in the char areas and on the eastern bank. Sandy areas grew in size, a cause for concern to both short-term and long-term agricultural production. Indeed, of the sub-district's (*upazilla*, as it is called in Bangla) area, about one-sixth lay in the embrace of the river and more than one-fifth comprised of useless sandy tracts. This meant that at least one-third of the total area was uncultivable.

In addition, erosion played a major role in shaping the physical shape of the place as well as the mental attitude of its people. Thus, in 1967-68, the entire settlement of Chilmari was completely eroded by the Brahmaputra. The population of Baoil Man Diar Khata Mouza dropped from about 8,000 in 1967 to about 1,000 in 1974. Currently, it is not more than 400.

The proud port where sea-going vessels and great river steamers once anchored, has all but vanished. Small fishing boats sit idly in the evenings. The devastation reminds one of Sadiya, a bustling river port in Assam at the mouth of the Dihang and the Lohit rivers which was swallowed whole by the river after a gigantic earthquake in 1950 sent a mountain of water down the Dihang. At least, Chilmari still exists. Sadiya is dead and buried under millions of tons of water, silt and rock.

The fierce erosion in Chilmari means that many people shift their homes not once or twice in their lifetime but as many as five or six times. It is reminiscent of one of life upstream too, in Majuli, the largest river island in the world, and in river bank areas near Jorhat, Tezpur as well as Dhubri, futher down the Brahmaputra.

These changes are part of a larger story.

Kurigram

Chilmari is part of Kurigram district, which was itself carved out of the larger parent district of Rongpur in 1983. It is in the poorest and most underdeveloped part of Bangladesh, itself by any measure a poor nation, with the highest density of population in the world. Bangladesh's population density per square kilometre is above 750. India's is 261, and Assam's is a measly 286 per square kilometre.

Few Bangladeshi civil officers from Dhaka or any other part willingly go to Kurigram on an official posting. A similar attitude can be observed in India where officials prefer to be located near a major metropolis that can guarantee them and their families security of jobs and the comforts of life, including good education for their children.

And the level of ignorance or lack of information about Kurigram is astonishing. 'It's poor and far off, I've never been there and I don't think I'd like to go either,' a prominent Bangladeshi editor told me over dinner at one of Dhaka's better hotels.[3] Indeed, the gap between rich and poor appeared to me to be more vivid in Bangladesh than in many other parts of the world. Or at least, we are talking of comparable levels of poverty as in the most

3   Conversation with author, Dhaka, April 1997

underdeveloped parts of India.

I remember one of the starkest sights during my first visit to Kurigram in 1997. I had taken a taxi from Dhaka because no local taxis were available. The only form of local transport were either cycle rickshaws or overcrowded buses which plied between Kurigram and its neighbouring towns, including the city of Rongpur which has a rich history of producing some of the great singers, bards, lyricists and musicians of the region. As I drove away from Kurigram and moved toward villages to its north, scores, perhaps hundreds of men (only men, no women), could be seen walking by the side of the road. It was an astonishing sight, late in the evening, and I felt compelled to stop and ask a local journalist friend who was travelling with me, showing me the lay of the land, about who they were.

'They are *Mohfiz, Mohfiz*,' he said, repeating the word for emphasis. The Mohfiz are the wretched of the earth, even in a place as backward and underdeveloped as Kurigram. They are the landless, their homes and properties destroyed by the waters of the Brahmaputra and its tributaries. It isn't certain whether the word has any any specific meaning, except a sense of hopelessness—a feeling carried by those who bear such a name.

These men, ranging from the young to middle-aged graybeards, carried little bundles of belongings on their backs. Regarded as the lower strata of society in Kurigram, a form of caste discrimination prevails against the Mohfiz. This I inferred from the instances cited to me. Thus, the Mohfiz are not allowed inside buses but have to clamber atop the vehicles which race over reasonably good roads at breakneck speed. And since they travel in groups, the conductor gives them a group concession on their tickets. For who knows when the next bus will come?

These are the men of passage, who travel long distances to make ends meet and ensure that their families have food at the end of the day.

I talked to a small group of them as we shared a boat ride from a Noonkhowa char on the Brahmaputra to the mainland. It was a two-hour drive to Kurigram and the road journey had been bad—sandy and dusty, barely metalled in many parts and extremely bumpy and hard on the back. It didn't help either that I suffer from cervical spondolysis.

As we talked, I became aware of the helplessness and hopelessness in which the Mohfiz were steeped. If ever there was fatalism, it was here. Man after man cited stories of how their families had been pauperized by the river. 'This is our enemy,' one of them said, staring at the water around us. 'We have lost everything here: my father was a big zamindar (landlord), we had much land and a good amount of money. Now we have no land, it is all in the middle of the water, we have moved five times in the past years and I have to travel elsewhere to earn and work.'

He fell silent for a short while after this outburst and spoke again. 'They call us Mohfiz, this is a word without honour—and we were not always like this, we had honour, we had property, we had money and now we must go like common labourers to work on someone else's lands.'

They were going to Comilla, he said. They would be gone for four months, during the harvest season and the sowing season. They would earn enough, he said, for the family to manage for the rest of the year. While they were away, their wives would work in the homes or fields of others, for keeping the family together.

When the water came, he said, conditions turn turned very difficult. 'We first put the food and clothes on the bed, when the water rise is not too much; then when it goes above the level of the bed, we put tables and planks together and live on top of that, or finally we go to the roof of the hut—with our families, goats and chickens.' How did they cook? 'Every day, we make one meal of *bhaat* on a chulah in the kitchen and eat it with salt and chillis and a little mustard oil.' The chulahs or mud baked stoves are set high above the ground—as much as two to four feet—to protect the homestead from suffering too much during times of flood. For those with boats—and most Bangladeshis in the countryside appeared to possess at least a dugout—life on land could move to life on the boat and then to higher ground such as roads or nearby towns. Unless the flood was of cataclysmic proportions, as that of 1988 and 1999, those affected managed to see out the worst days on one meal and bunched together in their homes.

From that conversation on the fifteen-foot-long country boat or nouka, the town of Comilla in Bangladesh's relatively better-off south-west appeared to be the favoured destination. All the men said they were heading to Comilla for not less than three or four months. They would stay through the entire agricultural season: from rice planting to harvest, threshing and milling before returning home.

Comilla abuts on India's Tripura state and its capital, Agartala, is hardly any distance from the international border. None of the Mohfiz spoke of the proximity of India, and especially, Agartala where daily and seasonal migrants from Bangladesh, coming in search of work for labourers, are seen moving across illegally but without any restriction every day. Although they did not talk about it on that boat journey, I am sure that many were considering the possibility of 'jumping' ship. A large number of travellers across the Tripura border are day labourers who work as rickshaw-pullers or at construction sites; they also sell fish, consumer goods and small items before returning home in the evenings.

What is of concern however are those who come to stay.

The Road to Tripura

Agartala is not much of a town to look at. It is, in one word, uninspiring. A town dominated by Bengali-speakers, it is sleepy and gives off an overwhelming sense of ennui. Its markets are desultory and small; its roads are bumpy and its climate is enervatingly humid, sticky and hot. Yet, this was once the home of the Tripuri kings who were great patrons of art and culture. They patronized Rabindranath Tagore and his university at Shanti Niketan. Tagore spent six years in Agartala, part of it in a villa put at his disposal by the royal family. Today, that villa is decrepit and crumbling, reflecting the sense of neglect and alienation that has spread through society in the state.

Tripura is a classic case of ethnic rage asserting itself in rebellion against unrelenting demographic and cultural pressure. In the space of a few decades, the aboriginal hill tribes (comprising of not less than twenty-one different groups, including Hindus and Buddhists and Christians) were pushed aside by a swift inflow of Bengali Hindu refugees and migrants from East Pakistan, now Bangladesh. The numbers grew even more swiftly after anti-Hindu riots broke out in East Pakistan in the mid-1960s. The result was that the docile Tripuris found themselves driven out of land and home by the aggressive Bengalis, many of whom were traders and farmers.

Kokborok, the main tribal language, spoken largely by the Tripuris, was ignored and Bengali instituted as the official language. This was partly the fault of the Tripuri royalty, descended from the Manikya clan, for they encouraged and even adopted Bengali as the language of adminstration. A range of professionals—from lawyers and teachers to accountants and doctors—migrated and settled in the state, which once extended into present-day Burma and West Bengal. Efforts were made to protect the tribal population by reserving land for settled agriculture but this did not work out very well, and led to extensive encroachments.

As the population density began to rise dramatically, the demographic profile of the state changed. At the time of independence, there was a slim tribal majority. By the end of the twentieth century, the Tripuris and other tribes were barely 28 per cent of Tripura's population. In less than 25 years (1947-1971), not less than 600,000 immigrants moved into little Tripura.[4]

Thus, in the space of less than fifty years, a tribal-majority state has become a 'mainland-majority' area, where the language, culture, land rights and political mandate of the original settlers have virtually disappeared and been replaced by an aggressive culture, drawing its moorings from neighbouring lands.

As political control slipped out of the hands of the 'natives' to the Bengali-speakers, a process of radicalization began in the hills. This was where the tribals now

4 B.G. Verghese, *India's North East Resurgent*, New Delhi: Konarak Publishers, 1996, p.171.

lived, to where they had been pushed, and where they found a breathing space, however inadequate. Efforts to restore lands to the original owners after the Bengalis had bought over or encroached upon large areas backfired in two ways. First, they were far from adequate and secondly, efforts by the state government to meet Tripuri concerns resulted in fears of dispossession and worse among the Bengalis.

Irrespective of whether the Communists or the Congress Party were in power, the situation has remained the same.

For many years, the Congress party ruled, but after the 1970s, Tripura lurched to the left. The Congress had an alliance with the TUJS, or Tripura Upajati Jamatia Samaj, which represented tribal interests. The latter rarely won more than a handful of seats. The Communists had several prominent tribals in the rank and file as well as leaders, such as Dasrath Deb who went on to become a chief minister in the 1990s but had to step down because of failing health.

Tripura's leftward move in 1978 coincided with a similar development in West Bengal. Since then, the Communist Party of India (Marxist) has controlled the state's destiny, although there has been a recent consolidation of Congress power.

Over the years, the emotional and political anger against the Bengalis has been building up. A series of militant organizations found voice but just as quickly died out, unable to sustain any momentum. In 1978, Bijoy Hrangkhawl formed the Tripura National Volunteer Force, with assistance from another insurgent group, the Mizo National Front of Laldenga.

The dominant tribal language, Kokborok is slowly

making a comeback although it uses the Bengali script for its written form. (Kokborok was to have been recognized in the Roman script as far back as the 1960s—but this did not come to pass).

Rabindra Sangeet, the sonorous lyrics and music composed by Rabindranath Tagore, is heard across the state, adding to the sleepy atmosphere. Few tribal chants are heard and tribal dances are presented as show-pieces before visitors, instead of being part of a vibrant tradition. These styles would have injected vigour into Tripura's culture. But it was not to be.

In 1980, I was recovering from an attack of hepatitis in an aunt's home in Guwahati when a phone call came from New Delhi, from Gene Kramer, then Bureau Chief of the Associated Press (AP). He urged me, health-permitting, to fly to Agartala and to report about the situation. At the time, I was working for the AP out of their New Delhi office.

My brother, Suzoy, was a medical specialist. He suggested that he would accompany me, as photographer, and also to keep an eye on my health. We arrived in Agartala and found that we had to share digs at the decrepit MLAs Hostel with other scribes, among them J.D. Singh of the *Times of India*, who was then quite a big name in Indian journalism. I had met him when he was the *Times* correspondent in London and he had lived abroad for many years, acquiring a larger than life image among young writers like me.

Every morning, we used to line up at the MLAs wash room, brushing our teeth, hawking and spitting before going in for a quick shower and then getting into our trusty Ambassador taxis and heading for the scene of conflict. Singh hawked and spat with us and shared the food that was dished out at the hostel. (I can remember toast prepared on a tava over a gas stove because there was no toaster, and then at a small restaurant, eating the best Mughlai paratha [a Bengali speciality comprising of a paratha with egg and meat] I had ever eaten, dripping in oil, as my brother watched. He checked me from having a second one saying that my system weakened by jaundice, starved of any food except boiled vegetables for nearly a month, would be unable to take any more.)

One supposes that the MLAs of Tripura at the time would have been well justified in going on *hartal* demanding better facilities. One can only presume that their conditions have since improved because now Agartala has numerous, reasonably good hotels (even with air-conditioning) and restaurants. Perhaps, it would be safe to presume that the lot of the MLAs has kept pace with other colleagues and contemporaries in the region.

Around us, as soon as we left the hostel, it appeared that Tripura was falling apart, riven by ancient hatreds stoked by recent angers growing out of land dispossession and the failure of successive governments to provide any facilities worth the name to the tribal communities, to nudge them toward economic development and improved lifestyles.

The Assam movement against 'foreigners' touched off a similar agitation in Tripura and militants in the tribal campaign were swift to seize the advantage. First, a Quit Notice was announced on all 'foreigners' (read here Bengalis) who had entered the state after 1949, when it merged with India. This was issued by none other than the moderate TUJS. Within three months, the campaign was out of the hands of the moderates and captured by Hrangkhwal's Tripura National Volunteer and its cohorts.

In an explosion of violence that charred villages and hamlets in the rolling countryside, Bengali men, women and children were hunted down and killed, their properties looted and torched. In retaliation, some Tripuris and other tribespeople also died—but the majority of dead were Bengalis.

One such site of a massacre was Mandai Bazar. We were brought there under military escort from Agartala and the major who led the convoy kept telling us, 'You won't be able to believe your eyes. It is horrible.'

Some bodies were still lying about when we arrived at Mandai, a village which also doubled as a major haat or bazaar for the neighbouring areas. Survivors told tales of a massive attack by tribals at night, of fleeing in terror through jungles and paddy fields and of how one tribal constable from the local police picket had rebelled and joined the rioting. A mother and child lay next to each other. Not far, a dao was plunged into the ground next to a human skull. Temples had been descecrated and looted. Three hundred and fifty died in those mad hours in Mandai. They were a prelude to the hatred and madness of Nellie and other killing fields in Assam.

The major wept like a baby when he came near the woman and her child. It was embarrassing to see a man in uniform break down uncontrollably, for very rarely does someone witness such sights. He perked up a little later where he took us to a nearby school building where two tribesmen were being held for their alleged role in the attacks. Both men were tied by rope to the steel bars in the windows. Their feet too were manacled.

'Look at the fellow, those are the eyes of a killer,' snarled the officer. I stared at him, appalled. Around me, most of the journalists, largely Bengali Hindus, were hanging on to every word, taking down his remarks as if they were divine incantations. Photographers jostled each other to take pictures. The next day, one of the manacled men, identified as Bijoy Hrangkhawl (which he certainly was not) appeared in a Tripura newspaper, his eyes stony as they stared expressionlessly at the camera.

No one bothered to ask them any questions. Neither, I regret to say, did I—although I did the ask army officer the basis for making the accusations. He said that the captured men had been tracked from the nearby jungles where they were hiding. They had since been identified by local villagers as having been involved in the mayhem. But surely, at night, when everyone is fleeing for their own lives, you don't have much time to identity your attackers, especially in the cover of darkness.

A couple of days later, Suzoy and I were returning in our car to Agartala. It was late in the afternoon, we hadn't eaten since morning and were quite hungry. But I had one more interview to conduct at the main army office before we could head for food. There was another army major here, extremely cordial who received us at the mess and asked us to have lunch.

I demurred.

'Have you eaten? If you haven't', then why not?'

We sat down to a quick meal, tossing questions about the situation and casualties at the officer. 'You can't name me as a source,' he said, 'But our figures are that not less than 1,000 people have died.'

Of course, the octogenerarian Chief Minister, Nripen Chakraborty, a veteran Marxist, stuck to a figure which was about half of the army estimate. Any challenges or queries were met with obstinacy and a flaring of temper. 'If you know so much,' he once snapped at me, 'why don't you tell me before you come to a press conference?' 'Are journalists to do the job of governments,' I asked. He stiffened with anger.

Barely a month later, an official inquiry into the devastation remarked that while the official toll was placed at 550 (of which 69 were tribals), 'according to the Chief Minister himself, over 1,800 are reported missing; many of them might be dead.'[5]

Eight years of intermittent clashes continued but the militants and their leaders were tiring. In 1988, a peace accord was signed between Hrangkhawl and New Delhi under which the TNV agreed to disarm its cadres, accept the Indian Constitution, review the problems of alienation of tribal lands and prevent further alienation, create development centres, and generate jobs for tribal young men and women.

That the agreement was inefficiently implemented is seen in the fact that Tripura, today, is perhaps the most violent of states in the North East with kidnappings, extortion, killings and rapes on the rise. Two major new insurgencies have risen from the ashes of the old TNV: the All Tripura Tigers' Force (ATTF) and the National Liberation Front of Tripura (NLFT) being the main striking arms of the militants. NLFT attacks on fellow tribals have been occasionally marked by gang rapes, another attempt at intimidation and control as they try and force conversions to Christianity.

Many issues have been mixed up in the process and the

5   Report of Committee on Tripura, Government of India, New Delhi, July 1980

demand for independence is getting more blurred by the day.

In addition, there are another fourteen 'militant' groups which officials and journalists in Tripura describe as essentially guns for hire. These are are deeply involved in vicious kidnappings for exortion rackets. The examples are countless and no one appears to be safe: a cabinet minister is shot when he goes to tackle his brother's kidnappers; a lowly tea-shop owner is kidnapped and held for a princely sum before his captors agree to a lower price.

Both major political groups, the CPI(M) and the Congress, are said to patronize various underground organizations. But this patronage is beginning to backfire as they and their cadres find themselves at the wrong end of a gun.

Twenty years after Mandai, Tripura is still burning and bleeding. This escalation in violence remains primarily rooted in the question of land and identity—expecially after the Bengalisation of the state. Over the years, it has become inextricably linked to the politics of ethnic cleansing allied with extortion and lawlessness.

In an effort to calm tribal demands, the Tripura Tribal Autonomous Council (TTAC), was set up in an amended form in 1988 and again in 1993 to provide them with a degree of self-governance. Reservations for tribal candidates exist in 28 of the 30 seats. In elections in February 2000, a pro-NLFT group known as the Indigenous Peoples Front of Tripura (IPFT) captured a majority. Over these past months, the NLFT has sought to widen its sphere of influence by driving away non-tribals (essentially Bengalis) from those areas abutting the TTAC, which itself comprises more than two-thirds of the state's total area. As this campaign continued in the year 2000, with occasional assaults on tribals reluctant to embrace Christianity, what is emerging is a state within a state, seized by democratic means but controlled by fear and the gun.

The future of such a political situation is unclear and potentially explosive.

On the one hand, it could lead to fierce conflicts with the Indian State, which could throw its military machine against such pro-independence groups holding power within Tripura. On the other, the current situation could force both tribals and non-tribals to accept changes from within the system and the new political equation. It is not possible to change the demographic map of Tripura. Yet, if political and economic power is distributed more equitably, with tribals controlling their lands and future within the provisions of the Indian Constitution, without heeding the demands of Bengali politicians, then there are good chances of short-term and long-term compromise. The participation and involvement of the IPFT in the TTAC is a positive sign.

There have been efforts to rouse the Bengalis by organizing such groups such as Amra Bangla (We are Bengalis) and more recently the Bengali Tiger Force. These are dismissed as inconsequential and without any bite to their bark. The latter group hardly has any weapons. This, however, may change if the ethnic assaults against Bengalis continue. A core of Bengali fighters, armed with weapons which are easily available for a price in the North East, could complicate an already complex and bitter situation.

These strands of discussion bring us back time and again to the basic themes that resonate in the North East and also in Bangladesh: land, migration and fears of loss of identity. The latter provides the ideological cover for crimes committed against human beings of different communities and creeds.

But is all this violence curbing the migration, which can be said to be at the root of the crisis?

Arunodoy Saha, a professor of economics at Tripura University, told me an interesting story. A student working on a doctoral thesis visited him, as the then Dean of Students, to seek his approval on his application. The young man had even selected his guide. As he scanned the application and the official papers which came with it, Saha noticed that an official note had been written on a Sunday. 'This is a fake document,' he angrily turned on the student. The latter was unfazed. 'Sir, in our country, Sundays are working days.' The boy was from Comilla in Bangladesh. Fridays are holidays there. There are hundreds like him who live in Agartala before either returning home or going elsewhere in India. The fact that they are Hindus makes detection that much more difficult.

It is barely a five-rupee rickshaw ride from near the border to Agartala. If you visit the official border post, you're unlikely to see more than a handful of people waiting to get in, or to go across as customs and immigration officials check their papers. But barely a hundred metres behind the checkpost, people are coming and going as if this was nothing but a daily ritual. It is just that for those who come into Agartala, working as rickshaw-pullers, daily labourers, supplying cosmetics and electronic goods, even fish, or buying Indian goods for sale back home.

In fact, one of the biggest exports from the Indian side, on the black market of course, is medicine. Drugs of all sorts are in high demand in Bangladesh because of that country's ban on major foreign medical formulations. Phensidyl, an Indian cough medicine, is a huge favourite. It is used more as an alcoholic stimulant rather than a cough syrup because of its high alcohol content.

Agartala, despite the fact that some of us from middle-class India look down upon it, is a magnet for people and business from Bangladesh.

Until 1998, Tripura was also a staging ground for an Indian-organized low level conflict conducted by Chakma tribal fighters against the Bangladesh Army. One need not go into details here on that; it has been described elsewhere.[6]

What is clear from all this is that the Bengali leaders of Tripura need to assure the tribal population of that state that they will accept some ground rules if conditions are to improve. These include the honouring of existing land deals, not acquiring more land or interference in customary laws, acceptance of tribal control over the TTAC region and its neighbourhood. In turn, the militant groups must recognize that, at least in the next decades, there is no future in seeking separation from India. If their armed campaign continues, they will hurt Tripura and their own fellow tribals as well as Bengalis. Their long-term aims are ill-served by such shortsightedness. The Indian State is unlikely to be damaged overmuch by their attacks. They too must recognize the weariness with violence that has settled across the state as it has in other parts of the world.

One truth endures. As Hrangkhawl wrote to then Prime Minister Indira Gandhi in 1983, and emphasized to

---

6   See Hazarika S., *Strangers of the Mist: Tales of War and Peace from Indias North East*, Viking/Penguin, 1995 reprint.

me nearly ten years later, if the question of immigration is not resolved then ethnic violence will continue to lay waste to Tripura. How is this to be resolved becomes important as the problem is part of a larger picture that embraces much of the region, and affects India more than is generally acknowledged.

CHAPTER TWELVE

The Story of Keramat Bhai

The car could travel up to the *chai dokan* on the edge of the village, on the dirt track that passed for a road. This was at a hamlet called Bepari Para, still a short distance from Chilmari Ghat. The day had been dry and hot, and sundown was but an hour or so away.

We had been looking for Bepari Para (meaning the neighbourhood of traders), for a little while. Our little group, comprising of a cheerful local reporter, Mamon Islam, a former engineer who quit his job because he could not stand the corruption in the government's irrigation and public works department, and me, had spent some time at Chilmari Ghat looking for Keramat Bhai and his associates, quite fruitlessly. En route to his village, Mamon, one of the most honest and helpful persons I have met in my life, suggested that we drop by a local politico from the ruling Awami League and have a chat with him.

So, we trooped into the home of the Awami Leaguer, who received us warmly. He was a member of the district council, known as the Union. After a few minutes of conversation, we found that the room had filled with unannounced visitors. These turned out to be the local headmaster and members of the village council who wanted to participate in the discussions. Foreigners, even

Indians, were rare visitors and someone who took a specific interest in local issues of flooding, displacement and land pressures was even more welcome.

We spoke of the need to improve relations between the two countries, especially in the field of trade. There was a ripple of laughter when we spoke of the illegal trade. Mamon Islam turned to me. 'When you had the transport strike in India, we were very badly affected in Bangladesh, especially in Kurigram.' He explained: 'Kerosene, sugar and salt—these are big items from India. They come by truck up to the border and then across by porters and boats, to be transferred to local transport vehicles. During the strike, the prices went up four, five times because of short supply and the greed of the *dalals*. Ah! They are so greedy!' said this simple man. Only now had the prices started to to come down. That was in 1999. The strike had taken place in 1997.

One of the Council members argued for open trade, saying that it was better to formalize the informal. Governments on either side of the border were losing money through their respective restrictions and regulations; the only people making a profit were the smugglers and their comrades, the border police on either side of the frontier. The customer was having to pay high prices because of this alliance between crime and the upholders of law and order.

I spoke about the large number of cattle which entered Bangladesh through 'cattle corridors' in West Bengal, Meghalaya, Assam, as well as Tripura.

The Union member smiled and spread his hands in a gesture of thanks to the divine. 'How great Allah is! You do not eat the meat of cattle but we do. But you have the cows while we need the meat. So, it makes good economic sense for you to send the meat to us and for us to buy it from you. This is the economics of the market; it is good common sense and it has existed in this region before anyone thought of globalization.'

Tea was served with biscuits in that small room which doubled as a drawing and dining room—and now a meeting centre. When we took leave, it was already late and we still had to locate Bepari Para to look for Keramat Bhai.

The village roads of Bangladesh are extremely bumpy and unpaved; they are as bad or as good as village roads in most parts of eastern India. We swallowed dust as we travelled and drew the curious stares of onlookers—it was clear that our presence and the car were novelties. We were not foreign-looking, certainly not by the colour of our skin. But the intense gaze of the people showed that they thought we were babus from Dhaka. It is apparent that not many babus or netas visited these parts except perhaps at election time—we also noted the trees of either side of the road that blocked out the hot sun and enabled the Bengalis to indulge in their favourite vocation: lounge and talk, a pastime known in Bangla as *adda*. This is something that is common to Bengalis on either side of the international divide, of all castes, creeds and dialects. Basically, they just love nothing better than a long gossip session.

We finally rolled up at Bepari Para very dusty and tired by the evening. We asked for Keramat Bhai and were told he was at evening prayers in the village mosque. So we chatted among ourselves and walked into the village to wait. At this point, Mamon came up and said he was surprised by one thing: many of the young men of the village spoke Assamese or *Ashamiya* as he pronounced it.

We talked to a few young boys; they could not have been more than eighteen, or a little over. They spoke Assamese reasonably well and had been travelling to Assam over the past years. 'Our fathers had gone there before us and we continue to go,' one of them said.

At this point, there was a sudden rush in the small lane from the mosque as the *azaan* ended. Children scampered out; a few graybeards slowly followed them. In the second, slow-paced group was Keramat Bhai too, in fez cap, lungi and shirt.

His face lit up with a delighted smile, revealing two rows of paan-stained teeth.

'*Ah, saar, apuni ahile? Ami to pura din apunar karona roi asilu. Kali khobor palo je apuni ahibo. Kintu bahut deri hol, iman deri kiyo hol?*'[1] In slow but clear Assamese, Kermat Bhai asked after my health, and added that they had waited the whole day for me since they had got word of my coming the day before. 'But it has become very late? What happened?' he asked.

We elaborated on the difficulties of locating his place, besides our meetings with the politicians and the teachers. All this while, Mamon smiled indulgently and listened to our conversation, surprised that he was hearing this at all in his own land.

My faithful researcher, Raquib of Dhaka University, had come to the village a couple of times and to Chilmari Ghat to talk with Keramat Bhai and his friends. He had given news of me and sent word that I would also be coming to the area at some point. 'He was a good boy,

---

1 All interviews of the author with Keramat Bhai and his fellow villagers, published here and in the previous chapter, were conducted in October 1997 and on subsequent visits in May 1999; follow-up interviews were conducted by researchers later in 1999.

very patient, he asked a lot of questions,' said Keramat Bhai as the villagers crowded around.

Since it was late, we decided to return to Bepari Para the next morning. It would be easier to talk in the privacy of his home, Keramat said. As we got ready to return, he stopped us and insisted on tea with biscuits at the *chai dokan* or tea shop on the edge of the main path, before a dusty diversion going into the village. The road could not have been more than 10 to 12 feet wide.

The next day, I returned, this time without Mamon Bhai who had to leave for some reporting, and asked to be excused. Accompanying me was Firdouz, a young and tall scholar from Dhaka University, who was taking the place of Raquib, who could not come because he was preparing for examinations. Firdouz wanted to take the civil service examinations and become a district magistrate and serve in the secretariat in Dhaka. 'I want to be an officer, then only can we do something for our people,' he declared, when I asked him why he wanted to join the administration. 'But, Firdouz,' I said, 'all across the subcontinent, people go into the civil service with such dreams only to see them dashed within a few years of entering the system. They become as venal, corrupt and inefficient as the earlier batches.' He only smiled, especially when I told him that, at least in India, many people from 'service' backgrounds were moving to management jobs in multinationals or large domestic corporates which paid far better. Or else, they were setting up their own, extremely profitable organizations.

Firdouz smiled again: 'Ah, sir, in India you have many opportunities, people can manage and do well in other fields. Here, opportunities are less, jobs are few, we have limited choices.' He was as fascinated by our interactions and the information that we were generating.

Before talking to Keramat, we had spoken with a number of householders at the Chilmari Ghat, both Hindus and Muslims, bonded by language and a history of shared suffering, for the river too had taken away their homes, time after time, year after year.

Thus, Nitya Kumar Ghosh, a high-school teacher, who said he was fifty-five, and lived on the river front at Chilmari, spoke of how his family had shifted six times because of the flooding. 'Four times in my lifetime and twice during my father's. The Old Chilmari lies in the river, some five miles from here.' His son teaches at a nearby school and Ghosh, wearing a singlet, lungi and with a few days stubble on his face, said that the river perceived people as an enemy. 'We are not its enemy but it pursues us—we go far away to escape it but it does not allow us to go, it follows us.'

Once, steamers from the Brahmaputra moved down to connect with the Ganga and into Bengal. 'At that time, the river depth was twenty-five feet,' Ghosh said.

Jute and foodgrains were unloaded from the boats and put on waiting railroad coaches. It was a sensible trading arrangement. Partition changed all that, standing common sense on its head and replacing it with bad economics. Communities which had been trading partners for decades and more were sundered. Road links were snapped and new markets were perforce created. Thus, a village found its farm lands in one country and its markets in the other. These days, the river is as shallow as a few feet in parts, filled by the silt from upstream. Where fields were once abundant, there are only homesteads. The homeless, displaced by the river, have set up house in Chilmari.

By the time I reached Bepari Para, it was late morning—it was a good twenty-five to twenty-eight kilometres from Kurigram. Firdouz and I had been delayed because of a long conversation earlier in the morning with the deputy commissioner (DC) of Kurigram, a large man who had fought in the Mukti Bahini during the Liberation war. He had insisted the previous evening that I go to a music programme by a woman singer who was visiting from Cachar in Assam.

Mamon had accompanied me and the guest of honour had been a tall, middle-aged blonde woman from a European aid agency. The woman singer, in a bright, shimmering green saree, was slightly off-key. Earlier, a dancer purported to perform her vigorous version of Bharata Natyam. Much of the time, she appeared to be a medieval soldier at a furious joust. A leap forward, then another back, sideways to the right and then to the left. This went on, but soon I started getting a headache, and, as politely as possible I slipped out.

The next morning, as I set out for my daily routine of exercise and walking—something I try and do wherever I am, I bumped into the DC. 'Ah, Mr Hazarika, how did you enjoy the evening music?' he asked. 'They were from your *Asham*.' I winced a little at the pronunciation of my home state and muttered something about how fascinating it was to run into similar cultures in a neighbouring country. Of course, the singer had sung only *Rabindra Sangeet*, and some Bhatiali or songs of the boatmen, which are popular in northern Bengal and southern Assam.

Then, he insisted, that we continue our walk together and he took me on a tour of the new office buildings. Parts of it were still being built; it was a Friday and so everything was shut. By the time the tour was over, it was well past nine and I had to hurry to get to Keramat Bhai's village. He must have wondered why I turned up so late every time!

It was close to noon when I landed at Bepari Para and was told that Keramat Bhai had gone home. A couple of his young neighbours took me to the place, past the masjid outside which we had waited the previous day, and then to a part of the village which was 'new'. It comprised of those who had been displaced by floods during the past decade and had moved to Bepari Para. There was some dispute about whether they could stay on these lands without proper allotment from the local government. The issue appeared to be one that would take some time to resolve, with the village and the local government officials being divided on it, right down the middle. The land was a gift from the river, from the surges that dumped large sand heaps on the bank. The river does not discriminate among those it displaces. A small gate and a low bamboo fence ringed his place. A few tall areca nut trees and coconut palms offered some shade. Keramat Bhai's home was a simple one. It comprised of three rooms including a kitchen. But as he welcomed us, his wife appeared a little worried. Apparently, soon after my researcher's last visit, a plain-clothes policeman also had come by to check things out. This was clearly bothering her and she said so to Keramat Bhai. He brushed her aside with a burst of irritation. 'I am not saying anything that is against the government, or against the country,' he snapped. 'What are you worried about? I don't care about such things. I am telling the story and it is better that the saheb knows the facts instead of hearing all sorts of wrong stories.' This did not completely satisfy her, but she stayed indoors after that exchange.

Keramat brought out a *murha*, a low stool made of woven cane. He squatted on the earth beside me. Firdouz, a cheerful young man with a ready smile, went off to talk to other villagers.

And this is Keramat's story, much of it in his own words.

'We used to live elsewhere, we moved here just four or five years ago. Earlier, we were living quite far away, on the banks of the river, at a place called Bolondiar Khata. Before that we were somewhere else. I can tell you that I have lost count, the number of times we have been displaced by the Brahmaputra. It won't be less than fifteen, sixteen, seventeen times. We really don't have a place we can call home.

'I have three sons and three daughters. All the boys are working as fishermen and in making and repairing fishing nets. That is a big business here still. The girls have been married off and live elsewhere.'

'I've been going to Assam for over thirty years. Actually, I first went thirty-five years ago and I have travelled the entire length and breath of the Valley. I have been as far as Pasighat and Nameri in Arunachal Pradesh and as close as Dhubri. There isn't a place where I haven't been in Assam. The Assamese are nice people, I didn't have much trouble there all these years. We would come and go quite easily. Pay a little on this side of the border to the guards, and pay a little over there to the Indians.

'Can I tell you something, saheb? I haven't been for about four or five years. But it was the Assamese who kept me on contract to catch fish and supply it to the local markets. I even stayed in Majuli for two years, helping build a boat near Kamlabari, the port. It was an Assamese contractor from Neamati Ghat who hired me for all those years. I would catch fish, help build the boat and even take the fish to the local haat.'

He paused. Memories returned in a surge.

The names of the villages and towns rolled off his tongue—Kamlabari, Natun Kamlabari, Dakhin Path. He had sold fish in Sibsagar, near the Shiva Dol, the large temple dedicated to Shiva, built in the seventeenth century by an Ahom king.

As mentioned before, the Ahoms came to the Brahmaputra Valley from the wedge between South-West China, South-East Myanmar and northern Thailand, and left an indelible impress on the countryside with their organizing skills, military prowess (especially as skilled naval commanders), the construction of sturdy buildings and roads, and a tough (at times downright brutal) and efficient administration.

Ravaged by Burmese invasions, the Ahoms sought British help. The price was the loss of Assam's freedom to the British. Today, questions of accession and colonial right, of the rights of successor states, of the rights of 'indigenous' communities, have returned to the centre of political debate in the North East as well as other parts of India. Communities, especially in the borderlands, such as in the state of Meghalaya, which have been placid all along, are now questioning the very Treaty of Accession signed by petty rajahs and chiefs of the Khasi and Garo tribes in 1947. They claim that they were never given a fair hearing and were not even consulted by the men who drew up the constitutional clauses pertaining to the North East. The framers of that document put traditional systems of governance aside and instead developed a structure of district councils for the hills of the Meghalaya, especially, which have led to little development and encouraged misgovernance, corruption and the devastation of the environment.

More than fifty years later, the successors of those adherents to the traditional systems—which still exist and are respected as far as land rights and property disputes are concerned—are demanding a say in the future of the Khasis and the Garos. These are questions which must be handled with sensitivity and attention to detail. The last thing that one wants is a knee-jerk reaction, from the state government or the Centre, which leads to more confrontation and conflict.

The question of migration is inextricably wrapped up with these issues and questions. The question of pressure on land, of holding onto one's identity in the face of the pressure of numbers from other 'majoritarian' groups, of the sense of being swamped by an 'alien' culture or cultures—these are facts and attitudes that make for a violent mix in the politics of such a diverse region, peopled by so many communities—a good number of which are small and unique.

It is not as if Keramat Bhai and men like him are unaware of such feelings. Indeed, he spoke of how during the height of the popular agitation against immigrants in the early 1980s, his employers hid him in huts near Kamlabari, one of the main towns of Majuli island. Later, they were assured by local students and other movement leaders that the Bangladeshis would not be harmed. 'They told us, "Don't worry, you are safe, no harm will come to you,"' Keramat Bhai said. He said the students knew that their presence was necessary for the local economy. In this particular case, they were building boats and fishing.

During his years in Assam, Keramat Bhai had voted in

elections, not once but several times. He was a bit dodgy on this. All he would do was to declare affirmatively: '*Vote disilu, sobe disile, kunuwe rokhuwa nain.*' ('I voted, others voted, nobody stopped us.') They gave their own names or changed them about a little when they were enlisted on the voting lists. He would not say where they voted. 'Other people will get into trouble.'

What, of course, is a source of not a little amusement is that a number of the places where Keramat and others lived and thus could have voted—and these included Jorhat and Nogaon—are strongholds of Assamese nationalists as represented by the Asom Gana Parishad, the regional party which Prafulla Mahanta and his cohorts in the student movement founded after they contested elections in 1985 and came to power.

There is devastating irony in all of this—Bangladeshis voting for a party that had their deportation at the top of its agenda! Politics does make strange bedfellows. The involvement of the immigrants with the winning side, even if it appeared not to have their interests at heart, was a sensible, strategic move making political overtures and aimed at reducing conflict.

The immigrants constituted a considerable chunk of the vote and the conciliatory moves of the AGP made sound political sense. Which party would not like a bank of voters delivered to them? When the AGP came to power for the second time in 1996, it had muted its opposition to immigrants and reduced its rhetoric on issues such as detection and deportation. It followed a safer line, one which made its policies hard to distinguish from those of other parties.

'We go quietly to Assam, we travel at night and go either

by the river or on foot,' said Mohammad Chakku Mian, a stocky fisherman who said he was twenty years old. The sturdy man said that he and his compatriots usually paid 100 Bangladeshi taka to the Bangladesh Rifles and 100 rupees to the Indian Border Security Force on the other side. 'Then there is no problem.'

Chakku Mian was also a good singer, a fact that he tried hard to hide much to the amusement of his fellow Assamese-speaking Bangladeshis and to his own discomfiture. Indeed, when they finally tired of teasing him, he summoned up enough courage to sing Bhatiali songs in a strong baritone. It was as we set out on a boat to Chilmari, to have a view of the damage that the Brahmaputra had inflicted on the land. 'People are going every day, even now they go,' Chakku Mian declared, without hestitation. He said that 'hundreds' were going every year only from this part of Kurigram. This was hard to quantify but certainly from Bepari Para and Chilmari Ghat and Ramna, one came across a number of men of different ages who bore this out.

Even at Keramat Bhai's village, I spoke with at least six others who were either currently living in Assam, or were about to go, or had been there. My researchers turned up five others.

And why not? If you can travel there, work there, vote there and come back with several months of earnings —this is virtual citizenship, without documents. It's hard to improve upon.

The shoreline near Chilmari Ghat showed signs of battering by the river. Thus, in many places, the bank was caving in and falling in chunks into the river or appeared to be on the point of doing so. Every year, the river gains one kilometre on one side and loses a similar area on the other. Sometimes, it is less than a kilometre; in bad years, it is much more.

During a visit in 1996, I remember talking to an old man in a tiny village near Goalundo Ghat, where the Brahmaputra and the Ganges meet. He claimed that at the time of independence (1971 from West Pakistan, not 1947 from the British), the river was more than ten kilometres from its current location. This was of course an impressionistic account of the river's progress.

But in Chilmari, the facts are known and visible. In the early summer of 1997, the port was already three kilometres from its earlier site. It had moved three years ago. The rapidity of the erosion was such that the Bangladesh government moved the river port down to Gaibandha, a further thirty kilometres to the south that very year. This was the final blow for Chilmari, a port that had seen the grand steamers come in from Dhubri and up from Narayanganj near Dhaka in earlier decades. These days, a handful of small fishing boats and *noukas* which ferry people over short distances are around.

One evening, a few of us travelled in a stout dugout to a char that had grown opposite Chilmari. It was called Manuh Mara Char or the char where people were killed. Obviously, the name had something to do with an incident that took place there, but no one really knew much about it. The moon shone on the island and the shoreline, not far away. And it was so still that the sounds of clatter of plates being stacked on top of each other, music from a radio aboard an anchored boat, and a brief quarrel between a man and a woman floated clearly across the water.

All was not desolate, difficult, impoverished and

depressing. The river and nature brought their own sense of beauty and richness to a neglected place like Chilmari.

Gaibanda was another three hours by road. The port was not picturesque here either. A long row of brightly-coloured Tata trucks (yellow and orange were preferred colours), laden with goods inched forward toward the ghat or moved away toward the hinterland. One was loading goods on to medium-sized boats and ferries. The ghat was also nondescript. It was certainly nothing like a river port that one had imagined; there were no jetties, no large, smart, sparkling vessels, no steamers, no harbours for the anchored boats.

The boats were medium-sized and sturdy, capable of carrying large loads of passengers and goods. They were made of teak, much of which had been smuggled across from Myanmar or Assam or Bangladesh's own Chittagong Hill Tracts. From here, the goods and people were transported down towards Dhaka and the east, along the old route of the Brahmaputra which flows by Mymensingh. This channel has become a shrunken, shallow stream that can be crossed on foot in winter.

And on foot, further north, when I was walking on Noonkhawa Char, near where the Brahmaputra flows into Bangladesh, I saw an old man with a bundle on his head trudging along the dry river bed. 'India is four miles from here, sir,' he said, identifying himself as Mahfuz Mian Bepari. For the past thirty-one years, Mahfuz Mian had trekked these shallow and unbeaten paths to sell a commodity from this region that is in much demand in Assam: tobacco.

Kurigram and Rongpur districts are well known for good tobacco. In his bundle, Mahfuz Mian had two packets: one contained the tobacco, the other a clean pair of trousers and a blue shirt. The old man, white bearded and wiry, said he did not know his own age but guessed that he was about fifty. He looked at least twenty years older—but then the climate of these places and the difficulties of their daily lives tell on the faces and bodies of men like Mahfuz Mian. Because of the low level of water, it would take him another two hours to the border. In times of flood, it would take barely an hour by boat.

At times, Mahfuz Mian said, one of his sons accompanied him. And they made the trip every two or three weeks, selling tobacco worth 400 taka or so each time. This amounted to a profit of about 80 taka, he said.

Imagine trekking through that pitiless terrain, in sun, rain and flood, at that age, to eke a living. The border drew Mahfuz Mian like a magnet because he got a better price at the haat there, at Narayanpur, than in Bangladesh.

This is the traditional route for commerce in the area. And no border can block it. It can only make the natural, illegal—just as it has done for migrants, for people like Keramat Bhai. But it cannot stop trade.

Keramat Bhai was quite frank. 'We go because we fulfil a need over there, we go also because it meets a need here. Your people need our skills and hard work, we need the money.' This sounded a bit like the Awami Leaguer and his explanation of the export of cattle from 'Hindu' land to a 'Muslim' society.

A cup of tea was sent out from the kitchen. I was tired of sitting on the murha. We had been talking for nearly a couple of hours, and it was time to stretch my legs. I walked to a nearby dwelling in Keramat Bhai's courtyard. This was a house without a roof but it had a raised floor, at least a foot or so higher than the ground level. A few clothes were hung out to dry and Keramat Bhai moved quickly to remove them.

Why this outhouse, I asked. 'When the flood comes, we move in here,' he said. That explained the higher level of the floor. But surely if the water rose much higher, how would they manage then?

Usually, they would get on to tables and planks. But, he added, the water rarely rose much beyond a particular level in this part of the village.

'Keramat Bhai, explain something to me: you have been going to Assam all these years,' I began. He interrupted: 'I stopped going about five years ago, it gets too difficult, I'm getting older.' He shrugged and appeared indifferent.

'But what was it that they wanted you for, what skills do you have that the Assamese fishermen don't?'

'Ah, sir, they don't know the *kaida*, the trick of being a successful fisherman. You have to know how to fish, gauge the currents correctly, know where to cast the net and when, and then work very, very hard,' he smiled. 'The Assamese don't know the trick. Another thing, you must have good nets.'

Keramat Bhai said he had stayed in places as far north as the Nameri National Park, fishing for the great golden mahseer in the Jia Bhoroli river. He knew the name of the river and the name of the sanctuary. The mahseer is perhaps the most majestic and powerful of the fresh water fish in Indian rivers. A wonderful, sporting fish, it grows to a huge size in the shallows, protected by the rocks that slow the speed of the flow. Catching it takes great skill and strength. Near Nameri, a group of environmentalists and businessmen have set up a camp for tourists and anglers who want to catch the mahseer. The organizers have developed it into an eco-friendly, educative and conservation sport where the fish is caught, weighed and then released into the water. Some of them have been not less than 22 kilograms!

Keramat Bhai said he had lived in the Nameri forests while fishing for mahseer. And, no, he did not do any eco-fishing! There is, thus, hardly any reason to speculate about causes behind the drop in the number of fish caught by anglers during these past years. Very simply, it is overfishing, and predominantly by foul means such as dumping poisonous chemicals in the streams, or using drag nets, or nets without any perforation, which kills even the fishlings.

Thus, while Keramat Bhai's point about the lack of skills of the Assamese fishermen is taken, there is much to be said against the use of illegal nets which catch not just the large fish but also the fishlings. This practice destroys the sustainability of the fish catch. It is harmful, in the long run, for local entrepreneurs, fishermen and consumers as it kills the diversity of marine life as well as the opportunities for its renewal.

Not many others are bothered about this aspect of fishing.

Upstream from Nameri, on the other side of the river, near Jorhat, a local Assamese contractor hired Keramat Bhai to work at Neamati Ghat and then moved him to Majuli. He was in constant demand because the Bangladeshis would catch more fish than the local fishermen.

'From Dhubri to Guwahati, Majuli, Jorhat, Sibsagar and up to Pasighat, I have gone with fellow villagers, I have fished and now I have come back. I've done it for thirty-five years and now others can go.'

Dhubri, he said, was a major staging point for further travel. Such distant travel does not merely mean the forests of Nameri, but a town like Pasighat which is also in Arunachal Pradesh. During my first visit there in October 1996, local residents spoke of Bangladeshi fishermen who were brilliant at their jobs. I thought it was a lot of nonsense, exaggerated xenophobia imported into the state from Assam.

I was wrong. It is men like Keramat Bhai who go there.

'Near the site for the bridge at Pasighat, about one or two kilometres from the town, that is where we used to stay on the bank,' he said.

His directions were accurate.

Keramat Bhai, Mohammad Shahid Ali and others have built a career in fishing in Assam. For those who don't go any more—both men are in their forties now—there are others who do. They travel in groups of three to five, rarely larger for fear of detection.

Keramat Bhai now spends his time taking goods down to southern Bangladesh on the large mahajani boats; these are vessels with high bows and fat bellies that enable them to sail steadily and carry a lot of freight. Other times, he fishes locally and sells the produce in the local market.

The trips south are on the boats of others. Three other men travel with him and they go from Chilmari to Dhaka and Narayanganj. The trips can last three weeks and he earns about 800 to 1,000 taka on each trip. His daily earnings as a fisherman are meagre in Chilmari: about 50 to 70 taka.

His gaunt, dark wizened features tell of struggle. But times were good in Assam. His face lights up when he speaks. 'We used to get work from the mahajans and local contractors. We never had a problem with work. At the end of the day, the total catch was shared by the contractor and us. We travelled during the season, September to December, but often we also stayed on.'

How much did they earn?

Four to five times whatever they were earning now in Bangladesh. 'Usually about 100 to 150 rupees every day; we used to save money, bring it back and spend it here. Nowadays, it's miserable.'

As we talked, a young man dropped by. He appeared interested by the conversation. Keramat Bhai greeted him and introduced me. He didn't volunteer the man's name. The man was visiting Bepari Para from another nearby village. That was nothing out of the ordinary. What was extraordinary was that he 'actually' come from a long way. 'He's come from Sadiya,' Keramat Bhai announced, watching my face for its inevitable look of surprise. Sadiya is in Assam and although that bustling river port was buried by the Great Assam Earthquake of 1950, the area is still known by that name. In fact, it is not too far along the Brahmaputra from Pasighat.

'Part of it is Kundil Ghat now,' I said. The visitor nodded vigorously and then said in Assamese that he had been there more than a year and was planning to return the following week. This was strictly a trip to visit family and friends.

How long did it take to come?

'Three days by boat and bus,' he said nonchalantly.

And when had he arrived here?

Another smile. 'Yesterday.'

With that bit of laconic information, the man stood up and left.

It's that simple to get across, even though Keramat Bhai and his older friends say that security is tighter at the border. It is also not as if everyone who goes across settles over there. They return to their homes from time to time. The village almost appears to be a kind of R&R (Rest and Recreation) Centre for veterans from the fighting front. One would not be surprised if both sexual activity and pregnancies go up at this time.

What emerged through our conversations was a picture of migrants—all of those who spoke with were male—with two homes. The ability of the men to speak Assamese reasonably fluently was also a considerable advantage in the process of migrating. They appeared confident and comfortable with their accessibility to either side. If we are to believe Chakku Mian, not less than 400 to 500 people leave this belt of Kurigram for Assam every year.

But what of those who say, especially Bangladeshi officials, that no one is leaving Bangladesh at all? One of Bangladesh's top demographers, Masihur Rahman Khan, remarked in a 1972 study that earlier efforts by demographers to 'obtain the birth and death rates of the population on the assumption that the population of Bangladesh was closed to external migration and that the age-sex data . . . reflected a stable/quasi-stable rate of growth . . . met with frustration because the assumptions on which the estimates were based were found faulty.'[2]

'Migration played an important role in the growth of the Bangladesh population,' said Khan. With the

---

2   Bangladesh Population during the First Five-Year Plan Period (1972-77): A Guestimate. Masihur Rahman Khan, Bangladesh Institution of Development Economics, Dhaka, October 1972

exception of 1901-1911, the area now comprising 'Bangladesh was losing population through net emigration mainly to India in all other decades.[3] This figure rose from 100,000 in 1911-21 to around 1.2 million in 1951-61 and the exodus was 'possibly high in 1964-66 due to and associated with the Pakistani war in 1965 with India.' Given Bangladesh's unsettled conditions in the 1970s, post-liberation and the trauma of the Pakistani crackdown as well as the war, the possibility of a 'continued net emigration flow from Bangladesh, though a smaller magnitude compared to that in 1940s and 1950s, cannot be ruled out.'[4]

Thus, without quantifying the outflow—and one must acknowledge that these were early days after the Liberation—scholars such as Khan and Sharifa Begum have indicated the significance of the movement into India.

Begum's figures, which one has written about and analysed in an earlier book, also must be taken note of. This we shall do in the next chapter.

But here one should return to Keramat Bhai.

Clearly, he was regarded as a spokesman for his people in the village. Few of the others were prepared to talk to us at any length because of the fear of being harassed by security officials for talking about a problem whose existence Bangladesh has officially and consistently

---

3   Ibid.

4   Hazarika, Sanjoy, *Strangers of the Mist, Tales of War and Peace from India's North East,* Viking/Penguin, 1995. Edition quoting two studies by Sharifa Begum: 1. Birthrate and Deathrate in Bangladesh, 1951-1974, Dhaka, Bangladesh Institute for Development Studies (BIDS), 1979; 2. Population, Birth, Death and Growth Rates in Bangladesh: Census estimates, Dhaka, BIDS, 1990

denied. But even Keramat Bhai had limitations: his was a micro approach, based on his experiences. One could not expect much more than that.

But when I asked him about possible solutions to the issue of migration, he smiled and spoke rhetorically: 'Can the river stop flowing? Can you block the rains? People who talk about such things do not know what they say. The Assamese need us, we need them.'

I talked to Keramat Bhai about my idea for a work permit for migrants from Bangladesh and how it could legalize temporary migration for purposes of labour. This is discussed in greater detail in the last chapter. Essentially, such a work permit regime would be aimed at developing a legal mechanism which would enable groups of migrants from Bangladesh (and other parts of the region, if necessary) to move into states where workers were required for the following: agricultural operations, construction and fishing and river-related work such as boat-building. They would not be allowed to settle permanently or have the right to vote or purchase land or housing. They would be given the opportunity to repatriate funds to their banks through a bilateral banking arrangement. At the end of one year, they would be given the opportunity to extend their stay by a maximum of one year. They would be housed in specific colonies set up for this purpose which would make monitoring that much easier.

Any 'leakage' of workers should bring the wrath of government upon the employer as well as erring district officials and responsible panchayat members. The system of local governance, especially through the Panchayats and Hill Councils, would be extensively used to control such movements.

Keramat Bhai thought about this idea for a while.

'If we have a *parchi*, (slip of paper) it will be of help; we will have an identification and we will be able to go and work and return without harassment or fear. It is a good idea. Many of us would be prepared to go under such a system.' The permit idea was more appealing than slipping across at night, not knowing whether one would be caught, or if one's contact was ready on the other side, not to mention having to pay out hundreds of rupees in bribes to border guards in both countries. The Indians were tightening up on the Assam side and he did not want to get caught.

There was another major factor in favour of the work permit: local people would get a feeling that the migrants could not intrude on their political and economic rights. It would create a sense of space and tolerance.

It was getting late and time to return to Kurigram. I don't know if I will see Keramat Bhai again, but if I do, I hope to see him in better conditions at Bepari Para. But then, I wouldn't be surprised if I bumped into him in Assam. He is not just a migrant; he is also an entrepreneur.

We have spoken of the difficult economic conditions in Kurigram. A reflection of the depth of poverty and the problems of local government is seen in a number of local roads there having been built by an NGO, the Rongpur Dinajpur Rural Service, rather than the government. There are not less than 34 NGOs, both Bangladeshi and international, working in Kurigram. And the best-run hospital and health extension programme is conducted by the Swiss agency. Terres des Hommes, People prefer not to go to the local civil hospital which is run-down and constantly short of medicines and equipment.

The core of the tragedy and hopelessness that blights Kurigram and parts of Bangladesh, which has moulded the lives of Keramat Bhai and many others like him, is summed up in the name of the Swiss agency Terre des Hommes: People without Land.

The rivers are the sorrow of Kurigram—the Brahmaputra, the Dudhkumar, the Dharla. Yet, every year, even as they strike with impunity and 'pursue' people, as Nitya Kumar Ghosh of Chilmari Ghat said, they also bring to Bangladesh the priceless gift of land and life.

CHAPTER THIRTEEN

Bangladesh: Standing Room Only

It was a clear, hot, humid summer morning: a bandh-less day in Dhaka. I was quite familiar with bandhs in the Bangladeshi capital. On such days, Dhaka would turn into a city where driving was a pleasure and even walking on the streets was comfortable! That is, if your vehicle was not being targeted by a stone-hurling mob, or you were not personally attacked. On a normal day, if you went around the New Market area or in Farm Gate, busy business centres, you would probably be swept off your feet by a rush of humanity, talking, rickshawing, cycling, driving, walking, and working. Especially, if it was evening. This vast, incoherent, swirling mass could be quite unnerving; on that day, I remember standing near the down-market Sundarbans Hotel, and staring with a mixture of horror and awe at the bedlam on the streets.

It was bedlam without violence. There was confusion, typical of Calcutta, multiplied by several times; Bombay's surging crowds at least three times over; and Delhi's aggressive drivers and rickshaws cutting in, swerving and violating every rule in book just to get ahead of the next guy. Small groups of policemen stood at the chaotic traffic roundabouts and lights, waiting to prey upon an unwary victim, while sharing a bribe and a joke.

The heat, pollution and dust compounded the confusion. Dhaka is one of the most overcrowded and polluted cities on earth. At times, especially near the main bus station, I have felt close ro suffocation, being an irregular sufferer of asthma. There are, of course, parts of New Delhi, Calcutta, Karachi and other cities on the subcontinent which are no better or worse.

The dominant feeling is that of being overwhelmed. There are people everywhere; the parks are overcrowded and early morning walks turn out to be public events with thousands marching up and down the fanciest or the grubbiest of roads and avenues; restaurants are full, not to speak of public transport and markets.

The best part about Dhaka is its creative people, who function under the most trying of circumstances—filmmakers and writers, singers and scholars, musicians and dancers, artists and teachers, and leaders of NGOs. Its cooks are no mean artistes in their own craft, conjuring up dishes of curried or steamed hilsa, that prince of river fish. Which brings me to another point: the next best thing to its wonderfully creative people is the smoked hilsa at the Dhaka Club.

Overcrowding is the basic problem in the country's main city as its facilities, built for a much smaller population, groan and falter. Residents of many metros of the Third World have to endure a similar, gruelling fate every day. What then is to be expected of other parts of Bangladesh, including the smaller towns? Here, roads are transformed into noisy markets. Vehicular progress becomes the equivalent of travelling at the speed of a bullock cart on an autobahn.

The 1991 Census of Bangladesh said that Bangladesh had a total of 112 million people. This was projected to grow to 120.6 million by 1996.[1] By 2006, this will have jumped to 135.7 million.[2]

What is the condition of people in the country? What is their accessibility to basic services and facilities such as medicines and healthcare, education and communications, drinking water and food apart from homes, roads and clothes?

If we were to take a set of statistics such as literacy rates for those aged fifteen years and above, the population of literates has significantly increased between 1974 and 1991. Overall it has risen from 25.8 per cent in 1974 to 29.2 per cent in 1981 and then to 35.3 percent in 1991.[3] Compare this with its immediate, large neighbour, India. The literacy index for this country is spotty with high incidence reported from the east and poor literacy in northern and central India, the so-called BIMARU belt (Bihar, Madhya Pradesh, Rajasthan, Uttar Pradesh), especially for women.

What makes especially interesting reading in Bangladesh is the official figures for adult literates on the basis of religion. While Muslims overall reported 53.47 per cent literacy, the Hindus and Christians showed rates of 61.89 per cent and 79.22 per cent.[4]

In the sector of drinking water, the Census said that only 4.30 per cent of the population had access to tap water. A majority depended on water from tubewells.[5] As far as rural female health was concerned, another study

---

1   Bangladesh Population Census 1991, Volume 1, Analytical Report, Bangladesh Bureau of Statistics, Dhaka, September 1994
2   Ibid.
3   Ibid.
4   Ibid.
5   Ibid.

showed that the percentage of women assisted at the time of delivery of the child by doctors was 2.2 per cent;[6] midwives and traditional dais provided the biggest support system: they managed 59.4 per cent of all deliveries.[7]

Yet, despite these drawbacks, Bangladesh still scores hugely over India when it comes to access to health infrastructure. It is number 88 on the World Health Organisation's country-wise list of health systems. India is way down at number 112, inviting an irritated reaction from Indian politicians.[8]

In the Human Development Report for 1999 which was released by the United Nations Development Programme (UNDP), Bangladesh is placed at the 150th position while India and Pakistan are at the 132nd and 138th spots, respectively!

The Bangladesh health survey estimated that the proportion of rural homes using electricity was a bare 8.2 per cent of the total.[9]

In the middle of all these statistics, several questions arise—how much are people in charge of their own lives? How secure are they in their present location, or how are they living? How do they respond to economic opportunities elsewhere? These are questions facing many underdeveloped countries, not least Bangladesh.

Over the years, the concept of human security has evolved beyond the physical safety of a person, community or country to that of exercising a range of

6   Bangladesh Health and Demographic Survey, Findings in brief, 1994 and 1995, Bangladesh Bureau of Statistics, Dhaka, June 1995
7   Ibid.
8   The *Indian Express*, New Delhi
9   Ibid.

choices in the development process.

The UNDP report outlines the two main aspects of human security:

'Safety from such chronic threats as hunger, disease and repression.

'Protection from hidden and hurtful disruptions in the patterns of daily life—whether in homes, in jobs or in communities. Such threats exist at all levels of national income and development.'[10]

For decades, it has been easy to characterize Bangladesh as the perennial poor man of Asia and especially of South Asia. The mental image is of a nation, reeling either from floods or dry spells, overcrowded, poor and badly governed. One of its foremost economists, Rehman Sobhan, says that in 1989-90 about 35 per cent of the population of the time or about 42 million people still lived in poverty.

'Life expectancy at birth has remained unchanged at 56.0 in 1988 compared to 56.9 in 1980. Infant mortality has fallen very marginally from 101.4 in 1980 to 98 in 1989. Chronic malnutrition has remained largely unchanged with 56.1 per cent of the population reported as chronically undernourished in 1985-86 compared to 57.3 per cent in 1980-81. Adult literacy has risen marginally from 25.8 per cent in 1974 to 33 per cent in 1987. School attendance ratios show that enrolment rates have risen from 5-9 years old from 18.7 per cent in 1974 to 22.5 per cent in 1981.' But for all age groups, barring the 20-24 group, they remained the same, indicating, Sobhan said, 'that marginal improvements in primary school enrolment have not ensured improvement in the

10   Human Development Report, 1999, UNDP, Oxford University Press, New Delhi, 1999

retention of children in these schools.'[11]

He declared emphatically: 'While the debate may go on about the exact percentage point of improvement or decline registered in our conditions of life, there is no debate that compared to most other countries in Asia, Bangladesh has registered a weak growth performance, has a rather large number of its citizens living in poverty and has a poor record of human resource development (HRD).'[12]

Assistance in terms of aid and grant assistance from bilateral and multilateral lending and financial agencies and institutions has reached millions of beneficiaries, including an estimated 500,000 poor rural women under the World Food Programme's Vulnerable Group Development. Many more have benefited from the Public Food Distribution System while rural works programmes, assisted by foreign aid, employed not less than one to four million every year between 1980 and 1988.[13]

Indeed, according to the Bangladesh government, the country is dependent on foreign aid for about 50 per cent of its development outlay. Exports pay for less than 50 per cent of its imports.

More recent statistics tell a marginally different story.

Adult literacy was 35.3 per cent nationally, a small but significant increase from Sobhan's 33 per cent. School attendance was up in spectacular fashion in the 5-year to 24-year group—from 8.92 million of the eligible population to 17.62 million in 1991. Yet, another 30 million did not go to school.[14]

---

11 Rehman Sobhan, *Bangladesh, Problems of Governance*, Konarak Publishers, New Delhi, 1993
12 Ibid.
13 Ibid.

Dwellings with electricity connections were listed at 19 million and acute malnutrition among children remained fairly high: about 14 per cent for those aged between six months and 71 months of age.[15] Infant mortality for 1996 was placed at 67 per 1,000 live births; this figure has shown a steady downward trend since the 1980s, falling from 116 in 1988. This is a remarkable achievement by any standards and has taken place because Bangladesh's rulers have given priority to child and women welfare.

Life expectancy was up from 56.4 in 1987 to 58.9 in 1996, again a very small rise in a decade.

The incidence of poverty (on the basis of a daily calorie intake of a minimum of 2,122 K. calories per person per day) was placed at 58.5 million in 1983-84, a figure that dropped steadily to 55.3 million in 1995-96. This means that Bangladesh has reduced the number of its absolute poor from 62.6 per cent to 47.5 per cent of the population, yet another major achievement.

But when it comes to population density per square kilometre and religious data, serious discrepancies begin to appear. Bangladesh's population density is placed at 755·for 1991, a quantitative leap over the 590 of the previous census.[16] In this demographic area, India's figure is 261 while that of Pakistan is 153. A comparison with earlier data points to another problem with Bangladeshi figures: they appear to be, to use a mild word, flexible.

Thus, in the early 1990s, when I worked on my earlier

14   Bangladesh Population Census, 1991, Volume 2, Union Statistics, Bangladesh Bureau of Statistics, Dhaka, December 1993
15   Women and Men in Bangladesh. Facts and Figures, 1970-90, Bangladesh Bureau of Statistics, Dhaka, July 1994
16   Bangladesh Population Census, 1991, Volume 2

book on insurgency and migration in the North East, the figures were the following for population density: 969 per square kilometre in 1991 and 624 in 1981.[17] These were not disputed although the 1991 Census places population density at 755 per square kilometre.

Human Security and Bangladesh

What is the connection between acute poverty in Bangladesh—which may be improving marginally, year after year—and the concerns of this book?

These lie in the description of human security as outlined elsewhere in the book. The UNDP report of 1999 said that threats to this security could either develop as a slow process or an abrupt emergency. This is an issue that has been discussed extensively in chapter four but it would not be irrelevant to talk briefly about it here.

Environmental pressures, such as those caused by overpopulation and land degradation as well as by poor economic planning, can lead to natural disasters and human tragedies. The UN list speaks of the following principal threats to human security, food and economic insecurity, health and personal insecurity, as well as environmental, political, community and cultural insecurity.

What rules govern the world that we inhabit? Whether it is access to drinking water, schooling, better nourishment and incomes, the countries of the South have remained at the bottom of the heap despite much-repeated declarations of support and assistance to the poor. This is not to deny that there has been assistance. There has been

---

17 Sanjoy Hazarika, *Strangers of the Mist: Tales of War and Peace from India's North East*, New Delhi: Viking, 1994. Reprint, Penguin, 1995

significant help. But it is a fraction of what is needed.

Deprivation and inequality create huge disparities within regions and countries. The United Nations[18] reels off a depressing set of figures with regard to the poorest and most vulnerable people in the world:

- Nearly 1.3 billion people do not have access to clean water.
- One in seven children of primary age school is out of school.
- About 840 million are malnourished.
- An estimated 1.3 billion people live on incomes of less than $1 per day.

There are some positive signs such as international migration and hard currency inflows as a result of workers' remittances. Thus, although India tops the world with its huge diaspora which sends billions of dollars back to the homeland, Bangladesh is not far behind either. India tops the charts with $ 9.3 billion, or one-sixth of all foreign workers' remittances, Bangladesh does not do too badly with $ 1.2 billion. Many of these workers are in the Middle East as also in South-East Asia and Europe. Yet, while India figures in the world's top fifteen nations for direct foreign investment and portfolio flows, Bangladesh drops completely out of sight.

Take another barometer of expanding economies and opportunities. Migration. The undocumented number of migrants are several times those who are documented, who come on visas and passports. The United States itself is home to not less than four million illegal aliens. There

18   Human Development Report 1999

are 700,000 of them in Malaysia of which not less than 70,000 are Bangladeshis.[19]

The number of illegal Indians and Bangladeshis in the United States and Britain are considerable. But the flow is not restricted to the rich West.

The *Independent*, a newspaper of Dhaka said that this situation was developing because Bangladesh found itself 'more and more overwhelmed with the problem of overpopulation and unemployment.'[20]

There is a growing acceptance and frankness about the outward movement of Bangladeshis to places such as the North East, West Bengal, New Delhi and other parts of India as well as to Pakistan. Indeed, the Bangladeshi migrant is moving illegally to new frontiers. With the tacit approval of host governments and communities, he is travelling to fast-developing countries such as Malaysia, as well as to one of the strongest economies in the world: Japan. These migrants include semi-skilled and unskilled workers as well as highly proficient specialists.[21]

These figures do not show up in Bangladeshi statistics. Nor do the remittances, or the movement to India. But there are ways of computing the number of people who have moved, with data from both countries.

In 1988, the Bangladesh Institute of Development Studies published a joint paper by three scholars who had studied poverty situation in the country. One of the issues they looked at was migration. Although out-migration to India did not figure, they referred to the size of the 'life

19 B.G. Verghese, *The North East Resurgent*, New Delhi: Konarak Publishers Pvt. Ltd., 1996
20 Ibid.
21 Interviews with Imtiaz Ahmed, New Delhi, and at Hikkedewa, Sri Lanka, 1998

time migrants' population in Bangladesh at four million (4.5 per cent of the enumerated population).[22]

One way to calculate the out-migration to India is to look at the history of Hindu and Muslim population growth, first in the area that is now Bangladesh and then in neighbouring Assam. In 1951, the population of East Pakistan was 41.9 million. Of this, 76.9 per cent was Muslim and 22 per cent was Hindu. The rest included Buddhists and Christians. In 1961, of a population of 50.8 million, the proportion of Muslims 80.4 per cent and that of Hindus fell to 18.5 per cent.

Every census year, the number of Muslims has risen, that of Hindus has fallen substantially. In 1974, the first census after the Liberation, Bangladesh counted 71.4 million people of which 85.4 per cent were Muslims and 13.5 per cent were Hindus. The proportions assumed greater disparity in the 1981 and 1991 censuses: 86.6 per cent for Muslims and 12.1 per cent for Hindus (1981) and 88.3 per cent for Muslims and 10.5 per cent for Hindus.

At the current rate of growth, it would not be surprising if the proportion of Hindus drops well below the double digit figure in the next years.

However, what makes these figures come alive is the fact that the physical number of Hindus have virtually remained at the same level for nearly thirty years. In 1991, the number of Muslims was placed at 93.8 million; that of Hindus was 11.1 million. In 1974, which was the first headcount after independence in 1971, the population of Hindus was 9.6 million. In 1981, it was 10.5 million. In 1991, it was barely 600,000 over the previous census. If

22   Atiq Rahman, Simeen Mahmud, Trina Haque, 'A Critical Review of the Poverty Situation in Bangladesh in the Eighties,' Bangladesh Institute for Development Studies, Dhaka, May 1988

we go to the pre-Liberation days, in 1961, there were not less than 9.3 million Hindus.

So, in reality, the population of Hindus has grown by a bare 1.6 million in 40 years. But if we take 1971 as the defining benchmark, then only about 1.5 more million Hindus have been born in these three decades. The Hindu rate of growth shows an erratic curve: a decadal growth rate of barely 3.1 per cent for 1974 which rises, unexplained, to 9.3 per cent in 1981 and crashes hugely again to 5.8 per cent in 1991. This means that in the 1970s, the growth rate per year was a bare 0.31 per cent, somewhat better at 0.93 per cent in 1981 and again extremely poor at 0.58 per cent in 1991.

Such figures defy demographic and common sense.

If we take an even earlier figure for Hindus and Muslims, we will find that the Hindu population has grown from 9.2 million in 1951 to 11.1 million in 1991 or just 1.9 million. This is impossibly low, given the 'Hindu rate of growth', according to R. Natarajan, one of our respected demographers. The Muslim population in this period increased from 32 million to 93 million, or an absolute increase of 61 million (nearly 300 per cent).

By no stretch of the imagination can it be argued that Hindus are less virile! Far from it, for they procreate at an alarming rate, all over the subcontinent, at Natarajan's 'Hindu rate of growth' of about 2.4 per cent per year or 24 per cent per decade. In the same space of time (1970s to 1991), a total of 32 million Muslims were added to the population at an overall growth rate of 24 per cent. Even to the most casual observer of the demographic scene, the inequality in these figures is obvious.

The 24 per cent decadal growth rate is held to be generally correct wherever Hindu populations exist, wherever they may be located. If we hold this as accurate, then taking the base figure of Hindus of 1974 (9.6 million), we are looking at a prospective population of approximately 14.7 million Hindus. But the census informs us, there are not more than 10.5 million. So where have these prospective numbers gone? No one is even suggesting for a moment that they have all converted to Islam or been butchered. The answer is much more simple: they have moved into India, which for better or worse, like it or not, is still viewed as the Hindu homeland.

This means that not less than four million Hindus who are missing have, to a near certainty, illegally settled in India.

The BJP likes to call them refugees. In my view, an immigrant who comes in illegally, without following the proper procedures, remains an illegal immigrant. The colour of his skin, or the faith he/she proclaims is not material, although those who have fled religious rioting have a better right to settlement that those who have just sneaked over.

One could quibble and say that these are 'Indian' figures. Let's look at what Meghna Guhathakurta, a Bangladeshi scholar, has to say about 'their' figures. 'The status of Hindus in Pakistan . . . became like "fishes in a water tank", as one Hindu milkman described his situation in the aftermath of a riot. In other words, they became hostages to the politics of the dominant society. They were kept alive' as long as the dominant society's interests were served, but were 'eaten' i.e. used as scapegoats or targets, whenever revenge was taken on India. 'Mass out-migration of Hindu population was estimated to be 5.3 million, or 538 persons per day since

1964, going as high as 703 persons per day during 1964-1971.'[23]

A study of laws in East Pakistan and Bangladesh which controlled 'enemy property and firms,' i.e. properties of Indians and then of Pakistanis who had left the country and vested powers in the national government to act as the custodian of such properties, showed that these have been extensively abused to pressure Hindus and force them to sell their lands at cheap prices or stop them from acquiring new land.[24] 'About 30 per cent of all Hindu households, or 10 out of 34 Hindu households, have been adversely affected by these laws,' it added.[25]

Guhathakurta, quoting this review of such laws, said, 'If there were no out-migration of Hindus from East Pakistan and Bangladesh during 1961-1991, there would have been 16.5 million Hindus in Bangladesh instead of the official figure of 11.2 million in the Bangladesh census of 1991. According to our calculation, a total of 5.3 million Hindus, i.e. on average 200,000 per year have gone "missing" during 1964-1991.'[26] The 200,000 figure seems to match with an Indian estimate, but the latter is for those crossing the border into West Bengal. Thus, it is likely to be an underestimate because it does not cover migrating Muslims.

In 1990, the Border Security Force detained more than 56,000 Bangladeshis trying to enter West Bengal. The rule of thumb for such outflows and seizures, say seasoned

---

23 Meghna Guhathakurta, Communal politics in South Asia and the Hindus of Bangladesh. Unpublished paper, 1999. Presented at Centre for Policy Research, New Delhi, Indo-Bangladesh Dialogue

24 Ibid.

25 Ibid.

26 Ibid.

security officials and diplomats, is that for every illegal person caught, four get through.[27] Their path is made easier if they are Hindu, or they pay a reasonable bribe to either side. There are other statistics too which give us an idea of the complexity of the problem as well as its scale.

Take Kurigram district which was a humble sub-division until the early 1980s. Its population has grown in a rather novel fashion. After registering a growth rate of nearly 80 per cent for the years 1961 to 1974, when its population soared from 4,80,903 to 1,291,325, it went up to 1,307,824, or a rate of barely 9 per cent for the period 1974 to 1981. Between 1981 and 1991, the numbers rose to 1,603,034, or a healthier 22.57 per cent.

If Kurigram had continued to grow at the rate of the 1960s, it should have had, in 1991, not less than 2,400,000 people, or about 800,000 people more than reported in the 1991 census. Of course, it lost substantial numbers to Lalmonihaat and Gaibanda which were hived off as separate districts. These statistics are not available to me, but interviews in Kurigram confirmed the view that many people migrated out of the area, into India and to other parts of Bangladesh, during the 1974 famine which was felt most severely there. This outflow continues to take place as we have seen earlier.

No wonder, even Bangladeshi academics such as Imtiaz Ahmed estimate the number of those crossing into India as substantial, no matter what the government at Dhaka says. Ahmed has estimated that 1.72 million people crossed illegally into India between 1961 and 1971, another half a million between 1971 and 1981

27 Ibid.

while not less than 600,000 crossed into Assam between 1981–1991.[28]

If we take his figures for Assam, then one would get an immigrant population of not less than 1.2 million which has come in after 1971, on the basis of 600,000 per decade.

This meshes with the figure provided by J.C. Bhuyan, a former Director of Census in the state. Bhuyan suggested in 1996, that with natural growth rate, the Muslim population of Assam should have grown from 3.59 million in 1971 to 5.2 million in 1991 instead of 6.3 million. He estimates the balance of 1.1 million as being illegal migrants. But this figure is flawed in its emphasis on the Muslim influx and omission of the statistics relating to Hindus.

Take another statistic for Bangladesh, that of voters' lists, a source of primary data in many countries. In 1973, the Bangladesh Election Commision said that there were 35.2 million voters. This increased to 38.36 million in 1979, 47.81 million in 1986, 49.81 million in 1988 and an all-time high of 62.18 million in 1991. The latter year was an election year which saw the end of President H.M. Ershad's reign and the return of the Bangladesh Nationalist Party under Begum Khaleda Zia.

The figures make no sense, especially the nearly 13 million increase in three years. One explanation was the massive rigging and inclusion of false names on the voters' lists during Ershad's time to ensure that his party

28 Hazarika, Sanjoy, Bangladesh and Assam: Land Pressures, Migration and Ethnic Conflict. American Academy of Arts and Sciences, University of Toronto, March 1993; Imtiaz Ahmed, Environmental Refugees, Reinventing Indo-Bangladesh Relations. Conference paper, December 1995.

returned to power. This did not work. In the 1996 elections, which saw the ouster of Begum Khaleda Zia and the induction of the Awami League under a woman leader, Sheikh Hasina Wajed, the number of voters fell from 62.18 million to 56.70 million, a drop of 5.48 million.

Where did these 5.48 million go? Where did they come from, in the first place? While a 1 to 3 per cent margin of error is acceptable, the 1991 list amounted to a discrepancy of nearly 10 per cent of the total population, making serious scholars question the quality of Bangladesh's electoral statistics, if not other data. Such unexplained 'gaps' make rigorous work that much more difficult.

The Indian Data

The office of the Registrar-General of India, better known as the Census of India, is tucked away in an unimpressive building of the British era, its offices filled with papers, files and computers. The style of the building does no credit to its importance: it looks little better than a military barrack. It is even more subdued when seen in the shadow of its giant neighbour, the opulent and sprawling Taj Mahal Hotel, its glittering five-star accomodation a place for the powerful and the wealthy to eat, drink, dance, sleep, conduct business and romance.

The Registrar-General's office does not merely house an accounting of the births and deaths in India. It compiles a vast number of statistics and social data relating to an exercise which takes place once every ten years, the Great Indian Census. In this endeavour, not less than one million people, largely government officers such as teachers, fan out across our towns and villages, seeking to interview every single man, woman and child living on the face of this country, on the very day they carry out their task.

Painstakingly, over the next years, every bit of data is collated from the village-level upwards, sent to the district and state headquarters, and then onto the Central office in New Delhi. They are checked for accuracy, fed into giant computers, analysed and then published, book by book, volume after volume. These volumes are a magnificent, low-priced tribute to the diversity of India. But equally important, they reflect the high sense of dedication and efficiency which exists in seemingly unimpressive offices.

In unpretentious English, one of the Registrar-General's documents of Assam sets out the basic facts and figures. To read it is like listening to a sonorous government official.

'Total population of Assam as per 1991 census is 22,414,322 including 11,657,989 males and 10,756,333 females.' Assam constituted a bare 2.65 per cent of India's total population and its geographical area of 78,438 square kilometres was 'a mere 2.39 per cent of the entire territory of the country.'[29] The average density of population per square kilometre was 286 with the highest being counted at Dhubri (470).

In decadal terms, the population growth was tabulated as 3.2 million in 1901, rising to 8.02 million soon after independence (1951), and then 10.8 million in the following census (1961), 14.6 million in 1971 and 22.4 million in 1991. As noted earlier, the census for 1981 did not take place because of the anti-Bangladeshi agitation.

---

29   These and other details are taken from various census documents of the Census of India, 1991, including Series 4 Assam (published by N.C. Dutta, Director, Census Operations, Assam, 1993)

The highest rates of growth in Assam were recorded between 1951 and 1971 when the population rose not less than 69.93 per cent or about 6.5 million. This is attributed to a sharp increase in migration from other parts of India as well as East Pakistan and Nepal. The subsequent increase of 53.26 per cent or about 26.63 per cent per decade for 1971-1991 does not appear large. In percentage terms, it is about 3 per cent higher than the all-India figure of 23.85 per cent.

The Census of India also publishes a series of volumes on migration data. These are extremely revealing documents—not in what they actually report but what they do not specifically disclose. Thus, the number of those resident in India who cited Bangladesh as their place of birth in 1981 was 4 million, excluding Assam, which did not have a census that year.

In 1991, the national figure dropped to 3,375,829. The highest contribution came from West Bengal which reported not less than 3.07 million people of Bangladeshi origin.[30] Assam reported just 288,109 people of Bangladeshi origin. What the reports do not say is whether people were born in Bangladesh and crossed over illegally, or whether they were born in pre-independent Bangladesh (i.e. East Pakistan), or whether they acquired citizenship legally, or not at all.

But there is other data which can help develop a better, more specific picture of these settlers. A key question is whether they have been in the state for under or over twenty years. We must remind ourselves that Bangladesh itself was born in 1971.

30 Census of India, 1991, Series 4, West Bengal, Migration Tables, Volume 1, June 1998.

According to the 1991 Census, those who gave their last place of residence as Bangladesh and who had lived in Assam for over twenty years were 1,98,460 persons, of which 1,08,594 were men. Another 16,200 had lived in Assam for between ten to nineteen years and of this a majority (8,920) were women. Those who had stayed in the state for less than ten years numbered about 12,000.

The largest number of those who acknowledged being born in Bangladesh were from the districts of Nogaon in Central Assam (43,171), Cachar (34,011), Karimganj (28,548), Kamrup (21,692), Bongaigaon (21,195) and Barpeta (20,470). Dhubri was some places behind with 13,202, after Darrang and Sonitpur. It is not without significance that the high population increases which we have discussed in earlier chapters, especially of Muslims, are from some of these very districts. These are official figures, culled from the heavy tomes of the Registrar-General of India, whose teams across the country undertake one of the most remarkable feats of mathematical, social and economic data-collection in the world—the Indian census. There is nothing which matches it in scale and scope barring the Chinese census. One can hardly expect Bangladeshis to acknowledge their nationality to Indian government officials. But more than 26,000 did so in 1991 in Assam. Yet, how many of those who did not spoke the truth?

As far back as the 1961 Census of India, the official report for Assam on migration said, 'Our experience during enumeration as well as during tabulation is that people did not correctly give their place of birth and so the interpretation of the data is very limited. True migration is often artificially deflated and remigration to place of birth is masked. It appears that the people who mostly concealed their birth place are those coming from East Pakistan.'[31] The report added: 'The slips in my Tabulation Office indicate that the Hindus gave their birth-place correctly, but among the Muslims almost everyone gave his birth-place as Assam.'

It says further that where the number of Muslim migrants cannot be 'ascertained from migration data, they have been netted from the religion data. So the demographic question relating to religion still has immense value and cannot be dispensed with as has been suggested in some quarters.'

The official report remarked that Goalpara district (since divided into the districts of Dhubri and Goalpara) is 'a sort of temporary halting place for some people who have come here from outside Assam and that these people again moved into the Upper Assam region after a temporary stay here. (This) heavy immigration and emigration together with the heavy density of population in this district completely prove that a big number of people must have come into the district from other parts of the subcontinent and that many of the figures of birth-place as given in the Individual Slip (a part of the census exercise to gather details about the individual) are mostly incorrect, if not completely false.

'Similarly, in the case of Cachar district, the same story is repeated though on a lesser scale.' It further quotes from 'A Note on Migration in the Eastern Border States' penned by S.P. Jain, described as the Census Actuary and Deputy Registrar-General, India.

Jain spoke of 'abnormally high growth rates of

31 Census of India, 1961, Registrar-General of India, New Delhi 1964, Chapter V.

Muslims . . . and of Hindus' (in 1961 over 1951). 'Generally speaking, they are on borders of adjoining districts. The magnitude of the rate of growth in each case leaves little doubt that there was a very substantial influx of Hindus and Muslims. The source must be East Pakistan as is shown in what follows. Every district in Assam (except two) and in West Bengal (except four) shows that the growth rate of Muslims was well above 27.5 per cent. Similarly, the growth rate for Hindus was well above 25 per cent in every district in Assam (except two) and in West Bengal (except three) . . . these growth rates nearly represent the upper limits and increases above them should be ascribed to infiltration.'

There is truth and wisdom in these words. They remain valid to this day, and Myron Weiner was only echoing their advice when he suggested the strategy of focussing on religious data for this book.

But why take religion as a basis for deciding the scale and issue of migration? The idea grew out of a conversation with him. Myron and I were sitting with another scholar, Thomas Tad Homer-Dixon from Canada, on the lawns outside the India International Centre in New Delhi.

It was a crisp winter morning in 1995 and both Myron and Tad were visiting South Asia for different workshops. Myron had written a book which partly dealt with Assam in 1978 called *Sons of the Soil: Migration and Ethnic Conflict in India*. Some even credited this piece of writing with inspiring the student movement and the later unrest. In it, Myron had analysed the Assam situation at the time and defined large-scale migration into the state as a reason for its high population growth (34.7 per cent between

1961 and 1971).

Tad had earlier asked me to do a study on migration into Assam from Bangladesh for the joint project run by Toronto University and the American Academy of Arts and Sciences at Cambridge, Massachussetts. Given this background, they had an interest in the project, especially Myron.

Myron pulled up his chair and leaned forward to emphasize a point. His face, the forehead furrowed with lines and surrounded by a greying crown of thinning hair, lit up with enthusiasm as he examined my outline. 'Sanjoy, I would concentrate very strongly on the religion figures.' I asked why. There were other statistics relating to urban/rural population, to the size of the electorate, to income levels which were surely as relevant.

The response was quick and unambiguous. 'People tend to lie about most things—their age, their wives, even the school they went to. Very few people lie about their religion.'

To get close to the truth, we would need to match religious data against birth place and actual growth rates.

Keramat Bhai and his associates have asserted that they were enrolled on voters' lists but never identified as Bangladeshis. Therefore, one can say with some confidence that the number of Bangladeshis who gave their place of birth as that country and who have lived for less than twenty years in Assam at the time of the Census is but a fraction of the real figure.

The 1991 census data for West Bengal also looked at the number of people who had given Bangladesh as their last place of residence. This is a total of 2.63 million. Of this figure, those who say they have been in the Indian state for ten to nineteen years is half a million (or 520,208 to be exact); those who say they have been for more than twenty years is 15.06 million. Those who had been in West Bengal for less than ten years were about half a million, according to the Census.

Again, there can be little doubt that those from Bangladesh are unlikely to identify themselves as such in vast numbers for fear of the wrath of the state and of simple harassment. Thus, again the 2.63 million figure appears to be an underestimate but not too far off the mark. It is certainly closer to the truth than the numbers for Assam. The Bengal figure is likely to be in the range of above 3 million.

There is another set of figures which we must consider when we look at migration from Bangladesh. These are statistics presented by the Government of West Bengal to the Supreme Court of India in January 1999.

West Bengal has a border with Bangladesh of more than 2,400 kilometres. In its response to a writ petition filed by the All India Forum for Civil Liberties against the Government of India and others (which include West Bengal, Assam and Mizoram), the state declared first that not less than 1.02 million Bangladeshis (including 667,500 Hindus and 349,738 Muslims) had overstayed their official visas) between 1972 and 1998.[32]

Secondly, it said that a detection drive had expelled just over half a million Bangladeshis of which over 400,000 were Muslim and 1,61,077 were Hindus.

---

32 This and subsequent data related to this petition is based on the Supplementary Affidavit/Status Report on behalf of The State of West Bengal filed in the Supreme Court by S.S. Rakshit, Joint Secretary, Home (Political) of the State Government, January 1999

This may cause some confusion. There are two sets of findings here: one, that more Hindus than Muslims overstayed their official welcome and settled in West Bengal; two, of those who were detected and deported, a majority was Muslim, suggesting strongly that more Muslims than Hindus come into the state illegally.

If we take even a 3:1 ratio for those not apprehended against those who have been caught, this makes for over one million Bangladeshi Muslims in West Bengal and about half a million Hindus who would be illegally resident in the state. These figures show that both streams of migration are taking place at the same time: legal and illegal, with large numbers of those in the former category also preferring to jump ship, once they have docked safely, and found their bearings. It would not be inaccurate to note that the number of Muslims detected who had come illegally was about three times that of the Hindus. Even by a conservative estimate, in West Bengal, one could have not less than 1.5 million illegals of both communities plus the 1.2 million who overstayed and vanished. This brings the figure close to 3 million just for that one state alone.

To get a national figure, one would have to add the missing Hindus of Bangladesh who have moved into India, primarily eastern India, plus the figures for Assam, other north-eastern states and as well as Bihar, Orissa, Maharashtra and New Delhi. The figure may not be less than 14 million. Governor S.K. Sinha of Assam quoted Home Minister, Indrajit Gupta as reporting to Parliament that there were 10 million migrants resident in India.[33] Governor Sinha in his report to the President of India in 1998, on the problem of illegal migration to Assam

---

33   Home Minister's statement 6 May 1997.

quoted from *India Today*. The latter had quoted Intelligence and Home Ministry sources for the following break-up of illegal migrants: West Bengal 5.4 million, Assam 4.0 million, Tripura 0.8 million, Bihar 0.5 million, Maharashtra 0.5 million, Rajasthan 0.5 million, and Delhi 0.3 million.[34]

The West Bengal government complained, 'Enquiries held at the addresses of their Indian referees (for visa holders) have revealed that in a majority of cases such addresses are either fictitious or that the Bangladeshi has never visited his referee after coming to India.' Not only this, but local people neither resisted the ingress of the outsiders nor cooperated with local authorities in detecting them.

While we are on the subject of numbers, let us consider another one which has been brought up by the Election Commission. In 1999, the Election Commission devised a strategy for Assam to pin down voters who could not give adequate proof of their identity and of their origins. It did so in response to the consistent demand by the students union (All Assam Students Union) to crack down on illegal settlers who were finding their way into voting lists, as they had been for decades.

A revision of the electoral rolls turned up not less than 320,000 persons of doubtful origin, who should not, in the view of the Election Commission, be allowed to vote. 'Most of them are Muslim, most of them are Bengali-speaking and none of them could give a clear explanation of how they came to be where they were,' said one senior Election Commission official. A check of references they gave for relatives and villages turned out to

---

34   Governor Sinha's report to the President, 1998

be false, as the officials in West Bengal too had found with many other cases.

Identifying foreigners is as much a question of legal procedure as anything else: the local police must file cases against these persons for giving false information to public servants, for entering the country illegally and for trying to get on to voters' lists. In other words, throw the book at them, including the Foreigners Act, and disenfranchise them till 2026, while allowing them to continue their economic activities.

These immigrants must be identified, registered and located in the areas where they are currently working. They should not be harassed but should simply not be allowed to move elsewhere, by making it mandatory for them to report to police stations every month and having the local authorities check on their residences. There is little point in trying to deport them. Bangladesh will not have them; in which case where can they be sent?

These measures may sound harsh and sweeping. But there are few soft options left. However, cases of immigrants and those of their descendants should be reviewed after 2026, when the proposed delimitation of parliamentary constituencies is to take place.

One would also need to assess what the 320,000 figure of 'doubtful voters' actually adds up to. There are usually two voters in a family of five or six, the average size of a family in India and Bangladesh. This means that for every person on the list there could be at least two others, who have not been registered. A simple calculation here brings up a figure of approximately 640,000 additional 'others' or a total of about one million people of 'doubtful' descent in the state.

An analysis of Assam's data for the growth of various

religious communities since 1947 is also instructive.

Between 1951 and 1961, Hindus grew at the rate of 33.96 per cent or from 5.8 million to 7.8 million. Between 1961 and 1971, their population rose from 7.8 million to 10.6 million, or at a rate of 34.76 per cent. Between 1971 and 1991 (at the risk of boring readers, let me repeat again that there was no census in 1981 because of the student agitation.) the Hindu population grew to 15.04 million, or a rate of 41.61 per cent over 20 years (decadal average of 20.85 per cent).

In the same period, the Muslim population went from 1.9 million in 1951 to 2.7 million in 1961 (a growth of 38.56 per cent); then to 3.5 million in 1971 (a growth rate of 29.96 per cent) and to 6.37 million in 1991, a jump of 77.33 per cent compared to the Hindu rate of 41.61 per cent. That works out at 38.62 per cent for each decade between 1971 and 1991. Or a rise that is comparable only to the period 1951–1961.

This is why it is hardly surprising that Assam is one of the three states in the country where Muslims number more than 20 per cent of the population. The other two are West Bengal and Kerala—there are historic factors behind this presence in Kerala, especially with large-scale migration of Muslims from neighboring states in the mediaeval period and Arab settlers.

Thus, the population of Assam has risen from about 8.5 million in 1951 to about 11.6 million a decade later; in 1971 it was more than 14.7 million.

Sharifa Begum remarks in an essay[35] that as many as 3.5 million people left East Pakistan for India between

---

35   Birth rate and death rate in Bangladesh, 1951-74, Bangladesh Institute of Development Studies (BIDS), 1974, Dhaka

1951 and 1961, the figure for 1961–1974 was placed by Sharifa Begum at 1.5 million. This underestimates the large number of Hindus and Muslims who fled that country in 1970-71 during the brutal crackdown on East Pakistan by West Pakistan. That tragedy led to the birth of Bangladesh; of nearly 10 million refugees who had left East Pakistan for security reasons, nearly 9 million returned to a new country: Bangladesh.

At least 1 million, both Hindus and Muslims, stayed back in India.

During the period after 1974, Begum also said that Bangladesh had lost substantial proportion of its population 'during migration and the famine of 1974-75.'[36]

Shapan Adnan, a Bangladeshi scholar, remarked in 1998 that while there is 'virtually no reliable data on the number and characteristics of all international migrants from (and to) Bangladesh,' there was also enough material at the micro-level to indicate 'a periodic exodus of the Hindu community to India in the past 40 years . . . Furthermore, cross-border out-migration of both Hindus and Muslims to India or Pakistan are reported to have taken place in recent decades from areas where poverty and landlessness have increased.'[37]

Adnan sketched this out further in his essay. Speaking of the hypothesis of extensive out-migration from Bangladesh, he describes this as 'not implausible' and that these are consistent with media reports of the 'existence of

---

36 Population, birth, death and growth rates in Bangladesh: census estimates, BIDS, Dhaka, 1990
37 Shapan Adnan, 'Fertility decline under absolute poverty: paradoxical aspects of demographic change in Bangladesh, *Economic and Political Weekly*, 30 May 1998.

men, women and children from Bangladesh in the slums, jails, brothels and other settlements of major cities of South Asia like Calcutta, Bombay and Karachi.'

Adnan postulates that this outflow is unlikely to affect Bangladesh's population growth to any significant level. That of course, is questionable for it has created such pressures outside of Bangladesh as we have noted and remains an explosive issue in India's East. But he makes a significant point about why people leave Bangladesh when he remarks that their movement out of the country 'provides an indicator of the desperation they must have faced before their departure. Unlike those who are sufficiently well off to be able to migrate abroad through formal channels for salaried jobs and education, these are very poor people who have, so to speak, walked across the porous international borders of the region.'

What has made people move is 'the desperate search for a means of livelihood . . . In principle, the socio-economic pressures generating this kind of international out-migration are unlikely to have been very different from those propelling internal out-migration by the poor, particularly to the cities.'

These views are backed up by international specialists. The World Watch Institute remarked in a major study in 1999 that 'population-induced land scarcity in Bangladesh led to conflicts that drove more than 10 million refugees into adjacent Indian states. These land-hungry Bengalis in turn exacerbated land shortages in the Indian states—leading to ongoing violent conflict.'[38]

Readers could be forgiven for believing that this

---

38 Brown, Lester, R., Gary Gardener and Brian Halweil, *Beyond Malthus: Nineteen Dimensions of the Population Challenge*, W.W. Norton Company, New York, 1999, p 98

passage could have come from the sharp-tongued Mullen of the 1931 Assam census fame. These words have been penned by Messrs. Lester R. Brown, Gary Gardener and Brian Halweil, three distinguished American environmental and social scientists.

If we follow the thumb rule of illegal migration through religious composition, we should look at the Muslim data.

The Muslim population has risen sharply in other north-eastern states, most spectacularly in the hill states of Arunachal Pradesh and Mizoram. These states reported a 135 per cent and 105 per cent increase in their small groups of Muslim resident between the 1981 and 1991 censuses. In the former, the numbers grew from 5,073 to 11,922 and in Mizoram from 2,205 to 4,538. Nagaland, Meghalaya, Tripura and Manipur reported growth rates of between 34 per cent to nearly 75 per cent. Only one state, Sikkim, reported a growth rate of less than 20 per cent. It was also the only state in the whole country to record such a low rate for this religious group.

In 1978, the Chief Election Commissioner of India, S.L. Shakdher, a slight Kashmiri Pandit, announced at the meeting of state electoral officers that Assam's alarming rise in population was 'attributed to the influx of a very large number of persons from the neighbouring countries.'

In the first categorical and brutal assessment by a senior Indian public servant on the migration problem in many years, Shakdher sounded a wake-up call to the country.

'The influx has become a regular feature. I think it

may not be a wrong assessment to make, on the basis of the increase of 34.98 per cent between the two censuses, then increase that is likely to be recorded in the 1991 census would be more than 100 per cent over the 1961 census. In other words, a stage would be reached when the State would have to reckon with the foreign nationals who may constitute a sizeable percentage, if not the majority of the population of the state.' Without mincing words, he added: 'Another disturbing factor in this regard is the demand made by the political parties for the inclusion in the electoral rolls of the names of such migrants who are not Indian citizens, without even questioning and properly determining the citizenship status.'

The IMDT Figures

Here, again, it is important to refer to the failure of the IMDT. It is worth bringing the figures listed earlier up to date. According to an affidavit filed by the Assam government[39] in September 1999, a total of 302,554 inquiries were initiated under the Act. Nearly all of them were completed and only 31,264 were referred to the tribunals for review and action. Half of these have been completed and only 9,625 were declared as illegal migrants. Of this figure, only 1,461 were physically deported. One would not be surprised if all 1,461 have since returned and are working industriously in different parts of India!

The governments, both in the states as well as at the

---

39   Affidavit on Behalf of State of Assam in the Matter of All India Lawyers
     Forum for Civil Liberties and Another versus Union of India and Others,
     1 September 1999 (for details, see Appendices)

Centre, cite inadequate forces as a constraint in tackling the inflow. But this problem cannot be handled by the police or by the normal law and order machinery. It needs much more, namely a vision for the region, and a practical step-by-step approach to make it a reality. Even steps being taken to identify immigrants run into problems, given the local political interests need of vote banks. The Congress Party has been most vociferous on this for its believes it stands to lose the most. It claims that the repeal of the IMDT would harm minorities.

Is the Congress the *thekedar* of 'minority' interests, in Assam or anywhere else? It has the advantage of being a party that has bent over backwards in the past thirty years to accommodate Muslim interests. This happened because the Muslims had little other choice. These days, that is changing both in Assam and in West Bengal. It is not just the 'secularists' who have 'minority' support; it is the regionalists and local groups, as well as the BJP to a lesser degree, that are wooing and winning this constituency. No single party or political alliance has the divine right to speak on behalf of any community, much less that of a state and a country.

Minority groups need to ask themselves and their leaders if their interests are best served by allying just with one political group. Even the United Minorities Front, which was set up in the 1980s and includes both Hindus (Bengali-speakers and others) and Muslims, now seeks accomodation on the issues that have grown around the IMDT. This is a good sign and can reduce the animosity that has existed for decades. Those animosities once erupted at the time of the Nellie massacres. They can still be ignited, for many hates still linger, in hiding for the moment perhaps, but waiting for a time to strike.

Knotty problems such as that of migration and of land pressures, which are aligned to many other factors—economic, environmental, social and political—need breathing space if they are to be tackled with any hope of success. Dialogue on all fronts, with all groups, including Bangladesh and its leaders then, holds the key. Without understanding the deeper issues and disseminating that understanding widely, efforts to address these key questions will remain at best short-term and thus doomed to failure.

A good gesture from Bangladesh has been the repeal of the Vesting of Properties and Assets Order (1972), which has been long resented by Hindus.

It is worth closing here with a visual that can bring to life dry statistics, especially the intelligence estimate which places the number of Bangladeshis in the Delhi/New Delhi area at not less than 300,000.

One would urge those who live near, or in the capital of India, to go near Pragati Maidan. Drive across the smelly, evil-looking Jamuna, corrupted and diseased by the muck and filth of millions of people and thousands of industries, large and small, along its banks. A smooth, Japanese-built bridge takes vehicles from the city centre.

Look at the river. A scene straight out of Assam and Bangladesh plays for us: giant fishing nets, placed on bamboo poles, rest easily here, raised or lowered by pressure from a leg. This is an enduring sight in Bangladesh as well as in Bengal. So is it of the Brahmaputra and its tributaries in Assam. But which

Assamese fisherman would come so far to cast his net, on the Jamuna? The Assamese are perhaps the least socially mobile of all major communities of South Asia.

CHAPTER FOURTEEN

Seeking Partnership, Renouncing Confrontation

The Bangladesh Foreign Minister, Abdus Samad Azad, once told a workshop on refugee and migratory movements that people who are 'determined to leave their countries for other places, for whatever reasons, will go to incredible lengths to achieve their objective.'[1]

Azad clarified his country's position on such migrations:

'The plight of undocumented migrants is a very real one and can neither be ignored nor be glossed over. It has to be addressed. We fully respect the sovereignty of all states to decide on their own immigration laws and procedures. There are certain aspects, however, that need to be highlighted in respect of undocumented migrants. Firstly, they are, by definition, daring, hardy and hardworking. Secondly by the very fact of their being undocumented or irregular in status, they cannot be a burden on the country of their destination and subsist at the expense of the taxpayer. They live in perpetual fear of

---

1   Fourth Informal Consultation on Refugee and Migratory Movements in South Asia, Dhaka, 10-11 November 1997

discovery but also work for a living, often for long hours and at reduced wages. In other words they are often subject to exploitation. Such people still manage to send remittances to their home country, which in turn have important effects.

'An international regime to manage migration or aimed at an orderly movement of peoples could possibly be an agenda of the future or even today. Bodies like the Commission on Global Governance and the Trilateral Commission have also evinced interest in an international framework to manage migration pressures more effectively. A buzz-word today is globalization and if this is to mean liberalization in the movements of goods, services and capital across national frontiers, then the question of movement of labour could also be a part of the international agenda.'

In May 2000, Sadako Ogata, the then United Nations High Commissioner for Refugees (UNHCR), made a landmark statement in New Delhi. The UNHCR chief spoke of the need to recognize the problem of what she defined as 'mixed migrations across national borders'[2] as one of the 'greatest challenges confronting all of us—including India.'

The dimunitive Japanese woman, who has become an internationally-recognized figure with her presence in refugee hot spots such as Rwanda and the Balkans, mingling with victims of violence, also asserted that nations while fulfilling obligations to genuine political refugees must also 'separate those fleeing from persecution or conflict, and those seeking economic

---

2   On the Humanitarian Frontiers. Lecture by Sadako Ogata, United Nations High Commissioner for Refugees, New Delhi, 5 May 2000

betterment.'[3] Her words lie at the heart of any search for a solution to the problem of the Malthusian flood of migrants from across the border in Bangladesh, Nepal and other parts of South and South-East Asia.

Take the impact of a small outflow from a neighbouring country into a small frontier state of India, Mizoram. This little state, with borders with Myanmar, plays host to about 20,000 economic migrants from Myanmar as well as a handful of political activists from there. The refugees in Mizoram—known political activists—are not more than about 100; a substantial number of these have been given identity cards by the local government to prevent harassment by police and Mizo public organizations.

The latter, led by the powerful Young Mizo Association, want the Burmese out of their region, accusing them of fomenting civil disturbances and organizing illicit stills, theft and drug running. Most of the migrants are of the Chin community, who are racially, linguistically, as well as by faith, (they are largely Christian) of the same stock as the Mizos. The majority are handloom weavers, labourers and domestics; some are petty traders, and few even have tea shops and restaurants. While some may be criminals, most are peaceful men and women, seeking to eke out a living with their traditional skills.

These include people who are born in Myanmar but see no problem in relocating themselves in Mizoram. I have personally met Mizos from Myanmar who came over to Aizawl in 1986 after a twenty-year-old Mizo insurgency against India ended. They were working with

3   Ibid.

the Mizo National Front, the Mizo insurgent group, then based in the Chin state of Myanmar. And when the other Mizos returned, they too went along and settled in Mizoram!

The population of Mizoram is about 700,000; it is supporting a migrant population of Chins and also of Chakmas from Bangladesh. While there are indigenous Chakmas, the rapid increase in population has placed them under suspicion of the dominant Mizos. The Chakmas are Buddhist, ethnically different and easy to spot.

As far as the Chins are concerned, the UNHCR recognizes and supports another 650 as Burmese political refugees in New Delhi, and there are demands from another 150 for refugee status. Even these figures are disputed by Burmese political exiles based in India, some of whom say that the actual number of refugees in New Delhi should not be more than 300. The others, they assert, are economic migrants who want to use their refugee status as a bargaining tool to get to a third country, preferably the United States, Australia, or Europe.

The problem is complicated by the involvement of Indian intelligence agencies such as the Intelligence Bureau, the Research and Analysis Wing, the Subsidiary Special Bureau and Military Intelligence, as well as the local state intelligence groups which seek information and leverage among the exiles, especially the political activists and military cadres based in North East India. Some of these groups are used as 'spotters' (security agents to identify hostile groups and individuals) and paid for their services—to check for information such as troop movements and other details of strategic interest.

Thus, even a small area like Mizoram shows the need to develop what Ms Ogata described, namely 'clear, recognized and practical mechanisms to separate those fleeing from persecution or conflict, and those seeking economic betterment . . .'[4] The movement out of Bangladesh represents more of the latter, even though the outflow of religious minorities is also a factor.

Let us look here a bit more closely at what she has to say because it is a good summation of some of the points I have made earlier.

'In much of the Asia region, and in South Asia in particular, the demarcation of the boundaries of newly independent nations, emerging from colonial rule, was often arbitary. The delineation of international borders by colonial powers, in many cases, took little account of the geographical and historical realities, of and past linkages of community and kinship between them. As a result, national borders have become porous in nature and difficult to secure. Morever, the ethnic, linguistic or religious affinity of communities has led to constant cross border movements of a significant scale. These include people migrating for economic reasons but also refugees and asylum seekers . . . Today . . . greater economic competition for limited resources is resulting in a hardening of social divisions. In many countries, this has been translated into an urge for a greater demarcation of communal or national boundaries, as each community and social group struggle to asset their access to resources and to defend their shrinking space.'[5]

Thus, the tolerance thresholds of host communities

---

4   Ibid.
5   Ibid.

shrink as the space for accomodation is eroded, setting the stage for social conflagrations.

Of course, we have the doubters like Shekhar Aiyar, who wrote an edit page article in the *Times of India*, 'Not numbers alone: enhancing quality of human capital.'[6] Shekhar, who teaches at Brown University in the United States and was an outstanding scholar, at St Stephens', Delhi, and then at Oxford University, debunks the Malthusian nightmare, declaring that the old man was wrong, just as all those who believe that larger, poorer populations are swamping other communities are shooting off the mark.

According to Shekhar, Thomas Malthus' theory that 'population growth would easily outrun the extra food available, leading to famine, mass deaths and a return to the original situation' is erroneous. Today, Malthusian arguments usually bemoan the fact that as numbers grow 'we will run out of something or the other—trees, coal or oil—and at that point we will face catastrophies of shortage and misery.' But, this, says Shekhar, overlooks the 'perennial inventiveness of humans' and the fact that as a resource grows scarce, 'its price rises quickly, leading to redoubled and invariably successful attempts to develop an alternative resource.'

Fair enough. But what is the alternative to land? As numbers grow, yes, we can improve food productivity, land use as well as distribution. But we cannot grow more land although that inestimable provider of joy and bounty, carrier of hope and tragedy, the Brahmaputra, and its numerous allies bring down silt and help 'grow land' in Assam and Bangladesh. Even these great friends

---

6   Shekhar Aiyar, *Times of India*, 13 September, 2000

have their limitations.

Yes, we need to develop non-land, non-agriculture-based economies, especially those relating to information technology. But if you have a shortage of land, an extremely impoverished rural population and money concentrated in the hands of a rich elite, then you have problems which 'enhancing the quality of human capital' alone will not help to solve. Land prices do rise quickly and this resource goes to those who can afford to buy it, or capture it by force.

Land is the resource over which different communities fight for it represents both a source of identity-formation and the last hope of economic security, if not survival. Where then are the alternatives in real time, in real places, for real people? Job creation in non-land-based activities is one, and this is an area of investment for domestic and international industry. This is unlikely to happen in large parts of South Asia for several more decades because of the reasons we have discussed throughout this book: the lack of infrastructure, the lack of growing incomes, local and regional disparities, the lack of adequate nutrition and the continuing gender bias.

What is the option? You pack up and go next door to where land appears to be a more equitable resource—or so it seems to you—and not under the kind of pressure that is faced at home. You inflict or carry the problems that you faced in your original home on a new community or set of communities, on new land.

A chapter in a recent World Watch book begins with these words: 'While economists tout record-breaking increases in global commerce in recent decades, more sobering statistics are being put forth by the world's leading biologists: the loss of living species in recent decades, they report, represents the largest mass extinction since the dinosaurs were wiped out 65 million years ago.'[7]

So, how far was Malthus off the mark? Not very, I would say.

Immigration Revisited

Immigration is a dynamic force internationally. Immigrants are a worldwide resource. They are changing the demographics of nations as economically, politically and militarily as powerful as the United States. It has been predicted with some certainty that the 'browning' of America is a fact and that in the not very distant future, the whites will become a minority. This is a recognition of all population flows and growth in the world. Indian-Americans number more than 1.5 million in the country of their adoption and they have the highest average household income of any Asian ethnic group. They are leaders in business, but especially in high tech industries, particularly information technology. The Hispanics or Latinos, those who speak Spanish fluently and are of Central and South American stock, now number 12 per cent of the population and their proportion in the US population is expected to go up to 25 per cent by 2050!

Every year, according to William Frankel, about a million people emigrate to the United States. Seventy per cent of them come legally. Thirty per cent 'will either have crossed a border surreptitiously or overstayed a visa

---

7   Hilary French, *Vanishing Borders: Protecting the Planet in the Age of Globalization*, World Watch Institute, W.W. Norton, 2000

limitation. In the case of the latter, the immigration authority is notoriously ineffective in rounding them up.'[8]

What Frankel does not say, but which is widely accepted, is that many of these illegal aliens are forced to work as daily wage labourers on farms, or in sweat shops as low-paid labour by unscrupulous employers who threaten to turn them in to the authorities should they squeal about their conditions. In numerous cases, the employers are their own kin or 'countryfolk', who have done reasonably well in life but are not above bending or twisting the law in order to do better.

Frankel makes another important point here—that the diasporas are forcing Americans to speak of 'multiculturalism', and no longer of assimilation. But a time will come, he warns, when ethnic assertions of separate identities will not be as easily tolerated as they are now and critics of immigration 'now unheeded, are likely in time to find more support.'

There are two timely warnings here: one, that while the force of numbers, of demography, will change politics and social conditions, they will also lead to clear assertions of separateness. Two, that even in developed countries, the walls against immigrants have gone up. Indeed, they have been up for many years and the far right in Europe and the United States, not leaving aside Africa, Asia and Australia, are poised to make major gains everywhere. Globalization does not necessarily mean that countries and peoples shed their ethnic and cultural biases along with tariffs.

The North East of India is a good glass bowl in which

---

8   William Frankel, 'Immigrants are a Powerful Force,' *Statesman*, Calcutta, 25 March 2000

to observe such developments. It is home to many splendoured, complex, even exotic, communities. In an extremely heterogenous and ethnically sensitive society, where the redressal of one group's grievances is seen as an assault on the concerns of another, these demands for small separatenesses will grow—but they will be marginalized by the numerically larger groups, whether it is the Assamese-speaking Hindus or the Bengali-speaking Bengalis, Hindus or Muslims. This is a reality and protecting these groups will become a major task, not merely of governments but of those very communities themselves. The most transparent and appropriate way of given true protection is to provide better governance, that brings about economic equity as well as meets basic needs. This must be backed up by a legal and constitutional framework that is sensitive to local concerns and accomodates them to the maxmimum degree.

Constitutions can be changed. They have been amended scores of times, as in the case of India. But the boundaries of a nation remain immutable. Millions of people, voting with their feet, may not recognize that. Their movement does not change the fact that a border exists. Indeed, their migration reinforces that reality, for it means that they have to resort to unfair means to cross a boundary and enter a different country. They may have made it legally. But they have chosen not to because they do not want to, and because they find this form of moving easier, even if it is riskier.

The worst way of 'protecting' identities is through the barrel of a gun. This alternative leaves no victors, only losers. Yet, this has been tried again and again in different parts of the world, including India's North East, with brutal results. Take the cases of the Kashmiris and the

Nagas, the Tamils of Sri Lanka, the Rwandans and Burundis, and the Bosnians, Croats and Serbs. The list goes on. The burial shrouds are endless, the cemeteries and cremation grounds are full.

The State strikes back, determined to protect its interests.

The majoritarian groups strike back, determined not to lose what they believe is theirs by right. The latter strategy can take the shape of preferential policies for their own groups, economic disincentives for others, and political alliances that give rise to blocks of sympathetic voters and supporters. This is notable in those espousing regional growth through regional parties, saying these are more sympathetic to local concerns. Yet, experience has shown in the past twenty years in India, that a regional government is not necessarily more efficient, sensitive to local demands or less corrupt than 'national party' governments. The key lies in whether that party or political coalition can bring about better governance. This has not happened in most states, barring limited areas of southern and western India. The hype always belies reality.

How can we bring about better governance? Clearly, one way is by devolving power to the lowest unit of government so that people are encouraged to develop a stake in running their own affairs instead of depending on the sarkar at the district, state, or national level to do things for them. This is an extremely difficult task as is shown in those Indian states (Bihar and Assam to name two) which refused to hold local body elections for years, despite court orders to them. They defied court rulings and the Constitution as well, for it is laid down specifically in the Great Book that such elections must be held every five years. Unless we develop ways of dispossessing such recalcitrant state governments of those powers which harms the Constitution and local governance, the changes which we seek will remain just that—in the realm of the sought.

It is local governance which will give us a more sensitive response to the problems of local conflict and representation of ethnic, religious and linguistic communities. This does not mean that we should not develop a national, even regional, macro-approach to these problems. We must. But the problems will have to be solved at the micro-level, where the action really takes place.

Migrants, refugees and internally displaced people are among the world's most vulnerable communities. There are three basic bonds that bind them:[9]

1. Disruption: Most have left behind the support of traditional values, extended families, friends, and familar ways of life. With limited means, they face new and uncertain situations.

2. Differences: Culture and language often set them apart from their new neighbours.

3. Difficulties of Access: Many are ineligible for health care benefits, are unfamiliar with family planning programmes, and unable to obtain information easily.

Over and above these concerns, migrants and migration, especially international migration, has become a 'critical issue for countries of South Asia, as it involves

9 Population Reports, Series J, Number 45, Family Planning Programmes, October 1998

more and more themes of nations and nationalism, particularly post-colonial nationhood in a region marked by massive population flows.'[10]

Note that phrase at the end: massive population flows.

The numbers we have spoken about in this book are huge. They may appear small if you compare them to the size of India's population or that of China, each over a billion strong. But the size of just the 'missing' Bangladeshi population is the equivalent of seven Bhutans, or nearly a quarter of Nepal.

Refugee Watch, a magazine which reports on conditions of refugee groups in different parts of the world with a special focus on South Asia, has commented that a study of South Asia's immigration problem would show 'how the flow of unwanted migrants and refugees results in the marginalisation of the nation—the nation they leave, the nation they enter.'[11]

Some suggestions for tackling these outflows lie in the UNHCR's document, *The State of the World's Refugees*, 1995, which spoke of the need to implement the 20:20 compact wherein donor nations pledged to earmark at least 20 per cent of their aid budgets and recipient states devote at least 20 per cent of their national budgets to human priority concerns, including basic education, primary health care and the provision of safe drinking water.

Other points which it stressed, included creating a UN administered human security fund to combat international problems such as environmental pollution,

10 *Refugee Watch*, South Asia Forum for Human Rights and Mahariban Calcutta Research Group, Calcutta, December 1998
11 Ibid.

natural resource depletion and communicable disease, financed by cuts in military spending and other financial allocations. A third point which has special relevance was to broaden the 'notion' of development cooperation between the West and low-income countries to include resource transfers such as private investment, trade, labour migration and debt payments as well as ODA (Overseas Development Assistance) allocations.

The Big Picture can be seen here.

But what does it translate into, for the purposes of this book?

In 1990, the Bangladesh Institute of Development Studies conducted a study of illegal trade between Bangladesh and India and Myanmar. In 1994, that study was updated with material from the same forty-nine research sites which were observed earlier.

On the basis of the data collected, Zaid Bakht, the author of the report,[12] pointed out that 83 per cent of all illegal imports were from India and valued at half a billion dollars for 1993-94. This was nearly 125 per cent higher than the legal imports from India of 413 million dollars. Illegal imports from India through official and unofficial channels amounted to 17.47 per cent of Bangladesh's total legal imports of 3.56 billion dollars.

And what item, pray, appears to be the biggest item on the agenda of Indian smugglers. This is a trick question that I often throw at audiences in India and elsewhere. The

12 These and subsequent references are from Zaid Bakht's study, *Cross-Border Illegal Trade in Bangladesh: Composition, Trends and Policy Issues*, Bangladesh Institute of Development Studies, Dhaka, October, 1996

answers range from tea and petrol to sugar and foodgrains. Only one person in all these years has got it right and that too at a lecture/discussion with the North East Study Circle in Bangalore in August 2000.

The answer is a six letter word: cattle.

Those skinny, tired-looking, bovines that slowly travel on the Guwahati-Shillong road, as they did during the days of my youth, are the providers of protein for Bangladesh's millions, especially at Ramzan. Our Awami Leaguer in Chilmari had got it right when he spoke of how economic considerations outweighed religious concerns. There are not less than 200 'cattle corridors' on the Indo-Bangladesh border for these animals. 'A staggering 1.7 million pieces of cattle are estimated to be illegally imported into Bangladesh every year,' declared Bakht's study. Of course, he meant head of cattle when he spoke of pieces. But language aside, Bakht clinically analysed the import of the animals into specific benefits for his country.

One of the important by-products of the trade in the animals was the availability of hides. Calculating that about 18 square feet of hide could be extracted from an average head of cattle, Bakht estimated an annual availability of over 30 million square feet of hide through illegal imports of cows, another 0.5 million or so square feet of hides and skin that were directly smuggled into Bangladesh. He also spoke of the impetus it gave to the availability of dairy products and meat in the face of rising demands. The supply of draft power to agriculture also improved as a result.

The list of illegal imports is imposing: there are not less than fourteen items in Bakht's list. Livestock, fish, poultry and related products are nearly 40 per cent of the total value of all such imports. Next come agricultural products, processed foods and tobacco and then textiles and electrical goods. Liquor and the cough syrup Phensidyl, which many Bangladesh take as a liquor or drug, comprise 2.44 per cent of the total value.

Bangladesh's total legal exports to India were a measly 21 million US dollars in 1993-94. Illegal exports to India constituted the sum total of the country's legal trade many times over: 126 million dollars worth of goods or six times the amount earned by licensed exporters and traders.

This means that Bangladesh's official trade deficit with India, at that time, was not less than 392 million dollars (413 million dollars for imports minus 21 million dollars of exports). With the addition of the illegal trade, this deficit rises to nearly 900 million dollars. There are other economists who say that the actual figure is over a billion dollars, because the under-invoicing of goods going legally out of Bangladesh is not often estimated.

To translate this deficit into a surplus, or at least bring it toward some parity with India, the following steps are a must. Smuggling cannot be stopped any more than illegal migration. But we must make a beginning that has the promise of improving conditions for a larger group of people on either side of the border.

One, the legalization of trade in specific items which are currently major income generators for both sides—cattle and fish, medicines and electrical goods as well as textiles. Some of these items are covered under SAFTA, the South Asia Free Trade Agreement, which has barely inched forward in these past years. Therefore, if India and Bangladesh can conclude bilateral agreements on these items, it will benefit a good number of people dependent on trade and also bring in official revenue for both sides.

Two, the setting up of border trade hubs which will become a focus of collection of goods and their export and import. These border hubs can also have separate labour force centres which will be manned also by immigration officials and district officials of either side who can authorize Work Permits, or the movement of people into specific areas of India—let us start with the North East and West Bengal—for labour-related projects and activities.

We will need a mesh of both economic development projects and political protection, with strong involvement of local groups, which will prevent this system from sliding into another set of failures.

It is a commentary on the long-term ineffectiveness of the anti-foreigner movement that twenty years after the agitation began in 1979, the same issues were still being paraded before the public in Assam by Mahanta's successors in the student body. Indeed, in April 2000, they went so far as to assert that there should be constitutional protection in state government jobs and for what they called 'indigenous Assamese.' This group was defined as those who could establish their descent from the 1951 National Register of Citizens (NRC).

That AASU could table such a demand in its official discussions with the Ministry of Home Affairs was another display of its short-sightedness. This pronouncement left a big question mark over those Indians who had moved to Assam after 1951 and whose names did not figure in the NRC. What would be their fate? How would they prove their identity and their Indian nationality? AASU's silence on this issue was an indication of its lack of an overall vision for Assam and its role in India and a biased perception of the realities of the border state. It created more confusion over an issue that has been surrounded by public anger and misunderstanding, media hype and social responses ranging from absolute hostility to total irrationality bordering on xenophobia.

AASU's former general secretary Samujjal Bhattacharyya, who took over as the President of the North East Students Organisation (NESO) in April 2000, went so far as to say that those Indians who had shifted to Assam after 1951 would be untouched as would be those 'foreigners' who had crossed over from East Pakistan until 1971.

The facts of the situation, or material presented as facts, are tossed out carelessly by political parties as well as the so-called non-political groups like AASU.

AASU's non-alignment to political groups is fiction. Its entire agenda is political. It is strongly linked to the Asom Gana Parishad (AGP) and in earlier days, some of its members had close associations with the banned United Liberation Front of Asom (ULFA), the insurgent organization. Those with such links included a member of Mahanta's own Council of Ministers although he later severed his connections.

In addition, AASU's various office-bearers and advisers have, some with undue haste and others with greater dignity, jumped over to the AGP or other political groups to contest elections to Parliament and the State legislature. In the process, they and the AGP have struck tacit deals with immigrant communities, standing their earlier theology on its head and creating further twists in an already convoluted situation.

The Indian Election Commission's proposal that all voters will have to identify themselves before they are allowed to cast their vote is also another step that will secure the value of the vote and identity of an Indian citizen. Until the Election Commission distributes its comprehensive Identity Card among all voters, and this will, take a number of years to happen, given the high costs involved, it should be compulsory for voters to carry a substitute proof of their identity—passport, ration card, electricity bill or telephone bill confirming their address—at the time of elections.[13] Tamper-proof Identity Cards have now covered 65 per cent of the country's electorate.

The Delhi High Court also has ruled that a person cannot claim citizenship merely on the basis of a voter's Identity Card or a ration card. In a ruling, on the pleas of eight residents of Yamuna Pustha in East Delhi (remember the explosion of violence against the deportation drive of the summer of 2000), Justice R.S. Sodhi said that the issue of a ration card or voters identity card 'does not ipso facto confer citizenship.' Justice Sodhi added that that citizenship could be conferred only under the existing laws.

There clearly needs to be a mix of several policy formulae that can defuse the situation and be practicable enough to implement. The following is a checklist of 'doable' programmes which could transform the region.

- Migration cannot be stopped completely; it can only be reduced, given the various pull and push

---

13   Chief Election Commissioner, M.S. Gill's press conference in New Delhi, 12 August 2000, reported as 'Voters Have to Prove Identity: EC' in State*sman*, New Delhi, 13 August 2000

factors. People, like water, tend to find their own levels and the phenomenon of migration is a global one not restricted to our part of the subcontinent. Therefore, there needs to be a larger perspective in which strategies and policies need to be developed.

- To view this as a cut and dried security issue is to completely miss the point. People are moving not because they necessarily want to but because of diminishing options: because they have to. It is primarily to be seen as a survival strategy not a conspiracy to create an Islamic state and increase the borders of Bangladesh. Those who are used as tools, informers or otherwise, by external forces are a few—although their numbers could grow in the next years.

Yet, the security dimensions of the outflow cannot be disregarded. According to the Director-General of the Border Security Force, Bangladeshi Muslims now dominate not less than five-to-ten kilometres of territory inside the West Bengal border, along Bangladesh. He told a meeting in New Delhi in October 2000 that this area was being used by Pakistan's Inter Services Intelligence agency for infilteration and subversion.[14] In addition, there are disturbing accounts of how the KLO and ULFA are entering North Bengal, almost at will, extorting funds from tea gardens and other businesses and using that sensitive corridor to slip into Bhutan and Bangladesh. This, if unchecked, could easily spiral out of control and create greater conflicts in Eastern

14 Director-General, BSF talk in New Delhi to civil service officers, 16 October 2000.

India, which would further extend the security forces, already hard-pressed and thinly spread out.

- Settlement, initially, is in the char or riverine, island and bank areas which are the most impoverished/underdeveloped of the region. The migrants then move on. Yet, these areas continue to be extremely backward and are becoming the soft underbelly of the region, with radicalism growing and alienation from Dispur increasing. If these feelings among old settlers (Indian nationals) are to be calmed, then short-term and long-term development projects under a special Char Commissioner with a team of experts from all over the region and the country should be created, with a committed group of NGOs to plan and implement ideas. A few examples are veterinary extension services, better rice and wheat seed varieties, vegetable and horticulture skills/technology, infrastructure and better designed homesteads which are 'flood-friendly'. A Char Development Authority already exists but is underfunded and virtually non-functional. The message needs to be out that Dispur and Delhi as well as the rest of the region care for backward char communities. Precise surveys of the needs of each major char should be conducted by teams of specialists with the help of local leaders and satellite mapping.

- Migration flows and refugee movements are two separate phenomena. A migrant may also be a refugee but a refugee, such as a Chakma of Bangladesh (coming into Tripura), is not necessarily a migrant. It is critical to differentiate these two outflows. The Central Government should draw up listings of both groups.

- Laws, however well intentioned and drafted, as well as improved policing (better roads, vehicles, larger forces, even fences) are not going to work unless the political backing is there. One does not mean simply support from the State Cabinet or the National Council of Ministers. One means support from MLAs, gram sabhas and panchayats, for it is these groups who can identify illegal settlers.

- However, there must be capacity to inflict punishment on them who connive at law-breaking.

- It should be written into law through Parliament and the State Legislature that any official, at any level, or any person, (be he/she a politician, a political supporter of any party), found collaborating or assisting in the settlement of such migrants be made criminally culpable. Officers can be suspended and dismissed from service, without pension and any facilities which they would be normally entitled to; politicians (at any level) can be debarred from contesting elective office for a period of not less than ten years. This process must be conducted by a retired judge of the State High Court, and a single appeal to a two-member Appellate Court (of retired judges). The problem until now is that not a single politician has been found responsible or proceeded against for such criminality, which amounts to nothing less than selling one's homeland.

- The Illegal Migrants Determination by Tribunal Act must be repealed without delay or at least the process of doing so begun; if this is taken up quickly, it will show that, even in the face of non-passage, the Government of India means business.

- ID-multi purpose cards must be made compulsory for all Indians resident in the North East region; intensive and extensive of election rolls should be held, first at the panchayat ·level under the State Election Commissioner or a Regional Commissioner under the direct supervision of the Central Commission.

- **Work Permits**

  Once Identity Cards are in place, then those from Bangladesh wishing to work in the region (or for that matter other parts of the country) can be issued Work Permits. These Work Permits or Job Cards can be issued at the border district level of both countries (Kurigram/Rongpur/Comilla to name just three adjacent districts in Bangladesh which border Assam, West Bengal and Tripura; see details in appendices). Through the connectivity provided by the Internet and software programmes written by Indian engineers, the Work Permits can become a reality. Each Work Permit should have a special number so that duplication is ruled out. Connectivity will be through the district headquarters in India and Bangladesh. In the North East, the Government of India has launched an ambitious programme, networking 446 blocks by computer, and which can be a base on which such connectivity can be built. Thus, there can be an accounting of those who come and go on both sides. This is the best recognition of a labour market and of a labour flow, which is what the migration is largely all about.

- The Work Permits/Job Cards cannot be individual ones to start with and must be issued to groups of not less than 15-20. There will be several parts of this Card, which will be more like a passport. One section, in visas will have the photo and signature/thumb impression of the prospective workers. A second part will give details of where the group is heading, the name of the employers, their address and local police station. A third part will say how long the group is going to stay. The group will report to the local police station upon arrival and once every six months. An application for an extension can be transmitted through the Internet and e-mail to the local district headquarters, for checking and a request for an extension of the Work Permit could be made at the local district headquarters. The extensions can be granted for a maximum of two years. Should any of the migrant workers go missing during this period, it should be brought to the notice of the local police and the concerned authorities. Criminal proceedings can be launched against specific employers. Punishments should be punitive, in terms of fines and the possibility of simple imprisonment. These can be part of a special act enacted by Parliament (see appendices).

- No worker will be entitled to such political rights such as the right to vote. But he/she can appeal against intimidation or a violation of basic human rights to the State High Court, the State Human Rights Commission, the Labour Commissioner and the Consulate of his/her country. They will not be entitled to buy immovable property or settle permanently in India.

- The right to vote will rest only with Indian nationals as identified through the ID-Card process.
- The names of those classified as D Voters (of Doubtful Origin) in Assam should be deleted from electoral rolls. They can be restored only if they can prove that they came before 1971. Otherwise, they should stay off the rolls and be moved to 'holding areas' on land acquired by the Central Government where they are kept like the East Pakistani refugees in Orissa (but without the vote), as repatriating will be expensive and next to physically impossible (Bangladesh will refuse to accept them).
- Improved surveillance facilities and better river patrol craft. Those held and pushed back at the border are the only ones who are likely to be accepted by neighbouring country.
- The above clause must include intensive and extensive involvement of local police forces in active patrolling and search operations at the border because they, more than any other security wing, know the routes and the middle-men who are making this movement possible. This is critical to the success of any scheme.
- A National Migration Law needs to be developed and I place a tentative draft (see appendices) for public discussion, which incorporates some of the ideas outlined above.
- Only those who have been registered as voters in the 1999 elections and their progeny as well as bona fide Indians who have migrated from other parts of the country (they will need to show verifiable documents of their last place of residence and the

names of referees who can vouch for them) will be entitled to vote until 2026.

- Better policing on the border with the involvement of local police—those who are detected as crossing illegally at the border will be the ones that can be pushed back and whom Bangladesh will accept than those who have settled on this side of the border.
- Development of a reliable network of police informers who keep the government abreast of latest social, political and security events in the region and improvement of the existing network in other parts of it.
- Implementation of a time-bound development programme for these areas that includes the building of good hospitals, schools and colleges, better boats and ferries, besides quick rehabilitation packages at times of natural calamity such as floods.
- The revenue administration rules must be changed appropriately to include inhabited chars in the regular revenue department so that it comes under the jurisdiction of the concerned district magistrate/collector. Otherwise, the chars remain out of the ambit of governance and are touched only by half-hearted, ad hoc measures.
- None of this can work in isolation. The river routes between India and Bangladesh should be opened up for transport and taxes levied in local currency on ships that use their waterways for travel and freight. Access to Chittagong Port through a railway line connecting Agartala, the capital of Tripura, would reduce transport costs and save enormous amounts of time, money and energy for people who want to sell their products in the best market for the best value.

- Bangladesh and north-eastern states like Meghalaya could collaborate in industries and fruit processing and marketing. Limestone from Meghalaya is already being shipped to Bangladesh where it is made into clinkers and cement and exported, as value-added items, to South-East Asian markets in hard currency. The fruit from the rich pineapple and orange orchards of Meghalaya and Tripura, as well as passion fruit from Mizoram, can be packed in India or even exported in pulp to Bangladesh, and packaged there, and re-exported. Rubber from Tripura is another commodity with a large market.

- Border trade could be encouraged so that the informal trade or smuggling becomes formal, giving communities access to more funds and better markets.

- The list of positive measure is long and one has mentioned only a handful. But it must be asserted here that international organizations such as the International Organization for Migration and other UN groups should consider compensating those countries which accept settlers/migrants with funds to help them strengthen their local infrastructure and resource management, on the lines of the Global Environment Fund (GEF).

- Finally, a massive programme of infrastructure building by focussing on transport through the waterways, roads and railway lines would generate huge capacity for employment and a vast range of ancillary industries. Many fresh avenues of employment would open up, with new townships springing up for the labour forces. These townships would need to provide basic services, including restaurants, dhobis, *chaiwallahs* and tailors to name a few. Traditional skills such as fishing and boat building would be encouraged. These endeavours would develop demands for large supplies of cement, iron, bricks, electric transmission towers, cables—the very nuts and bolts of development and progress.

- The roadways, waterways and rail lines exist: it is time to revive them and develop them to our natural advantage.

The stories of Mahesh and Keramat Bhai continue. For they are chapters which do not have full stops, no *ad shum*, no *khatam kahani*. As long as destitution and poverty prevail in our neighbourhood, there will be movements of people across borders (which they do not respect), in their hope of securing a better life.

In this process, demographic changes will take place, as we have suggested. Pressures on land will grow. Conflicts will arise. But with access to better information, nutrition, health care and other necessities of life, migrant-receiving communities and regions will be better placed to take care of their own interests without resorting either to violence or to subterfuge. We need to mandate such communities with economic and social powers as well as the detailed legal and constitutional mechanisms to achieve this.

'Local' communities which feel that their identities, if not their very existence, are threatened by the ingress of outsiders will find security not in force of arms or numbers but in constitutional safeguards which are imposed and implemented rigorously, even harshly. It has been as much the failure of the Indian state and its subordinate agencies, which have not honoured or kept their word, that is responsible for the fire that has swept Assam and other parts of the North East, as much as anything else. They say that a Constitution is as good or as bad as those who work it; the converse is also true. We need to stop blaming our instruments and start criticizing ourselves for the visible failure of governance around us.

Groups which migrate to seek a decent life will have some rights to work and to decent wages. They cannot have the right to vote and to citizenship. The dos and don'ts have been spelt out in the earlier pages. The *Rites of Passage* are not rights to passage. They are symbolic of our changed times.

Will Assam perish or will she prosper? I think we will see a combination of both. What Gandhi and Weiner advocate, perhaps more of the former. Let me clarify. In a message to Assam, Mahatma Gandhi, in 1944, said, 'If the people feel that the present policy of the Government on settlement and immigration is oppressive and anti-national, let them fight it non-violently, or violently, if necessary.'[15]

Myron Weiner remarked that while it was conceivable by the start of the twenty-first century that the global migration crisis would have abated, there was also the other possibility, that tolerance toward foreigners would have dropped even further and that as the pressure for emigration grew 'states are more rather than less likely to become restrictive.'

'What is uncertain is whether states will be effective at halting unwanted entries,' Weiner said, adding that governments were likely to face 'increasingly

15 Hazarika, *Strangers of the Mist*, p. 65.

uncomfortable choices, some of which require the balancing of potentially high economic, political and moral costs and uncertain benefits.'

Urging that humanitarian considerations aligned to national interests light the way for government policies, Weiner concludes that 'states will not and cannot allow others to decide who will permanently live and work in their own societies.'[16]

If Assam perishes, then who will live? Can India survive such a brutal body blow?

I do not know the answers to these questions. But they will be answered, if not in my lifetime, then certainly in that of the next generation of Indians, Assamese and Bangladeshis.

---

16   Myron Weiner, *The Global Migration Crisis: Challenges to States and to Human Rights*, HarperCollins, 1995

Appendices

Appendix A
Excerpts from Population Census Report.
National Volume.
(Bangladesh Bureau of Statistics, Dhaka, 1977)

BANGLADESH

Religious Communities: Table 20 focuses on the percentage distribution of the Muslim and Hindu communities from 1901 to 1947; all other communities are grouped under 'other'. It will be noted that Muslims and Hindus constitute together almost 99% of the total population in Bangladesh. The proportions of Muslims and Hindus, however, have changed continuously since the census of 1901. The proportion of Muslims was 66% in 1901, and it has increased to 85.4% in 1974. On the other hand, the proportion of Hindus was 33% in 1901 and has continuously decreased to 13.5% in 1974. The proportion of Hindus decreased each decade by at least 1 percentage point upto 1941 and then decreased more rapidly about 6 per cent during 1941-1951, 3 per cent between 1951-1961 and 5 per cent between 1961-1974. These decreases were paralleled by similar increases in the proportion of Muslims in the corresponding decades.

Table 20—Percentage Distribution and Percentage Variation of Major Religious Communities in Bangladesh—1901-1974

Year	All Communities Total	MUSLIM		HINDU		OTHERS	
		Percent	P.C. Variation	Percent	P.C. Variation	Percent	P.C. Variation
1901	100	66.1		33.0		0.9	
1911	100	67.2	10.9	31.5	4.3	1.3	49.1
1921	100	68.1	6.8	30.6	2.2	1.3	10.2
1931	100	69.5	9.2	29.4	2.8	1.1	-5.0
1941	100	70.3	19.3	28.0	12.4	1.7	76.9
1951	100	76.9	9.2	22.0	-21.4	1.1	-37.3
1961	100	80.4	26.9	18.5	1.5	1.1	22.3
1974	100	85.4	49.3	13.5	3.1	1.1	34.4

Sources: 1901—1961, Census of Pakistan, 1961, Vol, 2, East Pakistan, Statement 2—I, p. II—15.

1974, Census Data, Table 7.

The Muslim community constituted slightly more than 85 per cent of the total population of Bangladesh in 1974 and largely accounted for the overall growth of population of Bangladesh in all the past decades. They increased by about 9 per cent in the three decades upto 1931, when the overall population growth was about 2 percentage points lower. The unprecedented increase of 19 per cent in the decade ending in 1941, followed by the comparatively lower increase of 9 per cent in 1951, may be attributed to over-reporting in the 1941 Census. The number of Muslims grew by 27 per cent during the decade

1951-1961 and by 49 per cent during the 13 year period 1961-1974 as against the overall population growth of 21 per cent and 40 per cent in the respective periods. The fastest growth of the Muslim population (about 3.8 per cent per annum) thus occurred in the recent past.

In terms of percentage variations over the previous censuses, the Hindu community increased by 4% in 1911, 2% in 1921 2% in 1931, 2% in 1961, and 3% in 1974. Thus the growth of the Hindu population in Bangladesh has shown an almost uniform pattern over the last 7 decades. The greatest increase of the Hindu population in any decade was 12% observed in 1941. This figure is subject to doubt, since both the major communities inflated their numbers in the 1941 census. The number of Hindus, however, decreased by 21% in the 1951 census, which reflects partially the overcount in 1941 and mainly the migration of Hindus from the former East Bengal to West Bengal, on account of the partition of India and the creation of the independent countries of Pakistan and India in 1947.

The small religious communities viz the Buddhists and Christians formed only 0.61% and 0.30% of the total population of Bangladesh in 1974. Table 21 provides data for 1961 and 1974 on these two communities. The Christian community increased by about 45% during the period 1961-1974, while the Buddhists increased by 17% compared with the overall population increase of 40% during the period. The proportion of Christians in the population increased slightly from 0.26% in 1951, 0.29% in 1961 to 0.30% in 1974. On the other hand, although the number of Buddhists increased by 17% in both 1961 and 1974 over the previous censuses, the proportion of Buddhists decreased from 0.75% in 1951 to 0.74% in

1961 and 0.61% in 1974. This could be due to misclassification or to a lower fertility rate as compared to that of the general population. The large increase in the percentage variation of 'others' would imply that several Buddhists have been classified as 'others' in the 1974 census.

Table 21—Percentage Distribution and Percentage Variation of Various Religious Communities in Bangladesh 1961-1974

COMMUNITIES	per cent		
	Year		
	1961	1974	Since 1961
MUSLIM	80.4	85.4	49.3
HINDU	18.5	13.5	3.1
BUDDHIST	0.7	0.6	17.1
CHRISTIAN	0.3	0.3	45.0
OTHERS	0.1	0.2	136.2
ALL COMMUNITIES	100.0	100.0	40.6

Sources: 1961—Census of Pakistan, 1961, Vol. 2, East Pakistan, Table 5, pp. II-98 to II-99.
1974—Census Data, Table 7,

Table 22—Enumerated and Percentage Distribution of Population of Bangladesh by Country of Birth—1951, 1961, 1974.

Country of Birth	1951		1961		1974	
	Number	P.C.	Number	P.C.	Number	P.C.
BANGLADESH	41,065,863	97.94	50,189,972	98.73	70,718,414	98.94
INDIA	848,539	2.02	627,846	1.23	736,432	1.03
PAKISTAN	9,318	0.02	15,836	0.03	15,605	0.03
OTHER ASIAN COUNTRIES	8,204	0.02	6,203	0.01	5,201	*
OTHERS	405	*	378	*	1,977	*
	41,932,329	100.00	50,840,235	100.00	71,477,629	100.00

Source: 1951, 1961—Census of Pakistan, 1961 Vol. 2, East Pakistan, Table 8, p. II—116. 1974—Census Data, Table 8. * Negligible

273

Country of Birth : Table 22 gives the percentage distribution of the population by country of birth for the 1951, 1961 and 1974 censuses. The statement shows that almost 99% of the population of Bangladesh, as enumerated in the 1974 census, were born in the present territory constituting Bangladesh. Slightly more than 1% of the population was reported to have been born outside Bangladesh, of which the greater proportion was born in India, however, shows a decreasing trend, from 2.02 in 1951, 1.23 in 1961 to 1.03 in 1974. About 0.03% of the total population of Bangladesh was reported to have been born in Pakistan in the 1974 census. Only about 7,000 persons were reported in this census to have been born in countries other than the subcontinent area of Bangladesh-India-Pakistan.

Appendix B

RELIGIOUS COMPOSITION
6.1. Introduction

Population census 1981 like earlier censuses collected information on the religious affiliations of the population. Individual characteristics of each religious communities cross-classified by demographic and socio-economic variables are presented in this chapter. Aggregate measures such as over-all religious patterns, growth of population by religion over time, regional variations, urban-rural differentials etc. have also been discussed with the objective of measuring and evaluating the trend of social and economic development among the different religious communities of the country.

Source: 1981, Census of Bangladesh, Bureau of Statistics, Dhaka.

6.2 Population Growth By Religion

Numerical distribution and percentage variation of major religious communities in Bangladesh from 1901 to 1981 have been furnished in Table 1. The table shows that in terms of percentage variations over the preceding censuses, the Muslim community increased by 10.9 per cent in 1911 over 1901. On the other hand, comparatively lower increasing trends of this community have been recorded in 1921 and 1931. High mortality due to the occurrence of famines, droughts, epidemic diseases during this period might be the causes of these slow trends. A sharp decline by 10.1 percentage points in 1951 over the trend of 1941 may be explained by the net effect of migration. That is the emigrated number of Hindus after independence of 1947 was relatively larger than the immigrated number of Muslims from India. From 1961 to 1981 the rates of increase of Muslim population have been high. High fertility and moderately declining level of mortality during the last two decades may account for this rapid increase.

The decennial variations of Hindu population in Bangladesh have shown an irregular pattern over the census years 1901 to 1981. The Hindu population decreased by 21.3 per cent points in 1951. This may be due partly to the migration of Hindu from the former East Bengal to West Bengal on account of the partition of British India and the creation of the two independent and sovereign states of Pakistan and India in 1947 and partly due to the prevalence of relatively lower fertility among the Hindu population.

Table 1 : Numerical Distribution and Percentage Variation of Bangladesh Population by Major Religious Communities 1901-1981.

Census Year	Total population (000)	Muslim Number (000)	Muslim Per cent Variation	Hindu Number (000)	Hindu Per cent Variation	Buddhist Number (000)	Buddhist Per cent Variation	Christian Number (000)	Christian Per cent Variation	Others Number (000)	Others Per cent Variation
1901	28927	19113	-	9545	-	-	-	-	-	269	-
1911	31555	21202	10.9	9952	4.3	-	-	-	-	401	49.1
1921	33254	22646	6.8	10166	2.2	-	-	-	-	442	10.2
1931	35604	24731	9.2	10453	2.8	-	-	61	-	359	-18.8
1941	41999	29509	19.3	11747	12.4	-	-	53	-13.1	690	92.2
1951	41933	32227	9.2	9239	-21.3	319	-	107	101.9	41	-94.1
1961	50840	40890	26.9	9380	1.5	374	17.2	149	39.3	47	14.6
1974	71478	61039	49.3	9673	3.1	439	17.4	216	45.0	111	136.2
1981	87120	75487	23.7	10870	9.3	538	22.6	275	27.3	250	125.2

Note: (1) Hindus in this and subsequent tables include both caste Hindus and Scheduled caste.

... upto 1941 Buddhist and upto 1921 Christian communities are not available separately and as such these two communities have been included in 'Others'. Christian community is not available separately in the district of Sylhet in 1931 Census and as such they have been included in 'Other'.

It may be noted that due to the rounding of the totals in thousand, slight difference from the actual figures may appear.

276

6.3 Religious Composition Over Time

The comparative percentage distribution the population by different religious communities of the country from 1901 to 1981 have been presented in Table 2. The figures in the table show that the proportion of Muslim population in 1901 was 66.1 per cent which has risen to 86.6 per cent by 1981 and the composition of the Muslim population during the last eight decades since 1901 increased by 20.5 per cent points. Comparatively rapid increase in Muslim population are noticed from the census year 1941. The per cent variations of the composition of Muslim population between the census years 1941-1951 and 1961-1974 calculate to 6.6 and 5.0 per cent points respectively. It is observed from the table that the proportion of Hindu population has been declining from 33.0 per cent in 1901 to 12.1 per cent in 1981. The aggregate reduction in terms of percentage was about 21.0 per cent points over 1901. The differential growth rates between Muslims and Hindus, the migration of Hindus following the partition of the subcontinent in 1947, Indo-Pak war in 1965 and the Liberation war of Bangladesh in 1971 are the likely causes for decline in the Hindu proportion in Bangladesh. The Buddhists and the Christians are the minor religious communities in Bangladesh. The combined proportion of these two groups to the total population of the country is only 0.9 per cent. In terms of percentages the size of Christian population to the total population remained constant at 0.3 per cent while Buddhist population has declined from 0.8 per cent in 1951 to 0.6 per cent in 1981.

Table 2: Percentage Distribution of Population by Religious Communities, 1901-1981.

Census Years	Total	Muslim	Hindu	Buddhist	Christian	Others
1901	100.0	66.1	33.0	--	--	0.9
1911	100.0	67.2	31.5	--	--	1.3
1921	100.0	68.1	30.6	--	--	1.3
1931	100.0	69.5	29.4	--	0.2	1.0
1941	100.0	70.3	28.0	--	0.1	1.6
1951	100.0	76.9	22.0	0.7	0.3	0.1
1961	100.0	80.4	18.5	0.7	0.3	0.1
1974	100.0	85.4	13.5	0.6	0.3	0.2
1981	100.0	86.6	12.1	0.6	0.3	0.3

6.3.1 Urban-Rural Differentials

The per centage distribution of Bangladesh population of different religious communities classified by urban-rural and four Statistical Metropolitan Areas (SMA) as recorded in 1981 census is presented in Table 3. The distribution shows that the Muslims being the major religious community of the country, constitutes the overwhelming proportion also in urban areas. Their rural share is slightly less than the urban proportion. The proportion of Hindus in urban areas is marginally lower than their rural proportion. The proportion of Hindus in urban areas is 11.6 per cent as against 12.2 per cent in rural areas. It is evident from the table that like other areas, the Muslims constitute the major religious component in the SMAs also. Highest percentage of Muslim population in recorded in Dhaka SMA which has been followed by Rajshahi SMA. Somewhat lower proportion of Muslims is recorded in Khulna SMA. It is observed that comparatively higher percentages of Hindus and Buddhists have been enumerated in Chittagong SMA. The combined proportion of these two religious communities in Chittagong SMA is 11.4 per cent. It is also found in the table that proportionately larger proportion of christian population has been recorded in Khulna SMA. The Hindus and Christian jointly constitute about 13.2 per cent of the total population of Khulna SMA.

Table 3: Percentage Distribution of Population by Locality and Religious Composition, 1981

Residence	Total	Muslim	Hindu	Buddhist	Christian	Others
Bangladesh	100.0	86.6	12.1	0.6	0.3	0.3
Urban	100.0	86.9	11.6	0.5	0.8	0.2
Rural	100.0	86.6	12.2	0.6	0.3	0.3
All SMAs	100.0	91.4	7.4	0.2	0.8	0.2
Chittagong SMA	100.0	88.2	10.7	0.7	0.3	0.2
Dhaka SMA	100.0	93.5	5.8	0.1	0.5	0.2
Khulna SMA	100.0	86.7	9.5	0.0	3.7	0.1
Rajshahi SMA	100.0	91.9	7.2	0.0	0.6	0.3

6.3.2 Regional Variations

Percentage and numerical distribution of Bangladesh population by religous communities and by administrative Divisions and Districts are presented respectively in Tables 4 and 5. By Division it is found that

Dhaka Division has recorded the highest proportion of Muslim population which has been closely followed by Rajshahi Division both in 1974 and 1981 censuses. In both the censuses of 1974 and 1981, Khulna Division recorded the highest share of Hindu population. The highest proportion of Buddhist population is seen in Chittagong Division where they constitute 2.3 per cent. They maintained the same proportion in 1981 census. The proportionate share of Christan population in Dhaka Division is only 0.5 per cent which has remained almsot unchanged between 1974 and 1981 and this is the highest proportion of Christian population among the four administrative Divisions.

Table 4: Regional Distribution of Bangladesh Population by Religious Communities, 1974 and 1981.

District/Division	1974						1981					
	Total	Muslim	Hindu	Buddhist	Christian	Others	Muslim	Hindu	Buddhist	Christian	Others	Total
Bangladesh	100.0	85.4	13.5	0.6	0.3	0.2	86.6	12.1	0.6	0.3	0.3	100.0
Ctg. Divn	100.0	85.3	12.1	2.3	0.2	0.1	85.6	11.7	2.3	0.2	0.2	100.0
Bandarban	100.0	-	-	-	-	-	41.5	2.9	43.9	8.2	3.5	100.0
Ctg. H.T.	100.0	18.9	10.4	66.5	2.6	1.6	32.4	11.4	55.0	0.9	0.3	100.0
Chittagong	100.0	83.8	14.1	1.9	0.1	0.1	84.5	13.0	2.2	0.1	0.2	100.0
Comilla	100.0	90.2	9.7	0.0	0.0	0.1	91.6	8.2	0.1	0.0	0.1	100.0
Noakhali	100.0	92.8	7.2	0.0	0.0	0.0	93.0	6.9	0.0	0.1	0.0	100.0
Sylhet	100.0	82.6	16.9	0.1	0.2	0.2	81.3	18.0	0.0	0.3	0.4	100.0

District/Division	1974						1981					
	Total	Muslim	Hindu	Buddhist	Christian	Others	Total	Muslim	Hindu	Buddhist	Christian	Others
Dhaka Div	100.0	87.6	11.8	0.0	0.5	0.1	100.0	89.7	9.7	0.0	0.5	0.1
Dhaka	100.0	87.8	11.4	0.0	0.7	0.1	100.0	90.5	8.9	0.1	0.4	0.1
Faridpur	100.0	76.4	23.3	--	0.3	0.0	100.0	80.9	18.8	0.0	0.3	0.0
Jamalpur	100.0	--	--	--	--	--	100.0	96.8	2.7	--	0.4	0.1
Mymensingh	100.0	93.4	6.0	0.0	0.5	0.1	100.0	91.8	7.4	--	0.6	0.2
Tangail	100.0	87.6	12.0	--	0.2	0.2	100.0	90.6	9.0	--	0.2	0.1
Khulna Divn.	100.0	81.0	18.7	0.0	0.2	0.1	100.0	82.4	17.1	0.0	0.4	0.1
Barisal	100.0	82.8	17.0	-	0.1	0.1	100.0	84.5	15.1	0.0	0.3	0.1
Jessore	100.0	78.0	21.9	-	0.1	-	100.0	80.3	19.6	-	0.1	0.0
Khulna	100.0	71.2	28.3	0.0	0.4	0.1	100.0	71.9	27.2	0.0	0.8	0.1
Kushtia	100.0	95.2	4.7	-	-	0.1	100.0	95.1	4.5	-	0.3	0.1

District/Division	1974						1981					
	Total	Muslim	Hindu	Buddhist	Christian	Others	Total	Muslim	Hindu	Buddhist	Christian	Others
Patuakhali	100.0	88.8	10.9	0.3	-	-	100.0	90.3	9.4	0.2	0.0	0.1
Rajshahi Div.	100.0		12.9	0.0	0.3	0.4	100.0	87.4	11.6	0.0	0.2	0.8
Bogra	100.0		7.2	-	0.4	0.2	100.0	91.1	8.4	-	0.1	0.4
Dinajpur	100.0		23.7	-	0.5	0.7	100.0	75.9	21.9	0.0	0.6	1.6
Pabna	100.0		9.2	-	0.3	0.1	100.0	92.5	7.3	-	0.1	0.1
Rajshahi	100.0		13.0	0.1	0.2	0.7	100.0	88.6	9.5	0.0	0.4	1.5
Rangpur	100.0		12.0	-	0.2	0.2	100.0	88.0	11.6	0.0	0.1	0.3

Table 5: Regional Distribution of Bangladesh Population by Religious Communities, 1974 and 1981. (In Thousand)

District/Division	1974						1981					
	Total population	Muslim	Hindu	Buddhist	Christian	Others	Total population	Muslim	Hindu	Buddhist	Christian	Others
Bangladesh	71478	61039	9673	439	216	111	87120	75487	10570	538	275	250
Crg. Divn.	18636	15894	2262	427	29	24	22595	19351	2632	525	41	46
Banderban	-	-	-	-	-	-	171	71	5	75	14	6
Crg. H.T.	508	96	53	228	12	8	580	188	66	319	5	2
Chittagong	4316	3617	607	84	4	4	5491	4638	714	124	5	10
Comilla	5819	5250	564	2	1	1	6881	6307	565	4	1	4
Noakhali	3234	3000	233	1			3519	3549	263	1	2	1
Sylhet	4759	3931	805	2	11	10	5656	4598	1019	2	14	23

District/Division	1974						1981					
	Total population	Muslim	Hindu	Buddhist	Christian	Others	Total population	Muslim	Hindu	Buddhist	Christian	Others
Dhaka Divn.	21316	18666	2517	3	114	16	26242	23535	2553	5	121	28
Dhaka	7612	6684	867	2	56	3	10014	9067	890	4	44	9
Faridpur	4060	3100	944	-	14	2	4764	3852	894	1	15	2
Jamalpur	-	-	-	-	-	-	2452	2374	65	-	10	2
Mymensingh	7566	7062	456	1	38	8	6568	6028	484	-	45	11
Tangail	2078	1819	250	-	6	3	2444	2214	220	-	7	3
Khulna Divn.	14195	11507	2652	5	23	8	17151	14126	2946	5	63	11
Barisal	3928	3255	666	-	5	2	4667	3944	705	1	15	2
Jessore	3327	2595	729	-	2	1	4020	3227	787	-	4	2
Khulna	3557	2532	1006	-	16	3	4329	3111	1178	1	35	4
Kushtia	1884	1794	88	-	-	2	2292	2179	103	-	8	2
Patuakhali	1499	1331	163	3	-	-	1843	1665	172	3	1	1

District/Division	1974						1981					
	Total population	Muslim	Hindu	Buddhist	Christian	Others	Total population	Muslim	Hindu	Buddhist	Christian	Others
Rajshahi Divn	17331	14972	2242	3	50	64	21132	18475	2439	3	50	165
Bogra	2230	2054	162	-	10	4	2728	2485	229	-	2	12
Dinajpur	2571	1931	608	-	14	18	3200	2428	701	1	20	50
Pabna	2815	2546	260	-	7	2	3424	3167	251	-	3	3
Rajshahi	4268	3669	558	3	8	30	5270	4667	503	1	19	80
Rangpur	5447	4772	654	-	11	10	6510	5728	755	1	6	20

Appendix C

2.16 Percentage Distribution and Variation of Major Communities by Religion

Year	All comm-unities	Muslim		Hindu		Others	
		per cent	Variation	per cent	Variation	per cent	Variation
1901	100	66.1	-	33.0	-	0.9	-
1911	100	67.2	10.9	31.5	4.3	1.3	49.1
1921	100	68.1	6.8	3.6	2.2	1.3	10.2
1931	100	69.5	9.2	29.4	2.8	1.1	-5.0
1941	100	70.3	19.3	28.0	12.4	1.7	76.9
1951	100	76.9	9.2	22.0	-21.4	1.1	-37.3
1961	100	80.4	26.9	18.5	1.5	1.1	22.3
1974	100	85.4	49.3	13.5	3.1	1.1	34.4
1981	100	86.6	23.7	12.1	9.3	1.2	38.8
1991	100	88.3	24.4	10.5	5.8	1.2	18.1

Notes: Hindus include both Caste Hindus and Scheduled Castes.
Source: Census of Population. Others included Buddhist, Christian & others.

2.17 Former District-Wise Enumerated Census Population by Religion (Number)

Former District	1991					
	Total	Muslim	Hindu	Buddhist	Christian	Others
Bandarban	230569	109800	8105	87613	16769	8282
Chittagong H.T.	743876	320154	79701	337698	5437	886
Chittagong	6715387	5752206	808095	137448	7216	10422
Comilla	8206860	7609175	578022	7507	3701	8455
Noakhali	4626216	4339192	281730	1579	2175	1540
Sylhet	6765039	5605475	1122092	2683	20052	14737
Dhaka	13232427	12167099	985518	8686	59510	11614
Faridpur	5423847	4550652	848640	2478	17397	4480
Jamalpur	3013069	2919509	71589	1929	12422	7620
Mymensingh	7994204	7400925	514655	6078	53045	19501
Tangail	3002428	2747921	236106	1259	12140	5002
Barisal	5413078	4703565	691822	1224	14367	2100
Patuakhali	2049565	1870960	174217	3433	629	326
Jessore	4848023	4076541	760374	1256	6238	3614
Khulna	5039153	3833526	1175924	807	24130	4766
Kushtia	2801207	2698291	93559	429	7894	1034
Bogra	3434298	3146603	261166	2779	5844	17906
Dinajpur	3983103	3072588	835206	3120	25272	46917
Pabna	4183469	3741109	232490	1508	4985	3377
Rajshahi	6594298	5924019	548589	5262	32452	83976
Rangpur	8014876	7091719	871066	8634	14387	29070
Bangladesh	106314992	93881029	11178866	623410	346062	285625

2.17 Former District-Wise Enumerated Census Population by Religion (Percentage)

Former District	1991					
	Total	Muslim	Hindu	Buddhist	Christian	Others
Bandarban	100.0	47.6	3.5	38.0	7.3	3.6
Chittagong H.T.	100.0	43.0	10.7	45.4	0.7	0.1
Chittagong	100.0	85.7	12.0	2.0	0.1	0.2
Comilla	100.0	92.7	7.0	0.1	0.1	0.1
Noakhali	100.0	93.8	6.1	0.0	0.1	0.0
Sylhet	100.0	82.9	16.6	0.0	0.3	0.2
Dhaka	100.0	91.9	7.5	0.1	0.4	0.1
Faridpur	100.0	83.9	15.6	0.1	0.3	0.1
Jamalpur	100.0	96.9	2.4	0.1	0.4	0.2
Mymensingh	100.0	92.6	6.4	0.1	0.7	0.2
Tangail	100.0	91.5	7.9	0.0	0.4	0.2
Barisal	100.0	86.9	12.8	0.0	0.3	0.0
Patuakhali	100.0	91.3	8.5	0.2	0.0	0.0
Jessore	100.0	84.1	15.7	0.0	0.1	0.1
Khulna	100.0	76.1	23.3	0.0,	0.5	0.1
Kushtia	100.0	96.3	3.3	0.0	0.3	0.1
Bogra	100.0	91.6	7.6	0.1	0.2	0.5
Dinajpur	100.0	77.1	21.0	0.1	0.6	1.2
Pabna	100.0	94.2	5.6	0.0	0.1	0.1
Rajshahi	100.0	89.8	8.3	0.1	0.5	1.3
Rangpur	100.0	88.5	10.9	0.1	0.2	0.4
Bangladesh	100.0	88.3	10.5	0.6	0.3	0.3

Appendix D

Table 2: Population of Bangladesh by Religious Groups, 1901—1991
(Numbers in million)

Religion	1901	1911	1921	1931	1941	1951	1961	1971	1981	1991
Total	28.927	31.555	33.254	35.604	41.999	41.933	50.840	71.478	87.120	106.315
Muslim	19.113	21.202	22.646	24.731	29.509	32.227	40.890	61.039	75.487	93.881
Hindu	9.545	9.952	10.166	10.453	11.747	9.239	9.380	9.673	10.570	11.179
Buddhist	-	--	--	--	--	.319	.374	.439	.538	.623
Christian	--	--	--	0.61	.053	.107	.149	.216	.275	.346
Others	.269	.401	.442	.359	.690	.041	.047	.111	.250	.286

(percentage distribution)

Religion	1901	1911	1921	1931	1941	1951	1961	1971	1981	1991
Total	100.0	100.0	100.0	100.0	100.0	100.0	100.0	100.0	100.0	100.0
Muslim	66.1	67.2	68.1	69.5	70.3	76.9	80.4	85.4	86.6	88.3
Hindu	33.0	31.5	30.6	29.4	28.0	22.0	18.5	13.5	12.1	10.5
Buddhist	--	--	--	--	--	0.7	0.7	0.6	0.6	0.6
Christian	--	--	--	0.2	0.1	0.3	0.3	0.3	0.3	0.3
Others	0.9	1.3	1.3	1.0	1.6	0.1	0.1	0.2	0.3	0.3

Source: Population Censuses, 1981 and 1991.
BIDS WORKING PAPER
Working Paper New Series No. 5
Population Factors, Developmental Problems, Environment and Sustainability in Bangladesh,
M.R. Khan, September 1994

Appendix E

Bangladesh Population During the First Five Year Plan Period (1972-77): A Guestimate
By Masihur Rahman Khan
October 1972

Migration

Migration played an important role in the growth of the Bangladesh population. With the exception of 1901-11 decade when Bangladesh gained around half a million persons as result of net immigration from India, Bangladesh was losing population through net emigration mainly to India in all other decades. From an initial low net emigration figure of around 100 thousand in 1911-21, the net emigration rose to over 600 thousand in each of the decades of 1921-31 and 1931-41, to 1.9 million in 1941-51 and around 1.2 mill in 1951-61. Though no estimate of net migration could be made for the period after the 1961 census, it can be argued that Bangladesh was expected to lose population to India even after that date. The exodus was possible high in 1964-66 due to and associated with the Pakistani war in 1965 with India. Concerning the more recent migration, it is officially maintained that the exodus of around 10 million Bengalees to India from the then East Pakistan when she was still in the hands of Pakistan army was balanced out by a reverse migration of that magnitude to their motherland after the liberation of Bangladesh. In the post-liberation period there has been some inflow of Bengalees from across the border of India only possible for short stay as visitors. Given the present still unsettled socio-economic condition of the country, the possibility of a continued net emigration flow from Bangladesh, though a smaller magnitude compared to that in 1940s or 1950s, cannot be ruled out.

Rates of Growth

The rate of population growth is the balance between fertility, mortality and migration. The birth rate minus death rate gives the natural rate of population growth. Generally speaking, the natural rate of population growth in the past, until a couple of centuries or so, was very slow, at times negative, because a high birth rate (more or less constant) was matched by almost equally high (often fluctuating) death rate. Coming to the more recent period, the natural rate of population growth in Bangladesh was small during the decades 1901-11, 1911-21, 1921-31 and 1941-51, moderately high in 1931-41, and high in 1951-61. This pattern contrasts somewhat from that observed in the sub-continent of Bangladesh, India and Pakistan as a whole, because the incidences of the 1918-19 influenza death was lower and the 1943 famine deaths much higher in Bangladesh, compared to the rest of the sub-continent.

The rate of the natural growth of the population in Bangladesh in 1951-61 was 2.2 per cent per annum with net emigration the rate of growth was 1.9 per cent per annum.

Since 1943 Bengal famine, there has been a monotonic improvement in the mortality of the population, while fertility remained more or less unchanged at a high level. This resulted in an accelerated natural rate of population growth. Compared to the decline in mortality a model pattern of fertility change is that with a time lag of a number of years (the length of the time lag depending on the relative success of the family planning efforts of the people and the government) fertility start declining, though slowly initially and then quite fast. This simple pattern of fertility change is vitiated somewhat because of the dent in our age distribution as mentioned above. Even if we assume that our population have shown signs of declining fertility in recent years, the population growth rate will not decline during the plan period from its pre-plan period level.

Calculation of the Expected Population Size on January 1, 1973.

With the adjusted 1961 census population as the base and with the following assumption of the birth and deaths, the population of Bangladesh in July 1, 1970 should have reached to around 72.4 million.[1] With a

	Birth rate	Death rate
July 1, 1960 -- June 30, 1965	49.5	18.0
July 1, 1965 -- June 30, 1970	47.7	14.4

3.3 per cent rate of population growth per annum this population would have reached to 73.6 million on January 1, 1971. An assumed half a million deaths due to December 1970 cyclone would have brought the total size down to 75.1 million on January 1, 1971. An assumed yearly rate of growth of 3.3 per cent (without extra mortality) and an assumed extra deaths of three million due to the direct and indirect effect of the Pakistani army crackdown in Bangladesh during the occupation period of

1   Obtained by interpolation from Lee L. Bean, M.R. Khan and A.R. Rukanuddin, Population Projections for Pakistan, 1960-2000, Karachi: Pakistan (now Bangladesh) Institute of development Economics, 1968.

March 25 to December 16, 1971 would have brought the population size down to 72.5 million on January 1, 1972. At the assumed rate of growth, this population would rise to 74.9 million on January 1, 1973. The above calculations have been made without taking into account of the external migration. If it is assumed that the net emigration from Bangladesh during February 1, 1961 to January 1, 1973 would be around one million, the actual size of the Bangladesh population on January 1, 1973 would be around 73.9 million persons.[2] For the rest of the plan period a yearly rate of population growth of over 3 per cent can be reasonably assumed. At merely 3 per cent rate of increase, 73.9 million population on January 1, 1973 will rise to 76.1 million on January 1, 1974; 78.4 million on January 1, 1975; 80.8 million on January 1, 1976; 83.2 million on January 1, 1977 and 85.7 million on January 1, 1978.

2   In view of the uncertainties associated with the components of population change, it would be safe to assume that, at 95per cent confidence level, the population size of Bangladesh on January 1, 1973 will range between 73.9 + 1.5 million.

Appendix F

The Political and Institutional Issues

The politics of the SAGQ (South Asia Growth Quadrant) relationship and the specific implications of Bangladeshi labour being absorbed into the labour scarce economies of the north east of India merits discussion. If the north east is to grow to its full potential, it is conceivable that its own domestic labour force would be insufficient. This suggests that there is scope for temporary migrant labour from Bangladesh coming in on labour permits for fixed periods or to do specific tasks, as in the case of such labour flows to the Middle East. This review should explore the political acceptability and cultural sensitivity of the north east to temporary migrants, the scope for regulation, and the ability to contain abuse. Without full acceptance by the indigenous populations of the north east, such an agenda is a non-starter.

Careful attention thus needs to be given to the salience of both bilateral political pathologies which have constrained relations within South Asia. Here again the specific problems of the north east of India merit special attention. It would be both naive and counter productive to plan agendas for either the SAGQ or the BBIMN (Bamgladesh Bhutan India Myanmar Nepal) as if economic optimization were the only issue to be considered.

Source: Rehman Sobhan, *Tranforming Eastern South Asia,* Centre for Policy Dialogue, The University Press Limited, Okhla, 1999, p.165.

Appendix G

Copy of Express Letter No. 26011/16/71 – IC, Dated 29-11-1971 of The Under Secretary to the Government of India Addressed to the Chief Secretaries to All State Governments and Under Territory Administration.

Sub: Grant of Indian citizenship to refugees from East Bengal, who have crossed over to India after 25th March, 1971. Instructions that applications from such refugees for Indian Citizenship should not be entertained.

Refugees who have crossed over to India from East Bengal since the 25th March 1971 on account of the situation in that area cannot be treated a ordinarily resident in India. They are expected to return to their native places when the conditions permit. They should not be considered for registration as Indian citizens under section 5 (I) (a) of the Citizenship Act, 1955, read with the Citizenship Rules, 1956. If such refugees make applications to the Collectors who are the prescribed authority for purposes of registration as Indian citizens under section 5 (I) (a) of the citizenship Act, such applications should be rejected. Enquires on applications for registration under sections 5 (I) (a) of the Act should be made carefully to ensure that no refugees who has come after the 25th March, 1971 from East Bengal gets registered as Indian citizen by giving any false declarations claiming to be resident in India for long and from a date prior to 25th March, 1971, Suitable instructions may kindly be issued in the matter to all Registering Authorities under your control immediately.

Appendix H

Table 9

Growth of Various Religious Communities in Assam Since Independence

Religion	1951 Population	1961 Population	Growth Rate	1971 Population	Growth Rate	1991 Population	Growth Rate	Increase Absolute	1951-91 Percentage
(1)	(2)	(3)	(4)	(5)	(6)	(7)	(8)	(9)	(10)
1. Hindus	58,86,063 (66.65)	78,84,921 (66.41)	33.96	1,06,25,847 (71.04)	34.76	1,50,47,293 (67.13)	41.61	91,61,230	155.64
2. Muslims	19,95,936 (22.60)	27,65,509 (23.29)	38.56	35,94,006 (24.03)	29.96	63,73,204 (28.43)	77.33	43,77,268	219.30
3. Christians	4,87,331 (5.52)	7,64,553 (6.44)	56.89	6,67,151 (4.46)	-12.74	7,74,367 (3.32)	16.07	2,87,036	583.89
4. Sikhs	3,949 (0.04)	9,686 (0.08)	145.28	12,347 (0.08)	27.47	16,492 (0.07)	33.57	12,543	317.62
5. Buddhists	22,628 (0.26)	36,513 (0.31)	61.36	45,212 (0.30)	23.82	64,008 (0.29)	41.57	41,380	182.87

Religion	1951 Population	1961 Population	Growth Rate	1971 Population	Growth Rate	1991 Population	Growth Rate	Increase Absolute	1951-91 Percentage
(1)	(2)	(3)	(4)	(5)	(6)	(7)	(8)	(9)	(10)
6. Jains	4,169 (0.05)	9,468 (0.08)	127.10	12,917 (0.09)	36.43	20,645 (0.09)	59.83	16,476	395.20
7. Others	4,30,656 (4.88)	4,02,122 (3.39)	-6.63	062 (0.09)	-99.98	1,38,230 (0.62)	0.61	-2,92,426	-67.90
8. Religion not stated	--	--	--	--	--	10,083 (0.05)	--	--	--

Figures in parenthesis are percentage to total population.
Source: Census of India, Assam, 1991.

299

Appendix I

Table 5
Districtwise Percentage Decadal Variation in Population Since 1951 in Assam

State/District	1951-61	1961-71	1971-91	Average decadal growth
ASSAM	34.98	34.95	53.26	26.63
1. Dhubri	27.62	40.51	56.57	28.28
2. Kokrajhar	46.34	54.30	76.78	38.39
3. Bongaigaon	60.51	40.29	64.64	32.32
4. Goalpara	37.22	45.88	54.12	27.06
5. Barpeta	32.62	35.81	43.02	21.51
6. Nalbari	49.62	42.02	49.27	24.63
7. Kamrup	37.73	38.80	65.72	32.86
8. Darrang	44.75	43.24	55.63	27.81
9. Sonitpur	35.82	27.62	57.14	28.57
10. Lakhimpur	50.46	43.39	56.29	28.14
11. Dhemaji	68.56	103.42	107.50	53.75
12. Marigaon	37.89	37.51	50.90	25.45
13. Nagaon	35.91	38.99	51.26	25.63
14. Golaghat	26.04	30.85	58.12	29.06
15. Jorhat	24.17	17.47	33.10	16.55
16. Sibsagar	23.36	19.47	38.76	19.38
17. Dibrugarh	31.55	22.93	37.78	18.89
18. Tinsukia	35.92	31.02	47.03	23.51
19. Karbi Anglong	79.21	68.28	74.72	37.36
20. North Cachar Hills	36.95	40.00	98.30	49.15
21. Karimganj	22.96	25.13	42.08	21.04
22. Hailakandi	27.23	23.61	45.94	22.97
23. Cachar	22.60	23.96	47.59	23.79

Source: Census of India, 1991

Appendix J

Districtwise Population Percentages of Hindus and Muslims and other Religions in Assam - 1991

Name of District	Hindus (per centage)	Muslims (percentage)	Other Religion (percentage)	Total population
1	2	3	4	5
DHUBRI	3,82,817 (28.72)	9,38,789 (70.45)	10,869 (0.83)	13,32,475
KOKRAJHAR	5,31,477 (66.37)	1,54,801 (19.33)	1,14,381 (14.30)	8,00,659
BONGAIGAON	5,16,830 (64.00)	2,64,393 (32.74)	26,300 (3.26)	8,02,523
GOALPARA	2,66,499 (39.88)	3,35,275 (50.18)	66,364 (9.94)	6,68,138
BARPETA	5,57,929 (40.26)	7,76,974 (56.07)	50,765 (3.67)	13,85,659
NALBARI	7,87,485 (77.47)	2,02,653 (19.93)	26,252 (2.60)	10,16,390
KAMRUP	14,86,526 (74.32)	4,67,544 (23.37)	46,001 (2.31)	20,00,021
DARRANG	7,86,332 (60.54)	4,15,323 (31.97)	97,205 (7.49)	12,98,860
SONITPUR	11,47,228 (80.19)	1,89,859 (11.11)	92,200 (6.48)	14,24,287
LAKHIMPUR	5,98,946 (79.69)	1,09,010 (14.50)	43,561 (5.81)	7,51,517
DHEMAJI	4,49,492 (93.87)	7,114 (1.48)	22,224 (4.65)	4,78,810
MARIGAON	3,48,989 (54.55)	7,89,835 (45.30)	858 (0.15)	6,39,682
NAGAON	9,79,395 (51.73)	8,93,372 (47.18)	20,454 (1.09)	18,93,171
GOLAGHAT	7,13,131 (86.11)	58,859 (7.10)	56,106 (6.79)	8,28,096
JORHAT	8,15,320 (93.58)	37,651 (4.32)	18,236 (3.00)	8,71,206

SIBSAGAR	8,10,445 (89.25)	69,260 (7.62)	28,278 (3.13)	9,07,983
DIBRUGARH	9,51,763 (91.29)	46,814 (4.49)	43,880 (4.32)	10,42,45
TINSUKIA	8,67,825 (90.18)	30,095 (3.12)	64,378 (6.70)	9,62,298
KARBI ANGLONG	5,62,102 (84.81)	10,421 (1.57)	90,200 (13.62)	6,62,72
N.C. HILLS	1,09,957 (72.91)	3,340 (2.21)	37,504 (24.88)	1,50,801
KRIMGANJ	4,14,731 (50.14)	4,06,706 (49.17)	5,626 (0.69)	8,27,06
HAILAKANDI	1,96,269 (43.70)	7,46,016 (54.78)	6,763 (1.52)	4,49,049
CACHAR	7,70,803 (63.42)	4,19,150 (34.48)	25,432 (2.10)	12,15,381
ASSAM	1,50,47,293 (67.13)	6,73,204 (28.43)	9,93,825 (4.44)	2,24,14,1

Source: Census of India, Assam, 1991

Appendix K

Government of Assam Political (B) Department
Dispur, Guwahati 781006
No. PLB. 41/96/243, dated Dispur the 12th October, 1998

To
Shri Ambuj Sharma,
Director to the Govt. of India
Ministry of Home Affairs
(Foreigners Division), North Block,
New Delhi 110001

Subject:- Repeal of Illegal Migrants (Determination by Tribunals Act, 1983.
Reference: Your letter No. 14011/28/96-FVI, dated 25/8/98.

Sir,
Kindly refer to your letter cited above regarding State Government's comments and no objection to winding up of the Foreigners Tribunals under Foreigners (Tribunals) Order, 1964 in the context of repeal of IMDT Act, 1983.

2. Under Foreigners (Tribunals) Order, 1964, Foreigners Tribunals were set up in Assam (presently 16 tribunals) to adjudicate upon as to whether a person is or is not a foreigner based on the grounds furnished by the registering authority i.e., district superintendents of police. These tribunals were set up in Assam in a situation of peculiar problem faced by it as a consequence of influx of Bangladeshi nationals into Assam. Directives then received from Govt. of India required that Bangladeshi (erstwhile East Pakistan) nationals who had entered Assam prior to March, 1971 could not be sent back

whereas migrants who entered Assam thereafter would have to be identified and deported. The purpose of these tribunals, therefore, was to determine the nationality of the migrants who entered into the State prior to 25-3-71. These tribunals were not to deal with migrants entering Assam after 25-3-71. Post 25th March, 1971 migrants could be deported directly for which powers were delegated to the district superintendents of police and deputy commissioners under the Foreigners Act 1946.

3. After the enactment of IMDT Act, 1983, a new set of procedures were laid down for detection and deportation of post 25-3-71 migrants which nullified provisions of Foreigners Act with respect to direct deportation. IMDT Act, 1983 also required setting up of tribunals to determine the nationality of the migrants who entered Assam after 25-3-71, through elaborate procedure of detection, verification, screening and reference to the IMDT tribunals. Working through the IMDT Tribunals and experience of the State administration brought into focus various lacunae in the Act which created practical constraints and impediments in achieving the objectives of identification and deportation of illegal migrants.

4. The Assam Accord was signed on 15th August, 1985 which specified another classification of Bangladeshi migrants, i.e. foreigners who came to Assam between 1-1-66 and 24-3-71. The Assam Accord provided for detection of this category of migrants and deletion of their names from the electoral rolls for a period of ten years (from the date of detection) following which their names would be restored in the electoral rolls. The Assam Accord also provided that detection of this category of migrants would be done in accordance with the provisions of the Foreigners Act, 1946 and Foreigners (Tribunal) Order 1964.

5. As long as the Assam (Accord) remains in operation the State administration will have to carry on the work of detection, categorization, disenfranchisement (for ten years from the date of detection) and subsequent restoration in the electoral rolls of 1966-71 stream migrants in terms of the provisions of Foreigners Act, 1946 and Foreigners (Tribunals) Order, 1964. This will be a continuing task for quite some time till each case falling within the first stream, i.e., 1-1-66 to 24-3-71 is dealt with under Foreigners Act, 1946 and Foreigners (Tribunal) Order, 1964.

6. Continuance of Foreigners Tribunals is also necessary in the context of the Citizenship (Amendment) Act, 1985. Under this amended Act (Sec 6 AO) detection of a foreigner has to be done as per the provision of the Foreigners Act, 1946 and the Foreigners (Tribunals) Order, 1964 by a Foreigners Tribunal.

7. Therefore, in view of what has been stated above and having regard to the Assam Accord and the citizenship (Amendment) Act, 1985, Foreigners Tribunals set up under Foreigners (Tribunals) Order, 1964 will be required to function. Accordingly State Government feel that the existing Foreigners Tribunals should not be wound up at this stage.

Yours faithfully,

(M.S. Pangtey)

Additional Chief Secretary   Sd/-M.S. Pangtey
And Principal Secretary to the   Addl. Chief Secretary
Government of Assam
Commissioner & Secretary, IAA Department
(Border), Assam, Guwahati 22.

Appendix L

IN THE SUPREME COURT OF INDIA
Civil Original Jurisdiction

Write Petition (Civil) No. 125 of 1998
(Under Article 32 of the Constitution of India)

In the matter of:
All India Lawyers Forum For Civil Liberties (AIFCL) &
Another.

. . . Petitioners.
Versus
Union of India and Others.
. . . Respondents.

COUNTER AFFIDAVIT on behalf of the Respondent
NO. 3.
State of West Bengal

I, Saralindu Sekhar Rakshit, aged about 57, years, son of
Late Sudhangshu Sekhar Rakshit, by faith Hindu, by
occupation Service holder, personally working for gain at
the Writers Buildings, Calcutta, do hereby solemnly affirm
and say as follows:-

1. I am the Joint Secretary, Home (Political) Department
Government of West Bengal. I have been authorized by
the respondent No. 3 to affirm this affidavit on its behalf.

2. I am acquainted with the facts and circumstances of the
case and having access to the relevant records stated in this
affidavit I am competent to affirm this affidavit.

3. I have read a copy of the writ petition upon which notice has been issued and have understood the contents and purports there of.

4. With reference to Paragraph 1 to 6 of the Writ Petition in so far as the State of West Bengal is concerned, I may state the following:-

(A) The State of West Bengal has a very long land border with Bangladesh. Out of about 2203 long border, about 643.59 km is riverine. Most of the border is long flat terrain without any natural demarcation.

(B) There is no fencing, wall or any other kind of physical demarcation or barring. The arrangement for interception of infiltrators is not adequate for keeping continuous uninterrupted vigil along the entire length of the border.

(C) The task of effective sealing and closing the border is mainly done by deploying personnel of the Border Security Force which is a Government of India Organization. The sanctioned strength of the Border Security Force is inadequate to match with the problem of keeping continuous uninterrupted vigil along the entire length of the long border stretching over 2,203 kilometers. As of now, at the border, the deployment of Border Security Force has been much below the sanctioned limit provided for such deployment. In addition to Border Security Force, the Mobile Task Force of the State Government also, in co-ordination with the Border Security Force

Personnel, carry out the task of sealing and closing the border. It is necessary to augment Mobile Task Force. At the meeting convened by the Union Home Ministry on 24th August, 1998 which was presided over by the Union Home Secretary, these issues were highlighted. But as on date, there has not been any perceptible improvement in regard to the deployment of Border Security Force personnel or any augmentation of Mobile Task Force.

(D) It appears that between 1972 and 1997 a total number 9,91,031 Bangladeshi nationals entered into Indian territory with valid travel documents but they did not return to Bangladesh and have overstayed.

It may be noted that under First proviso to Section 2 of the Registration of Foreigners (Bangladesh) Rules, 1973, it is not necessary for a Bangladeshi national to obtain a registration certificate unless he intends to stay for more than 180 days. There is a consequent difficulty in ascertaining the place of residence of such overstaying Bangladeshi nationals. Sometimes, it is found that the local addresses furnished by such persons are fictitious and it becomes extremely difficult to trace them out. In some cases, they change their address quite quickly and renders it difficult to take necessary steps for their deportation. Strict enforcement of the requirement of registration of foreigners in the case of Bangladeshi nationals and also introduction of the practice of a rigorous scrutiny and verification of Indian sponsors of Bangladeshi nationals before visa is granted to them, may be considered by the Government of India.

(E) There has been substantial improvement in the situation and it will appear that between 1990 and 1997 a total number of 2,35,762 infiltrators who had entered into India through clandestine routes, have been detected and pushed back to Bangladesh. Such pushing back had been authorized and advised by the Government of India from time to time. This figure excludes the persons pushed back by other State Governments.

(F) The Government of West Bengal has all along been making every effort possible to stop infiltration and has been taking every possible step to push back or deport the infiltrators whenever detected. The idea of engaging Central Bureau of Investigation in such work is wholly misconceived and unwarranted. The nature of investigation CBI has the resources to undertake is not at all commensurate with the type of huge task of stopping infiltration of Bangladeshis and when detected deporting such Bangladeshis. Delhi Special Police Establishment Act which has established the CBI, provide for investigation of particular offences by the Officers of the Central Bureau treating such Officers as Officers-in-Charge of the particular area which is coterminous with the local police station. As such Central Bureau is eminently unsuited to perform the job.

(G) Recently with a view to preventing acquisition of documents for the purpose of establishing falsely that a Bangladeshi is an Indian citizen, West Bengal Government issued a notice in the matter of issue of new ration cards and has widely publicized the same through various newspapers. It has specifically been mentioned there that the certificates issued by any government officials, office bearers of Gram Panchayat, Panchayat Samity, Municipal Commissioners Zilla Parishad Members, MPs, MLAs, may simply be corroborative evidence but such certificates will not be conclusive proof. At the same time, absence of such certificates will not be deterrent to obtaining a ration card if on proper inquiry the applicant is found to be duly entitled. It has specifically been mentioned in that notice that if it appears in course of investigation that the applicant had entered into Indian from Bangladesh after 25 March, 1971, Certificate of Citizenship must be insisted before issue of such ration card.

A copy of the notice is annexed hereto and marked as Annexure.

(H) The Government of West Bengal has consistently been trying to have the Mobile Task Force augmented and the strength of Border Security Force increased. The efforts have not met with much success. On 18 June, 1996, in response to a Fax Message from the Ministry of Home Affairs, Government of India, a Fax Message was sent by the Joint Secretary, Home (Police) Department, Government of West Bengal, giving the details of financial implications of the proposal for augmentation of Mobile Task Force staff in West Bengal in the first phase.

A Copy of the said Fax Message is annexed hereto and marked with letter R-3/2.

(I) It may be worthwhile to mention that the proposal

for erecting barbed wire fences has also not progressed satisfactorily. There has been a proposal to erect barbed wire fences along 507 kilometers of land border. But this task has also not yet been completed. Moreover, erecting the barbed wire fencing at a distance of 150 yards from the zero line has resulted in leaving some of the Indian families in between the border and barbed wire fencing. In a letter dated 15 May, 1998, written by the Principal Secretary, Home Department, Government of West Bengal to the Secretary, Ministry of Home Affairs, Government of India, this problem was highlighted and it was pointed out that unless the fencing is carried out at zero line, serious dissatisfaction and despair among the people living between the zero line and the border will render ultimately the attempt of fencing infructuous. Besides, such erection of fences would have removed the grievances of the local people and would have quickened the process of completion of the task.

A copy of the said letter is annexed hereto and marked with letter R - 3/3.

(J) It may also be pointed out that Bangladesh Government has not so far shown any willingness to formally accept those who are sought to be deported in exercise of powers under Section 3 (2) (c) of the Foreigners Act, 1946. In fact Bangladesh Government has not shown even willingness to accept those who are sought to be deported on the basis of court orders. Consequently, all actions for pushing back infiltrators are turning out to be infructuous. Many of those who were pushed back re-entered into Indian Territory through clandestine routes.

Appendix M

Excerpts from Supplementary Affidavit on behalf of the Government of West Bengal.

6. (a) Passenger traffic along the border is regulated through International Check Posts. These International Check Posts keep a record of Bangladeshis entering into India with valid documents and submit periodical reports in respect of persons overstaying their visas. Between 1972 and November 1998, a total number of 10,24,322 Bangladeshis (Hindus 667500, Muslims 349738, others 7084) who entered into Indian territory with bonafide travel documents, have overstayed.

Enquiries held at the addresses of their Indian referees have revealed that in a majority of cases such addresses are either fictitious or that the Bangladeshi has never visited his referee after coming to India.

(b) A year wise statement of Bangladeshis who have overstayed their visas is enclosed marked 'AA'.

(c) Rigorous search for tracing them out have mostly failed. Until recently there was no local resistance, nor even cooperation of the local people in identifying Bangladeshis who have settled amongst residents of West Bengal.

7. (a) The number of Bangladeshi nationals who have entered India clandestinely without valid documents is likely to be much higher.

During 1972 to November 1998 – 5,73,334 Bangladeshi Nationals (1,61,077 Hindus, 4,08,349

Muslims and 3908 others) had been detected to have clandestinely entered into India and they had been pushed back across the border.

(b) A year wise statement of Bangladeshi Nationals who have been pushed back across the border is enclosed and marked 'BB'.

8. The responsibility of checking infiltration across the border rests primarily with the Border Security Force (hereinafter referred to as BSF). For operational convenience the border falling in West Bengal has been divided into two sectors (i) South Bengal Frontier headed by an Inspector General with Headquarters at Calcutta, is in-charge of the border in the districts of South 24-Parganas, North 24-Parganas, Nadia, Murshidabad, Malda and Dakshin Dinajpur, (ii) North Bengal Frontier headed by an Inspector General with Headquarters at Siliguri, is in-charge of the border in the districts of Uttar Dinajpur, Darjeeling, Jalpaiguri and Cooch Behar.

The South Bengal Frontier stretches over 1150 KMs including 150 KMs of reverine border and the North Bengal Frontier stretches over 1053 KMs including 109 KMs of riverine border. The sanctioned strength of the BSF for the entire border is 34 Battalions including two Reserve Battalions. At present only 20 Battalions are physically deployed at the border. The rest of the force has been withdrawn for duties elsewhere in the country. In all the BSF mans 405 border outposts along the West Bengal portion of the Indo-Bangladesh border. 226 of such border outposts are located in the Southern Frontier and 179 in the Northern Frontier. The average strength of these border outposts range from two sections to one platoon of force and between themselves they have to patrol and prevent infiltration over five to six KMs of the border. Taking into consideration the nature of the border, the BSF presently deployed at the border is absolutely inadequate to prevent infiltration.

9. (a) The Government of India had sanctioned the construction of 1597 KMs border roads and 507 KMs of barbed wire fence along the Indo-Bangladesh border, covering the vulnerable stretches. Till November 1998, construction of 1232.82 KMs of road and 455.14 KMs of fence had been completed.

(b) A district-wise chart is enclosed marked 'CC'.

10. There are in all 11 International Check Posts along the Indo-Bangladesh border to regulate passenger traffic across the border. Except for the Check Post at Haridaspur, all others lack elementary infrastructure like accommodation, communication facilities etc. The State Government has initiated steps to upgrade these International Check Posts with financial assistance from the Government of India. These International Check Posts keep a record of Bangladeshi Nationals entering into India with valid documents and submit periodical reports in respect of persons overstaying their visas. Enquiries held at the addressees of their Indian referees have revealed that in a majority of cases such addresses are either fictitious or such Bangladeshis had actually not come there at any time during their visit to India. Unless pre-verification of the referees is held before the issue of visas keeping track of such foreigners will continue to be difficult.

11. To detect and push back Bangladeshi Nationals who have succeeded in crossing the border unauthorisedly, the Government of India had sanctioned the creation of a Mobile Task Force for West Bengal. The present strength of this force is 1 Superintendent of Police, 2 Deputy Superintendents of Police, 11 Inspectors, 51 Sub-Inspectors and 100 Head Constables totalling to 165 members of the force. It need not be emphasized that the strength of this force is too merge to deal with the problem of infiltration emanating from more than two thousand KM long border. In neighbouring Assam the sanctioned strength of the Mobile Task Force is 3,153 officers and men. Government of West Bengal has repeatedly been entreating Government of India to augment this force, in keeping with the nature and volume of the task with which it has been entrusted. These entreaties are yet to find favour with the Government of India.

12. Till 1997 Bangladeshis intercepted in the bordering areas were being summarily pushed back in keeping with the instructions issued by the Government of India in their Circular No. 14011/8/96-F.VI dated 16-9-97. Thereafter the Bangladeshi authorities having resisted such summary push back, instructions have now been issued that such Bangladeshi Nationals, irrespective of the places of their interception, have to be prosecuted under the Foreigners Act and pushed back/deported only after an appropriate order from a competent court.

13. While it is relatively easy to detect, prosecute and push back Bangladeshis intercepted during transit, it is quite difficult to identify those who have already settled in the districts due to the following reasons:

(i) Their features, dress and language are largely similar to the residents of West Bengal;

(ii) Many of them have acquired ration cards and have been enlisted in the electoral rolls with the help of local touts and unscrupulous officials and politicians;

(iii) Many sections of the local people, including political leaders of all hues, harbour a sympathy for them and are reluctant to cooperate in their identification and deportation; and

(iv) The sheer number of such Bangladeshis believed to have entered into India after 1971, makes it humanly impossible to prosecute all of them under the Foreigners Act, get a conviction and a court order in respect of each one of them and thereafter push them back to Bangladesh.

Appendix N

Excerpts from Affidavit on Behalf of the State of Assam

14. That in the year 1983, the Parliament enacted Illegal Migrants (Determination by Tribunals) Act, 1983 (hereinafter referred to as the IM(DT) Act) to deal with the problem of influx of illegal migrants to Assam. Though this Act extends to the whole of India, it was applicable to the State of Assam only. That Act provides for the establishment of Tribunals for the determination of the question whether a person is illegal migrant or not to enable the Government to expel illegal migrants from India. The Act was made applicable to those illegal migrants who entered into India on or after the 25th March, 1971.

14.1. That Section 4 of the Illegal Migrants (Determination by Tribunals) Act, gives overriding effect to the provisions of this Act over other enactments on the subject including the Foreigners Act, 1946. Under Section 5 of the Act, Tribunals were constituted for the purpose of detection of foreigners and the member of the Tribunals could be only those person who is or has been a District Judge or an Additional District Judge in any State. Under Section 8 of the Act, detailed provisions have been made for reference to the Tribunal for deciding as to whether any person is or is not an illegal migrant. It is pertinent to note that application can be made by a person to the Tribunal only if he resides within the jurisdiction of the same Police Station where the suspect resides. Further, the application is required to be accompanied by affidavit of two persons and application fee of not less than Rs. 10/-

and not more than Rs 100/-. Under Section 8A, a person can make application to the Central Government for making a reference to the Tribunal. Such application can also be made only by a person residing within the jurisdiction of the same Revenue Sub-Division as that of the suspect. Under Section 14, an Appellate tribunal is constituted for hearing appeals against the orders of the Tribunals. The Appellate tribunal is constituted by a person who is or has been a Judge of a High Court. Under Section 20, the Central Government is required to serve on the illegal migrant so determined by the tribunal to remove himself from India. Under Section 20 (2), only an officer not below the rank of Superintendent of Police has the power to ensure compliance of the order of removal passed by the Central Government. Under Section 21, the Central Government may delegate its powers to the State Government. Under Section 28, the Central Government can make rules to carry out its provisions.

14.2. That under Section 21 of the Act, Central Govt. By notification delegated its powers under Section 5, 6, 7, 8, 8A, 14, 15, & 20 to the State Government.

14.3 That the Central Government in exercise of powers under Section 28 of the IM (DT) Act framed rules, namely Illegal Migrants (determination by Tribunals) Rules, 1984 (hereinafter referred to as the IM (DT) Rules). These Rules stipulate enquiries at various levels before a reference can be made to the Tribunal. Under Rule 4, a Superintendent of Police or a Sub-Inspector of Police can call upon a person suspected to be illegal migrant to give particulars in Form-I. It is however, pertinent to note that such police officer has no power to compel the person to give information sought for in Form-I. Under rule 7, the Inquiry Officer is required to submit his report in Form-II to Screening Committee constituted under Rule 8 which consists of the Sub-Divisional Officer and a Police Officer not below the rank of Deputy Superintendent of Police. Under Rule 8 (2), the Screening Committee scrutinizes the information received from the Inquiry Officer and after considering the relevant materials makes its recommendation to the Superintendent of Police as to whether the person mentioned in the report is or is not an illegal migrant. It is only if the Screening Committee makes its recommendation that the suspected person is an illegal migrant that a reference can be made to the Tribunal under Rule 9.

15. That under the IM (DT) Act, 16 Tribunals were constituted to cover 23 Districts of Assam. As per provisions of the IM (DT) Act, only the person who is or has been a District Judge or an Additional District Judge can be appointed as member of the Tribunal. However, under the Foreigners (Tribunal) Order, 1964 any person having judicial experience can be appointed as a member of the Tribunal. The State Government despite repeated advertisements have not been able to get qualified persons for appointment in some vacant posts as members of the Tribunal. The State Government has written to all the Deputy Commissioners to personally contact the retired District Judges or Additional District Judges of their respective areas who are not more than 63 years of age and obtain their willingness to join as Chairman/Member of the Illegal Migrants Determination tribunal. The State Government has also written a letter to the Registrar of the High Court to furnish the list of District

Judges/Additional District Judges (serving or retired) who can be appointed as Chairman/Member of the Illegal Migrants Determination Tribunal/Foreigners Tribunal.

16. That the status as on 31/5/99 with regard to number of inquiries made by the Inquiry Officer and the Screening Committee and the cases referred and decided by the Illegal Migrants Determination Tribunals is as here under:

01	Total number of enquiries initiate	3,02,554
02	Total number of enquiries completed	3,00,165
03	Total number of enquiries referred to Screening Committee	2,96,564
04	Total number of enquiries made by Screening Committee	2,93,636
05	Total number of enquiries referred to the IM(DT)s	31,264
06	Total number of enquiries disposed of by the IM(DT)s	15,142
07	Total number of persons declared as Illegal Migrants	9,625
08	Total number of Illegal Migrants physically expelled	1,461
09	Total number of IMs to whom Expulsion orders served	5,667
10	Total number of enquiries pending with Screening Committee	2,920
11	Total number of enquiries pending with the Tribunals	16,122

It is submitted that the Screening Committee under the IM (DT) Rules have rejected the cases for reference to IM (DT) Tribunals due to lack of positive evidence since under the IM (DT) Act it is the Government or the Complainant with payment of fees and affidavit who is required to establish by positive evidence that the suspect is an illegal migrant. However, to the contrary under the Foreigners Act, under Section 9, the onus is on the suspect to prove that he is not a foreigner. Section 9 of the Foreigners Act reads as under:-

"9. Burden of Proof: If in any case not falling under Section 8 any question arise with reference to this Act or any order made or direction given thereunder, whether any person is or is not a foreigner or is not a foreigner of a particular class or description the onus of proving that such person is not a foreigner or is not a foreigner of such particular class or description, as the case may be, shall, notwithstanding anything contained in the Indian Evidence Act, 1872 (1 to 1872) lie upon such person.'

17. That the IMDT Act is a discriminatory piece of Legislation, because it has made impermissible geographical classification for its application in a particular State only without justification/reason. The object of Legislation is to detect 'illegal migrants' which is species of foreign national, in order to deport such foreigners. There cannot be any geographical differentiation with the manner of defection and deportation as has been Practiced in the IMDT Act. As such differentia not pertinent to the object of the Legislation and the object to be achieved has no nexus to the classification.

Further, the IMDT Act, within its area of operation, introduced a new 'cut off date', namely 25/3/1971, for the purpose of defining 'illegal Migrants' who is inter-alia, is a foreigner. But for determination of such foreigner the

Constitution of India under Article 5 has already laid down such 'cut of date'. So without amending the Constitution, in respect of 'cut of date' as prescribed by the Constitution introduction of new 'cut of date' is wholly illegal and is not sustainable. As the provisions of IMDT Act are much more strict than provisions of the Foreigners Act, State of Assam found many difficulties and impediments in the implementation of the IM (DT) Act. Even the Hon'ble Governor of Assam submitted a report to the Hon'ble President of India in November, 1998 on illegal migrants and the impediments in the implementation of IM (DT) Act.

The Government of India in the tripartite meeting with the Sate of Assam and All Assam Students Union held at New Delhi on 1-7-1999 assured that the repeal of IM (DT) Act is under active consideration of the Government of India. In this meeting various other issues relating to illegal migration were discussed and decisions were taken. Some of the decision taken in the meeting are as under:

(i) The proposal submitted by Government of Assam for creation of additional posts for PIF/MTF was discussed. It was informed that additional posts cannot be considered.

(ii) It was noted that 1000 personnel of PIF/MTF have not been stationed as second line of defence so far. It was decided that 500 personnel would be stationed by July 31, 1999 and another personnel by September 30, 1999.

(iii) Government of Assam informed that 1000 posts are vacant in PIF/MTF. They requested that they may be allowed to fill up these positions not from ex-servicemen but from general category. It was agreed that atleast 500 of the vacant positions should be filed up as per existing norms so that delay is avoided.

Meanwhile, the request of Government of Assam would be considered and decision communicated.

(iv) It was agreed that Rs. 171 Crores proposal of Government of Assam additional roads and fencing is recommended for sanction.

(v) AASU urged that an Ordinance be issued for repeal of IMDT Act, 1983. Government of Assam representatives supported for issuance of ordinance in this regard. The repeal of IMDT Act, 1983 is under active consideration of Government of India. This has also been stated in the address of Hon'ble President of India to the Parliament in February 1999.

State Government has written to the Central Government on a number of occasions for either to repeal the IM (DT) Act or to make necessary amendments in the said Act in order to facilitate the State to detect and deport the illegal migrants.

18. That the major impediments faced by the State of Assam in the effective implementation of the IM (DT) Act are as here under:

(i) The onus of proof is on the prosecution under IM (DT) Act as opposed to the provisions of Foreigners Act, 1946 under which the onus is on the suspected foreigner.

(ii) There is no provision in IM (DT) Act for compelling the suspects to furnish the particulars required in Form No. 1 of IM (DT) Rules of 1984 and penal provision to deal with such suspects in case of their refusal to furnish information as required in Rule 5.

(iii) There is no provision for compelling suspects/witnesses to furnish information or statement to Police Officers making Enquiry and as such, taking recourse to action under Section 176 IPC is difficult in case of refusal.

(iv) The Enquiry Officer is not empowered to search homes/premises of the suspects nor can they compel the suspects to produce documents or give the necessary information.

(v) Prosecution witnesses do not appear before the Tribunals for want of necessary allowances.

(vi) Once Tribunals declare a person as an illegal migrant he/she becomes un-traced either before the notice is served or during the grace period of 30 days.

(vii) The notice/summons issued by the Tribunals cannot be served due to change of residence by the illegal migrants to some unknown destinations.

(viii) Expulsion orders cannot be served as the illegal migrants change their places of residence very frequently and merge with people of similar ethnic origin.

(ix) It is provided in the Act for filing a complaint against a person to determine as to whether the person is an illegal migrant, two persons living within the same police station are required and an amount of Rs. 10,00 has to be deposited with the application/complaint. This provision of the Act, puts a severe restriction in the matter of filing any complaint against any illegal migrant.

(x) The Tribunals after observing a long drawn procedure declare a person as illegal migrant who is to be deported from India. But very often, the persons declared as illegal migrants change their residence and shift to some other areas.

(xi) There are instances of strong resistance to enquiry officer conducting enquiries against the illegal migrants in Char Areas (Riverine areas) and other areas where there is a heavy concentration of immigrant population. The SPs Police who are otherwise busy dealing with law and order problems have virtually little force to spare for assisting the enquiry officers.

19. It is further submitted that even after detection of foreigners under the Foreigners Act/IM (DT) Act, the physical deportation of such illegal migrants has not been possible in most of the cases.

The Quit India notice is served on the Bangladesh nationals under Section 3 of the Foreigners Act, 1946 and under Section 20 of the IM (DT) Act, 1983 by the Foreigner Registration Officer for two categories of foreigners viz (I) Bangladesh Nationals who have entered India on or after 25th March, 1971 (ii) and persons who are declared as foreign nationals and deported and later on re-infiltrated as per provisions laid down under the laws. Under the present dispensation Quit India/ Expulsion is dependent on the verification report from Bangladesh Government as Bangladesh Rifles does not accept Bangladesh nationals unless nationality is again investigated by the Bangladesh Government. The Foreigner Registration Officers issue the Quit India notice or push back orders as per provisions laid down in the Foreigners Act and IM (DT) Act as mentioned above. But due to the insistence of compulsory verification of the nationality of the Bangladesh nationals by a Bangladesh Agency the desired result is not achieved. Besides this the State Government Authority (concerned SP) cannot keep a person (IM) in police custody for more than 24 hours under Section 57 Cr. PC, 1973. Further there is no provisions for meeting expenses resulting from keeping such foreigners/IMS until their deportation.

20. That the State Government has taken various steps to prevent future illegal migration into the Indian territory from Bangladesh. Some of the steps taken are as hereunder:

(i) Night curfew is promulgated which is in force at Border Districts of Assam and as a measure of deterrent to infiltration at night. In addition the works done by PIF Officers in identification, detection and deportation of foreign national are being quarterly reviewed and suitable instructions are issued to the staff of PIF Schemes for improving the performance.

(ii) Some illegal migrants are using Tripura and West Bengal as corridor for entering in Assam.

After detection these illegal migrants claimed to be the residents of Tripura. Inter State Check Post under the PIF Scheme have been set up one at Srirampur on West Bengal Assam Border and another at Churaibari on Assam Tripura Border.

(iii) In service training for the field officers are arranged at regular interval to improve their field efficiency by imparting lessons on essential acts.

(iv) Speedy completion of border roads and fencing.

21. The State Government respectfully submits that this Hon'ble Court may be pleased to give directions in the following regard to the Government of India both for the purpose of deportation of illegal migrants and for the purpose of preventing further illegal infiltration into the Indian territory:

(i) Repeal/substantial amendment in the Illegal Migrants (Determination by Tribunals) Act, 1983 in view of the impediments in detection and deportation of illegal migrants under the provisions of the said Act as pointed out aforesaid;

(ii) Reduce the distance between two BSF posts on the borders from 6-8 Kms to 2-3 Kms;

(iii) Creation of dedicated BSF exclusively for Assam and involving the local youth in the said Force;

(iv) Watch the borders with high-tech facilities like satellite surveillance, improving communication facilities, ensuring mobility on the roads as well as on rivers;

(v) Coordination with Bangladesh Government to accept the illegal migrants once they are determined as foreigners/illegal migrants by the Courts/Tribunals of our country;

(vi) Proposal of multi-purpose photo identity cards should be implemented forthwith particularly in the border villages. This work should be done in a time frame. Issue of Photo Identity Cards to the genuine Indian Citizen will go a long way in checking the illegal migration. The Election Commission of India's move to issue Photo Identity Cards to the Indian voters appears to be a step in right direction for checking the illegal migration from the neighbouring countries.

While issuing the Photo Identity Cards as above, a suitable process will have to be evolved to ensure that no illegal migrant retain his name in the Voters List and the names of such illegal migrants are completely deleted from the Voters List immediately after detection.

Photo Identity Cards as and when issued could also be used for grant of work permits to by duly authenticated by competent authority for engagement in non-governmental job, like contractors, labour, vendors, menials etc.

22. It is pertinent to mention here that in the recent past there appears to be a close nexus between the illegal Migrants and the Fundamentalist organization on the one hand and between the Fundamentalist organizations and

Pak ISI (Pakistan Inter-Services Intelligence) on the other. The Pakistan ISI has increased their nefarious activities in India whose action plan interalia includes subverting the Border Areas by utilizing the Fundamentalist Organizations in carrying out Anti India activities. The recent arrests of 4 (four) Pakistani Inter-Services Intelligence (ISI) Agents at Guwahati, Assam, has amply proved the sinister activities of the ISI and its well-laid plans in league with Muslim Fundamentalist Organization as well as ULFA and other Militants Outfits for destabilization of the State by indulging in large-scale subversive activities which is a cause of serious concern for the safety, security and integrity of the Nation.

The state of Assam assures this Hon'ble Court that it is taking the issue of detection and deportation of illegal migrants and prevention of further illegal migrants into Assam with all seriousness and sincerity.

Ganesh Kumar Kalita
Joint Secretary, Political Government of Assam
DEPONENT

VERIFICATION

I, the above named deponent, do hereby verify that the contents of above affidavit are true and correct, no part of it is false and nothing material has been concealed there from.

Verified at Guwahati on this 1st the day of Sept. 1999.

Appendix O

Draft of Proposal for an Indian Migrant Law

Article 1
Aims and Objects

A. to prevent illegal migration into India and the settlement of foreign nationals on Indian soil and the illicit conferring of citizenship and other rights on such nationals—which should be available only to Indian nationals;

B. to meet the concerns of Indians in different parts of the country, but especially the North East of the country comprising of the states of Assam, Nagaland, Manipur, Meghalaya, Mizoram, Sikkim and Tripura, Arunachal Pradesh, about such illegal settlement and to prevent the demographic changes that are altering the ethnic character of the NER (North Eastern Region) and to protect the rights of Indian nationals to their land, titles, vote, free movement and the acquisition of permanent assets.

C. to control future migration into the country by developing a set of rules that will enable legal, work-related movement of unskilled labourers for specific periods of time and limited to specific periods without conferring on such migrants any of the rights that are the privileges of Indian nationals—i.e. that of citizenship, of adult franchise, of permanent settlement or acquiring immoveable property.

Article 2
Definition of Migrant for the purposes of this Act:

A. an individual who moves (migrates) from any country

to India for the purpose of employment at a non-skilled level (define non-skilled as professions such as carpentry, mason, house building, road construction, farming, harvesting, fishing, boat building and river transporters etc.)

B. The individual is an adult, i.e. more than 18 years of age

C. He/she is not a refugee as defined by the National Refugee Law (a draft of this exists and is with the Government of India).

D. The individual is to live in India for a period not exceeding two years for purposes of A. and as defined in Article 3.

E. The individual will not be entitled to any permanent settlement rights such as Citizenship, adult franchise or acquiring of immovable property.

F. The individual may be a national of any of the following countries bordering on the North East: Bangladesh, Bhutan and Nepal.

(G. The individual must be a resident of a district in his country which borders the NER.)

Article 3
Control of Economic Migrants

A. The economic migrant will be entitled to move to a work place for pursuing occupations as those defined in Article 2 B under the following procedure:

1. He/she can apply to the Deputy Commissioner or District Magistrate in his district and indicate that he/she wishes to migrate for purposes of work in one of the occupations defined in Article 2B to the NER. He/she will be required to fill up a form where he must set down his/her name and address, father's name, age, bank

account number (if any) and desire for wishing to migrate and two passport-size photos of himself/herself. Required numbers of labour force will be indicated to the respective district authorities in these countries.

2. Once such applications reach a requisite/economic figure as may be decided by the district authorities, this information will be onpassed to authorities in the NER where a special unit (operations) locates labour force needs for specific areas and potential employers. Connectivity through the Internet will be the best way of communicating this information between authorities in the two countries. Once the location, agreed employers and numbers of workers are upon, Work Permits may be issued to the group at the border which are then transported (at employer's expense) to the site of work. Copies of that permit are filed with the respective Bangladesh/Nepal/Bhutan authority, with the employer and with the State Government at state capital as well as with local district police.

B. The Work Permits will be have three sections:

1. A Group Permit that attaches all the details (including passport photos) of the workers

2. Location of work place and identity of employer and the nearest police station.

3. The proposed duration of residence.

C. The Work Permits are not visas and do not entitle their holders to do any but the above prescribed jobs, occupations for a limited period. Any deviation will be punishable under relevant provisions of the law and lead to immediate repatriation.

D. The Employer will be made legally responsible if any

employee under the WP scheme is found missing.

E. WP members must report to the local police station in a group every 180 days without fail.

F. At the end of a year, if the WP members so wish, they can apply to the local district authority for a year's extension of the said permit. The permit will not be extendable beyond two years.

G. Foreign nationals under the GP system will be entitled to use Indian banking channels to repatriate Indian rupees to their bank accounts in their respective countries under a special bilateral agreement.

Article 4: Rules:

1. Those who migrate for economic reasons under the WP scheme will be entitled to the same rights as their contemporaries in India under existing labour legislation, including protection of their civil (human) rights under India law, such as

1.A. hours of work
1.B. areas of work (geographical)
1.C. occupation

Bibliography

PRIMARY SOURCES
Census and census reports

INDIA
Census of India, 1951, Assam, Manipur and Tripura

Census of India, 1961, Assam

Census of India, 1971, Assam

Census of India, 1991, Series 4 - Assam, Part VA and VB-D Series, Migration Tables, Volume 1, Directorate of Census Operations, Assam

Census of India, 1991, Series 4, Assam, Part VA and VB-D Series, Migration Tables, Volume 2, Directorate of Census Operations, Assam

Census of India 1991 Series 4, Assam, Aspects of Population Profile of Assam, 1991 Census, N.C. Dutta, Director of Census Operations, Assam

Census of India, 1991, Series 1-India Paper 1 of 1997 Language, India and states (Table C-7), M. Vijayanunni,

Registrar General and Census Commissioner, India

Census of India 1991, Series 4, Assam, Part IV-B (ii) Religion (Table C-9), Directorate of Census Operations, Assam

Census of India 1991, Series 1, India, Paper 1 of 1995, Religion, M. Vijayanunni, Registrar General and Census Commissioner, India

Census of India 1991, Series 1, India, Paper 1 of 1992, Vol. II Final Population Totals, Amulya Ratna Nanda, Registrar General and Census Commissioner

Assam Census Newsletters, Directorate of Census Operations, Assam, Guwahati

BANGLADESH

National Series: Bangladesh Population Census, 1991, Volume 1, Analytical Report, September 1994, Bangladesh Bureau of Statistics

National Series: Bangladesh Population Census, 1991, Volume 2, Union Statistics, December 1993, Bangladesh Bureau of Statistics

Community Series: Bangladesh Population Census 1991 Zila: Kurigram, November 1995, Bangladesh Bureau of Statistics

Zila Series: Bangladesh Population Census 1991, Kurigram, November 1995, Bangladesh Bureau of Statistics

National Series: Bangladesh Population Census 1981, Analytical Findings and National Tables, August 1984, Bangladesh Bureau of Statistics

Thana Series: Bangladesh Population Census 1981, Community tables of all thanas of Mymensingh District Part 1 July 1985, Bangladesh Bureau of Statistics

National Volume, 1974 Bangladesh Population Census Report, Bangladesh Bureau of Statistics, Statistics Division, Ministry of Planning, Government of the People's Republic of Bangladesh

Bangladesh Population Census 1974, Rangpur District, Bangladesh Bureau of Statistics

1997 Statistical Yearbook of Bangladesh, 18th edition, Bangladesh Bureau of Statistics

1995 Statistical Yearbook of Bangladesh, 16th edition, Bangladesh Bureau of Statistics

Census of Pakistan: 1961, Vol. 2 East Pakistan. Published under the Authority of Home Affairs Division, Ministry of Home and Kashmir Affairs, Karachi

Others

State of the World Reports, 1994, 1995, 1996, 1997, 1998, 1999. World Watch Institute, Washington

Supreme Court of India: Writ Petition (Civil) No. 125 of 1998: In the matter of All India Lawyers Forum for Civil Liberties (AIFCL) & Another versus Union of India and Others: Counter Affidavit on behalf of the Respondent

No. 3 (State of West Bengal); also Supplementary Affidavit/Status Report on behalf of Respondent No. 3.

Supreme Court of India: Writ Petition (Civil) No. 125 of 1998: Affidavit on Behalf of the State of Assam

SECONDARY SOURCES

Books and articles

Abramovitz, Janet M. 'Impoverished Future: The Decline of Freshwater Ecosystems', World Watch papers, March 1996

Barber, Charles Victor, *The Case of Indonesia, Environmental Scarcities, State Capacity, Civil Violence Series*. American Academy of Arts and Sciences and University College, University of Toronto, 1997

Baruah, Sanjib, *India Against Itself: Assam and the Politics of Nationality*, Philadelphia: University of Pennsylvania Press, 2000

Begum Sharifa and Armindo Miranda, *Data from the 1997 Population Census: A Preliminary Analysis*, Bangladesh Institute of Development Studies, Dhaka, Bangladesh

Begum, Sharifa, *Birth Rate and Death Rate in Bangladesh, 1951-1974*, Bangladesh Institute of Development Studies, Dhaka, 1979

Begum, Sharifa, *Population, Birth, Death and Growth Rates in Bangladesh: Census Estimates*, Bangladesh Institute of Development Studies, Dhaka, 1990

Brown, Lester R., Gary Gardner, and Brian Halweil, *Beyond Malthus: Nineteen Dimensions of the Population Challenge,* World Watch Institute, 1999

Brown, Lester R, *Tough Choices: Facing the Challenge of Food Scarcity,* World Watch Environmental Alert Series, 1996

Brown, Lester R., and Hal Kane, *Full House: Reassessing the Earth's Population Carrying Capacity,* World Watch Environment Alert Series, 1994

Change in Chilmari. Unpublished report. Intensive Rural Works Programme, Bangladesh. DANIDA, NORAD, and SIDA. October 1986

Economy, Elizabeth, *The Case of China,* Environmental Scarcities, State Capacity, Civil Violence Series. American Academy of Arts and Sciences and University College, University of Toronto, 1997

Gardner, Gary, 'Shrinking Fields: Cropland Loss in a World of Eight Billion', World Watch papers, July 1996

Khan, Masihur Rahman, *Bangladesh Population During the First Five Year Plan period (1972-77): A Guesstimate,* Bangladesh Institute of Development Economics, Dhaka, Bangladesh

Hazarika, Sanjoy, *Strangers of the Mist: Tales of War and Peace from India's North East,* New Delhi: Viking, 1994

Bangladesh and Assam: Land Pressures, Migration and Ethnic Conflict, American Academy of Arts and Sciences and University College, University of Toronto, project on

Environmental Change and Acute Conflict, March 1993

McGinn, Anne Platt, 'Rocking the Boat: Conserving Fisheries and Protecting Jobs', World Watch papers, June 1998

Renner, Michael, 'Ending Violent Conflict', World Watch papers, April 1999

Postel, Sandra, 'Dividing the Waters: Food, Security. Ecosystem Health, and the Politics of Scarcity', World Watch papers, September 1996

Samaddar, Ranabir, ed., *Reflections on Partition in the East*, Calcutta Research Group, Delhi: Vikas Publishing House Pvt. Ltd, 1997

Sobhan, Rehman, *Transforming Eastern South Asia, Building Growth Zones for Economic Cooperation*, Centre for Policy Dialogue, Dhaka: The University Press Limited, Dhaka, 1999

Sobhan, Rehman, *Bangladesh: Problems of Governance*, Centre for Policy Research, New Delhi: Konarak Publishers Pvt. Ltd., 1993

Suhrke, Astri, Pressure Points: Environmental Degradation, Migration and Conflict, American Academy of Arts and Sciences and University College, University of Toronto, project on Environmental Change and Acute Conflict, March 1993

Teitelbaum, Michael S., and Myron Weiner, ed, *Threatened Peoples, Threatened Peoples, Threatened Borders, World Migration and US Policy,* New York:

W.W. Norton, 1995

Van Hear, Nicholas, *New Diasporas: The Mass Exodus, Dispersal and Regrouping of Migrant Communities*, London: UCL Press, 1998

Verghese, B.G., *Waters of Hope: Himalaya-Ganges Development and Cooperation for a Billion People*, Delhi: Oxford and IBH Publishing Co. Pvt. Ltd., 1990

——*India's North East Resurgent*, Delhi: Konarak, 1997

Vital Signs, 1994, 1997, 1998. World Watch Institute, Washington

Weiner Myron, *The Global Migration Crisis: Challenges to States and to Human Rights*, New York: HarperCollins College Publishers, 1992

Newspapers, periodicals and magazines

Himal. October 1998 issue, The Price of Our Daughters. Kathmandu

World Watch. The references to Edward O. Wilson's work on consilience are from the special issue of March-April 1999

'Immigrant Adaptation and Native-Born Responses in the Making of Americans', Special issue, *International Migration Review*, Vol. 31, Winter 1997, Centre for Migration Studies, New York

'People in Camps', *Forced Migration Review*, August 1998, Oxford, UK

Index

Adis, 37
Adnan, Shapan, 232
Agartala, 169-78
Ahmed, Fakhruddin Ali, 56, 61, 64
Ahmed, Imtiaz, 218
Aiyar, Shekhar, 244
Akbar, 36
Ali, Mohammad Shahid, 197
All Assam Students Union (AASU), 25, 55, 60, 64, 67, 71, 141, 146, 229, 255-56
All Bodo Students Union, 39
All India Forum for Civil Liberties, 227
All Tripura Tigers' Force (ATTF), 173
Amin, Idi, 83
Amra Bangla, 175
Anam, Mahfuz, 151
Annan, Kofi, 18
Ansari, Abdul Barek, 143
Arunachal Pradesh, 32, 34-35, 38, 40, 87, 90
Asom Gana Parishad (AGP), 70, 141, 190, 256
Assam,
  Ahom rule in, 35, 37
  anti-immigrant movement (1980), 28-31, 255
  Bodos of, 38-42

communities of, 33-35
doable programmes to transfer region of, 256-67
elections in, 25-26, 57-58, 68
geography, 32
history of, 71-74
immigrants issue, 1, 28-31, 55-56, 59-70, 257-67
see also migration/migrants
land and people of, 16-48
languages used in, 35-36, 39
Motoks of, 42-43
oil and gas resources, 33
perception and concerns over migrants into, 25-28
population growth in, 221-25, 231
profile of, 31-35
primordial passions, 36-48
tea production in, 33
Tiwas of, 42-43, 45-46, 51-53,
tribal community, 38-53
under British rule, 37-38
Assamese nationalism, 26-27
Awami League, 90, 137, 179, 220
Azad, Abdus Samad, 239
Babur 36

Bakht, Zaid, 252-53
Bandihana Char, 149
Bangladesh,
    demographic statistics,
    204-11
    drinking water facilities,
    206-07
    health facilities, 206-07
    human security in, 211-20
    incidence of poverty in, 210
    life expectancy in, 208, 210
    literacy rate, 206, 208-09
    out-migration to India,
    213-20, 231-33
    population, 205-06, 210,
    214-20
    position on migration,
    239-40
Bangladesh Election
    Commission, 219
Bangladesh Institute of
    Developmet Studies, 213,
    252
Bangladeshis,
    identification problems,
    131-36
    illegal migration, 24-25,
    115-20
    in Assam, 1, 28-31, 55-56,
    59-70
    in chars, 102-13, 125-26,
    128, 130
    in Satrasal-Agomoni,
    137-45
    villagers views about,
    141-50
Barak Valley, 68-69
Bardoloi Gopinath, 26, 115
Barua, Jahnu, 128, 152, 154,
    156
Baruah, Paresh, 43
Basu, Jyoti, 118
Begum, Sharifa, 200, 231-32
Bengali Tiger Force, 175

Bepari, Abu Hossein, 149
Bharatiya Janata Party, 61,
    67, 99, 119, 141, 216, 236
Bhargava, S.N., 133
Bhattacharyya, Samujjal, 256
Bhowmick, Chandan, 147
Bhutan, 39-40, 54, 91-92
Bhuyan, J.C., 219
Bidekhi, concept of, 27
Blitz, 49
Bodo Sahitya Sabha, 39
Bodoland Council, 40
Bodoland Security Force, 41
Bodoland Tiger Force, 41
Bodos, 38-42
Borah, Gynanath, 27
Borbora, Golap, 29
Border Industrialisation
    Programme, 80
Border Security Force, 57-58,
    162, 96, 118, 122-23, 126
Borooah, Dev Kanta, 64
Bracero programme, and
    Guest Workers, 79-81
Brahmaputra Valley, 31,
    36-37, 39-40, 54, 56,
    68-69, 103, 105, 110, 112,
    115, 129, 140, 156
Brown, Lester R., 234
Cabinet Mission of 1946, 26
Cachar, 37, 39, 56-57
Carson, Rachel, 17
Centre for North East Studies
    and Policy Research, 6
Chakku Mian, Mohammad,
    191, 199
Chakmas problem, 87-91
Chakraborty, Nripen, 172
Chakravorty, Dilip, 107
Chaliha, Bimala Prasad, 60,
    62-64
Chapamara, 159

Char Development Authority, 259
Chars (Islands)
    Diwanis of, 113-15, 121
    immigration to 115-21, 125
    people and life at, 102-13, 125-26, 128, 130
Chatterjee, Sanjoy, 128
Chetia, Anup, 43
Chilmari Ghat 152-53, 156-61, 179-203
Chittagong Hill Tracts, 86-87, 89-90
Chowdhury, Moinul Huq, 56, 61
Chowdhury, Wazed Ali, 112, 115
Colonisation, scheme, 72
Commission on Global Governance, 240
Communist Party of India, 71, 168, 174
Congress Party, 52, 54-57, 61-63, 68-70, 119, 135, 168, 174, 236
Constitution of India, article 226, 134
Currey, Bruce, 159-60
Curzon, 71
DANIDA, 159
Daflas, 37
Daily Star, 151
Daimuri, Ranjan, 40
Dalu, 124
Darrang, 56
Darwin, Charles, 17
Das, Bharat, 144-46
Das, Mahesh Chandra 9-12, 122, 265
Das, Romen, 144-46
Das, Ronendra Chandra, 143
Das, Sushil, 137, 144, 146

Dasgupta Anindita, 100, 103, 105, 107-09, 112, 125, 131
Dawki, 13-14
Deb, Dasrath, 168
Debnath, Shanti, 150
Deoris, 37
Deve Gowda, H.D. 23
Developmental refugees, 87
Dhubri, 56, 100-02, 107, 109-11, 113, 120-22, 128, 130, 136
Diaz-Briquets, Sergio, 80
Dibrugarh, 56
Dimasas, 37
Economic migrants, 98
El Dorado, 97-98
El-Hinnawi, Essam, 78
Election Commission, India, 229, 257, 260
Environmental degradation, due to population growth, 20
Environmental displacement, 81-84
Environmental refugees, 77, 81-84, 87
Environmental Refugees, 78
Ershad, H.M., 219
Firdouz, 183, 185, 187
Foreigners Act of 1946, 134, 230
Franke, William, 246-47
Gaibanda, 193
Gandhi, Indira, 29-31, 52, 56-57, 63, 65, 67, 132, 177
Gandhi, Mahatma, 26, 266
Gandhi, Rajiv, 57
Gandhi, Rajmohan, 46-47
Gardener, Gary, 234
Geneva Camp, 86-87
Ghosh, Nitya Kumar, 184, 203
Gill, K.P.S., 58-59, 61-62, 94, 117

Glazier, 160
Global Environment Fund
  (GEF), 265
Goalpara, 56, 73-74
Goalundo Ghat, 192
Goswami, Sabita, 49
Greenpeace, 17
Guest workers and Bracero
  programme, 79-81
Guhathakurta, Meghna,
  216-17
Gujral, Inder Kumar, 24
Gupta, Indrajit, 228
Gupta, Shekhar, 68
Habi, Bhagduba, 51
Hajo, 129-30
Hajongs, 37
Halweil, Brain, 234
Hasan, Najmal, 49
Hazarika, Suzoy, 169
Homer-Dixon, Thomas Tad,
  225
Hrangkhawl, Bijoy, 168,
  171-73, 177
Humboldt Baron Alexander
  von, 17
Identity card, for voters, 257,
  260, 262
Illegal Migrants
  Determination by Tribunal
  (IMDT) Act, 70, 131-36,
  149-50, 235-37, 260
Illegal trade, 252-55
Immigrants (Expulsion from
  Assam) Act of 1950, 61
Immigration, as worldwide
  phenomena, 246-50
Independent, 213
India-Bangladesh,
  Gangawater sharing issue,
  21-24
India Today, 228
Indian Evidence Act, 134
Indian Express, 68

Indigenous Peoples Front of
  Tripura (IPFT), 174-75
Islam, Mamon, 179-81, 185
Islam, Nurul, 104, 107, 114,
  120-21
Jafa, Virender Singh, 72
Jain, S.P., 224
Janata Party, 64, 67, 71
Jinnah, Mohammed Ali, 26,
  74
Jorhat, 56
Kalapani, 146-48
Kamatapur Liberation
  Organizaton (KLO), 112,
  121, 258
Kamrup, 56, 68, 72, 74
Keramat Bhai, 116, 155-56,
  179-203, 226, 265
Khan, Liaquat Ali, 73-74
Khan, Masihur Rahman,
  199-200
Kramer, Gene, 169
Kurigram, 151-52, 162-66,
  218
Laldenga, 168
Land Settlement Policy, 73
Lathials, 113-14
Line system, 72
Lord of the Rings, 15
Machiavelli, Niccolo de
  Bernado, 7-8
Mahanta, Prafulla Kumar, 55,
  65, 190, 225-56
Mahfuz Mian, 193-94
Malthus, Thomas, 244, 246
Manipur, 32, 38
Mangaldoi, 64
Manuh Mara Char, 192
Meghalaya, 32, 34, 38
Migration/migrants,
  Bangladesh statistics on,
  213-20, 231-33
causes of, 19
doable programmes to

check, 257-67
economic migrants, 98
environmentally induced
    migration, 81-84
IMDT figures on, 235-37
illegal, 24
Indian statistics on, 220-35
life of migrants, 9-15,
    94-98, 155-56, 179-203
methods to deal problem
    of, 79-81, 250-67
mixed migration, 98-99
on move, 94-98
refugees as migrants,
    76-79, 83
rejected peoples and, 84-92
story of migrants, 9-15,
    94-98, 155-56, 179-203
unwanted, 92-93
vulnerable communities,
    250-52
work permit for, 201-02,
    255, 260-61
worldwide phenomena,
    246-50
Mills, R. Moffat, 69
Mir Jumla, 36
Mishmis, 37
Mizo National Front, 168,
    242
Mizoram migrants problem
    in, 32, 91, 241-43
Modhupur, 116-17
Mohammed, Noor, 107
Mohfiz, 163-66
Motoks, 37
Mugha ul-khand, 116
Mukti Bahini, 30, 83, 152,
    185
Mullen, C.S., 72-73, 234
Murshidabad, 118
Muslim League, 56, 73, 115
Myanmar, 32, 34, 91
Mymensingh, 54, 56, 72, 123

NORAD, 159
Nagaland, 32, 35, 38-39
Nameri National Park, 195
Narasimha Rao, P.V., 57
Natarajan, R., 215
National Commission for the
    Review of the Working of
    the Constitution, 6
National Democratic Front of
    Bodoland (NDFB), 40-41,
    121
National Human Rights
    Commission, 88
National Liberation Front of
    Tripura (NLFT), 173-74
National Migration Law, 263
National Register of Citizens
    (1951), 55
National Security Advisory
    Board, 6
Nations, dispariaties within,
    20-21, 212-13
Natural resources,
    vulnerability and
    dependence on, 18-21
Nehru, Jawaharlal, 26, 60
Nellie massacre, 24, 49-53,
    237
New York Times, 6, 94, 123,
    158
North East Students
    Organization (NESO), 256
Nowgong (Nogaon), 56,
    58-59
OXFAM, 86
Ogata, Sadako, 98, 240, 243
Orunodoi, 28
Osmani, Ghulam, 71
Overseas Development
    Assistance (ODA), 252
Palsane, Sudheer, 152, 154
Partition of Bengal, 71
Patel, Vallabhbhai, 26
Patwari, Hiralal, 64

Pesticides, impact on life chain, 17
Phukan, Brighu Kumar, 55, 65
Pilot, Rajesh, 40
Political refugee, 83
Population
displacement due to environmental factors, 81-
growth and pressure on basic resources, 18-20
growth impact on migration pattern
Portes, Alejandro, 2
Pradhani, Keshab, 140
Prevention of Infiltration from Pakistan (PIP) Act of 1964, 61, 63
Pua Mecca, 129-30
Public Food Distribution System, 209
Rabhas, 37
Rabindra Sangeet, 169
Rahman, Motalib, 50-51
Rahman, Sheikh Mujibur, 90, 137
Raquib, 182-83
Raychaudhuri, Ambikagiri, 27
Refugee Watch, 251
Refugees, as migrants, 76-79
Rejected people, as refugees/migrants from,
Afghanistan, 85-92
Balkans, 240
Bangladesh, 86-91
Bhutan, 91-92
Myanmar, 86
Rwanda, 85, 240
Sri Lanka, 86
Tibet, 84-85
Renner, 159
Revenge and Reconciliation, 47

Rongpur, 56
Rongpur Dinajpur Rural Service, 202
Roy, Bablu, 141-42
Saadulla, Mohammad, 73-74, 115
Saha, Arunodoy, 176
Sahay, Anand, 49
Saikia, Hiteswar, 31, 68
Samabhay Samiti, 147
Sankaradeva, 137-38
Santhals, 41
Sarkar, Subhas Chandra, 139
Satrasal village, refugees at, 137-45
Sen, Dipak, 141
Sen, Upendra Nath, 141
Shakhdher, S.L., 234
Shanti Bahini, 89
Shourie, Arun, 33-34, 60
Sibsagar, 56, 72, 74
Sikkim, 54
Silarai, 138
Silent Spring, 17
Singh, J.D., 169-70
Singh, Jaswant, 67
Singha, Purandhar, 37
Singhi, L.C., 148
Sinha, S.K. Gen., 228
Sobhan, Farooq, 151
Sobhan, Rehman, 208-09
Sodhi, R.S., 257
Sons of the Soil: Migration and Ethnic Conflict in India, 225
South Asia Free Trade Agreement (SAFTA), 254
State of the World's Refugees, The, 251
Sukhre, Astri, 77-78
Suleman, 122
Swiss International Development Assistance (SIDA), 159

Tad, Thomas, 225-26
Tagore, Rabindranath, 166, 169
Terres des Hommes, 202-03
Times, 169
Times of *India*, 49, 169, 144
Treaty of Yandaboo (1826), 37
Trilateral Commission, 240
Tripura, 52, 57-59, 91, 166-78
Tripura National Volunteer Force, 168, 171, 173
Tripura Tribal Autonomous Council (TTAC), 174-75, 177
Tripura Upajati Jamatio Samaj (TUJS), 168, 170
Tura, 124
Understanding the Muslim Mind, 46
United Liberation Front of Asom (ULFA), 43, 66, 101, 112, 121, 256, 258
United Minorities Front (UMF), 71, 236
United Nations Development Programme (UNDP), 78, 207-08, 211

United Nations High Commissioner for Refugees (UNHCR), 86, 91, 98, 240, 242-43, 251
Unwanted Migrants, 92-93
Vajpayee, Atal Bihari, 67
Van Hear, Nicholas, 76
Verghese, B.G., 22-24
Vesting of Properties and Assets Order (1972), 237
Wajed, Sheikh Hasina, 23-24, 90, 118, 220
Wavell, 74
Weiner, Myron, 19, 84, 92, 225-26, 266-67
Whewell, William, 3
Wilson, Edmund O, 3
Work Permits, 201-02, 255, 260-62
World Food Programme, 209
World Health Organisaton, 207
World Lutheran Organisation, 86
World Watch, 3
World Watch Institute, Washington, 17, 21, 233, 245
Young Mizo Association, 241
Zia, Khaleda, 219-20

PENGUIN ONLINE

News, reviews and previews of forthcoming books

visit our author lounge

•

read about your favourite authors

•

investigate over 12000 titles

•

subscribe to our online newsletter

•

enter contests and quizzes and win prizes

•

email us with your comments and reviews

•

have fun at our children's corner

•

receive regular email updates

•

keep track of events and happenings

www.**penguin**books**india**.com